# MAD CITY

## THE SAGE'S LEGACY

### BOOK I

## VICTOR VAHL

ISBN: 979-8-9859259-4-4

# STAY TUNED

First off, thank you for your interest in reading this copy of *Mad City*. This book is a love letter for the genre and concept of superheroes. An action blended with grounded drama and a mix of all the stories and lessons I've been inspired by.

If you've enjoyed this book by the end, you can stay tuned for more updates, special promotions and free content by signing up for my newsletter in the back matter of this book. This includes *Mad Vigilance*, a supplementary novella taking place after *Mad City*.

**I hope this book can give you a break, or some kind of reprieve and enjoyment, from the outside world.  Happy reading.**

~**Victor Vahl**

*"I REGRET NOW," SAID HE, "HAVING HELPED YOU IN YOUR LATE INQUIRIES, OR HAVING GIVEN YOU THE INFORMATION I DID."*

*"WHY SO?" INQUIRED DANTÈS.*

*"BECAUSE IT HAS INSTILLED A NEW PASSION IN YOUR HEART—THAT OF VENGEANCE."*

*From The Count Of Monte Cristo by Alexandre Dumas*

# I

## Isaac Sage

## June 20, 2022, 8:41 PM

The boxer's gatling-gun flurry lacerated his opponent's body. Every wound widening from consecutive, precise hits. From the TV screen, 22-year-old Isaac and the barside patrons could feel the ferocity of every hit.

His opponent's bloodied crescent smile said otherwise.

Isaac watched from the sidewalk, standing far out of reach from the dense crowd sitting inside the bar. A light breeze in the city brushed his unkempt hair, loose pants and grey sweater, the bar's glow reaching the sidewalk's boundary due to patio doors fully opened. The setting filled with an overwhelming, almost nauseating, warmth of camaraderie, splattered beer and obsession for watching fists collide.

The match was reaching the end of its penultimate round. Commentators reminded the public what was at stake. The victor would be declared the new champion over Obadiah Onyx, the retired champion. Two fighters that fought sixteen opponents to reach this point. Moises Sanchez, the rapid attacker, versus Ibrahim Gunner, the battered yet resilient defender.

Ibrahim maintained his advantage in terms of points from the earlier matches, but Moises's recent barrage had turned the tables. From the majority's perspective, Moises was ready to soon land a final blow.

Or at least he should have at this rate. While Moises' offensive yet inhuman prowess proved his place in the finals, Ibrahim's endurance, became definitive proof as well.

The audience's jeers at the referee reached outside the bar. Some prominent shouts detailed an investigation on Moises. Others were simply enjoying the even back-and-forth conflict, something worthwhile to observe in the moment.

Moises continued his onslaught, thick veins pulsating around his arms like a rattlesnake burrowed underneath the skin. He landed a straight punch clean on Ibrahim's shoulder.

Ibrahim's arm fell limp. The respective glove hung closer to the floor, swaying like a pendulum slowing to a stop. One patron cursed in shock.

Within one eye open, he danced around Moises almost as if there was an intended path; the grin expanded. It didn't exude arrogance, but pride channeled through a primal yet controlled frenzy.

Isaac would rather be home than standing outside a bar saturated with all this noise and so many people. But his dull, olive-sand eyes were glued to Ibrahim's energy in awe.

It may have been the super-heroic feats reminding him of the drawings he would make as a kid. But what evoked something more compelling was the wild nature behind his energy and significantly that bloodied grin. A liberation not felt in years.

Twelve seconds after the previous hit, the referee signaled at the judge. The bell rang with two minutes remaining for the round.

The referee gestured for the doctor to enter. Many exclaimed Ibrahim didn't need it; he still had energy to fight.

"Typical. Boxing's gone soft," one voice said throughout the noise.

But instead, the doctor went to Moises with a Q-tip in hand and brushed the cotton swab against a cut on his bicep. She pulled a vial from her pocket, filled with a clear liquid, and inserted the Q-tip into the vial. The doctor shook the vial for ten seconds until the liquid turned violet. The doctor shook her head, discontent.

The referee shook his head. He waved both hands at Moises and then grabbed a nearby mic. "Moises Sanchez was under suspicion of using performance enhancement," the referee said into the mic. "With this analysis, we can confirm traces of T. Dohrnum polluting his blood system. Ibrahim Gunner is your new champion."

Applause and groans clashed in the bar. "Not this M.A.D. shit again," one patron's voice stood among the noise, referring to T. Dohrnum as the slang, 'Mechanically Altered Drugs.'

"Maybe he was treating a sickness?" A woman murmured to her friend. "Like cancer?"

In the past, it would've been considered a cure for cancer. Now, M.A.D. was just as likely to be a mix of cocaine and LSD or anything else. For Moises's case, anything was possible.

Isaac planned to leave home to avoid being caught in the middle of the sea of crowds. Seeing them from afar made his heart skip beats, although tolerable. To be in them, however, was an extreme discomfort.

Then, the interviewer approached the stoic Ibrahim, the belt strung over his working shoulder.

"Ibrahim, although this ended in a disqualification, what a spectacular match," the interviewer said. "You took so many hits and kept standing, now you got the belt. But you don't look happy."

"This ain't my belt," said Ibrahim.

"What do you mean?"

"That this ain't my belt. I had it all planned; I was about three moves away. My entire life, man. It led to this. I fought tooth and nail from the bottom all the way here to win *my* way, y'know? This isn't my satisfaction; this isn't my win."

"Well, Ibrahim, looks like you're gonna be saying that from the top. Congratulations."

"I might relinquish the title but thank you." Ibrahim's primal stare from before dulled. His pride now replaced with mourning.

"Title or not, what's next for you in this career?"

Ibrahim flashed a smile. "That's always the hardest question when you're in these shoes now, isn't it?"

Everyone, including the interviewer, expected him to say more. His eyes wandered, seeming as though he looked for an answer in his corner or the crowd. With that, the interviewer awkwardly concluded the brief Q&A.

"Hey, yo," a shout directed at Isaac. He turned to find a man towering over him in a clean shirt and loose jeans, smiling with a glint in his eyes. "You're that Sage kid, aren't you?"

Isaac froze. The crowd surrounded them as the sea walked up and down the sidewalk. Flashes of the past sprinkled his senses in the form of a blanket of debris. The stress of the hallucination filled his lungs, forcing an urge to cough. The goal was to remain focused on this current reality.

"I am," Isaac managed to finally speak.

"You are, huh?" he gripped Isaac's shoulder with a maintained smile. "You know what you're saying?"

Isaac, unsettled, responded with a nod.

The smile snapped to a raging glare as he yanked Isaac toward him. Isaac broke away and tried to distance the gap.

"You all ruined everything!" The drunkard's slurred shout caught the attention of the moving crowd. He charged at Isaac as two men jumped out from the crowd.

"Tommy, get it together," one of the men shouted. "What the fuck are you doing!"

"I'm glad that bitch is dead!" The drunkard roared through a messy haze of spit. "Your dad too!" His irritated eyes glossed with tears.

Isaac knew instantly who he referred to as they were eternal constants haunting his life. No one other than Gemma Sage, the creator of M.A.D, and Samuel Sage, loving father and husband.

The crowd's motion pulled Isaac out of reach as the strangers continue restraining Tommy. Tommy hurled one of them to the ground and threw two punches to the back of their head.

Isaac extended his arm, trying to part through the sea to help the two strangers. He pushed and shouted to be let through. The crowd's refusal to comply, combined with the debris-filled hallucination, sent him deeper into the tides of the concrete streets.

Two cops rushed in from the side, breaking a part of the crowd to grab Tommy and slam him onto the sidewalk before cuffing his wrists and ankles. The drunkard screamed in anguish. Isaac continued his route home, the hallucination still clashing with him, sparking small doses of paranoia if the drunkard broke free from the cops and followed him now. But aside from a few passersby, the outskirts had begun to dissipate with the late night.

———

***

He arrived home at 12:01 AM. The tiny, flat studio home he owned for the past six years held a simple aesthetic with its bland porcelain tiles and blank walls that came with the house. He placed the phone on the tiny credenza by the entrance, entered his bedroom, and sat at his work desk.

The young Sage mustered enough energy to open the laptop and finish this ten-page report. Todd, his best friend, counted on him to complete it in time for class.

Words cluttered on the screen with every keystroke. It prompted Isaac's eyes to drift to a fragment of the past – A side-effect triggered by his medication. The fragment played out like a burnt silent reel of film, showing Gemma and Samuel consoling a young Isaac.

*'Focus,'* Isaac told himself, eyes locked back on the white screen.

The life Isaac chose was intended to be autonomous. Admittedly, his parents would dislike this choice. Despite all the work and success of growing a business into a world-changing corporation, they invested greatly in Isaac's health. Dr. Bukowski, his therapist, was the first to remind Isaac of this truth through their conversations.

Yet, a lingering guilt clung to him. A guilt of not dying with them, combined with the undeserving shame of living – or attempting to live – a fulfilling, thriving life.

Thus, a routine was set, from the most minute details to major beats. Take the prescribed M.A.D., in the form of bright-colored pills, as scheduled. Continue exercising in the morning or late evening. Attend therapy sessions and eat three meals a day comprised of proper nutrients. Continue academics and complete everything related, including the report, to graduate. Converse with Todd on anything and everything going on. Help ensure his success.

Last but most importantly – stay alive.  Dying early as a shortcut to join his family and be rid of these feelings were unacceptable.  This routine was the middle ground between living a full life and a mundane one. To cease every active thought and complete tasks, one by one, like a robot assigned to its duties until the limbs turned to rust, or its circuitry forced it to shut down. His mind was now set on completing this report, stopping intermittently to rub his eyes like a typewriter resetting after reaching the end of each line.

Once the tasks were done, he would ponder on what was next to come in the span of days, months and years.  Another school project. Housekeeping. Or, after graduating, a job where he could churn constant tasks for eight hours or longer, keeping him safe from most dangers.  He would live to reach an old age.  An ending that his parents were robbed of.

Dr. Bukowski had scolded Isaac on this mindset labeled as survivor's guilt. He insisted the goal should be to grow and thrive.  Yet, like an addiction, it pollinated Isaac's mind and sedated every ounce of constant worry.

Rampant knocks boomed on the front door. Isaac found the time was already 3:03 AM. Isaac wasn't expecting any visitors, let alone any strangers so late.

He rose to his feet and tiptoed to his bedroom door, listening to the booming harshen with each blow. The noise reached its peak with a splintering shatter, followed by a bang, seconds of silence and light footsteps. The sound of gurgling splashing followed. His nostrils became slowly overwhelmed by a bitter scent of gasoline.

New Manhattan wasn't a perfect city by any means. But Isaac was never in danger of being invaded until now. Could it be the drunk man from the bar? Did he follow Isaac home?

He nudged the door ajar. One shadow extended out of the bathroom.

*'I'll call the police.'* Isaac dug into his pocket for his phone. Nothing. He checked his other pocket. Nothing. His mind flashed back to the credenza. Isaac peered around the corner of the bathroom door. A scrawny fellow, masked by a cartoon pig helmet, poured a large, red canister of gasoline around the bathtub and toilet. He seemed cautious so as the gasoline didn't splash on his clothes.

———

The credenza was straight down the hall. Isaac continued his stealth. As he reached the end of the hall, a gargantuan figure in a cartoon rooster helmet stood in the kitchen area. It dropped a gas canister held in one hand. The towering eyes locked onto Isaac.

Isaac sprinted for the credenza.

"He's awake!" The Rooster shouted with a burly voice.

Isaac felt his body pull backward and careen toward the kitchen, slamming against one of the cabinets. The Pig ran out of the bathroom. Isaac yanked a frying pan out of a nearby cabinet, stood up and swung the pan against Rooster's head, leaving them dazed. Hopefully, Isaac thought, the force was strong enough to land a lasting concussion.

He chucked the frying pan at Pig and ran, nearly slipping, to the credenza. He snatched the phone and hauled halfway out the front entrance before being flung back inside, sliding across the floor. The gasoline soaked into his skin and clothes.

Isaac planted his hand on the counter to boost himself up. A sudden awful jolt resonated through his hand. He turned to find a butcher's knife, wielded by a panting Pig, cleaved into the counter. The large chunk of steel set in-between his pinky finger and the respective knuckle. Part of his ring finger caught by the blade in the form of a small gash. Blood poured out his wound, flooding the surface.

Frantic screams erupted, interlaced with rapid hyperventilation. Isaac's train of thought didn't leave much to plan other than an instinctive impulse to run and wail from the pain. Isaac smacked Pig once again with the frying pan that was within reach. Pig cursed through a nasal tone.

Isaac bolted down the hall, his sprint instant like lightning and heavy like thunder, aiming straight for the window.

*'No time to open it.'* Without stopping, he crashed through the window, his harsh landing softened by wet grass. He continued vaulting over a fence and sprinting another foot and a half before falling into a bush. His body, despite the storm of shock and fear, failed to stand up.

He conjured enough strength to fully extend his whole hand and claw into the ground, pulling the rest of his body to the anchored position, halfway out of the bush. As he released his hand from the ground to extend once more, a wave of dizziness smacked his head, blurring his vision.

In a split-second, Isaac saw his parents, still feeling the grassy dew on his body. They sat in the kitchen of their mansion over bread and butternut squash soup. Isaac handed them a drawing of a man with a cape, scrawled in red crayon. The upper half of the face was covered by a mask.

A memory playing not of choice, but rather as an instinctive muscle reflex.

*His mother and father examined the drawing. "A superhero?" Samuel asked.*

*Isaac nodded, focused on lifting the savory soup from the bowl into his mouth.*

*"It's a wonderful drawing, baby," Gemma said. "Would you want to be an artist?"*

*Isaac shrugged. "I'm just seven."*

*"Just seven, he says," Samuel replied with a smirk.*

*Gemma reciprocated the smile. "If you do, you can teach me how to draw."*

*A flustering heat overcame Isaac.*

*"Oh look, he's blushing!" said Samuel.*

*"No!" Isaac shouted.*

*Everything, from the soup to his face to Gemma and Samuel's laughter, warmed Isaac with peace.*

*"You know you can do whatever you want, Isaac," Gemma said. "Right? Just don't fear failure."*

Isaac's eyes opened to a white room, back in the present-day. A nurse and two police officers conversed with each other as other hospital workers scurried past the adjacent entrance. His maimed hand was now sewn up and bandaged.

The nurse and police turned to Isaac.

"He's awake," the police officer said. "Isaac Sage?"

"Where am I?" Isaac asked. "What happened to my house? I was at my house."

"Your house is gone, kid," the second officer said. "Most of it burned down." Isaac's skin paled, unable to think or process.  Now homeless, nowhere to go. He was fortunate to have the savings to fall back on. He found his phone on the nightstand.

"Can you explain what happened, Isaac?" The first officer asked with a notepad in hand.

Isaac recounted past the shock. "My house was…attacked. Two people attacked me; they dumped gasoline all over the floor, it was 3 AM. They cleaved my finger and– sorry, what are you writing?"

"Filling out notes for this investigation."

"I appreciate it, but I don't think it would matter."

"We'll do our sworn duty, son," the first officer said. "Anyone you think would have a motive to kill?"

"There was a drunk man that attacked me earlier on that same night. At the bar."

"What were you doing at the bar?" The first officer questioned.

"I was on the way home, but the fight had caught my attention, sir."

"The fight?  Ibrahim and Moises?"

Isaac nodded.

The officer rolled his eyes. "What a rip-off, that fight…"

"We know that drunk," the second officer returned to the main subject. "He was arrested before the incident."

"Then…I don't know."  In general, it could've been anyone that hated the Sages.

"Well with your house gone, we checked your records and saw your secondary address."  The first officer shared the address, being Isaac's former mansion.  "We shipped any items that survived the fire to there. We also notified the person living there and…"

Isaac's head simmered, muffling out the officer's noise as he thought about everything that needed to be done. Overwhelmed, unsure of what to do next.  He needed to gather his belongings.  But the idea of returning to the mansion made his heart race.

———

"Now then, why don't we take you to the station where we can do a proper interview?  It'll help find these arsonists."

Isaac reflected on the case of his parents' deaths.  Closed early, marked as a freak accident with no supporting evidence.  He wanted nothing to do with the police.

He checked the time. 10:21 AM.  There were more important matters anyway.

"No, thank you," Isaac gathered his belongings. "I have a therapy session to go to today."

"Can we get your insurance?" The nurse asked.

"It's okay, mail me the bill," said Isaac. "I'll be late if I wait any longer. Sorry, have a good day."

"Can't you reschedule it?" The officer asked. "Isn't this a bigger concern?"

Isaac shook his head, regaining some composure.

"Thank you, but it's fine," he said. "I just need to leave."

# II
## John Saint
### June 21, 2022, 2:27 PM

Summer heat forced the air conditioner's motor to stall. It forced a low grind in the ambience as detective John Saint laid back inside his black, rusted sedan.

The humidity dampened his button-up, tucked into grey pants, darkened with blots of sweat. The breeze mixed with several years' worth of bitter liquor and a variety of fresheners seeped into the car's interior.

Saint awaited a new case via the police radio, his phone set atop the dashboard alongside it. He re-tucked his light button-up into his faded mustard suit pants. The belt was decoration at this point. It might've been time, he thought, for a new waist size. He remarked it was time to shave after feeling stubble growing along his block jaw and thin cheeks.

This stagnancy recurred for the past few years, sans a few minor disputes. Compared to his past two decades of work with the New Manhattan Police Department, aka the NMPD, this should have been a good sign. But updates in the black market with little resolution implied the opposition improved their stealth.

He listened to the radio's crackling with one foot on the pedal. The slightest pitch would prompt him to ignite the car, change gears and make haste. First come, first serve, even for a twenty-year veteran.

A vibration shook the dashboard of the car. Saint broke his focus to find Edoris, his wife, on the caller ID.

"My sweet Doris," Saint answered.

"You left the cat in the bedroom, you ja—ugh, you dummy." Edoris spoke with a prominent New York accent.

Saint replied, "I love it when you talk to me that way."

Edoris tittered, spinning her tone into a scoff.

"What are you up to?" she asked.

"Nothing. Dead air today, and I've caught up on paperwork at the office."

"Come back home and I'll make you lunch."

A crackled voice emitted from the radio. "We're gonna need an investigator over here on the intersection of 31st Street and Bulldog Avenue, over," the voice said.

"I'm sorry, honey, I gotta go, I–"

"I know," Edoris said. "I love you. Attaboy."

"Attagirl." Detective Saint immediately hung up with a smile. He tossed the phone to the backseat, switched gears and stomped on the pedal, cruising through darkened streets that were once free of pristine and glistening smooth granite.

The architecture alone was a reminder of simpler days. Evil did evil things, and the good was there to stop that evil.

His father, Jacques Saint, was a hero that embodied this classic, altruistic philosophy in the law of New Manhattan and the city it was before, alongside Daniel Briggs and Catherine Carmichael.

Together, the legacy and reputation they invoked formed great systems. But Jacques' legacy alone shined just as bright. Every orientation and side talk would eventually bring up Jacques' heroism. He was immortalized into this folklore.

"It's simple good and evil," he'd say. "And when they're evil, they never win."

Saint recanted this to himself as he arrived at the crime scene; a brick town-house bounded by trademark yellow 'CAUTION' tape. No cars other than two police cars were around to his delight.

The detective weaved his square torso underneath the tape and waved his badge at the cop by the front door to proceed to the interior living room, smacked with an overpowering scent of sulfur and something else that made his lips sour.

The officers inside provided Saint intel on what was learned so far: The deceased was ID'd as Guido Rodrigues. Neighbors called around 10:50 AM, complaining about an alarming, potent smell of something rotten or overcooked. Officers verified the deceased victim at 2:30 PM where Saint arrived fifteen minutes after.

Learning more through background research and neighbor interviews, Guido's Spanish-Italian family had garnered a reputation for doing dirty business, unspecified.

It wouldn't be the first time unspecified dirty business related to something gang-related. And it wouldn't definitely be foreign for this to be a gang-related assassination. But although gang wars and drug cartels were a staple in modern culture, amplified by the expansion of altered, varying, occasionally unstable compounds of M.A.D in black markets, this deduction was jumping conclusions.

Saint examined the charred black corpse before it was sent to the morgue. The remaining flesh melted with the bone, fusing with the wool couch it sat upon.

Some areas like the feet were afflicted with first degree burns, while the arms were black and brittle, almost disintegrated by the air coming from outside. Half of the face drooped off the skull like hardened lava, while the other burnt-black half was intact with one open eye socket. Saint repeated the examination a few times, desensitized by normal disgust.

The body was incinerated on the spot. But the fire was controlled on specific locations. Guido didn't even have a chance to budge from his seat.

"What in the fucking Christ…" Saint muttered.

With permission, Saint shot photos of the crime scene. After, he searched for any flammable substance that could've been responsible for the sporadic burning, such as tanks for a flamethrower. All Saint found was a lighter.

The nearby cabinets in the living room included a few glocks with empty magazines. On the inside wall was a yellow note. Scrawled on the letter in black ink, it read:

*Hey, you need to stop calling me, okay? Stop freaking out or we're both fucking dead. I'll see you soon, hermano.*

The note left no name, but perhaps fingerprints of a potential lead were left behind. Saint returned to the car, content with this piece of evidence.

———

He checked his phone, glancing at a text from Edoris: "I'm making dinner. Show up please."

His current priority, however, sought more attention. The mystery of the case evoked thrills, like the addicted gambler getting close to cracking the invisible formula of hitting a jackpot.

Now, he would bring the evidence to the attention of Daniel Briggs, the commanding chief of the NMPD. Although Saint's position acted as more of a freelancer, freelancing was less free nowadays. A contract still meant reporting to a higher-up.

For all Saint knew, there may be a past arson case linked to this crime.

***

Chief Commissioner Daniel Briggs paced back and forth in the main cyan-tinted lobby of the NMPD as Saint arrived. The area was segmented by cubicles for staff. The 60-something Chief was weighed down by a slate button-up snugged into his dark jeans. The silver badge pinned to his shoulder shined more prominent by the contrast.

Officers and investigators approached him with reports and, like a maestro in command of an orchestra, Briggs waved his hand with a pen or open palm to either sign it off or deny it. One could forget his age from his active movement despite his wrinkled face and greyed hair.

As the sea of reports settled, he locked eyes with Saint, who nodded in the direction of the chief's office. Briggs raised three fingers, signaling his minute cue. Saint entered his office and sat down, meditating in silence.

Within three minutes Briggs entered and took a seat. He reached into his desk drawer and pulled out a fresh banana.

"Alright," said Briggs, "What do you got?"

Saint explained the details of the crime scene to Briggs, primarily the charred burnt corpse in precise detail.

Briggs's expression soured, placing his halfway-peeled banana on his desktop before rubbing his shut eyes.

"Jesus, alright. Did you come to tell me that?"

"I was curious if these details sound similar to anything recorded previously. Arson cases, for example?"

"No, no one's ruined my appetite quite this way, Saint."

"I need a lead." The lack of interesting work was getting to Saint. "Or even a direction. Something."

The soured discomfort in Briggs' face transitioned to focused concern. He placed a curled index finger to his lips and leaned back.

"Arson…"

"Arson?"

"Arson. Reports about one case every other month. And to have this be the second one in the past month… that's odd."

"What's the other one?"

"Something about a house being burned down. I think Jackson's got it logged by now. You think they're linked?"

"What did police find? Anything like the corpse? Or weapons, drugs?"

"Just an attack on the Sage kid. Drenched the house in gasoline, lit the stoves up and set it on fire. No residue of drugs or weapons found."

There was always enmity toward the Sages for the miracle drug being M.A.D. Could've been one extremist taking it too far. "I'd give it a five-percent likelihood. Otherwise, extremely coincidental. What about past cases linked to any homicide?"

"Never been linked to something homicide-related. Maybe one time. But again, that was ages ago."

Saint shared the letter he found. "It seemed like they were trying to hide from something. Or someone."

Briggs beamed an intense stare. A test of true character by noting any flinch of uncertainty. Saint remained stoic.

"So. Homicide?" Briggs asked.

"Maybe."

"How convinced are you about this?"

"Sixty-five percent. Close to seventy."

———

Several seconds passed.

Then, Briggs's glare softened. "You know I trust a Saint's judgment more than mine," he said. "Go ask Jackson Billows. Besides burned shit, there might be another pattern in those arson cases."

"I'll come back to you if I have anything new."

Before Saint exited, Briggs stopped him. "How you feeling, John?"

"Good."

"I know things have slowed. A lot. You feeling good to take this case on?"

Saint smiled. "Better than ever."

Briggs paused, assessing the detective once more. He knew of Saint's dull life for the past several years, combined with Jacques' passing. A lack of fulfillment. A yearning for closure.

"Alright, then. Get on with it."

There wasn't much Saint knew about Jackson Billows. He transferred from Miami PD a few years ago, accepting to go through the training program and re-familiarize himself. Afterward, Billows chose to be based in-house for the NMPD for most of his tenure after assisting in one M.A.D. raid operation that ended poorly.

Billows sat in a small, open-spaced cubicle with his own computer set-up, ten steps away from Briggs' office. His curly hair was slicked back with a glossy gel, sticking out at the ends. Being in the physical prime of his late twenties, he displayed a well-fit aesthetic aligning with the slim-fit, tucked button-ups he would always wear.

Without wasting any time, Saint approached Billows and asked for access to the arson-related cases.

"Manners might change my response," Billows murmured. He opened a drawer with rows of manila folders lined up, flicking through several of them before pulling out a folder with an orange sticker tab. He handed the folder to Saint. "Arson."

"Thank you."

Saint sifted through the files with one finger as he trailed along the head-quarters' narrow walkways.

———

At a glance, the five most recent cases presented similar traits of concentrated burns of multiple degrees with the house itself not being burned within three of the five cases.

*'How did no one notice this? It's too controlled,'* Saint deduced.

Before leaving, he made sure to drop off the bagged letter to forensics, hoping to find a lead from any fingerprints.

He entered his car and dove deeper into the files. That familiar sensation from past years surged through his body. Sparks of ideas and theories lit up in a chain.

Someone was killing people since last year and still roaming the city. It couldn't continue.

Then, Saint smacked the side of his head over a dumbfounded realization: Edoris's text.

He checked the message, bouncing back and forth between this and the folder for one minute.

*'Just another day.'* Saint let out a sigh and marked his house as the destination. *'It could wait just one more day.'*

# III
## ISAAC SAGE

## June 21, 2022, 11:16 AM

Isaac Sage's tired gaze drifted to a pool of blood on the carpet in Dr. Bukowski's office, snapping him alert. He focused on the source: his left hand, wrapped in crimson-soaked bandages dripping like a broken faucet.

*'One of the stitches must have popped,'* Isaac thought. It had been a stressful several hours of rushing after the police station. He covered the injury with the loose sleeves of his cotton-grey sweater.

The dark, hexagonal pattern of the doctor's carpet had withstood years of constant, predictable flow, now ruined by carelessness. Even with rigorous scrubbing, a bloodied hue would linger.

Dr. Bukowski, appearing in his mid-forties, pushed his glasses to the bridge of his narrow nose, sitting a few feet away from Isaac in his chair. At the sight of blood, he calmly pulled a few tissues out of his green shirt pocket and extended them to Isaac.

Isaac grabbed them and smothered his bloodied hand. A red stain spider-webbed through the white.

"Thank you."

"You could've canceled, Isaac," said Dr. Bukowski.

"I canceled last time. Didn't want to make a habit."

"Hm. Tell me what happened again."

Isaac readjusted to sit upright and explained the recent event.

"How do you feel?" Dr. Bukowski asked.

Isaac reflected on the silliness of the question before remembering the sudden spike from peace to terror. His hands trembled the longer he recalled it. He glanced at his backpack filled with only a replacement laptop.

The bloodied smile of Ibrahim – the champion boxer from the television – manifested as a mental image. It sparked an innate frenzy, like an unexpected glitch in a piece of equipment that, that passed as quickly as it formed when he felt pain from trying to ball his maimed hand.

*"Pissed,"* Isaac snapped. "That was my home."

"Try to look on the bright side," Dr. Bukowski expressed. His tone was understanding. "You lived."

"Me and my nine digits will remember that."

"Despite recent events, let's focus on progress. Have you been taking your medication?"

Isaac hesitated. The office's silence filled by the low hum of the air conditioner.

"The silence says enough." Dr. Bukowski leaned forward with a disappointing smirk.

"I do take enough, I just overthink my routine sometimes."

"Remember Isaac, that–those meds–help the sessions if consistent. And the sessions help you avoid those nightmares. Have they lessened at all?"

Isaac shrugged. "Somewhat."

Dr. Bukowski clasped his palms together. "It's not for me, but for you. I know the sessions take a toll. It's hard. But these sessions lead to embracing. Embracing means–"

"To recover."

Bukowski nodded. "Consistency. Let's simulate, okay?"

Isaac leaned back, eyes closed, reluctant to focus on the past. A deep reverberation vibrated across his torso, like sticks against a drum. His vision blurred Dr. Bukowski, and the surrounding room.

The blurs changed in color and shape before re-solidifying to a larger view of the city of New Manhattan. A sage-green obelisk towered over him, acting as a shield from the sun.

Re-immersion therapy, as told to him several times, was the only choice if Isaac wanted to move forward from his trauma. Relive the memories of his parents' death on February 19th, 2007, repeatedly, through his eyes, until he could accept *this* was his reality.

The memory often ran smooth like a film reel. But this time, the reel of the events skipped with erratic confusion.

Samuel and Gemma held his hands as they entered the building. His mind jumped to a pearlescent white lab with an array of mounted lasers firing at orbs of varying colors, each segmented in their own transparent cube. In a second, the setting burned away amid a sudden cacophony of screams, cutting between blue skies and grey plumes. A growing heat singed Isaac's skin as Gemma's screams and Samuel's anguish pierced his eardrums.

With a rising heartrate, the events accelerated into incomprehension before Isaac found himself at ground level, engulfed by a black mushroom cloud.

Dr. Bukowski shouted Isaac's name before the latter found himself in the office again, near-breathless from the feeling of debris in his failing lungs. He handed Isaac a bottle of water. Isaac snatched it and chugged half.

"How long?" Isaac panted.

"Two minutes."

Isaac gritted his teeth.

Dr. Bukowski nodded. "Your thoughts are probably clouded from recently. Why don't we call it a day?"

"I just got here."

"Please, Isaac," the doctor assured him.

Isaac relented. He rose from his seat, guided by Bukowski as he approached the exit in defeat. The decaying despair within lingered for so many years. The doctor, through these therapy sessions, reignited hope that it would work. All Isaac desired was a permanent solution to move through this routine without immense guilt.

"Doctor…" He turned back to Dr. Bukowski, bringing up this topic once more. "We've been doing this for a while. Has there *actually* been progress?"

"You feel the same again, don't you?"

"I'm sorry for being a broken record."

"It's okay."  Dr. Bukowski's comforting expression paled to melancholy. "Remember: Grief can be deceptive. It tells us that we must live in despair to make up for some apparent sin. Be it the sin of a deed or for being alive.

"I know your struggles. But I've seen your growth firsthand. You've had good days, but the grief makes you slither backward. It's normal. Don't let it conquer you. Let's talk about it next week, okay?"

Isaac nodded.

"Where are you staying at anyway?"

"Going back to my old mansion for now."

"Well, do me a favor and rest tonight, Isaac."

"Tonight…I have to finish these reports for my friend and…Shit!" Isaac smacked his palm to his forehead. "The charity event is starting soon."

"You got invited to a charity event?"

Isaac brushed through his messy hair.  "It's for the new Sage building. I promised myself I would go. *They* would probably want it."

"It's a great opportunity to socialize. I assume you have another outfit for the occasion?"

"Nope," Isaac said. He waved a bandaged hand. "We'll see if they understand."

***

Open stores and plastered posters of Obadiah Onyx's gym met Isaac's eyes down the streets of New Manhattan's design district before he found himself at the front doors of the Museum of Modern Art in Midtown district. Large vertical banners of the new Sage Foundation obelisk decorated the front facade.

Inside, purple-clothed tables and strangers were the most prominent and abundant. Scattered fixtures lit against the room's dark floors and stage podium.

Isaac's gaze wandered, struggling to find a comforting anchor. He fixed his clothes three times and straightened his posture while searching for an empty table to find solace. Stand around for a few minutes and leave. He could at least acknowledge he was there, then catch up on the rest of the tasks he needed to complete.

Then, a woman called out to Isaac. Eyes from the others tracked her, soon switching their stares to Isaac.

Her white curls set atop the slender shoulders of her suit, fashioned with a vibrant purple bowtie. One corner of her red lip was raised higher than the other.

"Isaac Sage? Is that you?" the woman asked.

Isaac nodded. Her silhouette rang a vague familiarity.

The woman flashed an exciting grin before she veiled her mouth with her left hand. She extended her right hand to Isaac. "Marley Darwin. I'm one of the shareholders. My friends call me Marley, as can you."

Isaac shook Darwin's hand. "It's nice to meet you, Ms. Darwin."

Darwin guided Isaac away from the crowds to an empty table set at a far corner.

"I heard on the news you were attacked in your home. Are you okay to be here?"

"Mostly in one piece," Isaac replied. News had spread quick. "Were you the one inviting me?"

"That is I. I'd been meaning to know what's going on in your life. Believe it or not, your father and I were excellent colleagues. I met your mother through him."

His memories followed. "And you've been at my house before," said Isaac. "With my parents."

"Oh, fantastic memory! I remember you were asking for your mother to tuck you in. You kept that shyness, I see."

Isaac flustered. "Sorry I never responded to your invites."

"Don't be. Were you living by yourself? What happened with your grand-parents?"

"Never heard from them."

"Other family members? Didn't you have a caretaker?"

"No family," said Isaac. "And I did, until I ended up moving into my own house."

"Alone? Not even a dog or a cat?"

"I think I can't be relied on for pets. It's not bad. I found plenty of time for reading and stayed occupied with school. The quiet helps–"

Darwin cut Isaac short, "You know we can help you."

"I'm sorry?" a stunned Isaac asked.

"We're aware of the work you conduct. Your purpose isn't that. Don't you realize it?"

Isaac noticed many sharp eyes still locked on him. Were they the shareholders? As a Sage, Isaac knew there were greater opportunities within reach for him compared to others. And he knew of others who would be interested in his predicament. But alas, the plethora of unknown eyes fixated on him was, to say the least, unsettling.


Flashes of February 19th, 2007 sped through his mind. Every set of eyes prompted a screaming echo. His fingers twitched. His sweater dampened. The sounds of chatter mixed with footsteps clambering against the floor. "I'm not sure if I agree," said Isaac.

Darwin raised one hand. "Look, I'm not giving you the position of CEO. You'll get to work, while learning more of the ropes behind the whole process."

"I'm open to donating some of my trust fund. It doesn't feel right of me to–"

"I understand," Darwin cut Isaac off, "I do. I also know of your schoolwork and career path, I'm no stranger to that. Think about it."

Applause filled the room as someone entered the stage. He spoke, but Isaac isolated him, focusing on Darwin instead.

Darwin continued. "Think about it and when you have time, ping me. Your father and your mother always wanted this."

Isaac fixated on a hypothetical. A scenario where they sat him down, trying to hold back the smiles forming on their faces, wrinkled from years of living.

"They did?" he asked.

Darwin nodded. A loud voracious voice emerged out of thin air. "We would like to take a moment to bring the heir of Sage Foundation out for a short speech! Isaac Sage, we thank you for coming here tonight."

A giant, intense light shined onto Isaac, dazing his vision. "How about a speech?"

"What did they say?" Isaac grinned. "Did they say anything else to you? What were they like?" He wanted to imagine the words and tone they were going to express to him.

"I'm sorry, Isaac, about what? Your place in the company?"

"Yeah. They must have said something for you to say this."

Darwin stammered. "It's more…it's more a feeling than anything."

Isaac's happiness deflated. Words from his parents, words he'd never been told before, thrilled him to have more pieces of them with him. Ibrahim's bloodied smile filled his mind.

"Then you don't know," said Isaac.

"How about a speech from the one and only Sage?" The host insisted once more.

Isaac knew his parents were proud of their work. He knew they told him to never fear failure, that they sacrificed a lot to give him a happy life, and they spent their last day on Earth with him. Knowing this alone made him more certain than Darwin did to work for this company pretending to continue his parent's legacy. He prepared himself to tell her this.

But then a sediment of grief washed over him. What good would it do? Would it bring them back? Would running the company bless him with the foresight to see them again? Isaac had accepted they were gone, and he had no time to amuse this PR stunt. That was it.

Isaac brushed past Darwin, her face sunken by melancholy, and exited the building with no concern to look back. A stuttered, awkward applause filled the stilted silence after the host thanked Isaac Sage for his appearance.

Outside, Isaac tried to clear his mind, only to be taunted by second-guessing. Maybe he was too brash, he thought. Perhaps he could've played along. He hailed a taxi to the mansion.

———

Those dull eyes drifted beyond the window, fixating on the sage-green obelisk erect in the distance. In the dark, it retained a pale aura. Like a ghost reclaiming its place.

But it remained certain to Isaac. No iota of his family's legacy lingered with him. No compound nor business nor philosophy to make him fit to run the business. His family's legacy died on February 19th, 2007. And as soon as things had settled again, he deemed himself fit for the same routine moving forward.

***

The trees replaced the buildings towering the sky. A sign the cab was on the private cobblestone lane leading to the mansion. The overhanging trees created a pleasant, otherworldly vista, even in the pitch-dark. Isaac recalled how his mother Gemma teased him for losing his thoughts in the trees.

As he immersed deeper into that self-reflection, her voice echoed from nothingness. A reel of this past memory played around him. He focused intensely enough, reminding himself this was only a memory.

Minutes passed before Isaac found himself stuttering whispers in the taxi again, parked in front of the mansion. It was a side-effect from the immersion therapy. One in which Dr. Bukowski warned Isaac to not sink deeper.

Isaac paid the driver and exited. The breathing froze once he faced the two-story mansion lit by the moon.

Vines wriggled along the house's discolored exterior, matching the steps leading to the front oak door. Isaac entered to find the grand off-white spiral stairway in the center. A 'Welcome Home' banner was hoisted above the stairway to his surprise.

A light switched on. Isaac turned to find a woman dressed in a light blue dress covered by a polka dot apron.

"Isaac?"

Isaac recognized that voice, baffled at the sound followed by the sight.

"K-Kara?"

25

She approached closer. His former caretaker's face was accented with light freckles and sunken curves under her eyes. The subtle smirk widened to a gleeful smile.

"Look at you, all grown up!" said Kara. "Come, I made food.."

Kara guided Isaac to the kitchen area, switching the lights on. The added brightness supported how Kara's appearance hadn't changed in the past six years. As if she never aged past twenty-nine.

She set two plates at the round table in the kitchen's corner. One plate with a sandwich and the other with chopped slices of apples and pineapples. Turkey, bacon, tomatoes, lettuce, pickles and mustard.

Isaac was filled with gratitude. "Oh, Kara." He smeared the mustard and pickles off as much as possible and took a bite, puckering his lips. "You didn't have to do this."

"Please," Kara smiled.

"I figured you moved out after I left," he said.

"Well, utilities never shut off, and… it was their house too, y'kno? I couldn't stop taking care of it."

Isaac offered a small smile. "It's nice to find it quiet again. Especially with no news media like before."

"No need to worry since *I* told them to fuck off."

Isaac chuckled over the thought of the news team's pitiful walk of shame. He chomped on a scoop of chopped fruit. Bright and refreshing to the palate. The static in his brain slapped him with fatigue.

"I still can't believe you're here," Kara continued.

"There's a lot I'd like to catch up on. My mind's fried."

"I can imagine."

Isaac's breathing eased as the food filled his stomach, now on the verge of yawning. Kara's joy added to the relaxation.

Kara continued. "So, your living situation here… It's temporary? Or–"

"Temporary."

"Are you sure?"

"*Yes.*" The warmth receded. To stay in this mansion again permanently wasn't an option. Every room and corner brought a painful reminder of the past. "It'll take a few months to find a new place and sign off on it and all that."

Kara's smile faded to a grimace. Isaac folded his arms, absorbing the harshness behind his tone.

He continued, trying to rationalize himself. "You know how this place makes me feel–"

"No, I get it." Kara forced a polite smile. "Well, we have time."

"Yeah–If you don't mind, I– oh!" Isaac thought about his conversation with the police. "I was told someone was going to deliver what they managed to salvage from my house."

Kara pointed upstairs. "The box is in your room."

Isaac proceeded upstairs, backpack in hand. He cut right at the peak, approaching his blue, bedroom door. Etchings were notched into the door frame, measurements scrawled beside each mark.

The box was set atop his cerulean-draped bed. Everything looked the same as he had left it, like if time froze in this room since his departure.

"There were times I thought about turning this into an extra den."

Isaac turned to Kara. "No hard feelings if you did. It was my choice to move out."

Kara shrugged. "Maybe you were better off here. Sometimes, it's too quiet."

The memories of this home soured like milk left in the sun. Isaac glossed his eyes away. Part of him felt apologetic if whatever Kara felt worsened because he left. But no words came. Only his limbs trembled.

"Why don't you get some good rest," Kara said. "I'll leave you to it."

"Good night, Kara," he said, eyes affixed on her reflection in the window.

"Good night, Isaac." Kara departed to her room down the hall.

Isaac opened his backpack, pulling out a new thin laptop. He scanned through the box, hoping the report survived the fire. Small figurines, a photo of his family and a charred Game Boy that surprisingly still worked.

'*This survived but not the laptop?*'

Isaac reached the bottom. No sign of the report. With his old laptop gone from the fire, it meant he'd have to pull an all-nighter. Todd was counting on this.

The last item was a new sight to Isaac. Snug in the corner of the box was an odd, bone-white card scrawled with smudged handwriting. Isaac picked up the card. The legible handwriting read "1316" and "Apricot Avenue." The address of Isaac's house.

He flipped the card to find the old logo for Sage Foundation: a green obelisk positioned beside the brand name in embossed, Roman-esque font. To its side was Samuel Sage's business information.

That card hadn't been seen nor manufactured in years. All scrapped after the incident.

Isaac settled down for the night, back in his old room. He booted up his laptop and typed. Intermittently, he paused to fixate on the card, unable to think about anything else.

He returned to stare at the card once more. From the smooth texture to the embossed ink, it was the real deal.

Five hours later, he finished the report. And still, the desire for sleep was outweighed by constant thinking. Every detail he conjured in his mind pointed to one thing: the attack on him was far from a random mugging.

The fog Isaac had imagined himself in for so many years was beginning to fade. Now, as the fog dissipated, a new path had revealed itself.

# IV
## Johnson Moore
### June 22, 2022, 12:06 AM

A white limousine sped along a highway lit against the dark sky. Three men sat in the backseat of the limo. Johnson, one of these men, held a white towel against his nose.

Johnson was a recent addition to a small-time drug smuggling gang, formerly working as a flower store clerk. On the second day while working at the store, he learned how much money he could make in cartels compared to all his other jobs combined. By the next day, he quit.

Unfortunately, Johnson had been prone to sporadic nosebleeds.

The other two men sat on the opposite end in individual revolving chairs – One was Frank, the Chief Financial Officer, dressed in a black-tie suit matching his receding hair. The other was a bald man, clad in a white suit with a glass of whiskey in hand. He sat with his torso twisted toward the window, half of his face shrouded in shadow.

Curious, Johnson watched as each cascading headlight passed by the window revealing a portion of the enigmatic man's appearance. The whiskey's clear amber color created a sepia tone-like lens.

It was the first time Johnson had met the man in the white suit. The only knowledge about him was Gus' instructions during onboarding: follow every single order given by this man to accomplish the mission that was approaching: A new deal with a Yakuza district.

The deal would provide an expansion in the district, leading to higher production and profit from M.A.D. in the form of the most euphoric-inducing variation created by the cartel's lead scientist. For the Yakuza, this defined the perfect entertainment drug.

He spoke in a dark, grizzly-like voice. "We need to make a return to Kingsbridge. Make sure operations aren't reaching over their boundaries. Make note of that."

"Noted," Frank replied.

The man in the white suit lifted an index finger and pointed at Johnson. "You. Your name?"

Johnson kept a stern expression, despite the towel in his hand. He enunciated his name.

The man cleared his throat. "How much longer do we have to bake in this fucking car, Johnson?" The grizzly tone in his voice changed to a more flamboyant husk.

"It'd be better if I ask the driver," said Johnson. "I'm not entirely sure—"

"Please, Johnson. First warning: Know every answer to every question."

"Yes, sir. I'm sorry."

"Fortunately, I give about 102 warnings. Frank gets it." The man waved his raised finger at Frank.

"It becomes part of the normal," said Frank with a half-smile.

The bald man turned away from the window, staring more directly at Johnson. He hunched forward, clutching his drink with both hands. "Christ..." he scowled. "Are you fucking bleeding still?"

"Yes..."

Johnson kept his gaze averted, feeling a flush of redness surging through his neck. Past instances reminded Johnson how much of an inconvenience he was for himself and those around him.

"You've been bleeding—hey, look at me, alright?"

Johnson caught the man's full complexion when he looked up. His vision examined every detail, like a human microscope trying to comprehend the sight in front of him. The right half of the face, from the cheek towards his eye, was scarred with varying degrees of burns in several ring-like layers. The passing streetlights revealed small patches of matte-like bone marrow around the bright red.

The eye of the afflicted half maintained the same pattern. Bloodshot veins of the same red hue filled the sclera, making the darkness in the narrow-slit iris more prominent.

Johnson accumulated an uneasy trickle of sweat the longer he stared down onto the man's tainted eye. For one flicker of a moment, it seemed an orange spark emitted from the eye.

But it didn't matter.  That calm stare evoked terror. As if the devil, or hell itself, had taken refuge inside this human's eye. If he were ever human.  Johnson did his best to maintain his composure.

"You've been bleeding for this whole fucking ride. Pull it together!"

"Sorry." Johnson's cheeks flushed red.  He lowered his head to try and reduce the visibility of the bleeding. "I've been getting these random nosebleeds for as long as I can remember. Y'kno?"

"Uh huh."

Frank flashed another polite smirk. "Lasting longer than I thought around Diablo," he said.

*'Diablo? Who has a name like that?'*

"Y'kno, maybe I should shove some tissues up there and say fuck it, right." Johnson smiled.

Diablo scowled. "Gross."

Johnson rolled his eyes down. The engine of the limousine purred among the smooth concrete. Then, the sound of a revolver's barrel spinning and locking in place caught Johnson's attention. Now, Diablo twirled a pistol, keeping the barrel pointed in Johnson's direction.

The revolver clicked. Johnson lowered his head and shut his eyes. The engine's hum occupied the lingering silence.

"Come on, Johnson," Diablo spoke more upbeat. "You're less gross than that. There's nervousness, I get that, what with all the blood and shit." He let out a reluctant sigh and continued. "My brother used to always say I had this commanding aura about me. When we were younger, we used to pull a whole bunch of dangerous stunts. More dangerous than that though, was our dad. If our dad caught us doing too much of that reckless shit, he would nearly beat us into a coma. And that was on his good days.

"One time we were climbing atop his tool shed. My brother was the first to parkour his way up and onto the roof. Mind you, it was made of the flimsiest wood. It's perplexing how that shed lasted through so many storms."

Diablo sipped on his whiskey. "Anyway, after he makes his way across, I go. I could remember being able to see the roof of our house and the neighbors' lawns. You imagine this is what kings see because you've been raised from dirt and you're short. It was about a second until I broke through the roof into that dust-filled shit hole.

"When my father stampeded into the shed, I screamed immediately. Terrified. Who wouldn't? I cried, 'I'm already hurt! I'm already hurt! Carlos deserves it more.' And if you could believe it, he listened. That day, my brother Carlos went to the hospital for spilling a pot of boiling water on his chest."

Diablo fell silent. Johnson struggled processing the imagery of that last sentence.

"That's… a shame," said Johnson. He held back any visible reaction.

"It's more hilarious in hindsight." Diablo cackled. The laughter eased Johnson for a moment, willing to share despite the continuous trickling of heat and sweat down his spine.

"My kid has that same energy, sometimes my wife and I don't know what to do."

"Frank's heard the story," said Diablo. "Right, Frank?"

Frank flashed another smirk. "Also part of the normal. We should go over numbers in case they get high and mighty, Diablo."

"Do you beat your child, Johnson?" Diablo rasped.

"Oh, god no!" Johnson responded. "How disgusting. I'd never imagine hurting my kid like that. She's a gem."

Diablo smiled. "You're a good man, Johnson. I knew it! I knew you weren't gross. Gross people never think anything is disgusting."

Johnson smiled halfway. He turned to Frank for reciprocation in the form of another polite smirk. However, his attention – split in awe and anxiety – directed to a revolver in his hands, checking each slot in the barrel was loaded.

A gun in civilian hands was a rare sight nowadays. Johnson knew dwindling production on firearms was a wide topic of controversy since its global announcement back in the day. Even black markets lacked the parts to make reliable weapons. For the cartel to have even a few was astounding.

*'It's just in case,'* Johnson assured himself. *'Just in case.'*

Johnson replied, "The reason why I wanted this job was for my family. I think I can do right with this."

"You're right, Johnson," Diablo placed his whiskey glass into a nearby holder. "You're in the *right* fucking place. You gotta get your hands dirty, though, and not from nosebleeds."

Beads of sweat accumulated on Johnson's head and neck. He chuckled. "I've already had to kill a few people." Johnson left out the detail that all those kills were accidents.

"Also becomes part of the normal," said Frank. Another polite smirk. "Stay focused, don't rely on luck."

"How long have you been a part of this, Frank?" Johnson asked.

Frank looked up to the ceiling. "Oh, it must've been–"

Diablo placed his revolver to the side and rifled through his pockets. "Frank. Hand me your gun. You too, Johnson."

Johnson unsheathed his revolver out of his pocket.

Frank batted a glance before he handed his gun. "May I ask why?" he asked.

Diablo's eye, bloodshot and vehement, darted around the car while the other calm eye focused on the task at hand. He emptied the ammo from each firearm. Frank sighed through his teeth.

"Let's play a game…" Diablo pulled out two golden bullets from his pocket. "Trick bullets. I will insert one into the chambers of each gun. The trick to these bullets is that some will fire and some will jam up."

He passed the revolver back to Frank and Johnson. Johnson's first impulse was to ask why, but the encroaching terror from before still held him back.

"You guys are fine to sit where you're at. Frank's right. Never rely on luck. And never assume something as coincidence."

———

Johnson looked to Frank for clarity. For the first time, Frank's composed expression was now one of concern.

"Like one of those old westerns," said Diablo. He clasped his hands together. "Quickdraw. Go in for the kill. If you hesitate, I'll kill you. Simple, right?"

"We've shared rides before, Diablo," said Frank. "I've been here for three years. Why put me in this with the rookie?"

"First, you were never the type to stay overnight, or longer. Second, you don't think I check numbers, Frank? Doesn't matter if that's your position. They're my numbers."

Frank squinted his eyes. "Are you implying I'm botching the numbers?"

"Well, okay, I don't check them. But thank God for Gus. *But*, but." Diablo turns to Johnson with a smile. "Get this, Johnson. Frank is no stranger to killing. But little do I learn that some of them he doesn't kill in exchange for personal loans. What do you think of that?"

Johnson remained silent.

"That's not a rhetorical question," said Diablo.

"Sh...shady," Johnson said. The hand holding the gun trembled. Even his toes trembled, reverberating into his knees. "Shady."

"And you, Johnson, well...nosebleeds. And the killings require more cleanup with you. Vomiting. Right?"

Johnson, flushed red, nodded.

Diablo clicked his tongue. "Count to ten with me."

Johnson's breathing hollowed as he tried to focus, counting.

"One...two..."

Frank had to be more experienced. His demeanor up until now showed it.

"Three...four..."

With Johnson's life on the line, it meant his family's life was on the line. They needed the money.

"Five...six..."

A confidence stirred from within. He gained certainty in his quick draw aiming.

———

34

"Seven…eight…"

All eyes darted along with the limo, zigzagging between one and another.

"Nine…"

Johnson's hand placed on the handle. Frank's gaze steeled with resolve. He nodded, leaving Johnson puzzled. Out of sportsmanship?

"Ten."

Silence. Diablo smiled. Frank whipped the revolver out first. Johnson, a second after. As Johnson pulled the trigger, Frank switched his aim to Diablo and pulled. The revolver clicked.

Johnson's bullet released, piercing Frank's liver. Frank planted one hand onto his wound for seconds, panting. He raised it, slowly, staring down at palm covered in blood.

Diablo pulled out his skull-engraved pistol and fired two shots into Frank. One in the neck and one in the head. Frank's eyes froze open as he expelled blurts of blood.

Johnson leaned his trembling torso into his seat, looking inward. Frank's stare wasn't the intent to kill. It was the intent to overpower Diablo.

"Huh," Diablo remarked, "Good work, Johnson. You made his life somehow hellish."

"I…I don't know."

"You don't need to worry about that."

Suddenly, Johnson felt three impacts against his torso. He looked up from his slouch and watched a line of smoke trailing up, originating from Diablo's pistol.

"What do I say? Um, this termination reflects your performance, et cetera, et cetera. You will receive no severance, yadda-yadda. Also, you look down too much."

Johnson mimicked Frank's shock, examining the severity of the wound based on his blood-drenched palm. He collapsed to the limousine floor at the same time.

Red seeped into the carpet flooring, some dripping off the edge of the cushion saturated in Frank's blood. Lumps of gum and mold clung beneath the seats. Some, to Johnson, looked like brain matter.

He thought of his daughter, lifeless on the floor because of this demon-eyed man. Blood, fluids, and the sweaty reek from the floor filled his lungs. Then, he thought about how to get home alive. That it was a necessity to not die here. If he managed to turn his body, then maybe he could cough the blood out. Diablo's sudden hyena-like cackle made it difficult to think.

The cackle settled. "El Ojo Loco del Diablo. I don't even know Spanish. Diablo. The name that stuck with me. I bet you couldn't care less since you never asked. Manners."

Johnson's hands grew numb. His nose began to bleed again. Wet iron trailed down his mouth like a waterfall.

An endless ringing overwhelmed his senses, shutting his body down. It eventually quelled to silence. Johnson's eyes rolled back, the wetness of blood soaking through his black suit.

# V
## DIABLO
### June 22, 2022, 1:45 AM

The enjoyment of death was visceral for the devil under the yellow streetlights. Surrounded by two corpses with a glass of whiskey in hand, it was another ordinary night of inciting his passions onto the world.

Within the drug operations, Diablo and his cartel's scientist manufactured a variety of substances. They were split into categories, also acting as code words. Rabbits, Tigers, Wolves, and their most volatile, the Dragon.

But a new substance, overseen by Diablo, was dubbed the 'Unicorn' for its mystifying properties, and its unique attribute of turning an ordinary flame purple. The downside was its rotten scent of what Diablo would describe as expired eggs complemented a mix of body odor. The Unicorn was now the main component of the deal that would win the interest of the Yakuza and help Diablo refine the element and extend his reach.

The moon shined on the destination: a rusted depot, hundreds of miles away from New Manhattan. The depot was occupied by groups of workers dressed in jumpsuits, transporting boxes with a handful of construction vehicles.

Diablo's limo circumvented the loading area and arrived at the massive front entrance. Inside, two men stood as two prominent navy dots.

Gus, Diablo's right-hand man, approached and opened the limo door. He was the kind of individual necessary for any business to succeed, and thus would never be in the position of Frank nor Johnson. Correct business etiquette, proper black suit attire–with a cord connected from the pocket to his ear for constant communication–a fascination with the patience of honing a blade. Impeccable skin care.

Diablo stepped out the limo with a nonchalant yawn.

"Evening, Gus."

"Good evening," Gus replied. "You're on time." The two entered the depot's vast facility.

"The meeting didn't start an hour ago?" Diablo asked.

Gus replied with a deadpan stare.

Diablo cackled in laughter. "That was funny," Diablo continued, "Better than your political jokes."

"Those aren't jokes…"

"Come on, I just got here." Diablo looked down to find a drop of blood on his suit. "And I got blood on my suit, fuck! This shit is harder to wash out than wine."

Gus turned back towards the car. "Where…*You did it again?*"

"Yeah, I did."

"Frank, too? It's better to have had them before. Probably would've died if this deal went uneventful."

"Why, so he could squeal the wrong numbers and flirt with the other side? They're ants. Too many of them around is a nuisance."

"Did Johnson go out quickly, at least?"

"Quick enough. Let's see, our clientele is…" Diablo squinted his right, tainted eye to get a good look at the group. One was well into his late seventies, while the other appeared to be in their prime. All of them resembled traits of Japanese descent. "The Chinese? I thought we were talking with Yakuza."

"Those are Japanese."

Diablo's vision returned to normal. "That's new. You think that—"

Gus interjected, "Nothing racist. We need this deal."

Diablo sighed. As the duo approached, the Japanese faction faced Diablo and Gus in a single file line.

Gus flashed a polite smile. In meetings like these, he was the better man to set the tone.

"Gentlemen," said Gus, "It's a pleasure to finally get this arranged. Let me introduce you to the man behind our operations. He is referred to as El Ojo Loco Diablo. You may call him Diablo."

"Diablo." The old man, in the middle, spoke and bowed. It was apparent from his accent he was raised in Japan, and he knew English at only a basic-level. He pointed to himself and smiled. "Kei Suguru." He motioned to the man on his right.

"I am Masao Kawasaki," he bowed. "I will be translating for Kei-Sama."

"We are so glad you and Kei-Sama appreciate the value that our product presents to the world," Gus said.

Diablo shuffled through his pockets and pulled out a stainless-steel lighter engraved with a funky-shaped grinning skull. A spark of flame ignited with one flick. *'Let Gus handle the talking,'* he thought, noting the lack of patience.

Gus continued. "I brought a suitcase with the formula your operation can use. We have sent it to test groups, and it is proving to be quite a best-seller."

He kept the lit flame close to his diseased cheek, numb to most sensations. The flame returned soothing sparks to those obsolete nerves. He struggled to keep the following adrenaline hidden, producing gleeful thoughts over future acquisitions. First Japan, then South Korea, followed by London and so on.

"As negotiated, you will provide us a monthly fee, twenty percent of the profits, to accomplish this transaction. If payment is unfulfilled, then, consider it an instant professional termination. Although I see us as thriving partners." Gus smiled.

Ambition was necessary in any business that wished to thrive. Diablo sought to execute with precision, be it partnerships. Or death.

Kei began speaking to Masao in Japanese. Diablo made a mental note of how fast and garbled it sounded. Masao spoke back. The exchange continued for another minute.

"We thank you for coming this far, Gus and Diablo," Masao said, facing the duo. "However, we have decided to not go monthly and would like only a fraction of the Unicorn for one payment."

Gus raised an eyebrow. "Interesting. You understand that you're losing the chance for a very lucrative deal?"

"Please, Gus," Masao raised one hand. "We understand the notoriety of your drug. But what if it is another trend? We cannot afford to commit to a long-term deal like you proposed."

Part of it was true. The trend of M.A.D. was a slippery slope, leading to a gamble of hit-or-miss in the black market.

But to Diablo, calling the Unicorn a trend was bullshit.

Kei continued to speak in Japanese, followed by Masao's translation.

"We'd like to leave with a deal. Not make this dishonorable."

The soothing adrenaline rattled into fury over the current downward spiral of this deal. How many times had they met to negotiate? Three? Four? It made Diablo's skin boil thinking about the amount of time wasted.

But he remained silent. Gus knew how to find alternative solutions. A signal was made in the event no solution could be found, however. Part of him wanted to see this signal.

"Alright," Gus said. "Boss?"

"Hm?" Diablo flicked off the lighter.

"Deal's done," said Gus.

There was a look of disdain on Gus' expression. It wasn't out of fear, Diablo knew that much.

Masao bowed. He grabbed a suitcase from behind them and handed it to Gus. "Here. Inside is your money."

Gus nodded and proceeded to walk back to the limo. Diablo turned to follow, catching sight of two Yakuza smiling, almost giddy that they pulled this deal off.

Diablo walked to Gus, ready to rant as Gus opened one side of his black suit, revealing a short sword, dressed in ebony, diamond-shaped wraps, tucked into his waistband. It was one of Gus' favorite swords to use in his hobby.

Gus flashed the blade. Diablo smiled. The signal that no other solutions could be found.

Diablo sped ahead past Gus in a frenzy, and then past the limo onto the open concrete. Diablo called over a passing forklift.

———

Upon stopping, he threw the driver out and got into the seat. Diablo turned the gargantuan vehicle toward the warehouse.

"Get moving!" he yelled to Gus.

Gus marched back and waved the limo driver to go away from the warehouse.

Diablo stomped on the drive pedal, accelerating the forklift into the warehouse where the Japanese duo still stood. Diablo roared, the air and heat rising from the base of his lungs and impaled the elder Kei into the wall behind him.

A barrage of bullets pierced the forklift's exterior, courtesy of Masao and his two semi-automatic guns. One round grazed Diablo, provoking him to curse in pain.

He pulled out his revolver and fired three shots at Masao. The third shot made an impact, forcing Masao to crumble. Diablo's right eye sparked orange waves of heat. Different sections of the warehouse interior combusted until only the center was free of flames.

The next target focused on Masao. In an instant, Masao's back erupted in flames.

The flame-lit Yakuza rose to his feet, letting out nonstop pain-filled shrieks, and lunged for an attack. Diablo reloaded his revolver when Masao's eyes widened, frozen halfway. He collapsed, revealing the blade of a short sword now plunged through his back into his heart. An unnecessary hail-mary throw from Gus, but appreciated.

Diablo unloaded bullets onto Masao's lifeless body until his revolver clicked dry of ammo. He plucked the sword out and waited for it to cool before he wiped the blood with the inside of his suit jacket.

And then, a strained yell echoed from behind him. *'Oh, Kei,'* he thought, *'Right.'*

He made a U-turn as debris continued to drop, sidestepping around it here and there. Kei was left immobilized from the metal still embedded into his torso. Blood and strained air expelled from his mouth.

Diablo aimed the gun at Kei's jaw. "You remind me of a funnier version of my father. Maybe prettier too. I mean, that's not saying much. Look at me, I'm the spitting image of him."

———

Kei spat blood on Diablo's white suit before the latter could make a snide chuckle.

Diablo responded with five impulsive gunshots to Kei's face, screaming numerous times over the unfiltered bang of the revolver firing. By the time his temper tantrum cooled down, Kei's eyes had lost their color and subtle movement. Diablo turned back, muttering how his suit was going to be in the cleaners for an entire week.

The limo approached Diablo, tossing out three bodies as the door opened; Gus welcomed Diablo inside. Diablo handed the sword to Gus and took a seat by the window.

All the workers looked at the burning depot in awe and terror as a purple hue ascended from the base. The work of the Unicorn being left to burn in there. The mass became invisible dots staring at a purple-orange glow on the horizon as the limo drove farther away.

Diablo always assured himself that he was better. Better than his dad or even whatever his brother imagined of him.

"Do we have any other meetings?"

"No. International ones are hard to come by. And the small cartels in the city refuse to do business with us."

"Not even Commander?" Diablo asked, referring to his friendly rival.

"You would be the last person he'd want to see."

"I miss that guy. Beautiful smile on him." His eye began to throb.

Gus acknowledged Diablo's discomfort. "Take some painkillers when we get back to the base. We recently got some strong stuff from a supplier that hasn't been mixed in with our M.A.D."

"Gus," Diablo growled, "Next time, make our fucking deal go through. There are no other options."

His father would say things like that, even when people were concerned for his well-being. Diablo acknowledged this reflection, rooted as part of his upbringing.

"Absolutely," replied Gus.

The highway lanes were bereft of traffic. A couple of red and blue lights strobing past the limo in the opposite direction.

Diablo was fixated on details of the business. After about an hour, he broke the silence.

"Hey. Puerco and Rooster were trying to go after a Sage. What's up with that?"

Gus sighed. "Let's discuss after we rest."

Diablo turned away to watch the dimming roads outside the window, his demonic eye illuminated under the cast of amber streetlights.

# VI
## TODD HYME
### June 22, 2022, 11:22 AM

Todd sat atop a bench table adjacent to his classroom. The canopy of summer leaves above rustled against each other, orchestrating a crisp whistle.

Manchester Manhattan University wasn't the grandest, but it provided enough for its students to study, socialize and enjoy pieces of nature within an urban landscape.

He traced a finger along his polo's fabric, stopping at a dark stain by his abdomen to his dismay. It was a similar residue to the glue he used for his projects.

11:22 AM, and Isaac was nowhere to be seen. It was their third year in college, both studying Advanced Engineering.

'*He'll show up,*' Todd thought.

At 11:30 AM, Todd entered class, where Professor Beige commenced her Advanced Engineering lecture.

Sixteen minutes later, Isaac tiptoed inside, dressed in a white tee, black sweatpants and unkempt hair, creeping to the empty seat beside Todd.

"Before you start," Isaac whispered, "Yes, I know I look like shit."

"Everything alright?" Todd whispered back, "I haven't heard from you all weekend."

"Had a bit going on. Lost my finger and my house."

"Ah. Does that mean you lost the report too?"

Isaac's eyes narrowed.

"I'm kidding, man." Todd said with stifled laughter.

Isaac smirked. He pulled out a full 20-page report from his backpack.

Todd scanned the documents. Fully typed and cited.  "So, you were joking about the fire, right?"

Isaac waved his bandaged hand. Four fingers extended outward, sans a pinky.

"Shit."

"We'll talk after class," Isaac replied.

Professor Beige hurled an eraser at Isaac's head, prompting complete silence.

***

Isaac shared with Todd what occurred to cause his disappearance, his eyes turning weary by the end of it. Todd offered Isaac half of his sandwich as the duo sat at a round table in the university café.

"I can buy my own sandwich," said Isaac.

"You need money for a new place, and you look like you're about to fall dead, eyes wide open, if you don't get something in your system.  I'm not keen on changing the trajectory of everyone's lives with an incident like that."

Isaac shrugged, becoming complacent as he engorged a third of his sandwich.

"Maybe we can get a little more time for this report," Todd continued. "I'll email Beige and let her know. Shit happens."

"Thanks." Isaac said mid-chew.  He rubbed his eraser-inflicted head. "Wish I had faster reflexes."

"The charity event happened this past weekend too, didn't it?" Todd leaned in.

Isaac nodded, his focus maintained on the sandwich.

Todd's eyes lit up. An impulsive grin formed out of pride for his friend.  For Isaac to own his family's company was a grand achievement.

"So, what was it like?"

"I showed up in sweater and slacks."

45

Todd squinted his eyes. He leaned back into his chair, his lips flattened. "Dude…"

Isaac cleared his mouth. "Maybe now, they'll stop sending invites. It's fine either way. We don't need shortcuts." Isaac tapped his finger along the table's chipped edges. "The woman that kept inviting me did say to think about it though. She wants me to be a part of what my family started."

"It *is* your family's company."

"That's the thing, it's not. Name and likeness only." Isaac took another bite of the sandwich. "I would've been the star of their marketing. I still think they're using me solely for that."

"Right."

"Yeah," Isaac replied, "I'll get to the top my way. *Our* way."

"I'm with ya." Todd and Isaac honed their skills to make it this far. They had been elected as candidates for big-tech engineering positions before. Their work applauded. Although Todd was adamant they were on the same level, Isaac swiftly swipe those claims away.

Footsteps echoed every time students walked in and out of the adjacent café, trays of different meals evoking savory and fruity aromas. Isaac's eyes were regaining their livelihood.

"You should probably rest."

"Got stuff to do." Isaac fidgeted his fingers on the table again, leaving four vertical smudges. "Wouldn't you want to find the people who did that?"

"Who? Your home invaders?" Todd asked.

"Yeah. Is that weird?"

He reflected on what would change from catching the culprits. How would that bring him closer to his goals? It seemed shallow and illogical.

"It's cool, but pointless," Todd admitted.

Isaac's expression turned blank. Simmering, the blankness turned into an angsty scowl. Not the response his friend wanted to hear. Todd tried to realign with him.

"Believe me, I couldn't imagine one person who wouldn't want that," Todd said. "But there are better things to pursue in life. Things you can direct that energy toward, like ways to lower crime rate. Or a better policing system, good surveillance technology."

"Finding and stopping them can lead to something else, can't it?"

"Feels more like a desire than a goal. Karma will get them anyway."

"I didn't take you for a karma person."

"When there's bigger things to focus on, I am."

He darted his familiar scowl away from Todd. It was his way of saying 'agree to disagree,' and leave it at that. Although Todd empathized with Isaac, he found no logic in his way of thinking. And thus, no rationale.

Being friends since grade school, Todd knew Isaac as a determined individual as opposed to the tragic moniker plastered by the media. He also knew Isaac's determination could be a wildfire if not controlled. But the honesty, as a longtime friend, came from solely good intentions. To keep the determination focused onto better goals and bring out the best nature.

"Hey!"

A familiar, brazen voice called out to Todd. It was Rosemary, a classmate from his Sociology class, standing out in a vibrant yet soft-colored floral outfit.

"Sorry to bother. You got the homework?" Rosemary asked. She fluttered her eyes to the corner where an entranced Isaac sat, then back to Todd. She brushed her fingers through her dirty blonde hair with one giant swipe.

"Oh, yeah." Todd pulled a sheet out of his backpack with her name. "It's got slightly different wording on the answers, but you should be fine."

Rosemary handed Todd a half-folded twenty-dollar bill from her pocket. "Thank you so much. By the way, um…" Rosemary pointed to Todd's abdomen. "Have you tried vinegar and water for that stain?"

"Ah, no, but I'll give it a try. Thanks."

"No problem," Rosemary smiled. "I gotta get going, thanks again. I'll see you in class tomorrow." She shifted her hazel-green eyes to Isaac. "Bye."

Isaac's expression snapped back to normal. "Bye."

Rosemary exited the café. Isaac leaned into Todd. "You have a girlfriend now?" he asked Todd.

Todd scoffed. "Nah. But *you* think she's cute."

Isaac's face flushed red.

"We've talked a few times in class," Todd continued. "I could tell her about you if you're interested."

"My head's in a bit of a jumble right now. Maybe not the best time."

"You should go for it. Before someone else does."

"We… need to keep working, yeah?" Isaac shrugged. "Focus and all that. Gotta make sure I don't fall behind on my other classes."

"Aren't they both optional at this point?" Todd asked.

"I got good at engineering. Not as good as you, but…I like learning about business, and new-gen chemistry. Gives me more insight into what my mom did."

"Kinda bizarre that you hear your mother being talked about like that. As a school subject."

"Bizarre…Maybe not the right word." Isaac scratched his head. "It feels like a eulogy. I get chills when they do bring her up in past tense. 'When Dr. Sage was around,' like that, you know? Sometimes Professor Beige glances at me when she catches herself saying it profusely." The puzzled look of self-reflection sunk to melancholy.

Todd pressed his lips. All the studies, isolation and now Isaac's recent event compacted into signs of fatigue. They'd spent all their time home or at the university this past year.

"We should do something this weekend. Something easygoing?" Todd asked.

Isaac shrugged. "I guess we could watch a movie. Although—"

"You'd prefer staying at home. Not much of a choice, is it?"

Isaac sighed.

"I'm sure I can get a couple others to join. Rosemary, for example," said Todd.

"Try not to make it obvious around her."

"I don't know how else to put it. I was gonna say you have a shrine of her in your attic, complete with religious prayers." Todd took a bite of his sandwich.

"Don't forget the part where I sacrifice a goat also while chanting her name," Isaac quipped.

They wrapped up lunch, Isaac finally admitting he needed to sleep for an extra 12 hours. Todd agreed. Before heading home, he scavenged parts – wires, circuitry and scrap metal and plastic – at the campus tech workshop before taking the subway station home. Isaac's missing finger sparked new ideas for a prosthetic.

***

Living at a complex in the eastern district of New Manhattan, was possible thanks to his scholarship and some extra help from his parents. Isaac urged to chip in, but Todd refused to let his best friend loan money, worried over the dynamic of their friendship changing. It was also a shortcut he wouldn't allow himself to take.

Erratic chatter emanated from a neighboring unit at 105, about two doors down from Todd's studio. His neighbor chatted with two people dressed in suits by the front door, his hands raised as a barrier. A woman, whose burly silhouette masked part of the sunlight setting in the west. And a man, pale frail and far short like a sponge left out to dry, kept one arm planted against the door frame, invading personal boundaries.

"I can pay… I need more time," was what Todd could hear from the neighbor as he reached his unit's door. Then, he averted his gaze to the corner, darting a shaken glance at Todd. Their eyes met only for a fraction of a second before Todd entered the unit.

A single room comprised of his bedroom, work area and the kitchen and bathroom at the far end. He sat down at his workspace. It consisted of a desk with drawers containing his parts in an organized fashion and a light hooked to the wall for the long nights.

He set a pencil, eraser and welding and soldering tools to the side and unrolled a two-foot blank canvas until it laid out smoothly on the desk surface.

He began considering every component, writing a list of desired goals. Optimal comfort, durable material, and efficient communication with the nervous system. As he thought, he wrote. Then he listed out the processes needed to achieve that goal, followed by sub-components.

Then, he sketched. Every stroke creating a line and beat, tapping against the wooden surface, flooded his ear dreams with a natural acoustic over a door from outside slamming shut followed by rampant shrieks, his chest pounding from the background noise.

*'It's not perfect.'* He used his thoughts to drown out the noise. *'But it'll be better than nothing.'* Todd knew the pinky finger might have been insignificant to Isaac at this point.

Gemma Sage's work instilled in Todd a conviction to invent. She contributed a worthwhile, innovative creation to the world for a while before the repercussions of *that* day. Todd believed she inspired others, including he.

No matter what noise or chaos existed, this is where he was most useful. Where his skills could sharpen, and, like a string of dominoes, create a long-lasting effect where maybe his neighbors wouldn't have to succumb to apparent loan sharks.

Finishing the rough sketch, Todd began soldering together the foundation of the prosthetic. He ignored the hours of sleep he would lose, immersing himself deeper in the process of cutting parts and connecting different materials. He relished the warmth of little sparks, the challenge of troubleshooting, and the flow behind repeating the process.

# VII
## John Saint

### June 22, 2022, 2:04 PM

Easing down the highway, Saint reflected on his dinner with Edoris. She was, for the most part, happy for him landing a new case.

"I know you're a professional, but I still worry," Edoris had said, adamant about communication. "Give me that peace of mind when you're working."

"I'll give it my all, with you in the back of my mind," Saint told Edoris.

"Attaboy."

To Saint, what this case would bring, was the satisfaction to move on. To compel him to say, 'I've done enough.' Where he could leave the city in the hands of others and find comfort in living a quiet life with Edoris. He affirmed all he needed was this satisfaction to attain that life.

***

Saint arrived at the police station. He patted down his white button-up and adjusted his coat. The folder of the Arson cases remained gripped in his hand as he stepped into the lobby. He passed by Billows's desk to drop off the manila folder.

"G'Morning, Saint," Billows said.

"Morning." Saint placed the manila folders on Billows' desk and kept going straight to Forensics for the results of the letter he'd dropped off, immediately pressing on to the next task. Every second of time spent was invaluable.

"You're welcome!" Billows yelled. He followed with a muttered 'jackass.'

———

Saint entered Forensics and learned of the acquired fingerprints. They ID'd Ricardo Rodrigues, the cousin of the deceased Guido and someone who had been arrested before over minor offenses. A notable feature of Ricardo's mug-shot was the absence of eyebrows on his pastel orange skin.

Saint then made his way to Briggs' office. The Chief shuffled through his papers, remaining oblivious to Saint's entrance. Saint knocked on the door to catch his attention.

Nothing. Two louder taps and Briggs jumped.

"Son of a bitch," Briggs yelled. "You're lucky you're a Saint."

Saint replied with a smirk. "I found a lead on this new investigation and some new hints."

"Alright, get on with it then and go."

Saint turned to exit.

"Wait!"

Only to be halted by another command.

"You're taking detective Billows with you."

Saint faced Briggs. "Why?"

He had no problem with Billows in general. Billows did his work and handled his baggage well. It was sharing the workload with another that Saint was disgruntled about.

"He's been cooped up here for too long, and he's read the arson files. And, well…" Briggs cleared his throat. "You haven't had a case like this for a while. I need someone with a good head on their shoulders to watch your back."

"Chief, I'm fine," Saint replied.

"You're smart. But that recklessness since when you started is something I was wary of. Even though you've matured, it pops up. I trust ya, John. I do. Let Billows tag along, offer an extra helping hand, and I'll make sure you have your freedom."

Saint clicked his tongue and tapped his foot, thinking of a counter. Seconds passed. Briggs' expression cemented. The detective exhaled through his nose, left the office and passed by Billows' desk.

"Meet me at my car in five minutes," said Saint.

———

"You taking me to a workshop on social etiquette?" Billows asked.

Saint smirked, locking eyes with Billows' deadpan stare. "Sorry. Get ready."

In the car, Saint explained to Billows what the investigation was about. Billows agreed to come along if it meant he wouldn't have to do paperwork for a long time.

***

Saint and Billows headed to Syracuse, where Ricardo's house resided. As they drove out of the city in Saint's sedan, the skyscrapers withered to flatlands extending beyond the horizon, divided by a single two-lane concrete road. The old sedan bounced up and down, one side rocking up higher than the other. Billows leaned half of his head out the lowered window, his nose pointed at the sky.

Saint flipped the radio switch to some bright, energetic pop music while he focused on case details and strategizing. Two seconds later, Billows turned down the volume dial.

"So, what do you plan to find? And who's handling the paperwork for this? Me?"

"An answer to this investigation," Saint said. "I'll handle the paperwork." He used his time in the car to meditate in his thoughts nowadays. And he enjoyed it.

The drive went on for a little longer, the radio still playing in low ambiance. Saint focused on the drive and processing his current clues for the investigation. Ricardo was linked to Guido. Guido was linked to a drug cartel. Given those hints and Ricardo's record, Guido got mixed up and was burned to death. But why? A simple mishap where Guido got greedy?

"So," Billows broke the silence, "what do you do when you're not investigating?"

Saint didn't respond. A simple mishap wouldn't lead to Guido's corpse being charred into burns of several degrees. A gunshot to the head would have sufficed.

"Looks like you're always in the field working," said Billows.

———

Saint presumed Guido might have messed with the higher-ups of the cartel. He tried to connect more clues into a cohesive web.

Billows coughed and continued. "I like playing basketball. Taking walks through the park. Books are cool, but I get distracted easily, y'kno?"

But Billows wouldn't shut up. His words collided with Saint's train of thought.

Saint gritted his teeth, ready to stomp on the brakes and shout at Billows. He wasn't going to allow any mistakes on this case.

"Action movies are nice. This one called Baby Driver, you should, uh–" Billows pointed at the radio with a sly smirk. "Is your favorite music pop?"

"Focus for me," Saint snapped. "I don't mean to be a jackass, but focus for me, please. It's not every day you find a burnt corpse in a town house. This is something affecting the city. It's…" Saint's mind lingered on the other similarly charred bodies in the reports. "It's important."

"We should know each other better. Music taste is a decent starter. How do you know it's important when we haven't started? Let me guess, this is your quest for *vengeance*." He said the last word in a mocking, melodramatic tone.

"Because more people will die from this if the bad guys win. We're there to stop them." If they didn't perform well, Briggs could transfer this case.

"Bad guys? What are you, a, erm—" Billows stopped his banter. *'Smart,'* Saint thought. "But it's no use getting worked up over it 24/7."

"Have you seen a burnt corpse?" Saint corrected himself before Billows had the opportunity to respond. *"In person."*

"When you see as many photos as me, it might as well be waived as seeing it in person."

The veteran detective let out a stressed sigh. "So let me get your take. It's bizarre, isn't it? The way he died?"

Billows scratched his head. "I'm no scientist, but I believe different parts of the body melt differently. Y'kno, with fat contents and all."

"Hm."

"But…To melt bones into a couch. And the fact most of the bones were intact other than the point of melding, *that's* strange. So, I won't say you're wrong. But you're being a bit of a jackass. So, take it easy, yeah?"

"Fine. Sorry."

Saint hoped he would find the feelings he wanted at the conclusion of this case. No more feelings of discomfort and unease with resting. Tranquility. He peered at Billows' head leaning out of the car, resting on the knuckles of his hand. His chest rose and sank, rhythmic like meditation.

"Y'kno," Billows said, "The best way to not be stressed from something as traumatic as a burnt corpse, or a dead body, is imagining it as something else. People usually say, 'try to think of something else,' but, I mean, a fucking dead body. How are you gonna think of something else?"

Saint sighed through his teeth. He yearned for time to think.

"The way I do it is after paying respect," Billows continued, "I imagine them as props. Make-up and CGI are so realistic nowadays. When you think of it as a movie prop, the brain eases. You can believe it and say, 'Damn, the make-up artist did an awesome job with that.' I would wear nose plugs though, for the smell–"

"Alright!" Saint shouted. "Alright. Can we meditate on this?"

Billows shrugged. For any case to be solved, every detail needed to be assessed thrice. If it were not to be handled properly, he questioned, what would his father think?

***

The ride diverted from the main road toward a hill leading to Ricardo's pale white house set at the peak. Saint parked just outside the front and approached the front door. Some of the white paint had chipped, revealing the beige wood foundation. To the left and right of the door were windows veiled by lavender curtains.

He knocked three times.

An eye peeked out of the right set of curtains then vanished. Then, the door opened. The face behind the door matched Ricardo's I.D. His appearance was aged, well-worn from three to four decades of stress. Some tattoos adorned his neck. Although he was ID'd as being in his mid-to-late twenties.

"Can I help you?" Ricardo asked.

"Ricardo Rodrigues," Saint introduced himself and Billows. They flashed their badges. "We're from the New Manhattan PD. We're here to investigate the murder of your cousin, Guido Rodrigues."

Ricardo's eyes widened, "Oh, God…"

"We're gonna need you to–"

"We're sorry for your loss," Billows stated, darting a brief glare at Saint. His desensitization had caught up to him. Saint lowered his head, absorbing the humility in silence.

Billows continued. "We found some evidence that looked like you may have some connection to the crime scene. May we come inside?"

Ricardo gestured them into his house with an extended shaky arm, guiding them into the adjacent living room. The house was bright and pearlescent with dated, ornate decorations.

Ricardo offered water as they sat on the suede couch. Billows accepted while Saint declined. He walked into the nearby kitchen and returned with two glasses of water, chugged his glass within seconds as Billows looked on surprised.

"Must be that good soft water," Billows chuckled.

"This is your grandmother's house, isn't it?" Saint asked, based on the address's records. The longer Saint analyzed the living room, the more he saw charcoal-like smudges on the wallpaper.

A crackling emerged from Ricardo's throat, like pop rocks on a tongue.

"My abuela let me stay here after I was evicted from my apartment. She moved elsewhere."

"When were you evicted?" Saint asked.

"Can't recall." Ricardo rubbed his Adam's apple. "Man. My mind is taking me back to when Abuela forced us to eat the stuff we didn't like, and we would try to feed it to the pit-bull. He got so damn fat." He heaved through a chuckle as if he was severely congested.

Saint replied, "There was a letter with your fingerprint on it. It said for Guido to stop calling you, or you'd both be in trouble. Can you explain that?"

"W-We were struggling with money," Ricardo stammered. "So, w-we went to a loan dealer that promised money in exchange for smuggling drugs. 'Special' drugs."

"M.A.D.," said Billows.

Ricardo nodded. "We settled our deal and got our pay. It would've been simple, but in that business…"

"We're no strangers," replied Saint. "Guido died from being burned alive, Ricardo. We need to know who would be capable of that."

The glass Ricardo held shook with his hands.

"I need—" Ricardo's dry voice sounded strained. "I need another glass of water if you don't mind."

Ricardo sped to the kitchen and took another giant gulp of water. Saint found there to be no sign of intentions to harm.

"Sore throat?" Saint asked.

"Recent flu." Ricardo hiccupped. Saint remained reserved, but careful of his surroundings. "Guido and I saw innocents get shot down. The job was supposed to be quick and then just leave it behind. But it got to Guido," his voice broke. Tears welled up in his eyes, his cheeks sunk into his grimace.

"Are you okay?" Billows asked.

"I'm fine," said Ricardo.

"Hey, we need you to focus, Ricardo," said Saint. "Do you know any affiliates of this gang–"

"The leader had the devil's eye," Ricardo sputtered, cutting Saint off. His eyes expressed regret as soon as he said it. Ricardo shook his head.

"I'm sorry, the devil's eye?" Saint asked.

"You don't know," Ricardo tried to keep his composure, "He took so much of it. And then they ramped the shit he took, and he took more of *that*. That's what they say." His hands trembled. "He's not like you, me, anyone. He has a guy that handles operations, um, Gus. We worked more with him, um…and, and then, um–"

"You're safe with us. It's okay," said Saint.

"So, this group," Billows asked, "they operate in New Manhattan, outside?"

"They move around, so it's hard to know where they're at. Wherever warehouses exist, they've probably operated there at least once." Ricardo coughed. "That's all I know."

Billows replied, "Understand, Ricardo, that you've committed crimes by being a part of these cartels. But like Saint said, we got your back. As the NMPD, we can drastically reduce your sentence. Help us help you."

"Jail?" Ricardo whimpered. "The fuck do you mean *jail*?"

"I'm sorry, Mr. Rodrigues." Saint stood up. "We can't let you slide with this. Police will be here soon. But as long as you cooperate, what Billows said is true."

Ricardo's coughing worsened. "I need a water."

"Go ahead, son," said Saint.

Saint pulled out his phone and made the call to the NMPD, informing them of the location and details, before mentally processing the latest evidence. A dangerous leader with an empire growing in the shadows of the city, during Saint's tenure. Infecting and killing innocent people.

"They've been right under our noses," said Billows.

"How the hell did we all miss this?" Saint questioned. This lack of knowing manifested a new realization. How could he have missed this? To be this blind and naïve.

Jacques' words echoed to Saint. "Justice is delivered when evil is unveiled. And evil hides behind many guises."

Then, he imagined the conclusion to this case. Bringing justice to the evil that he had missed this entire time. A sense of full, permanent relief. The kind of relief to close this chapter for good. Now, more than ever and for the sake of others whose lives were ruined by this cartel, this case needed to be solved.

Severe gagging followed, along with the sudden stench of burnt flesh singing through Saint's nostrils. The detective turned around to find smoke accumulating in the kitchen. Billows looked to Saint for confirming the level of danger.

The coughing continued, and a scruff voice growled in the smoke.

"They're gonna kill me!" Ricardo screamed. The heat ratcheted up in the house.

<hr>

Ricardo leapt out of the smoke, pale-faced, bent over as a pool of bright red-orange chunky goo and black smoke spewed from his mouth.

The red-orange goo was boiling. It pulsated and bubbled, singing a part of Saint's clothing. That's when he realized, to his horror, it was lava. The lava began to burn through everything it met, including the floor.

Ricardo met Saint with with bloodshot eyes irritated by the smoke expelling from his mouth. Saint reached for his gun when Ricardo charged and pinned him into the wall by his shoulders.

"Step away, Ricardo!" Billows raised his weapon at him.

"They're gonna kill me!" Ricardo shouted. "Like how I had to kill my Abuela! My brother! I killed him! I killed Guido! They didn't!"

His scorching hot breath stung Saint's skin. Billows yelled a final warning.

The man's grip tightened despite the warnings. "Do you want to see more? Like how I killed him?" A bright orange began to glow brighter from Ricardo's throat, "Like thi—"

The room reverberated with a sudden bang. Ricardo's grip around Saint released. His body fell to the ground.

The remaining lava poured out of Ricardo's mouth, instantly turning grey and brittle.

"What the fuck!" Saint shouted.

"I had to shoot him!" Billows shouted.

"Not that, the fucking lava! Holy…" Saint leaned back.

"If they all mutate like that, then…" Billows massaged the temples of his head. "I need a drink."

"Likewise. Likewise."

Minutes later, the squad cars arrived. Billows and Saint gave their stories that led to the shooting and death of Ricardo Rodrigues. And now, the first case involving M.A.D mutation had been documented.

It was unknown whether the news media would cover it. It was best to keep it a secret for as long as possible. Something like this would spur chaos in the world.

Outside, in the dusk, Saint sat with Billows. They basked in the blue and white lights of the police vehicles. Forensics and medics arrived ten minutes later to examine the corpse.

"Well, I think this case got important," Billows assented.

Saint nodded. "They'll get their justice. They all will." He stated it with calm certainty. "We'll start navigating through every warehouse."

"Good… after a drink."

"After a drink."

"And after you promise to please keep that corny justice crap to once every month. You sound like a serial character from the 50s."

Saint smiled, pausing for a moment. "Pop and rock."

"What?" asked Billows.

"My choice of music."

Billows squinted his eyes, then nodded, understanding the context. "Favorite artist?"

"Queen."

"That's a start."

The spark within Saint was alit despite the terror of the unknown. He felt alive, knowing this case could make the city safe enough for him and Edoris to have that peaceful life.

# VIII
## ISAAC SAGE

### June 24, 2022, 9:10 AM

'*Pointless.*' The sentiment Todd shared, mixed with fury and self-doubt, burrowed in Isaac's mind.

Step by step down the dense, daylit streets of West Village, he reflected on every second, minute, hour, and day spent drifting in the past.

Within that era of drifting, many treated Isaac the same as a tragic social experiment. The act of observing from afar, questioning what the orphaned child would do next. Or even strangers walking up to Isaac, a child, either expressing their condolences or confronting him, instigating how a loved one perished in the explosion because of his parents.

On the playground, Isaac found his comfort in isolation in contrast to being surrounded by loud, overly enthusiastic peers, egging him on with the most invasive questions.

Except Todd. Todd was initially quiet, yet receptive. Over time, his positive energy was a relief. Instead of offering rampant apologies, Todd joked with Isaac. Instead of invasive gossip, Todd snuck into movie theaters with him, discussing video game lore where parts of the movie dragged to predictability. Those times, among other worthwhile memories, made living more tolerable.

Alas, this was outweighed by the moments of stagnancy. The action of waiting for time to pass, removing most of the joys life could have been offered.

Additionally, the current tiny details were noticeable enough to spark speculation, including that ghostly card. That the incident haunting Isaac was more than a freak accident.

Isaac questioned. *'Coasting through life or chasing after the potential thing that took my family away. Which is more pointless?'*

<hr>

With each second, the balance shifted to one answer, impacted by more certainty. An act of something more than vengeance, but to enact the justice his parents deserved.

On this very morning, he commenced the first steps of any plan to ensure success: preparation.

First, gear. Isaac purchased the gear he needed through a hidden VPN on his own laptop yesterday.

Then, when to commence and how to move around. Traversal along the rooftops and upper levels in the night would be best to reduce visibility. Operations most likely initiated during dusk as well.

Third, who could be involved? The NMPD's history made them unreliable. Involving anyone else increased the risk of harming innocent lives. Thus, no one else could be made aware of his vendetta.

Indirect help though, in the form of training and resources, was effective. A good alibi would maintain the separation of this would and the underground.

Research for the most effective regimen led Isaac to the front doors of Onyx Obadiah's World-Class Gym, operated by the established retired fighter himself.

Obadiah was also well-trained in parkour, being a part of the group X-Ceed, run by the leader Chantal Freebes. Freebes and Onyx together held the Titan Quad-Fecta, an accolade handed to few for completing four of the world's toughest obstacle courses.

If Isaac could be trained under Obadiah, or someone like him, he would be in ideal shape for his mission.

Obadiah's gym was a compact cube of grey and red décor, with enough space for roughly fifteen people to train at once. Belts and framed photos of Obadiah's victories over the years adorned the walls, from boxing to Muay Thai, providing hard proof of his World-Class title.

A few boxers practiced with bright red punching bags on one side, while the other side stored a partition of faded gloves and mitts. Another open space was used for shadow-boxing.

Obadiah, in a slate tank top and knee-high shorts, worked a round of mitts with another younger, spry person in the ring, bounded by red rope. His white mosaic tattoos resembling gear cogs glistened against the sweat on his gargantuan, lean physique.

"Keep your hands up!" Obadiah shouted.  His tone cut through the air, catching the attention of many.

The student, though tired, pushed through the last few seconds with determination. The bell rang and Obadiah walked to his corner.

"Excuse me," Isaac approached the experienced boxer. "Do you have any free slots?"

Obadiah turned to Isaac. "First time here?"

"Yeah. Sorry to interrupt, but I was looking to see if you could teach me how to fight."

"Sorry, clients are full. Come by next month when I have a couple of slots. But you're more than welcome to use the gym for training. Thanks for considering Obadiah's Gym."

The bell rang again. "Listen, I really need to start now." Isaac shouted as Obadiah moved back into the fight. "Name your price!"

Obadiah turned back to Isaac, batting away his apprentice's combos. "What's your budget?"

Isaac hesitated. "Uh… a lot of zeros."

Obadiah squinted with a wary half-scowl. "We'll discuss it in my office after I finish."  He turned back and slapped the side of the exhausted apprentice's head.  "Hands up!"

After the round concluded, Obadiah guided Isaac to his office, lit with soft white light.  The space adorned with framed photos of a younger Obadiah over the years posing with a new belt, surrounded by his family. He shut the door and closed the curtains.

"So," Obadiah began, "elaborate on those lots of zeros."

"300,000," Isaac blurted. "And an extra 50K for a favor?"

"What would that favor be?"

"I understand you train with X-Ceed. Could teach me how to parkour?"

"You know you're asking for a lot here in *three* months."

"I do."

"What's your schedule even look like? Remember, I got other students lined up."

"Whatever schedule I need to be good at all of this in three months," said Isaac.

Obadiah crossed his arms, leaning his colossal mass against the wall, just opposite Isaac.

"I've known you for minutes, yeah?" Obadiah said. "I don't know you or your work ethic, if you're the type to commit or if you need to be coddled."

Isaac reached into his pocket and pulled out a check folded in a perfect half. "Then I'll write the check for 300,000 dollars now," Isaac said. "All upfront. Take that as good faith. If I pull out, the money's yours."

"How do I know that check isn't fake?"

"Teach me basics today, and I'll deposit it the day after," Isaac replied. "Look, I need this. I can't afford to wait."

"Why?" Obadiah asked.

"I… need to challenge myself," Isaac slipped a white lie. "Plus, my mom used to watch fights often when I was a kid. I always thought of this as the gentleman's sport."

"Doesn't answer why so soon."

Isaac paused, searching for a proper reason. "I spent too long sitting on my ass. I need this."

The soft buzz from the light overtook the seconds of silence.

Then, Obadiah replied. "Look, I don't do shortcuts. I'm not gonna accept the money until I see your worth. You ready to train today?"

"Absolutely."

"What's the extent you've trained before?"

"I've lifted weights and jogged a little."

Obadiah let out a chuckle rising in volume. "Oh, lord," the laughter settled. "Got our work cut out, then. Full exercise. Eight hours. I want to see you working nonstop. We'll cover the basics by the end of today. If we make it, then I'll take you seriously. Which means I'm turning you into a 350K fighter. It's a tango, though, through and through," Obadiah insisted. "Make sense?"

"Makes sense."

"Let's begin."

Obadiah didn't exaggerate the intensity of pushing Isaac to the brink of passing out on the first day. The grueling training regimen began with minute-long lateral shuffles–dashing from side to side–followed by high knees for another minute. A mere thirty seconds of rest was allowed before starting again for another two rounds.

Then came push-ups, relentless and unyielding, for a full minute straight with thirty seconds of respite in-between. The level of training was an understatement, pushing Isaac's brittle power and endurance.

His heart raced in rapid, hyperventilated beats, and his limbs trembled non-stop. Sweat-soaked hair weighed his head down. If there was another level of hell on earth, Isaac had found it.

But this had to be a test. If actions of resilience matched with the similar words spoken, then Obadiah would know his time wasn't being wasted.

It was also a reminder for Isaac. That the version of himself now and from the past was fully incapable of executing the desired goal.

Obadiah, relentless and unwavering, pushed Isaac to continue until he reached 300 push-ups. The first hundred were excruciating. To reach 200 took another hour of relentless effort, followed by several more grueling hours to finish the last remainder.

By the time Isaac reached the last painful push-up, only two students were training. His body, drained of energy, fell flat on the floor.

Obadiah, watching from a few steps away, approached Isaac and crouched down. "We've got a lot of work before us," he said. "We'll repeat this tomorrow. Have a good night and rest well."

Too exhausted to move, Isaac laid on the floor, nodding in agreement. He remained there for another hour, nearly falling asleep.

The next day, Isaac embarked on his journey to learn the basics of boxing for one week. Controlling head movement, learning how to move, punch, dodge, and initiate basic combos became his daily routine.

Isaac realized most of this would be forgotten in the heat of battle where naïve primal instinct would take over out of fear for survival. He rehearsed these movements after every session at home, striving for muscle memory.

———

Obadiah advised Isaac to continue training outside of the gym if he wished to see better results soon.

"Train as much as you can on your training days," Obadiah instructed. "And we'll make sure you rest for at least one day every week. You'll feel more pain and weakness than you've ever had. And it'll stay for longer than you'd like. Don't expect to be a changed man overnight."

The champion was, of course, right. Isaac's lungs still showed signs of frailty even after the first week of training. By the second week, the intensity of the basic techniques increased as Isaac gained familiarity with combining every learned defensive and offensive skill.

By the end of the third week, Muay Thai was incorporated into Isaac's training regimen. Obadiah expressed versatility was what made a mixed martial artist successful, not the mastery of one skill set.

There were days during these grueling sessions when he doubted, in his sweat-drenched fatigue, if he had the mentality to succeed, but he could feel Obadiah's unwavering gaze pressing at him to persevere.

During one mitt round, Isaac's body collapsed, and for the first time, negative thoughts kept his body grounded.

*'Give up.'*

*'This is too much. This isn't you.'*

A wave of shame washed over him until Obadiah crouched down.

"Look at me," said Obadiah.

Isaac complied.

"Remember what you signed up for. Not only did I sign up for it, but you're training faster than most of the other fighters here. Are you going to get up? Or was that all talk before? Was this all pointless?"

Isaac clenched his teeth and rose to his feet instantly, spurred from his internal rage buried beneath the fatigue.

There, an internal oath was formed. He would never revert to cowardice nor falter in the face of adversity again, even if overwhelming.

The following day, Obadiah got Isaac enlisted into X-Ceed, expanding his training to a new level. This was the professional level that fighters endured, amplified tenfold.

First, there was essential stretching to stay limber and avoid injury. Then came the control of momentum, a crucial skill for a runner who couldn't afford to slip on the edge of a rooftop or hesitate during a jump.

The sessions, from the routes and stretching to controlling momentum in every step and leap, were filled with unfamiliarity that required unwavering commitment. A lesson that Obadiah hammered into Isaac's head with multiple parkour sessions every week.

With each passing day, the intensity climbed. What had started as a dull energy sharpened into something grander and more lethal. His stamina increased with each training session, and by the end of the day, his muscles were once again exhausted.

These were the most tiring days of Isaac's life. During the time away from training, his studies in Physics and Engineering led him to discover new ideas that would enhance the safety of his mission. One of these ideas included gloves capable of inducing electric force upon contact, the user protected by a layer of insulation.

His research in New-Gen Chemistry provided insights into how M.A.D. was handled and its origins. The scientific name, T. Dohrnum, was derived from the self-regenerating jellyfish. Isaac delved into the compounds that made up M.A.D. and its incredible durability.

Isaac wrote every detail in a hunter green notebook, keeping it either in his backpack or snug into his desk drawer. While the sentiments of his mother that kept him bound to these notes, it was essential to know about M.A.D. Every detail could lead him to his goal.

He arranged meetings with Mikey, a M.A.D. dealer on campus, every evening at a discreet location.

Isaac studied each compound he obtained to spot any connection to the business card he had received. If there was even a slim chance of finding a lead, he was determined to pursue it.

So far, nothing. But just as he wouldn't be a trained fighter overnight, the results wouldn't reveal themselves either in similar fashion.

On the beginning of the second month, training reached a point of refinement on, the movements turning fluid with more ferocious power. Versatility and quick response, however, still needed work. It was backed by confidence after so much repetitive exercise.

Obadiah stated it was now time for Isaac to test everything he learned through sparring. He emphasized that a fighter's mindset also needed refinement, and achieving a state of flow was essential.

"The state of flow?" Isaac asked.

"It's what athletes and performers experience when they're in the zone," Obadiah explained. "It's what you'll experience when you're in the zone."

"What does it feel like?" Isaac inquired.

"It's like having the best dance of your life," Obadiah replied with a smile. "Reaching that flow state happens when you're performing a little beyond your abilities. So, we train in slow, rising increments."

"What if I'm not a good dancer?" Isaac asked. "Hypothetically."

"You'll be fine," Obadiah chuckled. "Get to your corner. We start now."

Every sparring match with Obadiah's students each carried a different style that led to learning from scratch. Every knockdown, every pummeling, and every clean counter marked a reset.

In exchange, a familiar, unsettling rage surged within him. A reminder that this wasn't fun and games.

Sloppy footwork transformed into commanding ring control. Stiff slaps transformed to tactical, disarming attacks. His two-dimensional mindset evolved, assessing every angle.

One by one, every student who pushed Isaac to his limit fell. Some by near-knockout, others by sheer ring control. Isaac had noticed tremendous improvement, as did Obadiah. However, the fights for him were patterns. Some more complex than others, but patterns that allowed him to examine his own flaws and polish them.

These very patterns also prevented him from this state of flow Obadiah expressed. Instead, it was a state of analyzing and responding. Isaac couldn't grasp this flow state.

The gauntlet that was once grand had narrowed down to only Obadiah's most skilled apprentice, whom had lost to Isaac three consecutive times.

On the tenth day of the second month, Isaac entered the ring , ready to fight the apprentice once more. Instead, he was nowhere to be seen.

Obadiah stepped into the ring, slipping each of his hands into scuffed boxing gloves.

"You've gotten familiar with everyone else's patterns," Obadiah said. He rotated each arm in a clockwise motion. "There's no time for registering in tournaments. So, your last opponent is me."

"I'm nowhere close to you," said Isaac.

"Exactly," Obadiah smiled. "Don't worry. I'm not gonna put you in a coma."

They sparred in five round sessions. Any time Isaac thought he had caught on to a pattern, Obadiah switched his stance, landing a clean, dazing counter. The punches were harsh, yet filled with the certainty that Obadiah was pulling each. He could bring down a cement wall if he wanted to.

It forced Isaac's rage to dig even deeper, responding with more determined hits. *'I'll be the one to knock him out,'* he thought.

Isaac gained the confidence to counter Obadiah's moves by the third session, although dispelled by direct blows to the head.

The following sessions repeated the same pattern. The eureka of discovering a pattern, only to be dissuaded once again by a new level of onslaught. On some days, Isaac managed to stand on two feet. On others he was knocked to the floor with such colossal force that he couldn't get up.

On the tenth session, Isaac crumbled from fatigue after a direct gut shot. After minutes sitting on the bench in recovery, Obadiah approached Isaac.

"You alright?" Obadiah asked.

"Yeah. Yeah, I am," said Isaac, his head bowed to the floor.

"You should be able to beat me by now. Or at least land a hit on me."

"I'm not a champion," Isaac replied.

"You think anyone with that headspace ever ends up winning? The moment you see your opponent as someone out of reach, you've already lost."

Isaac sighed in admittance. "Yes, sir."

Obadiah stood up. "I'll be honest with you. You've got ten more sessions to make this change. At least hit me with something that'll make me stumble."

Making Obadiah lose his balance was key to making this, all of this, realize it could lead to successful results.

Fighting past a sunken heart, Isaac tried heeding Obadiah's advice and his own intuition, incorporating counters, feints, and new combos while mixing in the familiar techniques.

For nineteen sessions, no matter what method Isaac tried, everything remained the same.

As much as he despised this feeling, this was the necessary path. For if he couldn't accomplish this, he didn't deserve to be on this mission.

***

Session twenty commenced on the first day of the third month, and as usual, both fighters entered the ring. Isaac hopped from side to side, loosening his muscles.

Obadiah gestured with his head for Isaac to take a lap around the ring.

"Before we start," said Obadiah, "you know what today is?"

Isaac slowed to his corner. "My last chance."

Obadiah nodded. "I'm your roadblock. Let's see what you've got."

The champion – his mentor – stood tall. He always refused to slouch. It was a detail that refined the steel of his aura.

Seconds in, the bell rang. Isaac and Obadiah paced toward the center with raised fists.

Obadiah began the round with a swift combo, jabbing at Isaac's head, followed by a powerful right punch and two consecutive left and right hooks.

Isaac stumbled from the onslaught, absorbing some blows with sloppy parries.

"Let's go!" Obadiah shouted.

With no time to think, Isaac focused on an iron defense, locking his muscles up for the remainder of round one.

The bell rang, signaling its end. Obadiah glared at Isaac as they returned to their corners.

Isaac could feel the trembling in his limbs, his unsteady eyes, and his heartbeat battering his deflated lungs. Fear held him back. The inner rage burrowing beneath his skin taunted him.

*'Embarrassing, for you and your parents. Do better.'*

He composed his frantic breathing. He assessed the tendons of his limbs for proper striking power within the next thirty seconds. The rage battered blood in and out of his heart.

The second round began. Obadiah took the initiative once more with a slower combo, providing larger openings to dodge and counter.

Isaac countered twice, delivering two jabs followed by a harsh right punch aimed at the champion's nose.

Obadiah parried the blows as if swatting a fly. "Remember, when you're hitting me," Obadiah reminded Isaac, "imagine you're trying to hit my spine or the back of my skull! Use the momentum of your whole body."

Isaac thought about Obadiah's words. Then, he thought about the next moves, and how to evade and defend Obadiah's attacks that were rarely predictable.

Then, this frame thinking grew tiresome. To a degree, frustrating. The energy he felt from watching Ibrahim's fight slowly re-emerged.

Isaac retaliated with raw power as Obadiah had advised. Two hits forced Obadiah closer to the ropes. A pattern emerged in the champion's rebuttal. Isaac parried and countered. Obadiah changed stance and deflected the hit.

The swift, harsh counter from the champion forced Isaac back on the defensive. The rounds continued with a similar back-and-forth pace, slowly rising in amplitude. Isaac struggled to ignore the in his heart. It was climbing the mountain all over again.

Obadiah increased his tempo, hitting Isaac with a force strong enough to fragment his vision into three. The strongest punch he threw out of all twenty sessions.

Isaac swung two massive, uncoordinated hooks like a feral beast. He crumbled to one knee after the last string energy wisped out of his body.

———

The bell signaled the end. Like clockwork, Obadiah approached Isaac.

"You're letting your emotions get the better of you, yeah?" Obadiah asked. "No need to hide it."

Isaac struggled to speak, let alone breathe. This was going to amount to nothing. This was the last session, and Isaac hadn't even made a dent against Obadiah.

"No excuses. You'll crumble even harder than this and put yourself at rock bottom with all the other failures if you lean on excuses." He extended his hand. "Clear?"

Isaac took Obadiah's hand and pulled himself up. They returned to their corners.

"Last round," said Obadiah.

The bell rang the beginning of the final round. Obadiah wasted no time, continuing his assault with the same tempo as his last punch.

This was the kind of training not for a fight but for a life-or-death scenario. In such situations, he couldn't cling to his fears or rage. It was the necessary training.

Then, a spark of *that* energy emerged, like the sight of Ibrahim's bloodied grin.

Isaac dodged one hit, took in the other punches and kicks, and began to find his desired opening. He maintained his stance, storing momentum as power. A jab, a straight punch, stepping back into a straight kick lunge.

Obadiah retaliated with a horizontal kick aimed at Isaac's torso, only to be parried. Isaac focused on that feral spark. For the first time, there was no deductive thinking. His eyes alone tracked Obadiah's attack and speed.

Another jab, straight punch, followed by two kicks to create enough spacing to evade Obadiah's next attack. Obadiah, this time, launched a ferocious combo. A splinter of fear nearly caused Isaac to paralyze as he did in the first round.

But he instantly countered, ignoring the risk of Obadiah's power. No thought, but instinct. Isaac expelled another string of precise attacks.

Isaac realized this was it. There was little time to think, but this had to be it. The state of flow.

An opening formed at Obadiah's head and torso. With clear-cut focus, Isaac held back his naïve excitement and homed in with a one-two combination at Obadiah's head, following with a straight kick aimed at his abdomen.

Obadiah's stance faltered from the combo. It was an exciting yet terrifying sight when Obadiah instantly rebounded with a flurry of attacks, forcing Isaac to crumble downward. Both knees hovered inches above the ground.

*'This wasn't the deciding factor,'* Isaac told himself. He weaved past Obadiah's oncoming straight punch, his cheek grazed from the swift microscopic fiction, and careened his right fist to another opening.

The decisive counter-punch, with slivers of breath. Only to suddenly be halted by his faltered lungs, inflating his disappointment as the deciding counter-punch flatlined.

The sound of the bell sobered Isaac as it simultaneously concluded the final round. Obadiah approached Isaac's corner. His white crescent smile bright against his bloodied nose.

Isaac's adrenaline brightened his astonishment.

Obadiah extended his hand, now ungloved, to Isaac. "That wasn't a 350,000-dollar punch. That right there was a strike worth three million dollars. You were almost there. Just need to control your energy."

Isaac smiled. "Thanks for everything, coach. I'll be back soon if that's alright."

"Keep it going. You're always welcome here."

He exited the gym, ready to collapse. A tandem bridge of comfort and discomfort. Isaac would continue his training periodically. Although he wasn't a master, he was ready to utilize what he had learned.

Near the end of the month, Isaac received the equipment he had ordered. For the next week, he missed school to build his gear. Kara checked in day and night, sometimes making small talk with him, while Isaac hid every trace of his work from her.

Kara handed him a manila parcel. "Todd dropped this off for you."

As Kara departed, Isaac opened the parcel, revealing an odd metal contraption with two thin straps connected.

Attached to it was a note that read, '*Another pinky for those promises. Figured it would be useful. —Todd*'

Isaac attached the device to the missing area of his hand, securing it with the straps. It was identical in size to his former pinky finger. Electricity buzzed around his palm as he commanded the finger to move.

*Twitch.*

Isaac managed to curl the finger with enough concentration. Curled in, then curling it back out. Soon, the device responded to where Isaac wished for it to extend or curl inward.

'*I don't know how the hell you did this, Todd…*'

Isaac yearned for a day when he was done with all this, hanging out with Todd, and even getting to know Rosemary, who still lingered in the back of his mind.

Wires, pads, two adhesive conductor boxes, and strips of clothing were scattered around the room, connecting with one another over time to form something more concrete.

First, the padded hoodie was assembled, composed of sewn threads and gorilla glue. Then came the pants, created in the same meticulous process.

Isaac moved on to the face mask, using scissors to create eye holes and then attaching a black lens to each hole using gorilla glue.

He extended the mask in front of him, juxtaposed to the other gear. Finally, it all came together.

Now, it was time to continue his research and search for clues. Isaac pooled his resources, hopeful to find something. '

Month by month, nothing came to light, and the results Isaac envisioned remained elusive. In exchange, that ever-present rage continued to etch deeper into his soul.

'*The moment would come.*'

# IX
## Isaac Sage

## October 1, 2022, 8:00 PM

Stagnancy found its way to slowly kill passion within people. The emotions Isaac held were awakened by the idea of someone causing him to feel pain for so many years. To bring premature endings to both of his parents. People who deserved a full life.

But after months of successful training, the months of research that followed led to no results. This stagnancy, at some points, had Isaac nearly receding back into dull normalcy.

Reminding himself of the cause was necessary to keep the passion alive, just as he reminded himself of his family for so many years prior.

But, in the span of one day, the stillness launched into full momentum with one simple clue.

On September 30, Isaac and Mikey met at their usual spot, standing underneath the fluorescent streetlamps that kept the adjacent roundabout lit.

Mikey rubbed his sunken eyes with lanky wrists and grinned.

"Did you finally take a hit?" Mikey asked.

"You know it's only for research," said Isaac.

Mikey chuckled. "To each their own."

"How's the apartment hunting?" Isaac asked. Connecting for a few weeks established some rapport between the two.

"Same shit, different day here. You?"

"School. Gym. Thinking on what to do next."

Mikey shrugged. "Don't we all?" He exhaled a beam of smoke, transparent against the light.

"Have you thought about it?"

"Maybe I'll make enough money and move to Japan.  Start a new life, new name and all."

"It's that shitty here?"

"Complete opposite.  But, there's always an itch to test a different life. What could be." Mikey snickered. "I don't know, maybe just high talk with my dumb ass. What've you thought about?"

"I got people wanting me to take my a job at the new Sage Foundation. They say my parents would *love* it."

"What's Sage Foundation?"

That was a first. Isaac pulled out his phone and showed Sage Foundation to Mikey on a results page.

"*This.*"

Mikey raised his eyebrows when Isaac showed him the logo of the building. "Oh, shit! I've seen that before."

"Yeah, I don't know how you could miss the tower."  Isaac glance at a soft, green line in the distance.  "You could even see it from here–"

"No, at where I pick up my stuff. They have a bundle of them on cards for some reason."

Isaac paused. "Who's they?"

"A few guys I meet with at this warehouse. Near the coastline, southeast of here."

The paused turned into ramped adrenaline. Months of no cross-reference between the card and the drug.  No location.  No origin points. But now, here it was, with someone Isaac had spoken with every day.  All it took was the right question.

"Are they there every night?"

"Doubt it. They only station there when the couriers are scheduled to show up."

"When's the next time they're there?"

Mikey squinted his eyes. "Why do you need to know that?"

"So… so that I know when you're coming back, obviously."

Mikey eyed Isaac up and down and followed with a shrug. "Tomorrow night."

"*Tomorrow?*"

Mikey nodded. "This supply today was meant for someone else."

Another burst of internal excitement followed that he refrained from showing visibly. If they handled the supply, they could know about other related warehouses. They could know about the process, and in turn, know who orchestrated the downfall of Sage Foundation.

"It's getting late for me, I gotta go," said Isaac. "Thanks, Mikey."

"Thanks to you."

"For what?"

"For the money. What else?"

***

The next chaotic 24 hours consisted of full preparation. Isaac double-checked all his tools and covered the rundown of his plan.

Capture one of the men, take them somewhere isolated, and interrogate them to get the answers. It wasn't the best plan, but it was the most concrete.

By night-time, Isaac pulled out the box of equipment from underneath his desk and suited up. First, the slate padded pants, then the onyx combat boots, followed by a loose dark grey sweater, and a thin black mask. Lastly, he slipped on the wire-riddled prototype gloves.

A reflection emphasized his outfit's amateur quality with the different shades of grey and black. The bulky clothing also stiffened his movement.

Isaac opened his bedroom window, lifting one foot atop the bottom frame. He paused, with mixes of fear and doubt roiling in his head. It was a lot to prepare within 24 hours. But, this may be the only chance he would have.

His time with X-Ceed provided discreet, alternate routes to the coastline, comprised of Rooftops, fire escapes and alleyways.

As he approached the coastline, the surrounding buildings and streets reeked of fish and seawater. Sea salt particles absorbed into Isaac's mask. Traffic dissipated to nothing thanks to an enforced curfew in this zone, based on the warning signs.

Far off in the distance was one of the few light sources flickering like a dying bulb.

Isaac reached the street level and climbed over a chainlink fence, landing on soft dirt. He crept toward the tiny warehouse shack, its single source of light continuing to flicker.

Doubt amplified with every step inching closer. What if the gear didn't protect him? What if he was shot in the head? Or if his stamina gave out?

Peering through the tiny square window, a few workers occupied the inside. It was livened with the low ambience of hip-hop and crashing waves outside.

Isaac's mind went blank for seconds before snapping himself alert. He counted three workers inside.

One of the men drifted outside, complaining about the light hurting his eyes. Isaac circumvented to the front, crouched low.

The lone, pale man focused on his orange-lit cigarette. The glow revealed a tattoo of a shark on his right shoulder. He exhaled rings of smoke, staring at the ocean. The dirt glued against his scuffed brown shoes.

Isaac continued his crouched, low approach through the shadow, lifting each foot so it didn't create any sound of drag. He repeated the plan and steadied his shock glove.

Seagulls cawed. Another set of waves slapped against the nearby dock.

He extended his arm out and slammed his hand onto the smoker's shoulder. The latter stood tall, jolting his attention with grit teeth and electrified eyes to Isaac.

With haste, Isaac flung a swift hook against his face, discharging a harsh electric shock. An encroaching burn spreaded through Isaac's palm. A miscalculation that left the electric currents too unstable, or not enough insulation

The man's eyes bobbed up and down before he collapsed. Isaac dragged him away further into the dark with a tight neck hold.

One of the buildings nearby was abandoned. It would be ideal to interrogate him there, get the information, leave, and then–

The smoker's body flailed out of control, breaking from Isaac's grip.

Isaac slipped past his adrenaline-filled swings before being blindsided on the cheek.

His gloves were surrounded by an aura of smoke. The wires burned frail strings of charcoal.

The man with the shark tattoo yelled an unknown foreign language with strained vocal cords.

The other men in the small warehouse ran outside, locking eyes with Isaac, startled as if coming across a wild bear.

Isaac bashed his former captive with one swift power punch and stampeded away to a nearby fence. The gear weighed Isaac down, exerting more effort to climb, struggling to increase the gap between him and the oncoming thugs.

All the fear conjured flashing thoughts as he propelled himself over the fence and sprinted, conflicted with stifled breathing and frenzy between his mind and body. Wondering if, were he left on the verge of dying and incapable of moving, someone would even find him in this abandoned part of the city.

How could they even know?


He tripped over a raised edge and hurdled through a nearby window of a nearby building. The dark room's leftover architecture implied this used to be a lobby.

Some of the shards sank into Isaac's arms and shoulders. His first impulse prompted him to shout and curse through clenched teeth. The faint stampede amplifying, however, made him fall silent.

Isaac ascended a nearby stairway. The rooftops would make the best distance. His movements shook the architecture beneath him. One misstep and he would be plummeting down to his enemies. The stomping's echoes had reached the building.

At the uppermost level, Isaac sprinted down the barren hallway, leaving a few new holes from his thunderous stomps. He charged through the final door, finding a row of cascading roofs ahead in his sight.

Isaac re-launched his sprint, finishing with a tremendous leap across the gap. His arc measured a decent landing on the ledge. He'll use his remaining energy for a leap to the next roof. That'll be enough distance to trek the rest of the journey back home.

Popping erupted from behind, disrupting his focus. Sharp wind whistled past his ear, followed by an impact of sheer pain in his core.

The measured arc from before vanished, as did all his forward momentum. His body plummeted into the alleyway.

The crash paralyzed him initially, like an ice pick twisting into his side.

*'Rest,'* his mind beckoned. *'Assess your injuries. Hide.'*

But the clamoring roars of the men continued, relentless in their pursuit.

Isaac channeled enough energy to force his dazed body to stand up. The alleyway and its walls tilted into mirage duplicates.

He leaned against one wall, using the streetlights at the end as his waypoint. A shock stronger than before surged through his right side and shoulder.

Isaac placed his hand on an area where wetness soaked through his sweater. He observed his hand to find the glove was glistening with something. It carried a strong, metallic scent.

The gradual realization forced an unrelenting tremor through his body, soon igniting his lungs with hyperventilation.

Isaac had been cut before but never shot. He was unsure of how long he had until his body bled out.

He covered his wound, forcing his weary body to saunter down the sidewalk. The nurse that treated his amputated wound told him applying on the wound combined with slow, controlled breath would reduce the risk of passing out.

The auburn sidewalk ahead dipped into a stairway, divided by a railway in the center. Isaac hobbled down the steps, using the railing as his crutch. A drop of blood dotted each step. His skin felt hot, like an intense fever.

An offbeat set of footsteps followed behind him. Glimpses of a stairway in flames encroached his sight, followed by bright blue skies and the voice of his parents. The reimmersion's side effects occurring at the worst time, most likely from the injury.

He persevered and crouched down to the stained subway floors, crawling underneath the turnstile.

The lights from the tunnel zoned in closer as the subway train made its stop. Its doors opened to reveal an explosive plume of smoke and thick debris. He stumbled forward anyway, convincing himself this wasn't real, despite how much horror it invoked into him.

Isaac removed his gloves, hoodie and vest. He dropped them into the narrow gap between the subway and the platform before the doors closed.

He sat down, hunched his body to cover his wound, and prayed. To Isaac, he failed his family. For drifting without aim for so long. For this mission.

A fusion of numbing aches and burning sensations carved lines across his face. He chose to focus on his breathing. Slow, deep. Inhale and exhale within 15 seconds. His sight now became a blurred blend between the visions and the subway's flooring.

As the subway alerted its departure, he could hear the three men jumping into the car, mere inches away.

All he needed was to remain hidden. Keep his eyes glued to the floor, veiled from anyone else.

While others seemed to be moving elsewhere, one was nearing closer. By the sight of the scuffed, brown shoes, it was the smoker. There seemed to be others in the car, from the way his legs were leaning, as if invading personal bubbles like a person with poor eyesight trying to read.

He sat next to Isaac. Isaac wiped his sweat away with his free hand. He fought to stay awake. The thug's line of sight wouldn't be able to see the wound.

He firmed his expression, the nerves calming numb. The vision had vanished, with the reality now fighting with darkness.

A pat on the shoulder snapped Isaac awake. It wasn't the touch, but the pain of his shoulder jolting him.

Then, a disarming chuckle emerged.

———

"I know the feeling, buddy," the man said.

When the subway reached the next stop, the group of thugs departed.

"You sure he wasn't here?" one said.

The smoker shrugged. "It was too dark anyway. Couldn't get a good look at his face. I wanna be this guy though." He pointed to Isaac with another laugh. "He was mumbling in his sleep!"

This was just another weeknight for them. The group departed at the next stop.

Isaac walked left into an empty car. He exhaled and covered his mouth to scream. He assessed his injuries. First was the shoulder, looser and less control in his movement. Isaac grasped his loosened deltoid, and with one brute force of movement, he almost forced the shoulder back into joint. A sharp, agonizing shock echoed through his arm and neck.

He tried again with grit teeth. This time, with even more power, he pushed his shoulder back into the socket.

*Pop!* The pain was immense but the weight had disappeared. He could at least walk home.

There wasn't much racing across Isaac's mind at this point. All he wanted was for this night to end.

***

Isaac found himself at the front of the mansion. He didn't remember walking here. His vision jumped again to lying against the base of the stairway inside the mansion.

A shrilled shriek followed. He bobbed his head around, confused to find the sound's origin until Kara stood in his line of sight, several feet away. A beat of silence followed as she stared with a shaky exhale.

Isaac mumbled through a smirk, "Good to see you." His eyes rolled back and his head thudded against the step.

The ground beneath him softened. Even the inaudible echoes felt like a soft cushion. The shadows made by the few lights, about thirty feet above, oscillated against the ceiling's blank canvas.

And then the following words solidified. "I think you need to go to a hospital."

Isaac's eyes jolted open, fully conscious. "Kara," he whimpered, "you can't take me to the hospital."

Kara continued to dial her phone.

Isaac strained to repeat himself, coughing when trying to raise his voice.

"Jesus, Isaac, look at you!" Kara shouted. "I had a damn feeling they would try to attack you again, I knew it." She raised the phone to her ear.

*"No!"* Isaac reached for the phone with no success. His body jolted in pain. "It was my choice!" He shouted.

"Your choice? What does that even mean?"

If Kara knew, he'd be putting her in danger. At the same time, the idiotic sloppiness of tonight could've put anyone at risk if this repeated.

"I...can't tell you," Isaac strained. "I can't go to the hospital. Please."

Kara looked away from Isaac, staring at the floor. Then, she locked eyes with him, now with a furrowed glare. Her silence was starting to make Isaac more lightheaded from his rapid-pounding heart.

Kara shook her head. "You've got broken bones and you've been shot. I have bandages to bind the fractures and sewing material to close the wound to stop the bleeding. There's leftover morphine to numb the pain."

Isaac nodded in immense gratitude.

"But you will tell me what happened. Why you've shown up to our house like this, what you mean by this being your choice. Everything. Or you can scream all you want while I call for the ambulance to take you to the hospital."

Before Isaac could mutter a word of acceptance, agreement, or even process a thought, he slumped into Kara's arms, nodding with the little energy he had.

# X
## John Saint
## October 3, 2022, 9:05 AM

Since the detective's encounter with Ricardo, layers of the simple case of sadistic arson unveiled itself as something more complex. Chief Briggs was stupefied when he received the report, specifically Ricardo's mutation.

Who else possessed this bizarre mutation? How much power did the linked cartel possess? Briggs allowed Saint and Billows to take full reins of the case and dive deeper.

In those months, Saint locked himself in his white, sleek office. Its wall was festooned with a makeshift web of red threads containing all the collected clues from past interrogations, searches and similar clues in past cases. He even skipped celebrating his forty-third birthday on September 24.

Being apart from Edoris filled him with melancholy and doubt. But to spend his time at home would be a distraction.

For the time being, Edoris understood the gravity of this case and its importance to Saint. The nightly phone calls eased their separation. And staying sequestered in this office forced him to focus and bring a true resolution to the case. The sooner, the better.

Main leads included the 'man with the devil's eye' and 'Commander,' another notorious cartel leader who'd been on the NMPD's radar in the past.

Despite his notoriety as the 'city's most dangerous small business owner,' Commander felt more like a red herring. It had to be the man with the devil's eye.

For now, all details branched to dead ends. There was no central clue pertaining to the culprit's whereabouts.

On the morning of October 3, Billows rushed into Saint's office an hour before their usual meeting recap.

"We got something," Billows stated.

Saint rose from his seat. "Where?"

Saint and Billows hopped in the car and headed to the location. On the way, Billows explained an undercover cop at the subway station spotted three men jumping over the turnstile, then traveling back to an abandoned tiny shack by the coastline of New Manhattan. They possessed firearms and seemed to also be stockpiling illegal substances.

When the duo arrived at the scene, about twenty-eight minutes later, two squad cars were parked with the arrested men sitting across. Clouds cast a sheet of grey over the area, desaturating the rich blue waters.

The on-site officers informed Saint and Billows not much was found within the warehouse other than the reported substances. Saint approached the arrested group.

"Gentlemen, if you'd be so kind as to answer my questions," Saint instructed. "Let's make things as smooth as possible."

Saint asked about the warehouses, processes, and their leader. The men's eyes wandered, unresponsive.

"I can give it a crack," said Billows.

"Let's have them think it over," Saint said aloud. "Certainly, they wouldn't be dumb enough to choose rotting in a jail cell."

Saint examined the other clues at the crime scene. A yellow tag was set on the far side of the warehouse, marking stray bullets scattered on the flooring. They were fresh, still set atop the dirt.

*'It can't be bullet practice,'* Saint thought. *'They wouldn't want to risk attracting attention with loud noises like gunshots. And who's the supplier for these firearms?'*

Saint marched back to the group. "Are we being vocal now? Maybe share with me a tale about those bullets?"

After minutes of a silent stand-off, the palest of the trio spoke. "You wouldn't believe it…" he said.

"A man nearly killed me with molten lava," said Saint, "try me."

"Some masked thug attacked us. It's why we ended up train-hopping, man. But we lost him… He could be from a rival gang. Maybe Yakuza?"

"Yakuza?" Billows repeated.

"Look, all we know is we weren't expecting shit that night," said the pale man.

Saint made a mental note of the masked man. He walked over with Billows to the edge of the concrete dock.

"What, like a vigilante hero?" Billows remarked.

Saint shrugged.

Billows seemed disappointed. "How anticlimactic of you."

"I don't know what their role is. For now, I consider it unremarkable. And this cartel has a supplier."

"A supplier with rare stock, like many cases. It was only two guns."

"Let's hope it's *only* that."

"Excuse me, detective." An officer approached Saint and Billows. "We might have one more person you could talk to."

"Who would that be?" Billows asked.

She pointed at a lanky teenager handcuffed by the cement dock pillar. "He was caught this morning. Walked in the warehouse empty-handed, came out with a parcel of drugs."

"ID?" Saint asked.

"He goes by Michael Wallace."

Saint examined the handcuffed teenager as the officer escorted them. His sunken eyes accented his drooping cheeks. The wind whipped around his stringy hair.

"Michael Wallace?" Billows asked.

Michael nodded his head.

"Nice to meet you, Michael," said Billows. "Listen, we need answers."

Michael gestured at his handcuffs.

"They're for caution," said Billows.

"You got relations in the drug trade, don't you?" Saint asked.

"What makes you say that?" Michael asked.

"Well," Saint pointed at the crowd of arrested men in the warehouse. "That gentleman over there–you see him, right? That gentleman was kind enough to give us your name and position."

Michael dropped his head in disappointment.

Billows continued the line of questioning. "Do you know the higher-ups in this operation, Michael?"

"You can call me Mikey. I just deliver what's needed. Everyone catches wind of the boss, though."

"And what's in that wind?"

"His face. A bit of a fucked up crazy guy. I never wanna meet him, or someone like that."

"For someone that crazy, he's good at hiding. Any idea why?"

Mikey shrugged. "Everyone's scared shitless."

*'They feel the chances of dying by his hand if they cross him are concrete,'* Saint deduced. *'Or maybe it's less 'feeling' and more 'knowing'.'*

Mikey continued. "I didn't even know they were delivering bad stuff!"

Saint sighed to alleviate the frustration of Mikey's obvious lie.

"I get it," said Billows. "So, you wouldn't know the main place then?"

"Nah," said Mikey.

Billows sat on the pillar next to Mikey. He leaned toward him, his hands clasped together.

"You don't wanna do this, kid."

"I'm… I don't know what you mean by that."

Billows' eyes squinted as another gust of wind flapped through the area. "Nah, you seem smart. Smart people know how to lie."

"I'm not lying!"

"You can tell me that even after the officer heard where you were delivering it to? You were going to *his* location. Right?"

Mikey shook his head. "I'm not lying."

"You know where this goes, right? You end up in jail, you go to court, you swear under oath not to lie. And you break that oath? Oh, man."

"I'm not stupid."

"No one's calling you stupid, and no one's calling you a liar. But you seem like a good liar. It's like when a CEO upsells the value of their business to investors without sharing any actual numbers."

Mikey lowered his head. The mop of string hair was still tangled from the wind. The veil of initial shame sank deeper.

"I just wanna go home," Mikey said.

"My thoughts? Tell everything you know," Billows advised. "Even if it's gossip, a rumor. Something could be helpful. And the reason, well…you ever had a bad night of sleep?"

"Yeah," Mikey said.

"Well, when you hide important information like that, the kind that can save lives, you'll have that itch waking you up. And you won't know why, until, again and again, it calls to you. Keeps you awake. No one wants to lose out on good sleep. I would know."

Mikey sighed. He fidgeted his fingers, forced together by his handcuffs. A red irritated circle formed on his wrists.

Billows looked on at him with patience. Saint observed with curiosity if Billows's words were enough to intimidate him.

"I was going to a greenhouse in the Bronx. It would've been my first time. They…they said *he* might've showed up there."

The Bronx had held bare granules of patrolling activity due to it being a blackout zone.

"*He,* being the boss?" Billows asked.

"Maybe. They might've been messing with me. That's all I know."

"It's worth looking into," Saint said. "Thank you, son."

"Last piece of advice, Mikey," said Billows, "Find something different. This won't lead to anything good."

Mikey nodded. As the duo headed back to the car, Billows advised the officer to free Mikey and run him off with a one-time warning.

"He's a good kid," Saint heard him say.

*****

The roads within the Bronx were weathered down to uneven shards of rubble, making it impossible to drive. Saint parked the car as soon as they entered the district and walked down the zone. They remained cautious of any hazards like sinkholes or fallen wires.

Zones that were over-reliant on M.A.D. collapsed from an economic standpoint. The struggle to rebuild dragged where the upkeep needed for properties exceeded the rate of rebuilding in many sections.

People left, as did businesses. Even the government concluded funds were being wasted, finding no value in upholding the area.

Different areas deteriorated into blackout zones at different rates. The Bronx collapsed eight years ago.

Many of the homeless remained. The criminal element used it as a base for operations, due to no one caring to monitor these dead areas.

Their walk led them to a suburban area with a cul-de-sac. A greenhouse resided at the end of the cul-de-sac, boarded with jagged 2x4's. A man-made tunnel, however, connected to a neighboring house. No door, but still held up with sound walls.

Saint and Billows entered the neighboring house. A vast living room with four columns spanning from foundation to crooked roof. A large sliding glass door was positioned at the far end, adjacent to upholstered walls. No sign of any entry point leading to that tunnel.

They double-checked their weapons, anticipating danger. The boss could be ahead. Saint knocked along the slate tapestry within the dismantled house, until an echo resounded at one specific spot.

He glided his hand up and down along the rigid area. His fingers found a raised, sticky edge. An adhesive camouflage.

Saint ripped off the camouflage piece by piece, revealing a door handle.

As Saint reached for the handle, a vibration went off in his pocket. He reached into it to find Edoris calling.

---

The racking of a weapon clanged from behind the wall.

Saint's eyes widened before instinct took over.

"Move!" Billows yelled.

Saint rolled to the side. Billows ducked behind the nearest column.

Shrapnel destroyed a majority of the door. Speckles of wood grazed Saint's face, irritating him with a stinging sensation.

Billows fired two shots. A thud followed on the other side.

"Hit confirmed!" Billows shouted.

Saint signaled Billows to flank from outside, and then marched down the hand-made hallway into the inside of the greenhouse, gun in hand.

Small, narrow gaps in between the wooden planks revealed the transparent dome. Fresh and rotted greenery flooded the dome's interior boundaries. Saint walked past one of the perpetrators laid on the floor, wounded by Billows' shots from before.

The detective checked his blind spot when, suddenly, a wide man charged at Saint with a sledgehammer. He was dressed in a white apron and black goggles. Tattoos of chemical symbols were scattered across his forearms.

Saint fired, grazing the man's shoulder. His swing smacked Saint's armed hand, launching the gun from his grip.

The white in the scientist's eyes expanded as he swung his sledgehammer again.

Saint rolled to the side. His gun was nowhere to be found. He rose to his feet and launched a straight punch at the wide man's abdomen, followed by a sidestep into a quick left hook.

The scientist dove away from Saint. Saint rushed in, keeping an eye for his gun. The scientist rolled around, grabbing something from underneath a nearby table. He whipped out the shotgun from before, aimed at Saint.

Saint crept back. His breath skipped a second while his mind focused on Edoris, thinking of that missed call.

The scientist stood up and gestured Saint to raise his hands. The barrel planted against his chest.

Two shots fired. What followed was a gushing wound that immobilized the scientist's trigger fingers, followed by another on his neck. Alas, he tried to pull the trigger.

Saint unfroze himself and launched two sturdy right punches, welting the scientist's face. The scientist clawed at the air, trying to reach Saint before collapsing.

Saint turned to find Billows standing by a shattered entryway. He had broken through from the other side: a vast backyard with one lone shed.

Two perps, dead from gunshot wounds. Saint's mind drifted to the leader. There had to be more.

"Did he escape?" Saint asked.

"The question is was he even here," said Billows.

Rumors tended to exaggerate. Saint sighed. "Let's find evidence."

He investigated the shed while Billows sleuthed around the greenhouse.

Saint discovered numerous scraps of paper, including a map of the entirety of New Manhattan. Red markers circled different parts on the map, including Florida village, Massena, blackout zones and more.

Billows confirmed the chemicals in the greenhouse lined up with narcotics.

Saint showed Billows the map. "It's denoting every warehouse. And in every warehouse…" Saint reflected on the scientist that they killed. Every scientist, no matter what, left a unique footprint to their version of M.A.D. "…a one-of-a-kind drug."

If the red etchings each confirmed a warehouse, then the amount was colossal. This operation infected nearly all New Manhattan.

"The obvious question is…" Billows remarked. "Which one's the main headquarters? Where our main guy is at?"

As they exited the shed, Saint found a card on the floor, pearl white in contrast to the muddied, run-down surroundings. He picked it up, noticing the old logo of Sage Foundation. On it was the name 'Samuel Sage' and his respective details.

"Hey," Saint called out. He caught up to Billows and showed him the card, "What do you think of this?"

Billows examined the card. "Did the Sages ever live around here once?"

"No. Their son lives in the old mansion near the city's eastern border."

"So, we go get him now?"

"Actually…" Edoris came to mind from the back of Saint's mind. "Let's call it a day."

Billows nodded. "Sure. Why don't you head out? I'll get the authorities here to clean up."

Saint walked back to the car, soaking in the amber sunset. He was struck with a mix of nostalgia and regret.

***

A glow of yellow flowed out the front windows by the raised porch. Edoris' silhouette moved in the kitchen area.

Saint entered, finding Edoris fussing over a stovetop decked with glistening brisket, fluffy mash potatoes and chopped carrots. Her back faced him.

He wanted to smile at the sight of her. Yet, there was the expectation of contempt for having been absent for so long.

Simultaneously, he expected to never see her again when the scientist held him at gunpoint.

Edoris washed her hands, paying care to her wedding ring. Saint approached closer. Within breath's reach, she jolted up, and spun around with two raised fists. She washed away her startled expression with playful anger.

"John, don't do that!"

"Do what?" Saint retorted.

"Scaring me like that. Jesus. Announce yourself next time."

Saint kissed her. She reciprocated with a warm smile.

"How have you been?" Saint asked.

"Good. I thought you'd be caught up working again."

"I wanted to see you."

"Well, sit down and talk. I can make the leftovers here as your plate. You know the drill."

"I'll be sure to have everything cleaned up."

They set the plates and sat at the small roundtable for dinner.

Saint bit into the brisket. "I don't know how you stay consistent after all these years. It's amazing."

"Come by more often and you won't miss out," Edoris quipped.

In retrospect, Edoris paid care to his work before. She helped him on the days he was running behind, or the days he couldn't get out of bed.

Even when Edoris worked outside the house, she took it upon herself to help Saint pursue his dreams. Past the occasional disagreements, she was always there.

As they continued talking, Saint was comforted by the warmth of the food, the delight of the conversation and the peace of mind with her around. There was always a peaceful life here with her.

After dinner, Saint washed the dishes. Edoris plopped onto the couch, in the living room, turning on the TV. She grabbed a nearby beige blanket and wrapped it around her body. Smokey, their grey cat, slept on the armrest of the couch.

"There's a new Queen documentary," said Edoris. "Have you seen it?"

"I've been a little occupied," said Saint.

"Right, right."

Saint chuckled.

There was a sense of envy in his adoration while observing Edoris. He had the case that, when resolved, would define him. But here she was, content with this simple, peaceful life now.

Saint placed the last dish on the drying rack, toweled his hands and plopped onto the couch beside Edoris. He wrapped one arm around her and kissed the crown of her head.

"I have a question," Saint asked.

"Yeah?"

"Do you ever miss the thrill of your job?"

"With the air force?  Or when I was a flight navigator?"

"Both."

Edoris shrugged.  "Nope."

"There's no feeling of wanting to…go back out there?"

Edoris let out a small chuckle.  "I had my adventure with that. You know this. And now my freedom. It's nice. You should give this early retirement thing a try."

Saint's smile soon faded thinking about the near future. He followed with a despondent sigh.

"I may be out longer in the next week or two."

"We've done this rodeo before, John. You gotta kick ass."  Edoris pressed her lips, her eyes turning dull. It was as if she wanted to come clean about something. An instantaneous expression of sorrow and self-doubt. Instead, she smiled. Her eyes brightened once again, as she intertwined her hand with Saint's.  "Case or no case, you know who will always be here right?"

"Yeah, the cat, whenever he decides to like me, thank God."

Edoris laughed, smacking Saint on the shoulder.

He then pointed at her. "Obviously," Saint continued.

"Attaboy."

"Attagirl."

Edoris kissed Saint. She pressed play on the Queen documentary. The opening montage rolled through, overlaid with striking rock-n-roll chords. In the back of Saint's mind, he recapped the details of the case and the possible solutions it could lead to.

# XI
## DIABLO

### October 7, 2022, 6:03 PM

Diablo kicked open the door to his office, wild and unbalanced like an inebriated bull. The spacious suite housed a tall oak wardrobe containing his other suits and a computer desk with a landscape view of the ocean touching the docks of Syracuse.

He plopped onto his chair and gripped the desk. Diablo wished this inebriation was for celebration. With the press of a few keys, two black monitors lit with visuals of two of his warehouses, apprehended by NMPD.

Diablo wasn't fond of negativity. The feeling was a stark echo of his childhood days filled with struggle. But his subconscious attracted to it, as if his mind was the positive side of a magnet. Perhaps, he thought, it was such a normal, customary feeling to gravitate to. Like the friend you can naturally converse with despite years of separation.

His head and shoulders tensed from frustration. He opened the nearby drawer and picked up one out of four syringes filled with a blueish-purple liquid, bubbling like a lava lamp. The right fix to rid this negative feeling.

He stabbed the needle into the right side of his neck. His heartbeat slowed, then spiked in less than a second. The feeling shifted to a wide hyena-like grin forming on his face. He cradled the back of his head, elbows lifted high, and rested his legs on top of the desk.

*'This issue can be fixed later.'*

A knock boomed from the door.

"Yeah?" Diablo yelled.

Gus entered, dressed in his suit and tie. He cleared his throat.

"I'm sure you're aware that two of our operations were busted yesterday," said Gus. "One in the outskirts of New Manhattan and the other in a blackout zone."

"I saw," Diablo muttered. "They're all arrested?"

"The ones near the main city were taken into custody. The ones in the Bronx blackout zone died."

"Our scientist…he's…The one in charge of Unicorn?"

Gus nodded.

Diablo sighed. *'Don't get mad, don't get mad.'* He slammed his fists on the desk. "Fuck!–er, um…We'll use what we have and try someone else."

Gus checked his watch. "It won't be the same."

Diablo ignored that comment. "Use our inside contacts to kill the ones that were arrested."

"On it."

Diablo pointed at his monitor. "You saw the camera feed? Before it went out?" Diablo re-ran the footage at the coastline warehouse of a bare silhouette attacking one of their thugs in the night, before being chased off screen.

"What about the detectives at the blackout zone?" Gus asked.

"Screw the detectives. Sure, they dented us, but we'll pivot and make sure they get their comeuppance. I'm on top of this like…"

Gus remained stoic while Diablo muttered his analogy haphazardly.

Diablo instead reflected on the assassination attempt on Isaac Sage.

"Did you talk to Bonnie and Clyde about that assassination shit-show?"

"Yes. I emphasized that cannot happen again."

"And no one on our end miscommunicated this?"

Gus shook his head.

"Moonlighting. Fucking moonlighting." The Sages were a remnant of the past. The business cards Diablo acquired were his own self-rewarded souvenir to remind him of his final job as a hitman. A successful finale at that.

"I can't believe them," Diablo continued. "God forbid this comes back to bite us in the ass. Are we cursed?"

"I suppose a curse would be a blessing at this rate. Yakuza might be trying to counter. Maybe we can adapt and reallocate funds."

"Reallocate?"

"We're losing profit."

Diablo flopped into his chair. He spun around to face the ocean. An ebb and flow between calm tides and violent waves. Production was thriving, but limited, nonetheless. If warehouses began shutting down, it spelled an imminent doom for Diablo's operations.

He spun back and impaled one of the monitors with a closed fist. The sparks charred his suit's sleeve. His phone vibrated, ramping his frustration.

Diablo answered, seething through his teeth. "What?"

"Hermanooooo."

He recognized the enthusiastic, laid-back tone as his brother Carlos. The date on his calendar didn't mark any birthdays or family plans.

Diablo cursed under his breath. "What's up, bro?"

"David," Carlos called Diablo by his real name, "You working today, man? I want you to come over here in a couple hours, I got some news to share."

"You can't share it over the phone?"

"Nah man, it's *news* news."

Diablo stayed silent, unable to find a plausible alibi. "I'll be there in an hour." He hung up, cutting off Carlos' enthusiastic response.

"You could always do mercenary work again," said Gus.

Diablo walked to his wardrobe and removed his suit jacket followed by his shirt. Scars and tattoos signified years of memories as leader of this drug cartel.

"And go back to my young and reckless era?"

"What was it, 25 million dollars?"

He plucked a Hawaiian dress shirt and khaki blazer from the wardrobe, nodding to Gus' question.

———

"A lot of money. But I can't risk what we've built." Diablo marched for the exit, patting Gus on the shoulder. "We'll talk once I'm back."

***

Emotional preparations were made as Diablo pulled up to Carlos' house. Meditation. A repeat affirmation of not to blow up, hence showing that side of his life. He wrapped bandages around the scarred part of his face. A never-ending medical procedure was his white lie.

Diablo approached the front door with a reluctant limp. Before he could knock, the door opened. Carlos stood at the doorway with a hyena-like grin filled with ignorant joy.

"David!" Carlos yelled.

His brother embraced him with his trapezoid-like, stocky body and mismatched clothes. Diablo kept his composure, tolerating Carlos' extroverted nature. "Come on in, hermano."

Diablo assessed the house's array of modern slate and dark oak, consistent from the walls to the tiniest décor as he was guided to the backyard.

The walls were plastered with frames of the same palette, ranging from Carlos and Vanessa's memories combined with their childhoods. Even, to Diablo's shock, an old photo of himself, Carlos and their dad.

"You hung that photo of us?" Diablo asked.

"All Vanessa's work." Carlos smiled. "She did great with the house, yeah?"

Outside, Vanessa set plates full of shredded pork with rice and beans. The thin veil of smoke indicated its freshness.

Vanessa greeted Diablo as they all sat at the table.

"So," Carlos covered his own right eye at Diablo. "Any progress?"

"Still nothing," Diablo replied.

"Ah, man," Carlos's playful expression deflated. "Keep your chin up."

"Have you talked to any of the other family, David?" asked Vanessa.

"You know me, Vanessa," said Diablo. "I'm the black sheep."

"Well, Carlos seems to think he's the black sheep of the family. What with his beer gut and all." Vanessa smacked Carlos' stomach.

"They're keg abs!" Carlos bellowed a laugh.

Diablo grimaced at the lovebirds' affection. "So, the news. *News* news."

"Read my mind. I wanted you to be the first to know…" Carlos placed his left hand on Vanessa's stomach. Her face blushed bright red like a flare.

Diablo exhaled smoke from the small opening made by his agape jaw, understanding the visual cue.

"Well?" Carlos continued with a chuckle, "Speechless?"

"So… speechless."

Carlos buried his face into Diablo's shoulder. The smoke spread into a thin aura outlining the drug lord as he forced his arms around his brother, as if shocked with paralysis. He firmly patted his back twice with a closed fist.

Diablo leaned away. "One second. I need to take a piss."

"Do you remember where–"

Diablo sped inside to the stairway, hurdling into a quick sprint once he couldn't see Carlos and Vanessa.

On the second floor, he entered the bathroom, blindsided by the pristine green and white décor.

Diablo planted his hands onto the sink. His eyes locked onto the open, rusted, drain hole as he formed a mental checklist.

Carlos was successful with his money. Diablo was on the verge of losing profit.

Carlos was married. Diablo had… Gus.

And now this.

Diablo broke the silence with a wild flailing, cursing at the top of his lungs. He fought past his hot hyperventilation and dug into his shirt pocket to pull out a vial of cocaine.

He lined the vial's snowy contents along the sinks edge and guided his nostrils down the makeshift lane with one sharp inhale.

———

Diablo's head shot back in self-reflection.  The amount of hours and humanity he invested into his line of work, all to impress his family.  "They have no idea how to appreciate this, *this*…" And then–

Calmness. Diablo's nerves softened as if a flurry of clouds bloomed out of nowhere to cushion his insides.

He washed his hands, humming a tune as he jogged out of the bathroom, walked downstairs and returned outside.

What was there to be mad about? Rather, there was only adoration for his brother and sister-in-law's newest addition to the family.

Diablo cleared his throat. "Carlos, Vanessa, I want to say thank you for inviting me over. The food is… fantastic. Incredible. And don't let my run to the bathroom make you think any differently," he let out a short cackle. "You guys are gonna make a great family with the new one coming soon, I have no doubts. Let's make a toast to that." Diablo raised his glass to the skies. "To a good and healthy future for you all and your child."

Carlos and Vanessa stared at Diablo, aghast. After a second, they broke their stare and raised their glasses. The glasses clanked, resonating through the silence.

Then, Carlos pointed at Diablo's face. "You have some stuff on your…"

Diablo wiped his face and brought his hand to view, white, chalky stain brushed on his skin. His face flushed with heat.

"So, dessert?" Diablo asked.

Vanessa sighed and walked into the kitchen.

Carlos leaned to Diablo. "Y'kno, bro, you should get into the medical industry," he said. "That M.A.D. stuff made it easy for non-medical majors to score big in the business."

Diablo mocked the irony of his brother's advice. "Why're you telling *me* this?"

"Well like, you know, you got the most potential out of anyone in the family."

"You don't know mean that," Diablo said with a flustered high. "Do you?"

Carlos nodded. "And bro, that Sage Foundation comeback made me think. That'll bring the medical market back to a huge profit margin. My stock trades will go wild."

Diablo's brother's words struck a nerve of realization. Big businesses like Sage Foundation reel in tremendous income.

In theory, if Diablo could manufacture and ship his drugs across the country through the covert guise of the new Sage Foundation, then… profit. A profit so grand Diablo would never have to worry about income loss. Ever.

There was one dilemma: How to get into Sage Foundations. Maybe killing Isaac Sage was the goal. Diablo then questioned what would that resolve? It'd be more consequences than benefits, with the number of resources and time invested to make it successful.

And then, another light bulb: the anonymous source that hired Diablo for the Hellfire Incident. The destruction of Sage Foundation, and the confirmed deaths of Gemma and Samuel Sage. All Diablo about him knew were two things. A name – Mr. Velcro – and his position being somewhere within the medical industry. He would be the best connection.

"What's on your mind?" Carlos asked.

"gotta head out. Getting late."

"I'll walk you out," Carlos patted his brother's shoulder, guiding him to the front of the house. "Be safe, man. Please. God is watching over you." Carlos hugged Diablo.

"You, too." The cocaine's effects were wearing off. And still, his excitement was at a high with this revelation.

On the way back, Diablo called old client. The same number he remembered even to this day. He advised to drop something into his mailbox, providing the address of the penthouse he would be residing in. An empty and insignificant area, but a place not far from Carlos's house.

Diablo wiped his nose, finding a blotch of blood painted on his head. He brushed it off as an aftereffect of the cocaine.

***

———

Diablo checked his mailbox the next day, fashioning a matching grey suit and bandages.  A bright purple stub slid out of the nearby compartment. He removed the card and read it.

*For the devil that told me to fuck off years ago,*

*Velcron Empire. Ask for Mr. Velcro.*

En route, Velcron Empire was an overstatement in Diablo's eyes. The glossy onyx and gold building still couldn't compare to the spire of Sage Foundation.

Diablo entered through the revolving door and approached the receptionist, set in a black cubicle offset by an ivory white interior.

"Hi there, how can I help you?" the receptionist chirped.

"I'm here to see Mr. Velcro."

The receptionist smirked.  "Is that meant to be a joke, sir?"

"No. Why would I be joking?"

"Mr. Velcro retired years ago, sir. Perhaps you mean someone else?"

"Are you sure?"

The receptionist squinted his eyes.  "Wait…wait, those bandages, ah—You are…?"

Diablo grinned.  "So, he is expecting me."

"I was so focused on spotting someone with a messed-up–" The receptionist halted his speech. "Anyway. Farthest elevator on your right."

Diablo entered the respective elevator, made from the same onyx-gold granite. The elevator descended, arriving within a few minutes.

Its doors opened to a pitch-black abyss, where a purple light source emitted in the far distance. A slender man hunched over a cherrywood desk sat in the light, writing. He was old, apparent in his frail, wrinkled hands. The angle of the light veiled the man's face in violet-saturated shadows.

"Hey," Diablo said from afar.

No response.

"Hello??" Diablo approached closer. A baton slid out of the shadows, blocking Diablo's movement.  "Should I be concerned about others hiding here?"

"Emin likes to work alone," The elder at the desk responded in a grim tone. "It's been a while, Diablo."

"Has it?" Once again, Mr. Velcro remained in the shadows. "You look the same."

"Why Sage Foundation?"

"I need an empire to expand my empire," said Diablo. "Simple as that."

"And your position?"

"C.E.O.?"

The man burst into laughter. "I love naivety in this line of work. Why would you even expect *me* to have any power over that? Wouldn't you be expecting me to burn down that building once more?"

"You mentioned once a lotta detail about which compounds made which profit. There's black market talk, but then what you described…I wish I could remember the specifics, but the feeling's there. *You* know your shit way more than any cartel."

Mr. Velcro remained silent for a few seconds before stopping his note-taking. "The answer's no. Continue your operations and grow. Don't leave any trail of crumbs. Then we talk business."

"Such as?"

"Sage Foundation will have a spot for you. Chairman."

The offer boiled Diablo's head. "That's not CEO."

"I'm aware."

"It'd be child's play to kill you right now."

Emin's second baton shot out of the dark, pressed against Diablo's neck. Diablo's eyes singed off parts of his layered bandages, ready to attack.

Mr. Velcro slammed the table, catching Diablo and Emin's attention.

"Do you have any earthly idea how many eyes I have watching you, Diablo?"

"What?" Diablo said, stunned.

"You don't. That's the answer. And the abundant resources I've provided. How do you think Gus has all those inside contacts? He's not even aware of it."

———

Diablo's face turned cold. Smoke exhumed from his head.

"*What?*"

"It was my gift to you for your last job. You exceeded my expectations." Mr. Velcro extended one hand to Diablo. "But I *could* tear what you have away. Be my guest."

Diablo's skin shivered. Then, a sudden revelation. Bonnie and Clyde's job.

"Bonnie and Clyde's moonlighting on Isaac Sage…That was…?"

"You're understanding."

His bandages erupted to ashes, filling the room with an orange light. "Have you been taking profit, too?! For how long? It doesn't make sense…How did I let you slip past me!"

Emin rammed his baton into Diablo's abdomen, stopping him.

Diablo's eye flashed an orange light. In an instant, Emin's baton melted to black, smokey goo.

Mr. Velcro laid down his pen. "Clean that up."

Diablo rolled his normal eye and flashed another orange light at the goo, evaporating it to smoke. The air filled with burnt plastic.

"Your business piqued my curiosity after the job. I toss some money, multiply it, and take it back in. I've also dropped foot soldiers into your operation to monitor it. Some of which you killed for fun, so, thank you for that."

"Why not mow me down and take over?"

Mr. Velcro raised his shadowy head, seemingly locking eyes with Diablo. "I'm only one man. Why waste talent?" Diablo rolled his eyes. "As I said. Let those warehouses of yours become an empire. Then we integrate it into Sage Foundation. Work toward this goal, and I'll promise you that."

Diablo simmered over the thought of the masked person. "I do have to tie up some nuisances."

"You say that as if that's my mess to clean up."

"Rambling. I'll get it done. I gotta be worried about that Sage kid taking my job or what?"

———

Mr. Velcro sighed. "That boy is *far* from getting to lead the new Sage Foundation. No chance whatsoever." His voice turned hoarse and loud. "Should've been dead by now."

"You're not trying to kill him again?"

"Between the company and that shitshow, the news media won't stop spotlighting features on the Sages now. I can't afford any more risk."

"Why kill a kid anyway?"

"He's in his 20's. And he's no different from any other Sage. If everything had gone right…I'd have prevent a future problem from manifesting in the new Sage Foundation."

Diablo sighed over the excessive drama. "How long do I got for this spot?"

Mr. Velcro opened a book next to him and flipped through the pages. "By next year, Sage Foundation will complete construction and be open for business."

"That fucking long?"

"Know your place!" Mr. Velcro's voice shifted to a vicious monotone. "Do not banter with me."

Velcro didn't have mutations to rival Diablo's. But he possessed power in his presence alone. Something impenetrable like a fortress. As if, with one twitch, his operatives would come striking down Diablo's weak points.

It was a demeanor Diablo was aware of for a long time. Rather, it had evolved. Cold, enigmatic, ruthless, and now meticulous in his operations. His reach was further than ever. He personified power in the shadows.

Diablo agreed to Velcro's terms reluctantly. He snapped back to the elevator. The mission was clear. A mission that added greater weight to his obstacles.

The elevator doors closed; the purple light vanished.

Diablo smirked, knowing deep down he could take down all of them—one by one.

His empire was within sight.

# XII
### TODD HYME

## October 14, 2022, 1:40 PM

At engineering class, Isaac didn't acknowledge his absence for the last two weeks despite his seemingly warm attitude. Nor the fact he didn't respond to any of Todd's messages or calls.

Now, two weeks' worth of assignments, including a new group project assigned last week, were set behind. The project, worth eighty-five percent of their cumulative grade, involved every student creating an invention from scratch.

If the project yielded enough success, they could be referred to pitch the invention to one of the high-tech companies.

The deadline was in two months. Despite all the illogical details, Todd remained reserved.

After class concluded, Isaac invited Todd to Posie's, a small bar a block away from campus.

Todd agreed with a simple shrug.

Posie's quaint atmosphere made it a great venue for events like trivia nights every other week or the occasional jazz night. The bar's interior was lit by autumn-colored lights paired with an aesthetic of birch wood.

They sat in one of the booths where Todd sipped on a glass of whiskey.

"I had no idea you were a whiskey person," said Isaac with his glass of water.

"Trying something new. I think I prefer gin, still." Todd pointed to Isaac's glass. "You invite me to a bar and you're gonna drink water?"

"On a diet. Hey, look, I know I've been out of commission. Sorry I haven't reached out."

———

106

The cloud in Todd's mind cleared, thankful for Isaac's acknowledgment. "Dude, what happened?" he asked.

"It's been a lot going on. Too much to say."

Todd sighed. "All you gotta do is let me know. I'm still in this, and I'm hoping you are too. Almost at the finish line and we got career opportunities flying out the window with each passing day."

"You're right," Isaac admitted. "What did I miss?"

Todd rotated his crystal glass. The amber liquid swishing back and forth in a clockwise motion. He explained to Isaac the project.

Isaac's eyes stopped blinking. "I'm sorry, what? From scratch?"

Todd nodded. "Two months."

"How heavy is the grade?"

"Eighty-five percent."

Slowly, Isaac withdrew. He wrapped his knuckles around his glass, thinking. "Can we use the prosthetic you made for me?"

"Those kinds of prosthetics exist. Has to be new. If we make a working prototype, it's an automatic one-hundred. But don't stress it. Tech companies might see our work."

"Did she say which ones?"

"Well, no," Todd pressed his lips, taking another sip. "But it's a way bigger opportunity than we've ever had before. Might be *the* chance. I can manage, but…"

"If a Sage was found inventing…"

"That's dollar signs for them. In theory, anyway."

"It'd be going against the 'don't take shortcuts' mantra."

Todd finished his glass of whiskey. "See, we're showcasing our hard work. It's not like we have nothing other than a name. The name is just additional leverage. We're taking advantage of how certain companies have a shallow mindset."

"A *nice to have,* but not a *need to have.*"

Todd pointed one index finger at Isaac. "Exactly."

Isaac sighed. "I'm gonna hold you back on this. My engineering isn't as innovative as yours."

"That's not true. I remember when you made stink bombs when we were kids. First time you thought of something that devious, too."

Isaac chuckled. "That's because that adult teasing us was an asshole."

"Still. That was you. You know how to engineer. Just follow my lead. Deal?"

Slowly, Isaac nodded, as if convincing himself that Todd was right. "Okay," Isaac chirped. "We can do this."

"Just don't ghost on me again, alright?"

"I got you. I'll try to brainstorm back home. Um…How's Rose doing, by the way? Have you heard from her?"

Todd raised a brow, thrown off by the sudden question. "I guess she's fine." He sneered, "Actually, most girls aren't fine when they're ghosted. You know I've been trying to set you up to hang out with her on our outings."

"I got a lot going on."

"And she probably does too. Find a balance fast, or the things you want won't work. Like *her*…"

Isaac stammered his hands around, struggling to find words.

Todd extended his hand. "Hand me your phone."

Isaac eased one hand into his pocket slowly pulled his phone with a look of hesitation. Todd snatched the phone out of Isaac's grip halfway out.

"I wasn't ready!" Isaac hurdled over the table.

"Don't worry, I'll keep it eloquent."

Todd selected Rosemary's phone number and typed a message. An introduction, followed by an honest request to chat more. Todd sent the message and handed the phone back to Isaac.

Isaac tilted his flustered grimace up, exhaling at the ceiling.

"What else have you got to lose?"

Isaac bowed his head with shut eyes. Todd understood his friend was the type to overthink on the wrong factors. All he needed was the right push, support, and trust.

Isaac let out a light sigh. "If it happens, it happens."

"You know I'm right." Todd raised his empty glass. "Now buy me another drink."

Isaac smirked. "Sure."

# XIII
## KARA CULVER

## October 14, 2022, 10:00 AM

Quiet summarized the past few days. The initial seconds it took to process what Isaac said–his reason for the incident, and the entire vendetta being the root of the incident–dragged like hours before turning into days of silence.

She tended to the plants while processing it all. Each green leaf's pigments shifted to yellow and orange, and the thin stems connected to each colored bouquet sprouted out of the small bushes by the patio entrance.

Dense, orange-red heads, coming from the two oak trees, provided another layer of cool shade. Her work included one lone lemon tree she dedicated to growing for years now. All the effort showed menial signs of visible progress.

Kara searched for a thought or some kind of reasoning to clarify the sanity, or insanity, of it all. Her mind drifted to a memory of when she worked at Sage Foundation.

Months before the tragedy, Gemma had an important meeting to with a group of investors. Gemma was going to pitch a new de-aging compound that would increase longevity and reverse-age in the human body. It would be proposed for use on pets before expanding it onto humans.

A wild idea that belonged in a sci-fi universe, but Gemma claimed she had the foundational groundworks to this ambitious compound. All she needed was the funds from the investors to expand.

Short on hands, she pleaded for Kara's assistance. While Kara tended to mostly housekeeping tasks, she agreed to help out of sheer gratitude for being given work in the first place. Kara produced all documents Gemma requested and arranged a simple slideshow per Gemma's guidance.

On the day of the meeting, Kara was informed to wait outside with Samuel as she presented to the investors. While Samuel helped with projects, he acted more as a pillar of support for Gemma.

His upright posture, draped in a rather loose, large suit, towered over Kara. His wide-rimmed glasses exemplified the softer features of his face in contrast to sharp features like his angled jawline and rectangular nose.

Samuel watched on with a subtle smile. It seemed like he was always proud of Gemma. The woman's most vivid feature, as Kara observed, was Gemma's firm, confident expression as she displayed her adept knowledge in her field, and a smile that compelled you to support whatever she was doing.

And then there was the masterclass work in refraining of show expression that others wanted, such as anger or jealousy. She knew how to control any room.

Once Gemma concluded her pitch, the discussion continued for some minutes. The investors proceeded to show Gemma some imagery before Gemma waved them off with a polite nod and handshake.

After, Gemma to Samuel explained the investors had chosen another competitor using the same exact compound of which she was in possession. There was a traitor in the company selling information.

Her rage, although subdued visually, leaked through her speech with visceral, sharp tones like a quiet, restrained roar.

A fire sparked in Kara's chest. Her heart hastened, fueled by a sudden anger toward the investors on behalf of Gemma. It was a familiar spite she held toward her parents. The very reason she preferred reprieve far away and in the streets and alleyways, even if it meant a harsher life.

As the calm diplomat, Samuel asked if there was a possibility that it was a grand coincidence. Gemma clarified that, yes, science had its definitive right and wrong answers. But like a painter with a canvas, there were key differences in the formulas, arrangements and so forth.

Gemma confirmed it was completely identical. She could double-check, or triple-check if she'd liked, but her work was buried in her subconscious. She stormed off into her office down the hall.

Kara spouted her frustrations. "What a piece of shit. There must be a way to—"

"They're not worth the air, Kara," Samuel replied. He turned, showing his same calm disposition she was accustomed to. "Sorry. If that came off harsh."

Kara shook her head.

———

111

"Gemma will get through this. She always does. We'll make sure it doesn't happen again."

"But *they* deserve it."

"We've all been through that feeling." Samuel affixed his stone stare onto Kara. "But things like that are a poison. You think you're following some goal. It'll spark you alive when you reach it. But that spark is what'll also make you burn."

Now, Kara found herself repeating those words Samuel told her in today's ambience. Arrhythmic footsteps of Isaac's recovering body. Water rushing and stopping. Leaves brushing together.

***

Kara went to the pharmacy to buy more medical supplies in case Isaac rushed to his doom once again. She stowed meals in the fridge for Isaac. Nearly two weeks of this and Kara was still unsure of what to do.

On October 14th, Isaac departed early in the morning.

Around noon, Kara tended to her usual gardening when knocks boomed at the front door. She stowed her gardening gloves in her back pocket and moved to the front door.

Two men –one with gelled curly hair, wearing a silk purple shirt and black pants and the other with a block-like face, dressed in a spotted beige trench coat, white button-up and khaki slacks–stood at the front door.

"Good afternoon, miss," the man in the trench coat spoke.

"Hi there," said Kara. "How can I help you?"

The man in the trench coat flashed an NMPD badge, as did his partner. "Detective John Saint." He pointed to his partner. "This is Jackson Billows. We were wondering if we could ask Isaac Sage a few questions?"

"He's not here right now. Is there a concern?"

"Everything's okay. Just questions we feel could help an ongoing case."

"What's the case?"

"Classified," Saint and Billows said simultaneously.

Kara nodded. She gave an expression of annoyance over the whole situation.  Isaac's sloppy actions bringing police to their doorstep.

"I can say he'll be available in two days," said Kara.

Saint raised a brow. "Not tomorrow?"

"He's a busy kid."

The detective nodded, then looked at his partner. The latter reciprocated the same expression. Detective Saint turned to Kara.

"Two days it is. Thank you."

"Have a good one." Kara shut the door.

Her heart began pounding. Isaac was lucky they didn't come to throw him in jail. Now, there had to be a conversation.

***

Kara heard Isaac's arrival by the early evening.

She entered the kitchen, finding him sifting through the fridge. Their eyes met once he exited with a carton of milk in hand. His eyes widened. His loose sweatshirt hung by his collarbone, drooping over his fitted sweatpants. His injuries had healed to bare visibility.

"Hi, Kara."

"Hi, Isaac."

"I made some food for us. It's in the fridge, so, it's cold."

"Right. Thanks."  Isaac turned to the pile of dirtied cookware by the sink. "Since it's already cold, maybe I can help you with the dishes first."

Kara shrugged. She handled washing while Isaac dried each pot and plate with a towel.

"Kara…I want you to know you have nothing to worry about. It won't happen again," Although his eyes focused on the plate, his hands trembled.  And the words coming from him resonated with sincerity.

Kara thought back to Samuel's words. She wanted to say it now to Isaac, to tell him that this path isn't meant for him. But she found herself drifting back to her old mindset.

She disagreed with Samuel. What she found, time and time again, was a return to that spark with a desire to find justice through revenge. It happened with her parents. It happened with the investors. And it lasted for years after Samuel and Gemma's passing.

Kara owed them her life.

When she learned on the day of the incident that only Isaac would be returning home, she felt all the blood rush down to her feet. She struggled to even focus on the tiny, important tasks like locking the door or re-sealing the cap on a milk carton for months.

Once Isaac shared his mission, the spark returned. Samuel had been right to some degree. Maybe she could find some reprieve in saying it aloud to Isaac. Be the mature figure he needed.

"Isaac…" She cleaned one plate, guided by the edge. "You should know…"

Isaac paused his actions. He stared Kara down from the corner of his eye.

She lamented on her isolation. Perhaps it was her way of moving through life, akin to Isaac. Perhaps they needed this spark o finally get closure.

Kara stopped drying the plate halfway and placed it on the damp towel. "A detective stopped by. He was asking for you."

Isaac almost dropped the ceramic dish. He placed it onto the stack of plates and planted his hands on the counter. "Wh-What did you tell them?"

"You wouldn't be back until the day after tomorrow."

"Did they say why they wanted me?"

"They wanted to ask a few questions. Kept it vague."

"Fuck," Isaac paced away from the counter. Kara kept her heart from pounding over Isaac's paranoia. "Fuck! I was so careless."

Kara mimicked inhaling with her arms, bringing them inward. "Take a deep breath." Then she brought them outward with a deep exhale.

Initially off-sync, he raised his chest with the motion of her hands and repeated with an exhale. Inch by inch, his expression eased.

———

"Kara," Isaac vociferated with passion, "if I stop this, I'll regret it for the rest of my life. What happened that night won't happen again." His eyes wandered to the dirt footprints among the clean marble tiles. "I made a mess."

Kara analyzed Isaac's conflicting expression. In her mind, she visualized a see-saw imagery of a peace of mind followed by Isaac's mission. Back and forth, increasing the tightness in her chest.

"They deserve justice," she said. "No one knows about this except us."

Isaac's downtrodden gaze lifted in her direction. "Kara...thank you," Isaac whispered through a lit smile. "Seriously."

"As long as you hold on to your promise. Never show up like that again. You need to get your alibi straight in two days to keep it that way. For both of us."

In this moment, clinging onto this mutual vengeance didn't feel poisonous. It was liberating. Easier, even, to breathe the air in the mansion.

"Any tips for the alibi?" Isaac asked.

"Don't fuck up."

# XIV
## John Saint
### October 16, 2022, 9:55 AM

"Could you imagine living in a place this huge?" Billows asked Saint.

Saint assessed the Sage mansion with his partner, enamored by the architecture. The blotches of mold pocketed in the exterior's bug holes exemplified its weathered age.

"Beautiful building," Saint replied. "But I could imagine how long it takes to clean."

"Weird that she takes care of the house on her own."

"If they continued to give her reserves of money, I wouldn't see a problem."

"Or maybe she can't let go either," Billows added. A sad perspective Saint hadn't considered.

Saint had compiled his research about Isaac prior to their visit. Dr. Bukowski, his therapist, refused to provide any intimate info due to client privilege. Records, however, provided a basic summary. Isaac endured sessions of therapy and was provided medication to deal with recurring PTSD. He was social but kept to himself with a microscopic circle of acquaintances.

His paternal grandparents, the sole living relatives, never contacted him due to an estranged relationship with Samuel. His maternal grandparents both passed away. And then, there was the recent assassination attempt. Prior to the assassination, Isaac left the mansion at the age of sixteen of his own accord.

Saint hoped the research could help discover something revelatory in this interview. Especially that business card.

Billows hammered on the door three times. Within seconds, Isaac Sage emerged from behind the door in a loose, long-sleeve sweater and linen pants. Parts of his muscles defined the loose outlines. His face was washed clean, and his messy hair was damp, falling around his forehead in patches.

Isaac smiled and waved one hand. "Good morning."

"Good morning, Mr. Sage." Saint introduced himself and Billows. "We were trying to catch you the other day, but apparently you were gone. I hope today is better?"

"Other than some work on my plate, today works perfect." Isaac gestured them toward the mansion. "Please, come inside."

"We won't take too much of your time," said Billows.

"Ah, it won't be until the evening anyway, it's fine."

The detectives and Isaac took a seat at the living room couch by a wooden coffee table.

"Answer as much as you can, if possible," said Saint. "The more detailed, the better."

"Absolutely," said Isaac, "Whatever way I can help."

Saint leaned forward. "You were living in another house back in June, right? And around that time, it was burned down by two assailants?"

"That's correct," said Isaac.

"How'd you escape?" asked Saint.

"I managed to hide out in some bushes," said Isaac. "And by hide, I mean I blacked out from blood loss. Believe it or not, my brilliant idea was to run to the hospital, and then come back to the house with the hopes of having my pinky finger there waiting for me."

"Got it fixed though, huh?" Billows interjected. Isaac's amputated pinky finger was replaced with a synthetic digit secured by nylon padding and straps.

"My friend Todd put this together."

"Got some great friends then," Billows smiled. "By the way, our team is hard at work to find those assailants and their motives."

"I can imagine," Isaac's olive-sand eyes remained relaxed. "Thanks. Has there been any good progress? Is this investigation linked to that?"

"Your situation may be linked in theory. What brings me to your house today is this…" Saint pulled Samuel's business card out of his coat pocket and placed it on the table in Isaac's view.

Isaac's dull gaze cracked into a tremor. The trembling progressed the longer he observed the card.

"We found this card during our investigation at a drug operation," Saint continued. "Do you have any idea why it would be there?"

Isaac shook his head.

"You don't have possession of any of these cards here? Not in the house?" Billows continued.

"All tossed years ago," said Isaac.

"What do you think of seeing this then?" Saint asked, probing for Isaac's reaction. The sudden tremble in his eyes signified one subconscious detail. It might have been shock. Or something more passionate.

Isaac let out a quiet exhale. He examined the card with a calm, piqued curiosity.

"I'm baffled. Where was this?" asked Isaac.

"We found it in a warehouse run by a cartel," said Saint. "Do you happen to have any clue as to why?"

Isaac held back his twitching lower lip, spurting out a split-second chuckle. "I thought they labeled it as a freak accident."

Saint knew Isaac referred to 'they' as the NMPD closing the case as such. "This angle could be a sign that…well, I'll speak on their behalf. We were wrong."

"Look, you know I'm not the detective here," Isaac pushed back. "Just trying to live my life. I don't want this here."

"As the son of the Sages?"

"I'd appreciate to be recognized beyond that."

"Apologies," Saint replied, "Detective habits. But it would be great to find out after all these years. Wouldn't it?" Saint asked. "Even my head is brewing new motivations for that incident."

The questions were intended as subjective. Simple, yet enough to incite a reaction. And Isaac's visual reactions contradicted with what he said.

A bead of sweat shed down the youth's forehead. His eyes continued to examine the card, the olive shade wavering within his pupils.

"Is everything okay?" Kara, the caretaker, asked as she entered. Isaac's entire expression recomposed once more.

"We're good, thank you," said Billows.

"It's a fairy tale scenario," Isaac replied. "Even if part of me would like to see justice, if that were possible, I can't hope for it. It was an accident we have to accept."

Saint nodded. He rose to his feet and adjusted his coat. "Last question. Can you tell us where you were on October 3rd of this year?"

"I was studying for some exam work and then watched a movie with Kara."

"What movie?"

"Ah," Isaac scratched his head. "Some *Edge of Tomorrow* rip-off."

He said it without hesitation. No internal reflection or time to think. Was it scripted? Or was he offended by Saint's 'label' of him and fed up?

"Good then," Saint shook Isaac's hand. "You let us know if you have any concerns or suspicions. It's our goal to bring justice to this case."

"Thank you for answering our questions, Isaac," Billows said.

"Thanks to you and all your hard work in this city." Isaac escorted them out of the mansion. "Be safe," he said as the duo entered their car and drove off.

"What do you think?" Billows asked Saint.

"I don't think he's fully off the list," Saint replied. "I have a feeling he wants something."

"You don't think you're reaching?"

"Could be. But sometimes you've gotta fish on the far end to net something substantial."

Billows responded with a look of skepticism. "Let's grab a bite and brainstorm."

***

Saint and Billows arrived in the city. The car coasted down the right lane amid dense traffic. Civilians sauntered the sidewalk underneath the color-changing greenery surrounded by the concrete.

Saint turned on the radio, playing Ranchera music. The subtle static of the police radio hummed in the background. The fall breeze cooled Saint's body. Billows had his eyes shut, head leaning against the window.

The radio emitted came to life. "Teams are proceeding to apprehended warehouses five and six, over."

"Copy that," another voice on the radio responded. "Proceeding to relay DEA."

Warehouses five and six. The duo had been so caught up in their investigative research that they hadn't realized progress was being made. Saint nodded in relief.

*'One step closer.'*

In the cacophonies of all the ambiance, an ear-piercing *POP* overpowered the music.

Grainy smoke sprouted from Saint's car as the wheel fought against him. The car careened toward the sidewalk, colliding with a sudden harsh force.

Saint's vision spun into a fuzzy blur. The daylight's sheer whiteness enveloped his sight. As his eyes adjusted, he found a nearby streetlight pole stopped the car's chaotic spinning, sunken into the corner of the front passenger side.

His popped eardrums ingested muffled echoes. He stumbled out of the car. Billows, crouched with his gun in hand, commanded Saint to take cover.

With his hand on the car's exterior, Saint crouched and guided himself to the passenger side past debris and reflective shards scattered around the floor.

A black bullet hole was now on the hood of the car, fresh with grainy smoke. More bullets whizzed through the air.

*'Sniper. perched somewhere high up and afar.'* Normal bullets were rare in the black market, but sniper bullets were even more of a rare commodity.

Saint reached the other side to find Billows now lying face down. He sped to Billows and verified his pulse. Blood pooled underneath his body.

Whoever had their sights locked on Saint and Billows didn't care about causing chaos in daylight, either. Saint turned to the inside of the car, finding a spark-filled hole in the walkie-talkie system.

Saint grabbed a fair-sized reflective shard from the floor, raising it above his cover. He rotated the mirror, observing every detailed reflected patch for an anomaly. In his view were desaturated skies and monotone buildings from his vantage point.

A split-second later, the mirror shattered in Saint's hand, scraping parts of his skin and head.

Scrambling to find the sniper would be a gamble for suicide. The bullets snarled through the air before pounding against Saint's vehicle.

An overwhelming burning oil smell singed Saint's nostril. He grabbed Billows and dragged his body to a nearby alleyway beside a dumpster. He would be hidden from the sniper's line of sight.

From the new angle, something in the distance changed. Or, perhaps, it was always there but hidden from the other perspective.

Saint squinted. *'Am I seeing things?'*

Distorted blobs of color floated in the sky. They shed an abnormal light at the top of one tower. It could be camouflage.

Saint maneuvered out of cover in a zigzag pattern. Two bullets grazed the fabric of Saint's button-up shirt.

The adrenaline wore on Saint's breathing, inflicting a sharp stab in his chest. Sirens swarmed the background, followed by an enormous boom. All he could focus on was running. He prayed Billows was far enough from the blast. The bullets shot through the wind at every turn, colliding against chunks of the nearby marble and bricks.

After a block and a half, two shots damaged Saint. One grazed his left shoulder, and the other hit some bricks where the debris impaled his right forearm. He focused on his pace and continued his zig-zag pattern. There wasn't time to rest.

Evading the bullets, and fighting his fizzling lungs, Saint arrived at the building after eight blocks. The entire base was made of glass, segmented into multiple rectangular arrays.

Without time, he ran inside, flashed his badge to the nearest employee and headed straight for the doorway labeled 'ROOFTOP ACCESS: EMPLOYEES ONLY.'

The stairway spiraled around the building to form a quadrilateral parallel to the building's geometry. Every door marked the number of a new floor. He ticked them off in his head to check every number he came across. Ten, twenty, thirty, forty, fifty…fifty-two.

He reached the top with shaky, gelatin legs. An open doorway revealing the blue sky.

The second he pulled out his gun, a sudden, sharp force knocked back against his nose. He stumbled back into the stairway against the railing, his arm holding the gun frozen in place. The force transitioned to the wounds in his forearm, as he screamed in pain.

Saint yanked one of brick shards from his forearm with his unarmed hand and swung it swiped through the air.

Another unseen force pinned him against the railing. Then, a small sliver of blood floated in mid-air. It crawled downward, forming a jawline before disappearing.

Saint grasped his gun's trigger and fired straight down the line of sight.

Blood spurted across the floor, out of thin air followed by patches. The patches connected to reveal a rugged disheveled, pale man. His long black hair extended down to his shoulders with a sniper rifle strapped around his back.

The sniper's face contorted in pain over the wound. Saint raised his weapon. "Don't move!"

The sniper threw his rifle toward Saint. The detective dodged and found the sniper gone once again. Rampant footsteps echoed in Saint's hearing.

One blunt blow knocked Saint's jaw, followed by tremendous pain digging into his bullet wound.

Saint swung a weak hook, albeit weak from low energy reserves. The sniper re-appeared, pulling out a sickle-shaped knife and swiping at the detective until he landed one horizontal slash across his chest.

The detective latched onto the sniper's presumed crown with one hand and headbutted him. In the moment of daze, Saint planted the gun underneath the sniper's chin just as he turned invisible.

"Show yourself. And don't. Move."

The sniper reappeared. Saint threw him to the floor and slapped cuffs onto his bony wrists.

A water bottle refracting sunlight had led to the light trick exposing the sniper's location. The sniper afterward was handed to the NMPD forces. Saint and Billows were driven to New Manhattan West Hospital, the nearest, leaving the former to wonder what else laid ahead.

***

Billows was taken to a private room on the fourth floor. Every entrance and stairway on each floor was guarded by two NMPD officers.

After careful examination and first aid from the doctor, Saint checked on the state of his partner. From the hall, he peered through the window into his room. Unconscious, Billows was covered in thin white blankets from his feet to his shoulders. Wires protruded from underneath the sheets, connecting to a heart monitor and IV tank.

The doctor, in his white coat and array of tools hung around his neck, entered the room. Saint followed, watching the doctor pick up the clipboard hanging from the bed and placing it back within the same minute interval.

"Reading's stable." The doctor's tone gave reprieve. He turned to Saint. "I assume you're a close friend?"

Saint nodded.

"He'll recover fine," said the doctor. "But he'll be in for maybe three to four months. Some take less, some take more. He may need invasive surgery. We found some lethal hollow-point bullet fragments lingering. Had any of those shards been a few centimeters to the left, he would've died."

The reply was so quick that Saint was unsure of how to process that what-if scenario. Fear of a premature death bubbled back in his gut. Quitting only felt easy in thought. The actual application, however, spelled for too much to be wasted in vain. Although it could be life-saving.

He could convince Billows to quit. *If* he needed convincing after what occurred.

"On behalf of all of us, thank you, Doc." Saint shook his hand. "Excuse me while I get some air." Saint removed his overcoat and tossed it onto the chair before leaving.

With heavy eyes, a parched throat and a frantic mind, he wanted a drink from the vending machine set in the hall. Hopefully, it would soothe him enough to slow the rate at which his mind was moving.

Footsteps followed behind him by the time he stood in front of the machine and tapped for the water bottle. A giant thud followed. A sip of the water brought a breath of fresh air.

Before he could take another sip, a voice caught his attention.

"It's been quite the commotion today."

Saint turned to the new voice. It was a man in light-blue scrubs, scarred from head to toe in bandages. Some patches revealed his open skin. His face, although clean of bandages, was swollen with purple-red lumps.

"It could've been worse," said Saint.

"Can I ask why?"

Saint squinted. "You don't know?"

The bandaged man shook his head.

"Good for you," Saint said. "Keep it that way. For your sake."

"Your area's surrounded by cops. A lot of cops." His bloodied right eye struggled to focus.

"They're with me."

The bandaged man's breathing thinned. The tempo in his speech steadied.

"What's…What's the reason?" he asked.

Saint grit his teeth. "You're being rather invasive."

The bandaged man moved closer to Saint, standing within an inch. "Hey, what are you–"

"I've been stuck in this hospital trying to stay hidden. I want to see my daughter." His voice turned shaky, exhaling rapid, uneven beats into Saint's eardrums.

"What are you, insane? Make sense or I can't help–"

"I heard mentions of cartels from the other officers. It's him, isn't it? Diablo?"

Saint paused, suddenly alert as if activated by a hidden trigger word.

The man continued, "He has connections to people like that."

"Who are you?"

"My name's Johnson. I was trying to make money in that business, in Diablo's cartel. Diablo tried killing me."

"You worked for him?" Saint grabbed Johnson's collar, infuriated. "And you've been *hiding*?"

"I-I want to see my family. But I haven't been able to because I don't want to risk getting them hurt. Eyes and ears everywhere. Even on the landlines I hear a click. I can tell you how you can stop him. I can leave knowing when he's dead. I have addresses. Please."

Saint paused. Perhaps it was Johnson's fear of avoiding anything at all that made him tick. But in dangerous situations like these, and with a family in mind, survival was key. He released his grip.

"Out with it."

Johnson pulled a folded sheet of tissue paper from his back pocket. "Both of these warehouses I had heard about. I worked at the one in Oswego."

Saint unfolded the paper. One in Oswego. Another at Kingsbridge, within the city. This seemed all too good to be true. "What else can you tell me about these places?"

"What else?"

"What are the operations there, what kind of brigade are we expecting? Think."

Johnson darted his gaze away with an anxious look as he reflected. "Well, Oswego is your typical warehouse operations. Most of the guys don't have firearms. Maybe about five, seven. Kingsbridge was something I heard Diablo mention to return to. I don't know outside of that. I'm trying to think if there's more but that's all I have. Sorry."

"Have you been approached?"

"I've been careful."

"And yet there are eyes and ears everywhere when you're out here in the hall?"

"It is a risk…but it's worth it."

Johnson's sweat glistened against the phosphorus lighting.  He analyzed his surroundings to find only them.

"Please," Johnson continued. "All I need to know is he won't be able to hurt them."

Saint leaned in and whispered, "For our sake, stay calm and keep hidden. Nod your head and walk back to your room."

Johnson nodded.  Saint watched him depart around the corner and enter a nearby room, then vanished from his line of sight after closing the blinds.  Saint pressed for the water bottle on the vending machine.

From the opposite end, Chief Briggs approached the vending machine and pressed for a sandwich. The new information began to infect Saint with enthusiasm.

"Man, what a day.  These sandwiches are a taste of heaven when you're starving."

"I suppose," Saint said, still absorbing Johnson's information.

Briggs shook his head. He glared at Saint from the corner of his eye.

"I wanted you to hear it from me. You guys are off the case.  DEA's taking over."

Seconds passed in silence before the sandwich dropped into the machine's slot with a giant thud.

"What?" Saint bemoaned.

"You're in their sights. I can't risk it. Don't worry. Carmichael will be handling it."

*'Carmichael.  One of enforcement's greatest.'*

"We were making great progress…" Saint's knees trembled with his energy on this conversation. "Our guys got two warehouses!"

Briggs raised his voice, "There's that fucking reckless head of yours. You went ten steps forward and then fifty steps back. You're done.  And you know Carmichael, there's no concern she won't close this case."

The Chief wasn't wrong. Saint's reason didn't align with not trusting Carmichael. It aligned with a more personal conviction.

"I… What am I supposed to do now?"

"You live your life. Find something else to do. You should thank me."

This was Saint's life for the past several months, costing him loss of sleep, and time with Edoris. All the sacrifice would be in vain.

*'Dad wouldn't shy away.'*

"Daniel," Saint referred to Briggs by his first name. He looked down at the floor, unable to look the Chief in the eyes. He fished for all the reasons to keep on in his head, his grip around the cold water bottle tightening. "I have two addresses. Locations of where the cartel's boss could be. There was a lead in the hospital the entire time."

"Then hand it to the DEA." Briggs bit into his sandwich.

"You know how much longer it'll take if we give it to them?" People disappeared from the hall and re-appeared. A sporadic pattern. But Saint retained his focus.

"All the document processing?" Saint continued. "The transferring of files? The new shitheads pretending to care over this. This is another coin in their bag–"

"So, your asset is withholding information." Briggs scowled at Saint. "Good thinking! What's your actual leverage, John?"

"My leverage is trusting a Saint!" he exclaimed. "What would Jacques think of this? You know how he would react if you handed off his case to someone, even if it was Carmichael?"

Briggs scoffed. He took another swift bite. "I thought you'd appreciate the relaxation."

"I'm my father's son. If the case is open, that word is nonexistent."

Briggs paused for several seconds as he simmered. His scrunched expression didn't soften.

"I'm close. This attack was a sign they're scared. And now with this address, we can–"

Briggs shot a pointed index finger at Saint. "*I* will speak to the DEA. *You* will provide that information to them. Be wary of putting your ass on the radar, John. I do this knowing Jacques would go AWOL if the same happened to him. Things will *not* get easier. Now, I'm going to enjoy the rest of this sandwich alone. In silence."

"Understood."

For a moment, all, including Briggs, disappeared from the hall and Saint stood alone. The hospital's pale walls and dim lights of the vending machine closed in around him.

A television in the corner revealed a newsreel reporting on the sniper incident. 'DETECTIVES TARGETED BY DRUG CARTEL,' scrolled over the lower third. A single light above him flickered.

# XV
## ROSEMARY DIER

### October 16, 2022, 7:27 PM

O range blossoms. Bright. Vivid. Pungent. Overwhelming. All traits of the scent that Rosemary couldn't rid from her skin. A prude, nostalgic scent she didn't wish to indulge in now as she sat on the edge of the sidewalk in front of the bills collection agency.

She chewed on the loose strap of her off-white backpack after negotiating the lowest fee she could pay for a late electric bill. The backpack wrapped around her floral-patterned button-up, the blouse tucked into high-waisted black jeans.

Clayton's over-reliance on M.A.D forced him into an inebriated coma throughout the evening after a full day of work. She imagined her father's misshapen, nonathletic stature alone in the dark, turning hysteric over why none of the lights were working. Rosemary did her due diligence to ensure that never happened.

The late fee, despite being reduced, left a dent in her funds. She wouldn't receive tuition money until next month. Asking others to lend her money was her personal taboo.  It would take two hours to walk home without a bus or train to rely on.

Underneath the violet sky, she removed her backpack and brought it to her front, searching inside for spare cash in the mess of scrap sheets and notebooks.

*'Stressing over five missing dollars,'* Rosemary shook her head.  *'You're better than this, Rose.'*

The longer she searched, the idea to start trekking home before nightfall became more convincing. She rose to her feet, continuing to search her backpack while paying attention to the road.

———

129

At the bottom of her backpack, a wrinkled Ziploc bag came into view, snugged between a crevice. She pulled the bag outward, stunned with the slow realization of what this was: Green-yellow chunks of M.A.D. Euphoric scents of lime and fresh herbs leaked from the tiny holes of the bag.

Rosemary thought she had thrown out every bit of M.A.D. before she left for rehab half a year ago. Like an expensive haircut gone wrong, she was disappointed at the sight. And more disappointed as, by impulse, she salivated over the though of the drug's rich, numbing acidity. Followed by the lulling nature that calmed every sense of paranoia.

Her rehab helped her understand the drug's effects was more like stockpiling instead of curing. She was still healing, in fact. A tint of dark circles under her eyes remained from insomnia. The fullness in her cheeks was thin and still healing. The skin kept some light, faded dots from syringe use. The drug called to every part of her craving for the calm.

Her fingers twitched, deciding on the right decision.

Then, a bump broke her focus. She re-focused to find a man wearing a wrinkled, light blue sweater with grey dress pants.

"I am so, sorry, I–" she examined the face closer. Shaped yet messy hair with dull olive eyes and light bruises. It was Isaac Sage. "Oh. H-hi."

"Hey there," said Isaac. An awkward silence filled the air. He was a familiar presence, yet unfamiliar at the same time. They texted back and forth ever since Isaac messaged her on one random afternoon. Harmless conversations, overall. Small talk over what they were doing. Joking, banter, some small slices of life interjected in-between. They were the best distraction Rosemary received in ages.

Yet, Rosemary was nervous to see him in person.

"By the way, sorry," Isaac flashed a smile. "You're not mad, right?"

"Sorry?" Rosemary asked. "I'm not following."

"I meant to text you back. Just got caught up with other things."

Rosemary squinted her eyes. "I thought *I* hadn't texted you back?"

Isaac glanced away, then back to Rosemary. "No, that was…that was me, I think."

Rosemary let out a playful sigh. "Thank God, I'm not the villain here for once."

Isaac laughed. "To what, the rats in the city?"

"They are my arch nemeses, is that obvious?"

Rosemary and Isaac chuckled.

"What brings you here?" he asked.

"About to head home."

"By train? There's a train station right there," Isaac pointed to the G train entrance in the opposite direction.

"Walking. I'm broke."

"For one train ride."

"Yes." Rosemary looked on with a straight face, feeling a red flush overtake her.

"I could give you money if you need that."

Rosemary smiled. "No. But, thank you. I'll walk my way home."

"It's only five bucks."

"I insist, no, thanks."

"How long is your walk?"

"It's not that long." Rosemary examined the sky turning dark. More streetlights turning on, one by one. In the back of her mind, her route could bring her into a blackout zone if she wasn't careful enough. But she refused to ask for help. "I'll be fine."

Isaac gazed at the sky, along with the road down ahead. He locked eyes with her. Rosemary smiled, trying to remove any hint of worry.

"Listen, I, uh…can we make a deal?"

"What do you mean?"

"Let me give you five bucks. All I want is this…there's this diner, Starlight Diner, down the street. I've been dying to go, but I'm worried I'll get mugged."

"Oh, so you need me to protect you?" Rosemary smirked.

"You remember in our texts, right? How you would make a fantastic body-guard. Resume-worthy stuff. Would you be willing to guard me? It's on the way to your home. I'll even pay for a milkshake."

"Are the milkshakes to die for?"

"To *die* for."

"But you haven't been there."

"I…hear things. It'll be complementary for being my bodyguard."

Rosemary paused. Isaac's intentions were obvious. But the kindness behind it compelled her to agree. Her father, she thought, should be okay for a little while longer.

***

After thirty minutes, Rosemary and Isaac arrived at Starlight Diner. The location maintained a 1950s retro design with a vibrant palette of marble white and hot pink. Even the anchored TVs maintained the aesthetic of CRTs.

They entered, sitting at one of the pink booths beside the landscape window.

When the waiter arrived, Isaac ordered a Cookie Crisps milkshake, while Rosemary ordered the Fruity Pebbles Bonanza shake. The waiter scribbled the order into his black notepad and left to the kitchen.

Rosemary's eyes averted to the window. She was content with starting conversations. But now, her mind was fixated on when she'll return to the stress. She was reminded of how her mother, Cher, would ease her stress. Her presence alone was its own natural sedative. From the soft manner in which he spoke and the scent of orange blossoms in the perfume she always wore.

"Todd told me you're into fashion," Isaac broke the silence.

"Yeah," Rosemary replied. She averted away from the window. "It's my form of escapism."

"Nice."

Rosemary nodded. "I would do it day and night if I could."

"When was the last time you did it?"

"Months, maybe?  Too much going on."  She chose to keep any response centered around her worries flat.

It was odd sharing her worries with Isaac, specifically. While the year of the Sage Hellfire was Isaac's worst year, it was Rosemary's best year. Her last vacation with Cher.

"Maybe you could find a studio?" Isaac asked.

"Don't have the money."

"Right. Sorry."

"It's fine."

The waiter returned with their order. Isaac placed the tip of his left thumb to his lower lip. His eyebrows furrowed, almost as if he was trying to move the milkshake in front of him.

"Are you trying to practice your psychic powers?" she teased Isaac.

His focus cracked into a flush, nervous smirk. "I was thinking. There must be a way to enable you to do what you wanna do."

Rosemary stirred her milkshake with the striped straw.  "I could be your bodyguard full time. Stock up on those five-dollar shifts."

"I could get you a job at Sage Foundation, maybe."

"Guess I am that good of a bodyguard."

"No," Isaac laughed, "like a job job.  Really, they've been wanting me to work there, I could include you in as part of the package."

Favors acted as a last resort. Relying on others weighed a sense of guilt. Her old friends made sure to hang that bag of guilt around her to their advantage.

"You don't have to do anything," said Rosemary. "But thank you." Isaac shrugged, tracing a line through condensation layered on his glass. "I'll wait it out until there's a moment to get back."

"You should be able to follow your goals."  He drank from his shake. "That's all."

Rosemary squinted her eyes. Was it a ploy to buy her attention? He darted his eyes to the window, almost as if angered by the idea that someone else was experiencing this.

———

133

"You seem to be passionate about this," said Rosemary.

He looked back at her with alit eyes. "People should be where they deserve to be," he said with directness.

"If everyone was born from the same cloth, sure."

Isaac's expression deflated. His eyes drifted to the corner, then shifted to another corner with two fingers and a thumb holding his tilted head. He wrapped his knuckles against the table with his other hand.

"Todd tells me you're a hermit," Rosemary said.

Isaac broke out of his trance, looking aloof. "He said that?"

"Verbatim."

"So, the engineer is our one and only source for gossip."

"Yeah…we suck."

"Don't pin that on me!"

"Hey, we're in the same boat unlike our social engineer."

"He can engineer his way out, he'll be fine."

Rosemary and Isaac laughed in unison. When it died down in laughter, she noticed a softness in his eyes. A rare sight to find in someone's glance, through her life anyway. Something more natural than what that piece of M.A.D. would've done.

Rosemary continued. "Here, you have milk around your nose." She pulled a napkin from the nearby dispenser and wiped Isaac's nose.

"Thanks."

Isaac angled up at the TV behind Rosemary. The gentle aura in his eyes gradually faded the longer he stared at the screen. Rosemary turned around. On the screen was a news headline: 'JOHN SAINT: DETECTIVE TARGETED BY DRUG CARTEL.' The newsreel followed with footage of an apparent sniper being thrown into custody.

Rosemary turned to Isaac. "Do you know him?"

Isaac brought his attention back to her. "Not really, no. One insane thing after another in this city."

"Gets crazier when it gets later, but that's always been the same–" Rosemary looked at the time.  11:03 PM. "Shit! I'm sorry, I gotta make sure my dad's alright."

"Let me walk you out. I'll cover the bill."  Isaac pulled a twenty-dollar bill from his pocket and left it on the table as he and Rosemary exited the diner.

They stopped at the adjacent sidewalk underneath the yellow streetlight. Rosemary's knuckles softly brushed against Isaac's, guided by a subtle, passing gust.  He, with a sudden pink-flush face, escorted her to a nearby train station.

"Hey, if I got intense at one point, sorry." said Isaac.  The intercom signaled its arrival as they stood at the entrance.

"You were. It's okay."

Isaac turned red.

"So, my bodyguard duties are over? Nothing more needed from me?"

A warmth in her core expected something more. From the way Isaac looked as if wanting to embrace her, it could go to either something passionate like a bonfire or vile like horrendous burns.

Then, Isaac shook his head. The dull-olive shade of his eyes softened underneath the warm light.

"Talking to you made my night better."

The sudden response warmed Rosemary.

Isaac flashed a look of surprise for a split-second, followed by another smile.  "You'll be okay heading back home?" he asked.

She nodded with a smile.  "Thanks."

"Text me when you're home. Bye, Rose."  He walked away, vanishing into the dark background beyond the glowing patches.

Along the way, she checked her back pocket, finding a folded, pristine five-dollar bill.  *That wasn't there before.'* She turned back once more toward the gate, passing through.

***

Rosemary returned home to the stench of orange blossoms and whiskey. Even Clayton couldn't be rid of that nostalgic scent. The lights were back on, and the air conditioner let out a small hum throughout the house. Everything was functioning.

And, to Rosemary's shock, Clayton stood tall, swaying back and forth in the middle of the kitchen. The blanket she had draped over him hung on his large back. His body let out small, sporadic wheezes of air.

"Dad?" Rosemary called to Clayton, keeping her composure. She walked across the stained carpet. Clayton's eyes were unfocused yet awake. "Let's get you to bed."

Clayton swatted her hand away. He rubbed the inner corners of his eyes with his free hand. It was a familiar calm before the storm, bringing an unsettling prickling sensation.

"I can't find your mother," said Clayton. "Where is she?"

A ghost-like hand tightened her vocal cords, unable to dispel the proper, desired words. The dire symptoms of the M.A.D. he ingested caused temporary dementia.

"She's…out of town, dad. Let's get some rest."

All she needed was for him to sleep and the amnesia would be gone come morning.

"Why…are you *lying*?" Clayton asked.

"Wha…?" Rosemary stuttered, trying to find her ground. "I'm not–"

"The calendar…" Clayton lifted one finger and pointed it at the fridge's door. "It says October 2022. I thought it was a typo. The other months say the same year."

Rosemary remained silent, focused on the overpowering aroma absorbed into the carpet. Her lips frowned.

"Daddy, I'm sorry–"

"*Get off*!" Clayton pushed back Rosemary with his roar.

In the reflection of his dark gaze, Rosemary saw a terrified child; And like a terrified child, she cowered to the animal resembling her father.

"I don't know you," Clayton shouted. "I don't know you! Get out!"

———

He threw a frame at the wall adjacent to Rosemary. Clayton continued blindly smashing memoirs against others around the apartment with no concern for coordination. The clashing glass created an explosion of microscopic shards that blitzed through the air, just grazing one of Rosemary's eyes by the bare surface.

She scurried to her room, avoiding the shards in the carpet, and grabbed a few of her necessary belongings, tossing them into her backpack. Charging cables, a handful of clothes, and a photo frame of Clayton, Cher and herself.

From the haste to the efficient packing, this was a natural instinctual response to a recurring incident. Cher would've stood her ground, if it was instead a downspiral for a deceased Rosemary. She would've consoled him and nurtured him, forcing him to stop his addiction and be a better man.

But Rosemary, as she reminded herself repeatedly, was not her mother. Now, where to go? She opened her phone, noticing a text from Isaac. He wrote:

*Wanted to make sure if you made it home?*

Rosemary refused to ask for Isaac's help. Seeking solace in him felt too soon. She scrolled through her contacts, finding Mikey, her former plug.

*'Better an acquaintance than a friend,'* she rationalized. As she sped out the apartment, she called Mikey and got a hold of him.

"Hey," Rosemary said, hyperventilating from the stress. "I need some help." She used a small, white lie. "Contractors are taking over my place. Please."

***

Rosemary and Mikey sat on the sidewalk outside his apartment. Once again, she found herself staring at the Ziploc bag with the green-yellow substance. She asked him if they could sit here to take in the air. Her lungs still heaved from the quickness of the events.

They shared words for several minutes. But her heart still weighed heavy with despair.

The streetlight, an obnoxious white color, exemplified Mikey's pale skin.

"Thank you," Rosemary muttered.

"No worries. Those contractors need to be more professional and warn you ahead of time," said Mikey.

Talking didn't work. She needed help to ease this stress now, before it overcame her senses. Panic was on the rise.

"You could get your money reduced, too. I know this guy–"

"Mikey," Rosemary interjected, "Do you have a lighter and pipe?"

"Of course."

She pulled the green-yellow M.A.D substance out of her backpack. "Smoke this with me?"

Mikey nodded. "I also have this acid-y stuff." He reached into his pocket and handed Rosemary a vial filled with a shiny, jelly-like texture. "You wanna try?"

Rosemary popped the cap open. A sudden stench of rotten eggs and sulfur overwhelmed her nostrils. "No thanks, Mikey." She soured, almost gagging. "Your nose has gotta be broken, what the *fuck*."

Mikey shrugged. He took one chunk of the green-yellow substance from the bag and placed it into the hole of a translucent green ornate pipe. With a lighter, he ignited a flame over the substance.

The chunks crackled with the expanding fire, bubbling up as Mikey inhaled from the pipe. A fume of green-tint smoke exhaled from his mouth.

Mikey passed the lit pipe over to Rosemary. She inhaled the smoke and exhaled. Again, once more. The sharpness of the stress dulled.

She repeated four more times until every negative feeling was insignificant. She handed the pipe back to Mikey.

"When do you wanna go inside?" he asked.

"I…just wanna lay here," Rosemary replied with a familiar lightness in her body. It brought her back to a night she was on a Ferris wheel with her family.

When the Ferris wheel reached its peak, the trees and mountains were fixated in the horizon. It was the first time she saw the world on a grander scale.

Cher exclaimed to look farther, and she could see the mountains. Look higher, and she could see the stars. She could envision anything she set her mind to.

Her face twitched between an expression of euphoria and melancholy. And then, in the white, blaring light, a striking silhouette called out to Rosemary. The light faded to reveal distinct lips and golden hair belonging to no one other than Cher.

# XVI
## ISAAC SAGE

## October 21, 2022, 2:04 AM

Vibrant, cyan neon glowed through the pitch-black skies. Its colors stemmed from the grand sign of *The Tipsy Tapp,* a West Village nightclub across from the rooftop Isaac stood upon.

Isaac's mind rushed to a sudden re-immersion of the past, manifesting around his reality. A recollection of a recent session with the doctor earlier today.

The night sky dissolved to the warm palette of Bukowski's office. Isaac's fingers ran across a new carving next to three similar grooves on the green velvet chair in Dr. Bukowski's office. An egg-shaped timer ticked aloud.

Dr. Bukowski removed his glasses and cleaned the lenses with a tiny microfiber cloth. "I am glad you're doing well, despite my worries of not hearing from you at all," he said with an echo reverb.

"Sorry about that," the Isaac of the past said in a similar echo.

"You've been able to focus on life. Where do your parents reside in your mind now?"

Isaac knew the doctor referred to the grief. "They come and go."

"Meaning?"

He sighed. "Sometimes I realize I haven't thought of them for a while. So, I do what's best. I start thinking about them again. Most of the time, it hurts."

"What's the reflection focused on?"

"What…uh…what I've lost, I guess."

In a way, forgetting what was lost felt like the ultimate form of disrespect. To reel the guilt back like a fishing rod hooked onto seaweed was more deserving.

"Where does Isaac Sage fit into life now?"

Isaac scratched his head. He withdrew his hands halfway into his navy sleeves, rubbing his clothed palms.

"Yeah. You lost me," said Isaac.

Dr. Bukowski gestured inward, in self-reflection. "We may tend to look at things myopically based on our past traumas and beliefs.

"For example, this pain. You may see it as this unfortunate weight handicapping you, me, and many others even though you feel guilty to be rid of it. Thus, your subconscious decides you fit in life as a burden or mere static." Dr. Bukowski raised his index finger. "But if you take a step back, just one, perhaps you'll begin to see your pain in a different light. Where you may fit into a role that's more deserving."

The timer buzzed, snapping Isaac back to present-day reality, still perched on the ledge.

The question wouldn't stop buzzing in his head. Where did Isaac Sage fit into life now?

In the back of his mind, however, was Rosemary. He wanted to keep thinking about her, mostly about the little things. Watching the corners of her smile gradually form and simultaneously, the glimmer in her eyes. The way she bites the straw on her milkshake. Her sense of humor sparking a carefree joy.

Like this mission, this dream was among the first things he felt within reach. To be done with this soon was key.

He reminded himself to focus. Thanks to Kara's scouting around the city, and her past familiarity with many locations, the Tipsy Tapp was at the top of the list. Kara emphasized to investigate, not instigate.

By the luck of timing, Halloween season made it easier to blend in. A crowd of neon-dressed partygoers approached the front entrance, overwhelming the bouncers with drunken excitement and chanting songs.

Isaac descended and found an opening through the crowd's center. He narrowed his body and snaked through the gaps, past the distracted guards distracted as partygoers demanded to be let through without an ID.

Similar neon-drenched dancers filled the dark blue interior space. Sweat, alcohol and cigarette smoke coagulated into one abnormal scent. No signs of a drug operation yet despite the excessive drugs.

Isaac reached the DJ's booth, catching a view of the dense sea of people from the elevated platform. Behind the booth, as noted in Kara's investigation, were two uneven slats on the floor behind the LED equipment.

Isaac grabbed the narrow crevice and yanked open the doors. No one paid any mind as he descended into this underground bunker, shutting the uneven slats behind him.

Orange lights filled the room, bouncing off the concrete walls and dark grey floors. It was a single path branching out. Although, one path with a shadow stretching outward caught Isaac's eye.

Isaac peered from around the corner. Hundreds of stacked crates formed a maze in the room ahead. Each crate had its own symbols of rabbits, roosters, and dragons.

Inside were four masked men huddled in a circle. The masks resembled blue neon renditions of Day of The Dead Skulls.

A table, adjacent to the maze, was lined up with smudged vials of the most common variation of M.A.D. and bags of cocaine. Two katanas covered in a black sheath wrapped with off-white sageo hung above the table.

Isaac crept into the room, only to be blindsided from behind a second after. Another guy, dressed in a neon clown mask. He cursed under his breath, thinking back to his attempt last month, fearful of the same result now.

The thugs unsheathed hammers, bats and crowbars, cursing aloud.

*'Not this time.'* His gloves were repaired. His gear was fortified. The same mistake wouldn't happen again. Isaac dodged and side-stepped past the first attacks, connecting combos with evasions, leading into wild, animalistic back-to-back blows.

The hurricane of counters from the thugs followed with their beast-like grunts and roars. Isaac conjured every ounce of speed to block and counter before throwing himself with two thugs through the crates into the middle of the maze, concussed by the electricity in his grab.

His left glove emitted wild sparks, singing some of the adjacent thugs and part of his sleeve. Isaac took advantage of this slim opening and launched another set of attacks until he was struck to the floor at the end of the maze.

*'Don't stop,'* Isaac thought.

He parried an oncoming attack as he rose to his feet and continued, absorbing direct blunt blows to his chest, and a severe battering across his arms, legs and face. It turned into a blind, frenzied brawl for survival.

Isaac leaned on whatever wall to recover his wobbly stature before bouncing back with energy at the three chargers, exchanging a swing with an uppercut at the first charger with the second and third chargers dazing Isaac.

The vigilante, returned the momentum with three electrified hits on the third charger, and finally, several electrified blows against the second's ribs until he fell on the floor unconscious with everyone else.

Isaac lifted his mask halfway and inhaled until the air reached to the pit of his lungs.

Then, exhale. Again, and again. He stared at the five semi-conscious foes on the floor, rolling and twitching in pain.

He turned to the table, startled by one man standing by the doorway over the pool of bodies. A sudden weight pressed on Isaac's chest.

The man was silent, gazing around the room with an upright stature. His dark, slicked-back hair reflected against the lights above, matching his fitted suit and thick-rimmed spectacles.

He marched around the outskirts of the maze to the table of drugs and removed his coat, followed by his tie. He laid them flat on the desk's surface, free of any folds and wrinkles, and reached for both katanas.

The man slid one katana across the floor to Isaac's feet.

"Pick it up," the man said.

Isaac re-adjusted his stature. "What?"

"My name is Gus. You ruined my bunker." Gus unsheathed his katana, revealing the blade. A metal so clean that the ceiling's lights shined off it with brilliance. "That is all."

"What?" Isaac stared with a blank expression as Gus's calm force turned visceral with one fell swoop of his blade toward Isaac.

Isaac unsheathed half his sword, stopping the strike inches above his head.

Gus retracted the blade back to his abdomen in an instant and lunged forward.

Isaac feinted. Gus' controlled power still managed to cut Isaac's right arm.

Gus shifted between different stances as if his limbs were made of water, whittling Isaac's last-minute grand counters and strikes. He stumbled around the pool of bodies, where some of Gus's strikes slashed away his defensive armor.

As Isaac recovered an ounce of energy, his footwork was pulled back. He looked down to find one of the thugs gripping onto Isaac's ankle with a wry grin.

The second-long distraction was enough for Gus to launch a diagonal slash, decimating majority of Isaac's padding. The next strikes would decimate his organs.

Isaac lashed out of the thug's grip and threw two barbaric horizontal swings, leaving Gus open. If he was going to fight with a weapon he was unskilled with, he might as well use his own style.

Gus angled his blade, flashing a blinding light at Isaac. As the light enveloped his sight, a burning sensation swarmed through his left outer thigh.

Isaac hopped back, clearing his vision. A horizontal gash, fresh and red, seeped across his dark fabric around his left leg.

It hurt. So extremely that he wanted to fall. Instead, he screamed with sheer adrenaline allowing Isaac to hold his weight with one leg.

Gus rang his blade against Isaac's, locking their stances. He followed with a knee strike at Isaac's core and then an upward slash, cleaving Isaac's blade in two.

This was going to go one way at this rate: Isaac would exhaust himself more, trying to find balance with a broken sword, while Gus would become more acclimated than he already was to this fight and find *the* opening.

The opposing blade lunged at Isaac. His leading foot tripped past an unconscious thug.

Gus could become acclimated to the fight, but not the environment. As Obadiah said, conserve one's energy like a marathon, not a sprint.

Isaac pivoted and smacked Gus' sword away. The blade's new path impaled a nearby crate.

Gus gritted his teeth as he jerked the sword around, unable to pull it out.

*'Only one shot.'* Isaac twisted his torso, winding his fist back, and swung it into Gus' abdomen before he could release the blade.

Isaac launched another power punch, cutting Gus' cheek, followed by electrocuting his head with both hands, flowing into one lethal knee-strike against Gus' head.

Gus stumbled backward before he slipped and collapsed. He struggled on all four limbs, unable to get back up.

The room was cleared for exploration. Isaac ignored the semi-conscious Gus and limped around the room searching for evidence.

Sterile alcohol and harsh chemicals overpowered the underground bunker as he smashed all the vials against the walls and flooring. He used some of the alcohol to sterilize the fresh cuts and wounds, cursing at the intense pain of it for seconds.

Isaac searched the steel cabinets, finding several dark-colored serums, and a manila envelope containing documents detailing a list of chemical compounds and how each should be handled. No details constituted any trial-and-error experimentation.

M.A.D. had a reputation of having uncontrolled results. But what if there was a set ingredient Isaac could trace back? It was worth a shot in theory. He looked at the other dark-colored serums secured in a rack, each with a different label. Isaac decided to take the one labeled 'X.'

After securing the vials and documents, he grabbed each gas canister, pouring it all around the shipment material and equipment, leaving Gus and the unconscious thugs untouched.

The slick trail routed from the rooms to the center hallway. Isaac found a small pink lighter in one of the men's pockets. He ignited the flame, ready to set everything ablaze.

Memories of the tragedy suddenly sped through his mind. A visceral imagination of Isaac himself once again surrounded by erupting fires with fear of not escaping. The people here not escaping.

Instead, he smashed everything to leave nothing but debris and loose chemicals in the room.

Isaac returned to the surface, flooded with the same dancers from before. Now, exhausted, he was ready to head out and push through the crowd.

The crowd gasped in horror as Isaac continued. Behind the cloth mask, he rolled his eyes. *'It's not like I'm a problem.'*

---

Then, he froze with deer eyes. Cold steel impaled his left shoulder and slid out. The pain radiated through his body, lighting him on fire. Isaac shouted in agony.

He turned, furious, to find Gus. The swordsman held his blade high, unable to keep it steady. One open, bloodshot eye locked onto him.

With both hands, he hovered his sword over his hyperventilating breath.

The dancers, still shouting, dispersed in different directions. Their scattering left an open space for Isaac and Gus. It seemed the bouncers were too occupied with the swarm.

Isaac examined his own strength. Fizzled. Stiff. Unable to lift his left arm. He raised his right fist, heavy like a cinderblock. The electricity surged once more.

Their fatigued breaths synchronized. Slow, then frantic, almost as if their own muscles were revving to accelerate for the attack.

The screams, breathing and techno music all crashed together to a mountainous avalanche as the two opponents let out their battle cry. Isaac's heavy body prevented him from evading the strike. This was a losing man's attack.

Then he saw it. The pattern in Gus' attacks.

The blade winded back and swung outward, before careening to the target. An opening that allowed for a well-timed overhead shot.

In two seconds, Isaac took his gamble. Take the attack but step forward to keep the blow from deepening.  This would allow him to land his overhead shot. A created opening.

Isaac, with ferocity, wound his right arm back. The blade reached the height of its arc and careened downward. If successful, the diagonal strike would destroy majority of Isaac's organs. He'd have to wait another year before he could function again.

The overhead shot launched. Isaac moved his leading foot toward Gus. The blade sunk into the point between the collar bone and the shoulder.

His electrified fist continued flying until it crashed into Gus' face, staying in place to continue electrifying him.

His blade moved down by half an inch. Isaac clamped his jaw, committing to the punch until the electricity stopped. Smoke exhumed from Gus' charred face. His bloodied grip cracked loose. The focus in his bloodshot eye dissipated.

Gus collapsed. Isaac looked down with contempt. The blade, still sunk in Isaac's body, was no deeper than a knife cut a chef would incur. Isaac removed the blade and calmly walked outside through the frantic storm of patrons, leaving without anyone noticing.

***

The next day, Isaac staggered out of bed patched with stitches, ointments and bandages thanks to Kara. The pain around each bruise and sewn cut still reverberated through his body as a dull ache.

He walked downstairs and sank into the couch grabbing the remote and flipped through the channels with lightheaded high. Last night was a success. What he procured was, he hoped, another step forward.

On Channel 10 News, there was a report of the Tipsy Tapp in flames. Isaac's eyes widened.

The news coverage reported two people died in the fire, and narcotics were discovered. Witnesses stated a man in a white suit was close to the wreckage, but no footage was found of his appearance.

Isaac shut off the TV, perturbed by the news. For them to make such a move in less than twenty-four hours was massive. For all he knew, they were onto him. Isaac's mind went to 'Compound X.'

If the ingredients could be traced back to an origin point, a likely source could be found. And the source could be that much closer to the perpetrators.

The best he could think of right now, as a starting point, was finding the chemist behind the instructions.

Isaac skipped class to focus his time on cross-analyzing compound X. He found a microscope stored away in a box of Gemma's former belongings. With his laptop, searched through Sage Foundation's T. Dohrnum database through archives saved by internet historians.

Sage Foundation archives could contain the compounding instructions, followed by whom the compound was patented to and the creator of said compound. The creator would've had to sign off on the patent, address included. It was a long shot and didn't guarantee a result, but it was worth a shot.

Isaac popped open the vial. A rotten stench engulfed the room. It was mixed with…

*'Sulfur.'* Isaac procured a tiny sample, recapped the substance and filtered through the results of the database using Sulfur, narrowing over 600,000 to less than 100,000.

He opened his New-Gen Chemistry notebook, skimming through the scrawled notes, including how M.A.D. variants may use regular compounds as their base.

Isaac handled the square with care and placed it on the base underneath the scope.

He viewed the surface first. A dark, white-dotted purple hue compounded by a light violet membrane.

Zooming closer, more of the molecular structure strung with each other. An odd detail was their slight vibration. Isaac was unsure if this was the microscope malfunctioning. Confirmation proved it was set properly.

With the longest scope, the sulfur molecule was attached to two other molecules.

Then, it clicked.

"Hydrogen. Hydrogen sulfide!" Isaac narrowed down the results in the database by half.

Hydrogen sulfide was normally in a gaseous state. Additionally, another molecule, or set of molecules, would bind around the hydrogen sulfide, acting as a barrier.

But this M.A.D. variant did bind, despite being composed mostly of Hydrogen sulfide. Without a barrier, and its normal gaseous nature, it could imply something volatile. Or explosive.

"Hey!" The sudden shout startled Isaac.

His hands darted out, smacking the nearby vial, the contents shattering all over the floor. The aroma of rotten eggs and sulfur contaminated the room.

Emerging from behind the door was Todd.

Todd's positive gesture then soured. He covered his mouth and nose with his shirt's collar.

"What the hell is that smell?" Todd asked. "Are you okay?"

Isaac responded, "You gotta knock! Did Kara let you in?"

Todd apologized. "I knocked, but the door was unlocked."

Isaac presumed she must've been in the backyard gardening.

Todd continued, "Didn't know you were caught up in…whatever the hell this is." He coughed, covering his mouth. "You missed class agai–Seriously, what is that smell?"

Isaac sighed. "Research for another class. Let me meet you downstairs, I need to clean and pack this away."

Todd exited the room. Isaac turned to the shattered vial on his bedroom floor. The area the chemical touched sizzled, bubbling around the edges as the center portion corroded the floor, forming a hole.

Isaac's heart raced as the chemical emitted purple sparks. He ran to the bathroom, neutralizing the liquid with dish soap.

# XVII
## TODD HYME

### October 22, 2022, 7:17 PM

A potent scent of rotten mold and expired food lingered in Todd's nostrils since his meeting with Isaac. It branched into the other senses, causing his eyes to water and his head to throb with a low migraine.

He hunched over a sheet of paper laid out across his desk underneath the warm-white light. His baggy shirt and polka-dot pajama pants brought enough comfort while seated in his wooden chair.

Back at the mansion, Todd proposed his idea to Isaac about the nanobots. While Isaac was supportive, he was, in some irony, adamant about the stress the limited time would create on a project as ambitious as that.

Isaac's counterpoint was a helmet that could detect every moving nerve in advance. However, the proposed purpose was confusing. How would it be helpful? Why would the model be so dense around the face? It wasn't like these doctors were welders.

After Todd expressed his doubt and skepticism, Isaac clarified it could be used for complicated surgeries, predicting certain maneuvers that may cause side effects to other parts of the body. Visors were necessary to house all the complicated wire and circuitry.

Todd countered. Isaac insisted further, more than he ever had with anything else.

Todd, although disappointed, conceded. He sketched every mechanical interface and wire that would compose the helmet, line by line.

Through his sketches, he realized the helmet would need an insulator. Another section needed more anchors. Todd questioned if his proposed material would work. If not, what else?

Grand ambitions tended to frighten many away once they envisioned failure on the horizon. Whether it's the sheer process of revisions that manifested this, or the growing abundance of work. Todd watched colleagues so affected by it that their instinct was to switch careers. Then, they ended up failing in that career.

For now, simplicity was Todd's current goal. A pair of black lenses, connected with electromagnetic synapses.

If, in a ten-meter radius, the brain could detect oncoming motions per its muscles and nerves, doctors would be able to assess the functionality of any human body for better precision. A deeper analysis could uncover critical symptoms early before they worsened.

An aching heat spread through Todd's head as he continued drawing, the rest of his body being chilled by the A/C. The more he focused on that rotten smell, the more the heat intensified. He pinched his nose, trying to force the scent out.

His hand slashed an unintentional line across the sheet of paper.

A heaviness pressed upon his eyes. His body lightened with every pencil stroke. Though he urged his body to continue, his eyelids fought against him.

He ability to create routed from an adamant dedication for it. A creator needed to sacrifice sleep and promote isolation to accomplish creations. To do anything else was observing the world, all its glory and flaws.

These hands were that—not of an observer, but of a creator.

***

The next day, Todd arrived to class two minutes before Professor Beige commenced. He found himself slumped on his desk, irritated by a blaring alarm. Nine hours of nonstop work caused him to oversleep.

Despite his lingering lethargy, he made it. A complete, prototype schematic of the helmet.

Seconds later, Isaac tiptoed through the entrance past Professor Beige in a baggy striped sweatshirt and grey pants, complemented with disheveled hair.

*'Speak of the devil.'*

The darkened scars and purple-black bruises creeping out of his clothing had lightened by a shade or two.

"Hey man," Isaac said. He pointed at the rolled-up poster on the desk. "Is that it?"

"Prototype," said Todd. "It's basically there, the vision and all."

"Can I see?"

Todd slid the poster to Isaac.

Isaac plucked half the binding tape off the paper with his thumb and unrolled it across the black desktop. He brushed his hands through his hair, smiling.

"Dude, this is incredible!" he said.

"Thanks, man."

"Everything is perfectly lined out." Isaac's gleeful smile widened. "You could've fooled me and said this was the final thing."

"Looks like you owe me big on this."

"There's a *book* worth of things I owe you now. How much more time do we have to finish again?"

"A few weeks."

"Every day counts. I'll be coming in again next week. We'll start going over the report piece by piece?"

"I'll hold you to showing up to class then."

At the end of class, Isaac offered to hand the poster to the professor for review.

"I have to speak with her about the missed classes. Might as well knock both out."

Logically, it made sense. But there was an odd suspicion over why Isaac chose to hand the poster himself. Todd cast those doubts aside.

"Sure. Let me know how it goes."

After a few minutes of waiting outside, Isaac came out of the classroom.

Todd motioned a thumbs up. "All good?"

Isaac motioned back a thumbs up. "She was lenient on the missed classes, thank God. Project's good too." Isaac handed the rolled-up poster to Todd.

"Groovy." Todd struggled to form sentences and stay on track as the fog in his thoughts intensified.

***

As the week passed, Todd continued working, fighting past his weary senses. With each day, he lost more sleep to revise the schematics.

Hallucinations of his family followed. Some were phone calls asking him to come home, vivid enough to where he could visualize their name on the call history. Or he'd peer through the peephole after a few knocks on the door to see his parents. And then when he pulled away from the sight to open the door, there would only be a vast nothingness, absent of any building, street or light.

One night, the knocks boomed against the door once more. He opened the door, dazed in expecting the dream to repeat.

Instead, it was the NMPD, with the usual streets, buildings and lights visible in the background. They questioned Todd, now sober, on the whereabouts of his neighbor at unit 105. He had been reported missing for the past two weeks. Todd was unsure.

The officers departed an hour later. The hairs on Todd's skin stood tall. It wasn't his responsibility for his neighbors' safety. Yet, some itch compelled him to think otherwise.

***

On November 4th, Todd woke up in a cold sweat. He showered it off, then realized he slept through his alarm. Todd freshened up, left and arrived to class only ten minutes late, his lungs ready to burst.

Professor Beige glanced at Todd with an expression of concern. Even she knew this behavior was unlike him.

As time passed, Isaac was nowhere to be seen. *'Keep faith,'* Todd thought. They'll go over this project and succeed. *'He'll show up as promised.'*

Todd double-checked his phone after class concluded, finding no messages from him. He was fed up, and for the most part, exhausted from all the working and thinking.  His mission now was to sleep for the rest of the day and forget everything.

He entered the subway and simmered in his self-reflection. Even holding onto this contempt drained Todd. Energy could be diverted to focus on better things. Let karma hound Isaac for his lies.

The train's sudden chime startled Todd. Half-dazed, he realized he had fallen asleep.

Todd examined the current stop: 56th Avenue Station. His stop, Belleview Street, was five blocks ago. He got off as soon as the train stopped. The next train to arrive was fifty minutes, delayed from police apparently finding a dead body on the tracks. Walking home was the best option.

Each step dragged along the concrete. Passersby circumvented around him, meshing into blobs. Honking cars inched through traffic, a parade of humming motors. Each soundwave worked together to overshadow the people's chatter.

Then, a low shriek pierced through the loudness, prominent like an off-sync instrument in an orchestra. It filled Todd with panic. An incessant cry for help coming from a nearby alleyway.

Curiosity urged Todd to move to the source. Logic said otherwise.

Todd crept further into the dark path.. He traced his hands along the brick wall, leading to a corner turn.

Around the corner was a man pinned against the wall by two thugs.

Each of the thugs wore helmets. A chicken on one and a pig on the other, both with exaggerated cartoon traits. Todd found himself in a familiar, uncomfortable scenario reminiscent of his neighbor's dilemma. He shouldn't be here. He should still be dragging along the concrete to get home.

But now, he couldn't help but feel a gripping urge to help. He was, in fact, tired of waiting. For others like Isaac. For others in actual need of help now.

The pig-face thug towered over the victim, while the chicken-face was shorter and frail, holding a knife up to the victim's neck with a wrinkled, wiry hand.

The man pleaded for forgiveness, his eyes darting about as the pig-faced thug clamped down his neck. His frantic eyes locked with Todd's stare, standing still in the moving crowd.

"Please…" the man strained his vocal cords.

The chicken-faced thug punched his nose, sending the back of his head into the brick wall.

Todd grabbed a broken bottle on the floor by the dumpster, his eyes planted at the group.

Would throwing work? Lunging? Todd wished he could lay out a rehearsal of the scenario.

Then, the sound of cracking glass echoed through the alleyway. The bottle was beginning to crack from the strength of his panic-stricken grip.

The two thugs shifted their attention, shouting muffled curse words underneath their helmets. They released their grasp and attention, allowing the bloody-nosed victim to sprint off like a rabbit escaping its predator.

Todd chucked the bottle at the floor near the duo. He ran back into the crowd, hurdling through each narrow crevice created by the passersby, careening past a couple cars through the busy intersections.

The lack of sleep and strenuous exercise intensified the tearing in his chest.

Then, a force yanked his body backward. Something coiled around his mouth and nose. His shriveled lungs were soon overwhelmed by the pain of his head being slammed into the adjacent wall.

He was thrown onto the dirt-covered floor layered with trash. It was the alleyway. Todd never ran. He froze, his hallucinogenic mind deceiving him.

The thugs pummeled his body. Todd gazed at the light beyond his reach. He tried to call for help. That, maybe, someone would notice and rush to his aid.

Yet, if they were anything like he, who would rush to his aid? Who would fight past that frozen state and confront this duo?

The vicious strikes stopped his breathing. A potent iron scent clung to his nose.

As sirens approached and Todd's consciousness faded, the beatings against his body dissipated. His hair rubbed against the dirt as he curled inward, trying to ease the pain. He wanted to bury his face and scream the pain away. Then, he wanted to slam his hands into the dirt floor, out of self-spite, until the bones shattered.

He blacked out. His last sight revealing worn, scuffed scrapes and swellings on his purple-reddened hands.

# XVIII
## DIABLO

### October 26, 2022 – 11:23 AM

Since Diablo's last meeting with Mr. Velcro, he worked with Gus on the proper counter strategy toward the NMPD. They reflected on Gus' encounter with the vigilante in his office.

*"Un-Fucking-Believable."* Diablo's quiet roar shook the room. He rotated his chair to fidget away his temper. Gus stood across from him, patched in bandages and tiny stitches with one eye still tinted light with blood. Almost like a poor imitation of Diablo.

"I should've notified you as soon as it happened," Gus replied. His tone remained steady in its usual calm diplomacy.

"You had him! You had him, didn't you? But you had to do this whole fucking honor shtick? Since when? You know what it's like listening to a person saying the same thing repeatedly?"

Gus, stilted, responded, "I…underestimated him."

"I am taking away all your swords. I cannot fucking believe this. And no sign of his identity?"

"He lifted his mask halfway, but that's as much as I can recall. Let's focus on the DEA though. An inside contact informed me they're on the case now. Did you get the reports?"

"I know damn sure that I know well enough. Someone got them for me." Diablo leaned to the drawers, pulling out the documents. One of the reports went into detail over the subject receiving lava-like salivation. Name, Ricardo Rodrigues. Reports delved into his affinity with the Rodrigues mob and most of his life being raised between Mexico and New Manhattan.

---

Then came experiment results. Contact with outside surfaces seemed acidic at first until it ignited into flames. Survivability was written with a scrawled 'unknown,' next to '0%.'

Another document entailed a subject reducing his visibility to a mere 0.2%. The subject resided in Russia and made a living as a hitman. Name, Fyodor Gustov.

Gus examined the reports and responded. "It'll keep the trails hidden."

"As long as there are no duplicates. I would be more peeved than I already am if that's not true. We've got a lot on us. Whatever map they have, though, shouldn't house every location." He rose out of his chair and proceeded to exit. "Walk with me."

Gus followed. "Such as?" They stood on the steel balcony watching over the workers handling their crates. Diablo rested his hands on the steel railing.

"The prototype warehouse in Queens for Compound X. Haven't been there in a while. We should tighten security there."

"I'll take care of that. Speaking of security, the next topic I wanted to address…" Gus adjusted his glasses. "I received information that a worker found a Yakuza hiding among us."

Diablo exhaled through his nose like a bull covered in red paint. "Continue."

"After they were caught messing with supply, they forced him to undress. Make sure he wasn't stealing anything else. There was a symbol on his back. An elongated red koi fish with the head of a blue dragon."

The fibers in Diablo's body tensed up. "Which clan is that?"

"Which one do you think?"

Images of the deceased duo back in June of that year flashed across Diablo's mind.

"They're still occupying the Kingsbridge warehouse, too. Do you remember that?"

Diablo nodded. "Well, you're 1-1 for ideas, the win being hiring that sniper," said Diablo. "Anything else in mind? Should we inspect all our workers for fishy tattoos?"

"I have, possibly, more efficient ideas," said Gus. "But I need to verify something after this meeting."

Diablo rolled his eyes.

"In other news, your two favorite goons messed up a job again. There's a man who still hasn't paid a loan from us, and they let him escape. Francisco Pierre."

Diablo's head turned hot and slammed his clenched fist onto the steel rail. "Un-fucking-believable!"

His vision blurred and split into fragments on impact. Clarity returned after a split-second. Old flames seeking vengeance. Pieces of the business malfunctioning.

This business was akin to a Jenga tower. Pieces were pulled, swiped, flicked, tossed and planted and slammed.  If anyone dared to risk the tower crumbling, they became dead on arrival. Diablo had allowed his free rage to continue gambling on this tower.

Up until now. The tower was stumbling, its foundation unsteady.  The next moves required meticulous precision.

"Will you be personally handling this?" Gus asked.

Diablo double-checked the revolver in his suit was loaded. "Handle your things, I wanna reconvene later. Text me the address."

***

The address brought Diablo to a run-down townhouse near a busy intersection in the city. Diablo bounded white bandage around his right eye and exited the vehicle, ascending the steps to the front door.

He knocked a rhythmic beat. Footsteps echoed from far and above, nearing close to the door. The door creaked ajar.  The woman's frail, wrinkled head poked out the slim opening. Her blue eyes shined like bright sapphires.

"Can I help you?" she asked.

"Hello, madame," Diablo said. "This is the Pierre household, correct?"

The woman remained silent.

He continued, "You must be Mrs. Pierre, yes?"

"I assume you're looking for my husband?"

"My apologies, *that* should've been my opening," Diablo smiled, "I'm looking for Francisco Pierre."

He noticed the woman struggling at making steady eye contact, darting at the bandages.

"I must apologize for this." He pointed to the bandages. "I have a condition that severely burned my eye, and it's sensitive to the open air."

"Ah." The woman turned red. "I'm sorry, I didn't mean–"

"You know how contaminated this city air is," Diablo interjected. "May I come inside?"

With a puffed exhale, Mrs. Pierre opened the door, revealing her dirtied shirt and an apron draped around her thin body. She walked Diablo inside through the living room past a stained brown couch and CRT television before entering the kitchen. The open square space was lit with obnoxious fluorescent lighting.

Mrs. Pierre offered Diablo to an open seat at the nearby round table as she poured a glass of water. He assessed the remainder of his surroundings. To his left and right were exits to the living room and backyard. Behind him was a stairway.

"Honey!" a man's voice emerged from upstairs, thick with a heavy classic New Yorker tone. "Who are you talking to?"

Diablo's vision broke into blurred duplicate fragments of Mrs. Pierre. He tried to re-clarify, placing his hand against his head. White spots flashed in his vision like a camera going off every few seconds.

"You have a friend here, Franky!" Mrs. Pierre shouted back, "Come downstairs!"

Rapid thumps banged from above, then stopped.

"I don't see anyone!" Franky shouted back, unseen. "You better not be joking."

As Francisco emerged from the doorway with a brace covering his nose, his eyes froze as if a semi-truck was charging at him full speed.

"Mary, what the fuck!" Francisco screamed. The frail man sped for the front door.

Diablo fought past his fragmented vision and unwrapped the bandages around his head with one hand, letting them fall to the floor. With the other, he unsheathed his revolver.

He ran out the kitchen entryway, hurdled over the couch, and smacked Francisco's head before he could open the door.

"Sit down!" Diablo roared. Mrs. Pierre screamed in terror, pleading to stop.

Francisco plopped onto the couch. Diablo pressed the gun against Francisco's forehead.

Diablo let out another roar. "I want my money back!"

Francisco placed his two palms together. "I- I don't have it, I don't have it, look, you got the wrong guy!"

Diablo removed the barrel from Francisco's head and shot his upper thigh.

Francisco shrieked. Rapid footsteps followed and a door slammed shut from down the hall. Diablo turned to find Mrs. Pierre gone. He couldn't risk anyone calling law enforcement.

"*Hey*!" Diablo rushed down the hallway. "Get back out here, or I will blow your brains out!" He pressed his ear to the door. Hysterical crying filled the room with Mrs. Pierre assuring everything will be okay.

Diablo burned off the door hinges with his right eye and kicked the door down. He aimed his revolver dead-center at a terrified Mrs. Pierre, crouched.

But then, the adrenaline crawled to a slowing halt. The heat in his head dissipated, along with the glow from his eye.

A little girl–probably four or five years old–hid behind Mrs. Pierre. Strands of her thin, blond hair swayed in front of her shivering, tear-filled sapphire eyes stared at Diablo.

Diablo lowered his pistol. The rage subsided in exchange for a subtle melancholy. His mind brought an impulsive image of Carlos' unborn child, grown and living in fear at night knowing people like Diablo exist in this city.

A light, soothing warmth emerged and extinguished in seconds.

———

He turned back and approached Francisco. "If you tell anyone what happened here, I will find you and kill you," Diablo growled.  "And if you so much as mistreat your kid, I will find you and kill you. My people will be watching until your very last breath. *Have a lovely day*."

Diablo paused at the front door. He turned and shot Francisco in the other thigh. "Consider that even." Diablo departed to his car, revving the engine before bolting off.

***

Diablo parked on the side of the warehouse at Onondaga Lake and checked his suit to find no blood or scuff before walking to the entrance.  Gus stood by the entrance while workers tended to their shipments.  His black suit jacket was draped over one shoulder, with the first few buttons of his shirt were loosened.

"Were you waiting this whole time?" Diablo asked.

"About thirty minutes," said Gus. He pointed at the lake, its body of water absorbing the sky's violet and pink hues.  "I got to enjoy this view for once."

"What if I never showed up?"

"I enjoy the view."

Diablo squinted his eyes.  He observed Gus further to see if he was getting high off the stash.  The whites of his eyes were tinted with light pink.  "You're too at ease."

"For that reason, let's talk. Do you have time?"

"I'll make time." Diablo followed Gus to the edge of the docks.

"How'd your excursion resulted?"

"We can make up for the losses." Diablo let out a sigh.  "Talk."

"There was a reason for my errand, as you may have expected."

"Don't.  Just get to the point."

"There was another leak. But…" Gus flashed a rare eccentric smile. "What if I told you there was a way to take care of all three problems.  The vigilante, law enforcement, and the Yakuza."

Gus's words, stricken with confidence, ignited a spark in Diablo. He looked at him, curious of what he was about to say next. "I'm listening."

"First, I can't guarantee how smooth this will go but your involvement will raise the odds of success. I don't have time to make bombs or anything."

With every detail, this plan became more enigmatic. "I'll do what I need to do, now talk."

Gus smirked. "Last question: would you be willing to play pretend?"

# XIX

## Rosemary Dier

### October 27, 2022, 3:01 PM

Gusts danced with Rosemary's hair as she struggled to keep the loose strands away from her rocky road mint ice cream. Every frigid bite and lick stung her mouth.

She sat beside Isaac on a bench in Bryant Park, watching a flutter of pigeons pick up spotted crumbs of bread.

After a little more than a week since their last outing, they arranged another one, almost ending with a kiss. Mikey would be creeped out by how abundant and abrupt Rosemary would smile out of thin air.

Days passed in bliss. And now, for their third date, Isaac suggested to explore the coastal side of New Manhattan near a dock and a handful of warehouses. After, they relaxed at the park.

Talking with Isaac distracted her from the current chaos of bouncing between her apartment and Mikey's. It was the last thing she wanted to think about.

New scars were etched on Isaac's face, composed of a few narrow slits and light bruises.

"You doing okay?" She massaged one bruise with her thumb.

"I think that's the third time today you asked," Isaac replied. "Remember, I spar. And I suck at dodging."

"If you can't learn how to dodge, then why not quit?"

"And not get any more face massages?"

Rosemary's lips filled with a smirk. "Weirdo."

"What's a weird thing you've done?

"I had a boyfriend in fifth grade. I dumped him for not believing in aliens."

"Aliens?" asked Isaac.

"A phase."

"What, did he make fun of you for it?"

"He was actually nice. I just really liked aliens back then."

"Did you at least break up with him privately?"

"I mean…" Rosemary's face burned pink hot. "He didn't believe in aliens, Isaac."

Isaac exhaled through his nose and licked some of the melt running down his fingers. A few drops attracted two of the cooing pigeons.

"You probably gave him PTSD. Now he's the biggest alien conspiracy channel somewhere."

Rosemary smacked Isaac's shoulder. The latter laughed.

The trees were as still as the lake Clayton would force her to fish at. She was awful at it, but the lake breeze and her father's jokes made it a worthwhile memory.

"What's your family like?" Rosemary asked.

"I don't remember a lot, to be fair," Isaac said. "Mostly time in the mansion. But there was always that safe feeling. It's something you can only have with your parents. Mom was hard-working to a passionate T; knew how to handle nearly every problem. Dad was calmer and controlled his emotions. Sometimes my therapy would reveal memories I had forgotten." Isaac observed his half-finished ice cream cone, trying to kindly shoo away the pigeons. "And you?"

"My mom is…was the best. You can be a stranger and still feel safe. The kind of person that would, as naïve as it sounds, pick up any hitch hiker because everyone has a bad day."

"*Was* the best?"

"Been gone for a few years."

He looked down, stopping most of his motion. "I'm sorry."

"It's okay."

"And your dad?"

She wanted to bring up the warm memories of the past like fishing or watching fireworks on top of his shoulders. Instead, Clayton's hysterical breakdowns ran through her mind.

Suddenly, one word slipped out. Hate or something. Then another word slipped and another until Rosemary found herself venting about her father's addiction, followed by her own addiction and rehab, and how her father never stopped.

Isaac looked surprised. Rosemary didn't blame him. Not even she expected to say all of this on the third date, let alone any date. Regret consumed her as the wind filled the silence. She expected him to change the subject.

"I know you'll manage to find a solution," Isaac replied. "I'm far from a therapist but you're courageous, bright, headstrong. You have the strength your dad needs. Sorry you both are going through that."

The soft light poking through the makeshift foley ceiling shined on Isaac's face, bringing out the color of his dull eyes to a luminous glow. Like a dark green king's tide soothing the sand's rough texture.

That familiar warmth from the first date intensified and the spark from the second date lit ablaze.

She yearned for this natural feeling to be permanent. It was comparable to the artificial happiness her M.A.D. produced, or the first bite of any sweet treat like the ice cream in her hands.

"Someone must be dealing your dad that substance," Isaac said out of the blue.

"What are you suggesting?" asked Rosemary.

"Oh." Isaac blinked. "Thinking out loud. Sorry."

While obvious, hearing those words sparked Rosemary's mind. There was a supplier out there feeding Clayton his addiction.

***

Rosemary reflected on that idea further, returning to Mikey's apartment. She asked him if he could provide any insight on dealers and suppliers.

Mikey explained how dealers worked in their network. The less they knew about each other, the better, in case one of them were ever arrested. "You never know which one will crack and snitch on the rest," he said.

Rosemary decided for another insight that was more personal. Ingesting M.A.D. again allowed her to immerse into what she called crossing to the other side. Every time, she would find Cher in a cloud of white smoke on a lone bench.

They'd sit on the bench and talk. Rosemary would share her stories, as did Cher. It was one of the few tangible happy things in life.

Rosemary explained to Cher about Clayton. Her mother expressed dismay over her father's addiction. Cher encouraged Rosemary to move forward. If she could change her father back to the man she fell in love with, then she could rest.

Rosemary saw Mikey check the ammo in his gun one night.

"They don't give couriers a lot of bullets," he said. "They're rarer than M.A.D."

"Self-defense, then?"

Mikey nodded. "Part of the job, that's all. Not to k…" He struggled to even utter the word 'kill' aloud.

Later that night, Rosemary took the gun and snuck back to her apartment.

****

Rosemary tailed her father around the city the next day. It appeared to be an ordinary schedule: Clayton would leave the house and take the subway to his office job. He'd grab lunch at a nearby deli, work more and then return home. At no point did Clayton interact with anyone suspicious.

Rosemary returned to the apartment, frustrated with herself. Clayton stood in the kitchen.

"Rosie, where have you been?" Clayton asked. "I was about to call the police."

"Everything's fine. Thanks."

Rosemary locked herself in her bedroom. She repeated the same process the next day with no success.

Her phone vibrated as she gazed at the gun on her nightstand. It was Isaac. Rosemary wiped her tears and exhaled.

"Hey," Rosemary answered.

"Hey Rose," Isaac replied. "How are you?"

Rosemary kept her voice low. "Not…not good."

"What happened?"

"I tried finding the dealer. And…I got nothing. I don't know what to do." Clayton's muffled shouts outside raced her heart.

"Things will work out, just…keep trying."

Rosemary nodded. "I miss you."

"Miss you too. You free to talk more?"

"I'm gonna sleep early now. Hearing your voice helped."

"Sleep well, Rose. Good night."

Tomorrow was another day. She lulled into a slumber with the comfort of her luscious sheets and pillows.

A slam jolted her awake.

Did minutes pass? She checked the time.  2:02 AM. A few hours since she fell asleep.

Another slam shook the apartment, followed by receding stomps. Rosemary opened the door to find her father gone.

Clayton never left the house whenever his memory reset. The loud noises must've stemmed from withdrawal.

*'The dealer!'* Rosemary realized. With time running out, she got dressed, grabbed the gun and scurried out the apartment.

Rosemary caught up to her father, enough to see enough of his silhouette in the yellow-lit streets. She slowed her speed to maintain a steady distance. Her surroundings were familiar for several blocks until Clayton turned into barren, dark roads.

There were multiple train stations and bus stops along the way. Most likely, Clayton didn't want anyone tracking him.

Clayton cut right, marching down a narrow road of broken pavement set between two vacant buildings. The warm yellow of the streetlights had long since been exchanged for the light grey glow of the moon.

A single, wet drop fell, followed by another and another until rainfall dimmed Rosemary's sight and hearing.

Rosemary no longer kept track of the distance or direction. Her focus was on not losing sight of her father. The rain forced her feet to steady on the slippery gravel. Clayton's shadow extended and thinned to a sliver.

A rattling from above startled Rosemary, The rooftop of a building to her right was vacant. Perhaps, Rosemary presumed, it was thunder nearby.

What would the outcome be if she confronted the dealer? Shoot him dead on the spot? She pondered on this more.

Finally, an orange light ignited in the distance, revealing one silhouette standing at the end of gravel road.

Rosemary stopped. Nowhere to hide. She pulled out her gun, ensuring it was loaded. She tried not to think about the scenarios, but the questions began halting each footstep. When to fire? How many bullets? The weapon trembled in her hands.

"It's weak!" Clayton's shout froze Rosemary as she was about to stow the gun away. "The stuff you gave me is weak! I can't go on like this."

"*Lower* your voice," a raspy voice replied.

The rainfall was so harsh, Rosemary couldn't hear her own footsteps. She marched closer to find the dealer's silhouette, dressed in a high-collar coat, next to Clayton.

She raised one hand, trying to call out to her dad in the rainfall. The dealer broke his stance, stumbling back two steps.

Before Rosemary could reach for the gun again, the dealer shrieked, "You idiot, you were followed!"

Her finger froze on the trigger. The act to pull felt heavier. Rosemary struggled to exert the effort.

Another silhouette crashed from above onto the space between Clayton and the dealer. The silhouette, crouched, rose to his feet.

Clayton sprinted back down the road, not even glancing at Rosemary.

Moonlight revealed some features of the new silhouette, such as a basic mask and a grey hoodie and gloves covered in wires. Her eyes locked onto him, uncertain of his next move.

The masked man gestured to the road's entryway. "Go!!!" He yelled.

The dealer swung a hammer strike down onto the masked man. The masked man absorbed the strike with his forearm, synchronous with thunder booming through the sky. The strike grazing his head.

"*Go, now!*" The masked man repeated his warning. She became invigorated with sudden adrenaline, and sprinted down the gravel road, slipping once onto her knees and elbows.

She turned back on instinct, uncertain if she was in danger. It was near impossible to discern who was who from this distance. One silhouette was ready to collapse.

Then, as the opposing silhouette attacked again, the defender launched their whole body, sending both to the floor.

The defender pinned his opponent with his lower torso, swinging consecutive hooks. Each blow erupted splashes of water like a geyser.

She sped to the concrete sidewalk, stomping against the asphalt until she headed to Mikey's place, uncertain of who won.

Rosemary banged on the door. With every minute, she knocked harder and faster.

*'Come on, come on...'*

Mikey opened the door with narrow-slit eyes. "Dude..."

She entered and stowed the gun back to its respective drawer.

"I was in over my head. I'm sorry, I'm an idiot."

Mikey approached Rosemary, rubbing his eyes. He opened the drawer, as if checking to make sure what he saw had happened.

"I'm glad you're okay." Mikey yawned. "Go the hell to sleep."

The next day, Rosemary reconnected with Isaac. He was inquisitive, leaning his body around Rosemary as if he was checking every angle of her.

"How's your dad doing?" Isaac asked.

"Not sure yet. I did what I could."

"It'll get better. You tried."

All she could do was wait and see if Clayton would get better. Rosemary bubbled with warmth from Isaac's kind words.

Isaac continued, "I like to think that those actions make change."

"Thank you. You never had to say all of that."

"Well, I mean…I like you." Isaac paused for a moment. Then, he slowly extended one hand to hers.

She wrapped hers around his. A force–no, an instinct– brought her body closer to his, the smile she expressed internally gradually becoming visible.

"Me too."

***

The following morning, Rosemary awoke to the smell of freshly cut fruit. Outside was a bowl of pineapples and mangoes, juxtaposed with a jug of orange and lime-zest avocado toast.

Clayton cut the last piece of bread, tossing the worn knife into the sink.

"G'morning, Rosie," Clayton said with a smile. "How'd you sleep?"

His smile prompted Rosemary to reciprocate. "Good. You're looking bright today."

"Yeah, I woke up feeling good for once. No sweats in the middle of the night, no hangovers. Here." Clayton gestured at the plates of food. "Have at it."

She sat at the stool and grabbed a plate. "Thank you, daddy."

"Listen, I don't know what your plans are for today," he replied, looking down for a moment, then turned back to her. "But if your schedule is free, let's go fishing. We haven't done that in a while."

She took a bite of the salted avocado, giddy from the few drops of lemon juice and her dad's words.

"I would love that."

Clayton sprung up like an energized light bulb. "Great! Good, good, good." He hurdled past the kitchen. "I'll get the gear ready in the car, you focus on your breakfast."

Clayton shuffled around the house to bring the bait and fishing rods to the car. He was active, enthusiastic. Normal.

***

Clayton pointed to the Hudson River sign as they arrived. "Big City Fishing. There are more than seventy species here."

"Kinda small, don't you think?"

"For the Hudson? Not at all."

Rosemary's worn sneakers toed the park's greenery. She held a rod in one arm while Clayton carried the other gear. Spry dogs, joggers and families huddled around picnic blankets filled the park's liveliness.

They reached the railings barricading the ocean. Rosemary and her father set the bait down, preparing their fishing rods.

Then, like second nature, the voices of a past memory whispered close to her ear.

*'Snug onto the string. Lift the rod over your shoulder. And then lunge and release that string.'*

Her black line propelled out far into the river's depths.

"Wow!" Clayton exclaimed. "You've been fishing without me?" He tossed his line, landing behind Rosemary's.

"Never."

The sun flared high over her father. She was re-living the past she wanted. No tricks. No hallucinations.

"I love you, Daddy."

Clayton smiled, moving in closer to shade her body. He bent down and kissed her crown. "I love you too, baby girl."

# XX
## KARA CULVER

### November 2, 2022, 9:26 AM

"**I** might have found something," said Isaac. His hand hovered over the steam from his cup of coffee. His eyes, relaxed, set on the windowpane that revealed the morning shine. His body slumped into the chair by the roundtable.

Kara leaned against the kitchen counter, across from him.

"Where at?"

"Queens. I registered some footprint of a scientist at a building there. Not fully concrete since there was multiple locations he worked. But it was the most jarring out of his portfolio. Hopefully, I find something tonight."

Isaac set his cup down. "With everything going on, I've been feeling over my head."

"*Now* you're feeling that way?"

Isaac chuckled. "If I threw away every daily aspect of my life, I wonder that I might feel better. Definitely get some more sleep."

"You have had your late nights."

"Ah. Did I wake you?"

Kara had woken up in the middle of night, hearing Isaac soldering and buzzing together something. Isaac hadn't explained what it was for, or what it's related to.

"Don't worry," she said. "You should catch up on sleep."

He wiped his warmed hand over the sunken curves underneath his eyes before letting out another exhale. "When all is said and done."

"You sure you want this?" asked Kara.

Isaac's fatigue expression suddenly sharpened. "Are *you* having doubts?"

"I've got no reason to.  I can't fathom how no one else acted on this for years. We're resolving something that should have been resolved ages ago."

The sharpness in Isaac's expression softened to a somber calmness, like steel becoming pliable with enough heat. She could see the combined work and burden consuming his energy.

"If not sleep, then study," Kara continued. "Go to school today."

"School…" Isaac sighed.  "Alright.  Maybe I have some doubts."

"Go on."

"I'm doing this to feel like my old self. But is it doing too much harm?"

Kara tilted her head.  "Don't overthink with tired thoughts."

"This one's been racketing around.  That new tool I've been working on…I convinced Todd to draw it up."

"You told him about…?"

Isaac raised his hands, shaking in disagreement before folding his arms together. "No, no.  I convinced him with a small lie.  But I lied to him.  I keep disappearing, too."

"There's a reason for not letting them know, isn't it?  Just like there's a reason for doing all this?"  Kara leaned back and looked at the windowpane to compose her thoughts.  Isaac's emotions may be brittle from the trauma.  But he had gifted potential.

"I can't endanger them."

She turned to Isaac. "You are smart.  You make stuff many others struggle to even connect."

Isaac blushed. "Simple stuff.  Todd is the better one."

"Electric gloves are *not* simple."  Kara chuckled.

Isaac struggled to lock eyes with Kara, instead pinning his eyes to between the lower corners.

"You're right," he said. "Once this is over, I'll make up for these mistakes."

"Will you tell them the truth?"

"I would've if there were a reason.  This side of my life is for mine."

"It would be lonely."

"Good thing I have you to talk to about it." Isaac smiled. "I appreciate it."

"Well when this chapter of your life ends, you can tell them."

"Or maybe there's some good out of this. And being a part of Sage Foundations at the same time. Darwin's kept that door open, and–"

"Isaac…" Kara sighed. She could feel Samuel's words of revenge holding more weight. "You can go to Darwin, that…she's been to this house before, right? That Darwin?"

Isaac nodded.

"Do what you want with that if that makes you happy. But when this ends, it ends."

Isaac paused, moving his mouth around as if trying to find the right words to respond to. Then, he stopped. "Of course."

"You stowed the new supply, right?" Aside from medical supplies, Kara found an adrenaline booster for Isaac to use in case his fatigue got the best of him.

Isaac nodded. "Ready to go. What are your plans today?"

"Tend to the house. Maybe work on the garden. I'll find something."

"You always do." Isaac chugged the rest of his coffee. He stood up and made for the exit. "It's probably gonna get worse."

Kara tilted her head. "Probably."

"You're okay with that? The danger of it?"

"It'll be worth it once those assholes get what's coming to them. Or am I wrong about you?"

Isaac shook his head. For a moment, she saw a reflection of his father's somber expression. And then, another memory of Samuel hugging a young Isaac, whom held onto a stuffed superhero doll.

"You mentioned feeling like your older self when you're done," said Kara. "How sure are you?"

Another memory flashed of her standing in the meeting room with Samuel. An echo of his words reverberated. 'A poison.'

———

Isaac squinted his eyes for a split-second before responding. "It has to. It will."

Kara remained silent.

Isaac smiled as he turned away. "Be safe."

"You too," she said before the door shut.

# XXI
## John Saint

## November 2, 2022, 9:44 AM

Saint sat in the interrogation room with Briggs and Catherine Carmichael, one of the NMPD's legends assigned as captain of the cartel case. Her folded arms, tied hair and mute expression evoked a reserved nature, complementing her simple buttoned professional attire.

The detective had shared the information about the warehouses and proposed a full-stage raid with his involvement. The DEA took their time to prepare instead of charging in as soon as acquiring the information.

They interrogated Johnson, the informant, ensuring he told the truth. While he might have stuttered and appeared like a pissing chihuahua, as Carmichael had told Briggs earlier, Johnson remained true with his information.

"Why do you want to be involved so much?" Carmichael asked. "Is it a personal vendetta?"

"None at all," said Saint. "I need to see this case to its end. On my terms."

"Sounds like Jacques," said Carmichael. "You vouch for him, Daniel?"

"I do," said Briggs. "He's…dedicated is a nice way to put it."

"Dedicated." Carmichael nodded. "Dedicated's not exactly the clearest term."

"I'll follow your orders, ma'am," said Saint.

"I'll assemble two squads of twenty and have scouts confirm both warehouses are exhibiting some kind of activity. We need to seize both to remove any threat or even an ounce of suspicion. Meet us at the northwestern border of the main city at 3 PM sharp three days from now. A grassland. You'll come with me to Kingsbridge."

Carmichael scribbled something using a pen and paper stowed in her pockets. She continued, "This is my number in case you change your mind."

"No need to worry about that," said Saint.

"Take it anyway. I won't ask again if you want to be a part of this or not. Your punctual attendance will say otherwise. This will not be a smooth operation. You know this better than anyone that these are violent people we're dealing with. Casualties can occur."

Saint obliged, saving the number on his phone. "Understood."

"Then make your rounds for what you need to do before then. Kiss your loved ones, leave behind letters, all of that." Carmichael left the room. Briggs let out a despondent sigh. He looked at Saint, about to say something. Instead, he turned and left in silence.

***

Home was always the beacon back to comfort and safety. It was also the place that lulled him into a false sense of completion.

At the end of all this, he would be back home. Through all these years, he was still beckoned by the wisdom of his other half.

Saint entered the house, finding Edoris' lit grey eyes tracing along an open, worn book by the corner of the kitchen. Her hair was tied in a bun, held further back by thin glasses.

Edoris' eyes glossed up. She folded a corner on one page and closed the book.

"Honey, it's eleven o' clock," Edoris said.

Saint kissed Edoris on the forehead. "Never too early to be with you. Is lunch with you on the table?"

Edoris nodded. "I'll spruce something up."

She put together toasted sandwiches made of chicken seasoned with salt, pepper, garlic and aromatic herbs. The redness of the tomato glistened over the oozing gouda cheese and the peppered, golden-brown chicken, all set on a white, ceramic plate.

The taste reminded Saint of arriving at a local diner made of family-owned furnishings. The aroma incited a disarming comfort.

It tickled Saint with a gnawing anxiety to speak what was on his mind.

"I keep telling people about this case…" Saint paused, finding the least confusing way to process his thoughts. Smokey entered the kitchen, purring against Saint's leg.

"What about it?" Edoris asked.

Saint petted Smokey with his one free hand. A way to ease his nerves.

"That I'm getting closer to the end. I don't know if I'm telling myself the truth."

Edoris' smile faded. She stiffened her body.

"Which is?"

"If this end is worth chasing." His subconscious averted to another question.

'Will there actually be an end? One where this desire for legacy is fulfilled?'

Edoris removed her glasses. She stared at Saint, those grey eyes matching the muddled weather visible through the adjacent windowpane.

"You've accomplished so much already. At this point, all you can do is your best and appreciate that."

Edoris' lips twitched to a familiar frown, dispelling the warmth that came earlier.

She reformed her smile. "You still have me."

Saint pecked Edoris' cheek and left for the hospital minutes after to check on Billows and Johnson. He claimed he was running behind schedule.

***

Saint had a couple exchanges with Johnson since their initial encounter. Johnson showed Saint photos of his wife and daughter with small fun facts for each of them. Like how his daughter smiled after saying the word 'bubba.' Or his wife's love language being the collaborative effort of working on single-color puzzles. He was blissfully ignorant of whom he shared this information with.

At the hospital, Saint headed to the floor Billows resided, walking past a vacant room set with starched, tucked sheets.

A vague familiarity rang before it clicked: This was Johnson's room.

No guards were present either. Saint waved down a nurse.

"Excuse me, do you know when the guy in this room got cleared?" he asked.

"Name?" the nurse asked.

"Johnson Moore."

"Ah..." The nurse glanced downward. "I'm sorry, but he passed away."

An uneasy dryness stirred in his tongue and lips.

"Jesus. When?" Saint asked.

"Late last night. It must've been about three or four in the morning."

The detective's breath hastened. "There were guards. Where are they?"

"I haven't seen any guards since last night."

Saint tried to calm the panic in his voice. "Damn it!"

He marched away from the nurse and halls, entering an adjacent stairwell. Paranoia directed him to call Carmichael on his phone.

"Hello?" Carmichael answered.

"It's John Saint," he kept his voice lowered. "Johnson's dead. Guards left their post."

A pause of silence left static chattering in the background. Carmichael didn't need anything more than that.

Carmichael responded. "Then we commence today. 3 PM."

*"Today?"*

"We have to make haste."

Saint checked the time. Two hours from now. "That's...I–"

"No excuses. Either you show up or you're better off not here."

Carmichael hung up. Saint glanced at the vacant bed, then back to the clock. *'Deep breaths,'* Saint instructed himself. He needed to think with a calm mind. A distraction.

He made his way to Billows' room.

Inside, Billows cursed in frustration over an ongoing basketball match playing on the small CRT television. He rubbed the bandages covering his areas of injury. At least he was able to find a distraction from all the recent chaos.

Saint knocked on the open door, catching Billows' attention.

"Yo," said Billows.

"Hey champ," Saint replied, maintaining his focus on this conversation. There was a faint hum from the ceiling fan, set at medium speed. "They couldn't bring you a better TV for this room?"

"Right? Can't see shit on this thing. What's the score now? 2-1?"

"For a basketball game? Score says 66-40. How the hell do the Knicks still exist..."

"Nah. I'm talking the score of saving each other's ass."

Saint's eyes lit up. Billows let out a voracious laugh.

"Come on, at least you're on the board now," Billows bellowed. "Can't believe I ended up stuck here for a month. I missed Halloween."

"You didn't miss much, other than Edoris and I seeing the best costume of the night. A box."

"A box?" Billows replied.

Saint mimed a box over his head. "A literal box."

"I need that optimism."

"Or stupidity."

Billows grinned, holding back a laughing fit.

"What's your situation?" Saint asked.

He pointed at his injury in the form of a faint red dot. "Hollow bullets are a bitch. I got a week here. Didn't you get shot too?"

Saint shrugged. "Slight graze."

"Lucky."

"For once."

"Anything new with the case?"

"They handed the case to the DEA the day we were attacked."

"Son of a–" Billows gripped his chest.

"Easy. Earlier that same day, there was a new lead in the hospital."

"What's his involvement?"

"New hire by the cartel, only to get shot and left for dead by the prime suspect. He gave the location of two warehouses. Now he's dead."

"We've taken down *six* and there's *two* still?"

"The map at the blackout zone probably only showed some territories. State's infested."

"Then, the plan?"

"Our plan is to raid both."

Billows squinted at Saint. The hum of the fan felt louder for a moment. "What do you mean our plan?"

Saint paused. The seconds to think and assess allowed him to decide. "Joining the raid on Kingsbridge. It's at the northern end of the city."

"I know where Kingsbridge is at," said Billows. "Honorary DEA…What's Chief think of this?"

"On the same boat as you. We're close."

"You know I've done a raid before. Have you done one?"

Saint shook his head. It was detective work up until now. He would never compare his stand-offs or chases to a raid. It was a whole other animal.

Billows continued. "A raid means people don't come back or watching people come back. *That* stays with you. You said it, the DEA has it under control!"

"I'm not a rookie, Jackson. I have to see this through."

Billows grit his teeth. "You have someone waiting for you."

Edoris. "And I'll come back to them."

Billows looked down.  His expression mellowed at his wounds, still healing.  The machinery and fluids still hooked into his body.

"I can't bury another person I know," said Billows.

"It won't be your duty even if it does happen.  But thank you."

"When does it happen?"

"Today."

The exclamation in Billows's expression was interrupted by his chest pain.

Saint continued, "I'll be heading there as soon as I leave here."

Billows' anger mellowed. "Saint…"

"I'll be fine," he smiled.  "Let's keep the score as 2-1."

As Saint left, Billows sat desolate on the bed.  His harsh, focused expression stared at the comforters.  Possibly thinking of every factor that could go wrong.  Saint's mind began to operate the same way.

***

Two black convoys and a crew of twenty armored officers occupied the grassland, lit orange by a few surrounding streetlamps.  Saint parked not too far where Carmichael looked at him, alert like a hawk.  Her professional attire was covered by light ballistics gear – a vest and padding strapped around her limbs with additional pockets to carry extra ammunition and weapons.

Carmichael greeted Saint. "Made it a minute early," she said. "Good."

"When do we move out?"

"Now.  Get some gear on."  One of the officers provided Saint with the same equipment Carmichael was wearing.  Aside from his issued pistol, he equipped an automatic rifle.  It was one of the many heavy weaponry Carmichael's team was carrying.

She roared at her soldiers the commands to move out. Her brigade listened and reciprocated the same energy with ease. The first black convoy departed as quick as it loaded off to Oswego. The other soldiers entered the back of the second black convoy.

"You'll sit up front with me and the driver," Carmichael ordered Saint. He followed her to the front seats, where the driver was already positioned. Carmichael banged the back panel once. Two thuds boomed from behind the panel.

"Move out," Carmichael told the driver. Saint was impressed at her squad's quick mobility. Carmichael checked her watch. "Eight years of doing this and we were two seconds slower. They'll be getting a lip full of it later."

Saint smirked. The moment of relief was soon outweighed by the familiar tension. The engine started, with the vehicle crawling into its speed over rough and smooth terrain.

For twenty minutes, they sat in silence. Saint could only imagine what they were all thinking. The idea of becoming accustomed to this, and choosing to return to this, felt incomprehensible to Saint. Saint pondered that perhaps they were driven by the same ideal that drove him with the desire to be on this raid. The one time to be surrounded by a whole crew of alike people, only to sit in silence.

Around the last leg of the route, Carmichael spoke. "If you do have a vendetta with this guy, you're more than welcome to say it now."

"I told you the truth. No vendetta. My reason is to finish the case I started. Because–"

"Because dad would've done the same?"

Saint fell silent. He nodded.

"The insanity…" Carmichael shook her head. "I had a feeling. I like to have all the answers right before events like this."

"Why's that?"

"Times like these, we all know we're standing at death's door. Everyone in this convoy. I'd like to die knowing every question I had was answered. That's what most of them think, too."

A hint of sorrow inflected Saint's tone. "You think we'll die?"

"There are chances, *high* chances, you'll die in any mission.  The actions we conduct are drastic and are met with even more drastic counters. Guaranteed consequences are bound to occur."  Carmichael smirked.  "Something tells me you have a lot of faith in my team."

"You're one of the NMPD's finest."

Carmichael's smirk faded.  "Everyone has their time limit, John."

"Well, it's simple good and evil.  And in this case, evil never wins."

The engine's hum filled the silence for a few seconds.  The driver chuckled, and then Carmichael blurted out a laugh.

Saint lowered his brow.

"You even got a reaction out of him," Carmichael pointed to the driver.  "What are you, in your forties?  You really believe that?"

The detective maintained his brow positioned to his scuffed shoes.  He held confidence in his voice when he replied to Carmichael.  "If I remember correctly, my father was saying this and he was older than me."

"I don't recall *you* saying that."

"We were never really drinking buddies, were we?"

"No, I never got that sort of attitude from you either."  Then, Carmichael's brazen tone shifted to a somber note.  "When did you start saying that?  After Jacques…?"

Saint looked at Carmichael perturbed before he looked down then at the window.  "I…I hadn't thought about it."

The longer he sat with the thought, the more he realized the sudden usage of that line of reasoning intermittently just a week after his father passed.  Then, a month later, it ran constant, bleeding into his methodology and philosophy.

The detective deduced his own line of thinking and drew conclusion minutes later.

"You have that same expression," said Carmichael.

"As my father?"

"Yeah.  You know what else he kept saying?"

Saint shook his head.

"He used to say that one day this'll all slow down. Between you and me, well…I don't need to say. We all miss him."

Carmichael nodded. What the detective would've shared, had it been right, was a worry that hovered over him ever since the death of his father. That if every essence of his father, from conversation to things in writing, disappeared over the years, to the point where one day Saint would wake up and not have a single thought of him at all.

To not be remembered was more permanent than death itself.

The convoy parked in front of a barren silo. Majority of the cylindrical structure was corroded in golden rust. Carmichael signaled one of the soldiers to position a drone above the structure. The soldiers relayed there was no entry from above. Ground-level scouts found no signs of any tripwire bombs and only one entry way in the form of a double door.

Plumes of thin grass surrounded the flat dirt the silo was set upon. "No movement around the outer boundaries," said Saint. Saint noticed something glimmer from around the silo. He leaned, noticing the glimmer coming from a camera.

He tapped Carmichael's arm and gestured the glimmer to her.

Carmichael turned to the troops. "Form up on the entrance. Saint, stay close to me." She handed Saint a gas mask and equipped it. She equipped one herself.

Chances were it could be a fluke. This location could be empty. Or a whole gang was waiting on the other side. On that golden snitch of a chance, Diablo could be in there right now, ready to rain hell. Most likely, they had their supplier for weaponry from a black market.

For a safer city, and to be rid of evil, this was the chance. Saint and the others would know soon.

Carmichael, Saint and eight troops formed two columns of five rows at the sides of door. Carmichael was fourth in line on the left side, while Saint was last.

The troopers at the front –wearing infrared masks – stuck two clay bombs to the door. They raised four fingers on one hand. After readying the bombs, they nodded to each other, and counted down the fingers to zero.

Another trooper in the second line pressed a trigger. The door catapulted inside the silo. Two troopers at the third line tossed smoke bombs into the silo.

The leading brigade motioned their arms forward.  In two single file units, they entered through the smoke.  Saint inhaled, crouched low with the rifle ready in hand, his sight focused on Carmichael's silhouette.

Bullets pierced through the fog creating hollowed rings with booming gunfire following seconds after.

For the first minute, the group cleared through a few members waiting on the ground floor. Once the smoke dissipated, Saint and the others assessed the silo to be five floors in total, with the upper four covering the outer ring, creating an open center.

More bullets rained on the squadron before they could find a stairway, leading to a massive maelstrom from both ends.

Saint's best mindset was to focus on what was in his control.  Take out the enemies within his reach and protect the teammates closest to him.

He took down two gunmen on the second floor before taking cover, as the rest of the troop shot at other enemies in his blind spot.

The leading brigade troops were soon shot in the head, as confirmed by a nearby trooper.  The remainder defended themselves at different points of cover. Saint remained close by Carmichael and three other officers.

The gunfire was dying down.  This was the moment to recoup and strategize based on what was discovered and lost. Saint leaned to Carmichael, and–

Suddenly, the lights went out.  Pure darkness. The sole reliable sense being sound.

Footsteps from above echoed down to the floor level. More seconds passed in the darkness.

A whistling of smoke rang from the sky, down to the floor with the sound of a clatter. Grenade explosions followed. The floor filled with light and gunfire.   Some of the officers screamed in the distance, followed by another clash of bullets.

Carmichael moved out of cover, using the flashes to her advantage.  Five quick gunshots incapacitated three. They were approaching fast.

"Move out!" Carmichael shouted.

One man, brandishing a katana, could be seen appearing in the flash and vanishing with each fade into dark, creeping toward Saint's group.

Instead of following Carmichael, Saint made a gamble to protect his team. He approached toward the man.

Another flash lit the space. The man swung the sword toward Saint's hip. Saint grabbed the man's wrist and fired his gun point-blank range. The man's chest was riddled, turning his white shirt to pure dark red.

The detective now stood alone in the dark. More footsteps ran toward him. He fired, creating light for himself. Three gang members simultaneously shot as he sprinted out of the line of fire. He fired his rifle in an arc motion.

A flare dropped from above, revealing all three attackers dead on the floor with its red glow. Gunfire from above continued to fill the ambience. The stairway was within sight, snug in a tight corner.

Saint ascended to the second level. Just as he exited the stairway, he was suddenly shoved and pinned against the railing by two gang members, losing his rifle. One plunged their sword into Saint's arm just when a stray bullet flew through their head. The other gang member turned to kill the source. Saint unsheathed his pistol and shot the distracted gang member's head.

He continued his rain of fire to the third level, where he followed two gang members approaching a room and riddled both of their backs with bullets. In front of Saint, Carmichael shot up from cover, relieved at the sight of Saint. Her collarbone was drenched in blood. Saint went around for cover with her.

"Where's our medic…" Saint whispered.

"*Shut up,*" Carmichael whispered back. "It's a graze." Right beside them was an trooper and gang member's corpse. The trooper's brains spilled out of his head, while the gang member's eyes were frozen, one eye pooling with blood.

The gunfire shifted to dead air. Carmichael's reserves revealed she had less than one-third of a magazine left. Saint had at least one clip for his pistol.

"In here…" Someone blurted in the room Saint and Carmichael hid in, gasping for air. "In here!"

Rampant footsteps moved to their location. Carmichael examined the corpses. She patted around, finding a smoke bomb on the trooper's kit, and a grenade on the gang member's belt. She threw out the smoke grenade to the entrance, veiling the entrance as she fired.

No response. She shot again, then met with fire on the enemy's end.

Carmichael pulled the pin of the grenade and chucked it into the smoke. An explosion rang, followed by painful shrieks. Carmichael, crouched, sped into the smoke. Two gunshots killed the silence.

Adrenaline was thinning. Was that it? Were they all subdued?

"Clear," Carmichael emerged out of the smoke. Her and Saint remained silent until the remaining troops regrouped. Out of the twenty, six remained. It was a blessing, Carmichael admitted, that six survived.

Carmichael and Saint investigated the fourth level. A lab was used as one room with an array of compounds being tested. A few of which were M.A.D. An officer gathered samples of each compound to bring back to HQ.

Another included a few desks with multiple documents laid out on the table. A window was positioned on the far end, filling the room with natural light. Nearby, two maps were pinned against a corkboard. One each marked with different X's.

Saint examined some of the documents. A few contained briefs detailing meetings with other cartels with the hopes to collaborate and expand outside the area. One included information on Diablo. Whereabouts of the main warehouse were circled around the familiar Oswego and new areas including one in Syracuse.

Among those details were spray painted symbols on certain parts of the silo, including this room. The symbol was a blue koi fish with a dragon's head.

"Something's off," Carmichael said, looking at the document regarding Diablo's position. "The context of the documents doesn't make sense. Says our esteemed members *met* with Diablo and didn't return?"

"This isn't a part of Diablo's cartel," said Saint with a racing heart. "It's a god damn rival."

Carmichael scoffed. She threw the documents to the floor. *"Fuck!* "The others need to know."

Saint wondered if the same applied to Oswego. He spited his own frustration and carelessness. A rage toward Diablo festered. Was Johnson in on this? Or was he fed the wrong information without knowing?

Carmichael pulled out the walkie-talkie. "Oswego, this is Kingsbridge, what's the situation? Over."

Static.

Carmichael switched channels. "Oswego, this is Kingsbridge, we were led to a false location, proceed with caution and provide your status, over."

Saint turned to the entryway, finding a gang member rushing toward Carmichael. The sword wound back around his torso, aimed at her neck.

"That's not good…" Carmichael said, oblivious to the oncoming attacker.

"Move!" Saint pushed Carmichael aside. The blade cleaved through Saint's left eye. He fired his pistol, missing before losing balance from the sheer pain. The detective shrieked, stumbling around, losing sense of his surroundings. "Carmichael, watch out!" Saint screamed.

Carmichael unsheathed her gun, finger squeezing the trigger. The gang member's sword passed through half of the gun and her neck. Her head plopped on the ground and rolled to a quick stop, motionless eyes glued wide open. Officers ran inside and shot the attacker until he fell to the ground.

Saint continued stumbling back, and back. Soon, he slipped and crashed through the lone window, feeling the slivers of glass sink into his skin. His body bounced off a railing before plummeting to the ground.

***

Saint dreamt he sat in a room where blank-faced people were passing by him and Edoris.

Edoris' eyes were red, as if she had been crying up until now. Saint realized he was leaving somewhere.

But where? An older reflection of himself appeared in a vast area of red dirt. He had an identical square jaw with a thinner build. The man turned, revealing himself as his father, Jacques.

Jacques reminded Saint they were going on a trip into the canyons, set beneath skies cascading with light flickering through pockets between the clouds. A rather odd nostalgia.

Saint was conscious enough to know his father was dead. Yet here he was, walking.

Many questions blared in his mind, unable to pull one distinct thing to ask him now. Instead, he looked at his father's calm, still eyes, lacking judgment or contempt.

Jacques patted Saint's shoulder. "Good to have you here, kid. Someone needed to take out the rest of the bad guys."

A ticking rattled in Saint's chest. A panic-inducing countdown.

Saint then found he and Jacques were venturing through a canyon with two encroaching paths. Dusk was settling. The incessant ticking alone alerted Saint with dread.

Jacques bathed them in an orange glow from a lantern he was carrying. It formed a ring of fire, protecting them from the surrounding void. The array of stars above scattered in the night sky, with prominence.

"Tell me, kid," Jacques said, "What's happened, hm? Kids? Please tell me something more than detective shit." Jacques laughed.

"Edoris and I will try again one day," Saint said.

"Will?"

"Yeah. You need to come back to the city one of these days. It's not the same without you."

Jacques smirked. "I like it here. It's finally slowed down."

The canyon path branched to multiple paths. Jacques checked his gourd of water, swishing around what was left.

"Pay attention to your light," Jacques continued. "Thank God it's finally slowed down."

The lantern began to flicker. No matter what Saint did, the light was diminishing. Jacques walked further ahead.

"All the work I did," Jacques muttered, "It's had to have slowed it all down."

Soon, Saint's body refused to respond. His light diminished. The orange glow from Jacques' lantern faded as he marched into the canyon's depths.

The light dimmed until it disappeared. A deep void swirled above. It swallowed the stars.

Saint wanted the orange glow to return. Something. Anything. But nothing.

# XXII
## ISAAC SAGE

## November 3, 2022, 2:08 AM

A harsh, phosphorus spotlight beamed onto Isaac, warming his vigilante gear. He breathed through his new tool; the sleek black helmet constructed from Todd's schematic.

Vitals on the lower right HUD indicated Isaac's stress. The visuals held a retro aesthetic like old computer software filled with jagged pixels and polygons, and the helmet was bulkier than its original schematic. It further solidified while Isaac had the adept skills to engineer complex work, Todd's innovation and entire understanding of engineering were on another plateau.

Isaac ran into a small, enclosed cubicle in the Queens warehouse after subduing two guards.  It was a challenging night.  The scientist, his prime suspect, was nowhere to be found. Security was heightened, far more advanced that what Isaac faced at the Tipsy Tapp. And the vertical layout of the facility forced Isaac to hasten his adaptation.

But challenges were to be met with anticipation, not shock.

The cubicle room housed a scuffed desk, an entryway on the other side and a control center. He stumbled with jittery nerves, searching the room for his next clue.

A guard, equipped with thick, black ballistic gear in the form of plates, rushed into the room from the other side, charging at Isaac.

Once again, the gear was put to the test.

A wireframe pattern of the guard appeared on Isaac's HUD. The wireframe threw a wild right hook.

Seconds later, the guard threw a hook.  Fully identical to the wireframe. The helmet's concept was to predict real-time movements, and it was succeeding.

Isaac closed in, grabbed the hook and fired an electrified punch to the nose. The guard careened to the steel flooring behind him.

With space to breathe, Isaac patted around the helmet's sleek surface, ensuring no cracks or dents were incurred so far. The slotted holes weren't clogged. The interior protective padding was sound.

Never-ending experiments in his bedroom-turned-mini-workshop converged morning and night together. Were it not for Todd's blueprint, Isaac estimated an additional six to eighteen months of work to get it this far.

Isaac rummaged through the control room, while sporadic gunfire filled the ambiance.

The confidence outweighed any anxiety. The results were consistent. And the reason behind his mission rejuvenated him. Isaac sifted through the drawers and space cluttered with documents, blank paper and then–

A sticky note. Different shapes –a triangle, square, circle and hexagon– were scrawled onto it, followed by an adjacent phone number for each respective shape. 'The boss' was written next to the hexagon line.

Isaac tore apart the room further, finding a map. The map displayed facilities marked by the shapes, including the hexagon.

Jackpot.

Six guards, dressed in new high-collared coats, swarmed in from both sides before Isaac could analyze the locations. They lacked armor like the other guards he encountered.

Isaac electrified the nearest guards. The current's strength and close vicinity sent a chain of shocks across the group. A path to the window was straight ahead.

Isaac stowed the map and hurdled out of the guards' grasp, making a running leap to crash through the window. Glass clung to the sweater and pants' fabric.

The bullets from submachine guns whizzed past him before his body began to tumble toward the ground. It was rare to have this much weaponry in one location. The HUD could only predict muscle movement and nothing more.

Last resorts were set, just in ase. He removed his left glove and unplugged two wires before tossing it upward.

The glove disintegrated, releasing a harsh, light-blue shockwave. Every gun in the warehouse would be ineffective now for twenty minutes.

A second later, the HUD alerted an oncoming attack. Isaac managed to look up and block a silhouette striking him from above. Although blocked, the attack sent him crashing to the ground.

Isaac rose back up to find a man fashioning blond cornrows. His long-sleeve, high-collar coat and baggy pants made his figure appear grand. The lean structure of his face said otherwise.

Armored guards lay on the floor dead. The blonde gazed down at Isaac. A matching grin poked out from his high collar. Men of similar attire, about ten, surrounded the duo, forming a circle.

"Alright," the blonde raised a steel-covered hand, holding the map Isaac had acquired.

Isaac patted his body, only finding the sticky note. "Shit."

The blonde pulled a lighter from his other pocket, flicking it on. He moved the flame close to the map.

Isaac's confusion erupted to an infuriated lunge at the man. He pivoted away from Isaac's attack with ease.

"I got you riled up. Good." Commander stowed the lighter and map.

Isaac gathered himself, seething. "Are you the scientist behind compound X?"

"Ah?" The blonde stowed his hands in his pockets. "Ah, nah, I don't work here. I'm Commander."

"You work with the boss of this warehouse?"

"Nope." Commander squinted. "Are you fucking with me?"

"Then you're not my problem."

"Nah, I definitely am now." His smirk filled with disdain as he looked away in reflection.

"I've been staking this spot out to finally one-up the big guy. You decided to go and beat up one of *my* people a month ago."

Isaac recalled fighting the dealer to Rosemary's father around that time. He sighed.

"Couldn't keep your eyes off me or what?" Isaac asked.

Commander laughed. "Wouldn't you like to know?" He winded his arms in a clock-wise motion and continued. "You make that tech? What's your wattage on those gloves? That's gotta be a durable metal on your helmet, too." A drug dealer and an apparent science geek.

"Maybe you can ask me out on a date first and I'll indulge you," Isaac quipped.

"Either way, I guess we both wanna see head honcho burn."

"Head honcho?"

"Tell ya what, I'll give you this map. *Indulge me*. Papa's gotta show his crew how it's done when someone fucks with one of us."

"What do you know about the boss?"

Commander grinned. "Indulge me."

Isaac's patience thinned. His muscles tensed around his shoulders and arms.

"That tech's all mine when I win too, yeah? Not that you'll need it when you're dead or in jail–"

Isaac rushed Commander, landing a three-hit combo through a jab, electrified straight, and a knee to Commander's chest.

Commander reeled back and headbutted Isaac. The latter stumbled, waiting for the static on his HUD to return to normal.

Commander flashed his smug, annoying grin again. Whatever that steel was on his hand must be on the rest of his body.

Isaac refused to relent. The two clashed back and forth with fast-paced attacks. Isaac's HUD helped predict Commander's combo strings of three to four hits. One hit in exchange for a block. A block for a dodge. A dodge for a counter. In this back-and-forth struggle, Commander's elusiveness matched Isaac's ferocious hits.

By the fourth blocked combo, a sudden force knocked the air out of Isaac's abdomen. Isaac should've predicted that strike.

"Predictable!" Commander shouted before being grappled into a headlock by Isaac's left arm. Was saying that a coincidence? Or did Commander already figure it out?

Then, Isaac's entire body flew back from another unknown force. It was so harsh that the collision with the surface nearly snapped his bones. An aftershock of orange dust surrounded Isaac, blotting his clothing with the pigmented stain.

Isaac winded back his legs and catapulted his lower torso into Commander's face. The momentum sent Commander rolling to the center of the ring.

Commander ripped off his jacket. Bright, titanium alloy layered his lean arms, each one sporting three circular indentations. The alloy started at the base of his neck and stretched to bracers on his knuckles. Air whistled in and out of each indented hole.

"You never know when weapons can run out these days," Commander said, "But this lasts forever. I wanna know if you agree or not."

"Will you shut up?!" Isaac snapped, aggravated.

"Don't get scared, now!" Commander launched a flurry of strikes with a shot of a compressed air after every certain hit.

He landed another shot, caving Isaac's chest. One arm and his legs, stretched across the dirt, kept Isaac up.

In the back of his mind, Isaac knew of this danger. The more he dove into this side of the world, the more enemies he would find. But naivety hoped that luck would steer him clear of these dangers.

Commander maintained his tempo while Isaac paced the timing of his shots over weary breaths.

Sweat accumulated on Isaac's gear, the growing heat hampered his reaction timing. Regardless, Isaac measured the timing. Every shot of compressed air delayed one and a half seconds between the initial sound and the boom that confirmed the shot.

Determining the activation pattern wasn't observing a pose, but a sound. With enough focus, Isaac could hear a low whining indicating the start-up sound. The whine lasted one second, with the air shot fired half a second later. Isaac sidestepped the shot, the air bruising the surface of his ribs on one side.

He waited once again for the final hit in Commander's next combo. The start-up sound commenced.

Isaac threw an electrified uppercut at the center of Commander's core and kept the fist planted against his body.  Electricity surged through Commander.  He screamed until, after five seconds of continuous voltage, Isaac released. Commander fell to his knees, laced with charred marks.

This was it. Isaac reached for the map in Commander's pocket.

Four waves of air hit Isaac's body all at once. His vision greyed, the agonizing shock of the blow carving down into his nerves. He flew against manmade boundary and was shoved back into the ring by the thugs.

Air surrounding Commander distorted. His smug grin and lax eyes turned wild, set above a bloody nose.

"Diablo's got nothing to worry about."

*'Diablo?'*

The circular indentations on his arms sank in as he aimed his knuckles at Isaac. The makeshift ring clamored for their leader.

This was the face of an animal who would fight tooth and nail for the win. An admired leader and, ultimately, a parasite who's corrupted more people aside from Rosemary's dad.

The prior rage narrowed to a new goal adjacent to Isaac's current vendetta. Take down Commander and make him incapable of corrupting anyone else's lives.

Consecutive shots of air fired while steam protruded out of the machinery. Isaac ran around the ring to dodge the shots. A tube of air cut past his forearm.

Despite the simultaneous shots, there was still a start-up delay. Isaac used the noise cues and rolled past the wave of shots, the yellow dirt clouds staining his clothes, and closed to land an electrified punch.

The electric sparks traveled past Commander's skin to his machinery. A wide grin filled his face. The wireframes showed opportunity to attack was in Isaac's favor.

Isaac ducked past the next strike. He feinted, followed by another hook.

Commander countered with a swift back hand strike, creating enough distance to fire more shots of compressed air. He lunged his spark-covered body toward Isaac with two swings before firing another air shot inches away from Isaac's shoulder.

Isaac ducked with a deep gash inflicted on the crown of his shoulder. The pain in his body screamed a thousand times over, like fire ants burrowing into his shoulder, down his arm and up his neck.

The fighter's flow was the sole factor that kept his brain lit with adrenalized electricity. His helmet had its uses. But ultimately, it couldn't be a foolproof solution for everything.

Commander's eyes narrowed. That euphoric grin vanished. A look that said he knew he missed. The vibrant lighter poked from his pocket. He wouldn't miss next time.

Commander, still jittery, composed his stance. Isaac did the same. Like two coyotes in the Old West, ready to lunge with the last inch of stamina, assessing when to strike based on the shift in the end or a twitch of faltering movement from the opposing end. Every factor leading to the decisive outcome.

Both shots catapulted. Commander fired three shots. Two gashed Isaac's left arm as he closed in and snatched the lighter from Commander's pocket.

The low-start-up emitted again. Air shuffled, picking up more orange clouds of dust. The in-and-out motions in the emitters were invisible.

It was a gamble, but Isaac had a feeling the compressed air used some form of combustible gas. If it meant incapacitating his opponent now, then Isaac was willing to risk it.

*Flick.* Isaac positioned the lighter's open flame in front of Commander's next air shot.

Commander's eyes widened. He flung his mechanical arm outward, firing the shot into one of the thugs.

Isaac fired a colossal straight punch at the opening. Commander's ribs cracked. Another attack collided against Isaac's jaw.

The fist remained planted as Isaac uppercut Commander's core twice, following up with a third uppercut to the chin. The makeshift ring of goons broke, homing in on Isaac from different angles.

Commander grabbed Isaac's collar. The latter aimed to finish this. Two more jabs to the face and one electrified overhead, jaw-shattering right punch.

Commander fell to the floor, rolling out of reach as the thug's wireframes filled the HUD with chaos.

*'Fight,'* Isaac dodged some attacks and tanked the others. *'Fight until my limbs turn stiff and cold.'*

A clash of symphonic blows followed. The collusion of wireframes meshed with his vision leaving Isaac blind to the swarm of high-collar goons.

A hand covered his vision, which Isaac yanked off,

Then, instead of fighting the crowd, he stood outside a blazing inferno consuming the warehouse.

Commander was gone alongside majority of his crew. A few of them limped away in the distance.

Isaac looked around in shock. *'What the hell happened?'* His heart raced, assessing the loss in time. *'What the hell is going on?!'*

Soon, his eyes froze in horror at the pyre in front of him. Like a child meeting its nightmare.

He repeated to himself the fires wouldn't consume him to subdue the encroaching terror. That he was far enough. That it wouldn't repeat again. It couldn't.

Isaac checked if the map was in his grasp. Nothing. He was close. His progress stonewalled because of Commander. He was furious.

"Ah…ah…"

Isaac turned to spot the unknown voice. The moonlight and orange flames encapsulated what he first thought was a memory: A scrawny fellow wearing a pig mask. The other, more bulky, wearing a rooster mask.

"You're kidding…" Isaac muttered. The same people that attacked him and burned his house down.

They charged, screaming in unison.

Isaac sidestepped Pig, launching both electrified fists into Rooster's torso. Rooster fell to their knees.

"No, wait, please!" Pig yelped before Isaac pinned him down.

Isaac removed Pig's mask, revealing a pale, stubbled man with sunken cheeks and bulging eyes. Isaac grabbed the back of his head and slammed him against the concrete multiple times.

"Where is he?! Where's your boss?!"

Pig hyperventilated.

"*Answer!!!*" He roared in point-blank range.

"Massena!" Pig whimpered. "He's at Massena!"

Sirens blared in the distance. The rising smoke from the warehouse was a visible beacon now.

"You got lucky." Isaac chucked Pig to the concrete and ran to a nearby scaffolding, leaving the two culprits to fend for themselves.

He ascended to the rooftop, facing a sudden downpour of rain slamming against his body. The lack of friction forced Isaac's muscles to tense to the point of nearly losing his footing.

'*Calm yourself,*' Isaac told himself, hyperventilating. '*Just one minor slip.*'

Isaac pushed onward. Despite the self-imposed resilience, his body failed to adapt. At the edge of the rooftop, he propelled his body off the roof toward a fire escape. His body bounced off the metal rails before into the alleyway.

He snapped himself up, panting. His helmet lay by his feet. The locking mechanism must have malfunctioned from the rain.

Just as he picked up the mask, the sight of one man halted his motion. The man's round, sunken eyes locked onto him in equal shock. Almost a reflection, were it not for the messy tuft of bright blonde hair hidden beneath a hoodie and the Ziploc bag of M.A.D. in his clenched grip.

Isaac hoped the downpour created a veil that shrouded his face. But the man continued staring with shock.

Eventually, he shook off his own surge of surprise and re-equipped the helmet, climbing up to the roof once more with caution.

As he run further, his mind fixed onto the face. The silhouette. The familiar features. Then, it finally connected. That face. *That* face.

It was Clayton, Rosemary's father.

***

Isaac entered the mansion, catching Kara's attention from the couch.

———

"What happened?" she shouted.

Isaac removed his helmet. "Some scratches."

"I'm not talking about that."

Kara pulled her phone out, showing a news headline. *'Eighteen Officers killed in planted explosion, two critically injured.'*

A helicopter camera showed a birds-eye view of the ruined warehouses, then switching to a sketch of the supposed culprit. The reporter shared a sketch based on what enforcement had seen on the team's HUD prior to the explosion. A masked vigilante, covered in a black mask and grey hoodie. Isaac's outfit.

"So, what the hell happened?"

"I…I was careful," said Isaac. "No one could have connected me to this. I'm the one that's been burning the warehouses, why would I…" Isaac screamed. "It's him. It's him!"

"Who?"

"The leader!  I'm so stupid–" Isaac flinched from his injuries. Kara guided him to take a seat, and then helped him remove his gear. She returned with an advanced med kit in hand and began patching his deep wounds.

Isaac continued. "They were there."

"They?" Kara asked. "The scientist?"

"The people who burned my house down."

Kara's eyes widened. "Wha…What did you do?"

Isaac buried his hands into his face.

She paused midway through a stitch. "Don't tell me that you…did you?"

"No. I wanted to, but…no."

Slowly, she resumed. "You wanted to?"

"I'm not sure why I didn't go through with it when they deserve worse."

"Jesus. Well, you did the right thing," Kara leaned towards him. "I get that it's a lot. I do. But besides the leader, no one needs to die."

"How can this be safe?  Kara, the further we fall into this, the riskier it gets."

"I know, I…I can't have this mission be your downfall."

"Well, it's not. I got the boss' location."

"We're still close then?"

Isaac nodded. "What I'm doing can lead to good things. Hell, I helped Rosemary not too long ago."

"What are you talking about?"

"I found her dad's dealer and stopped him."

Kara poked into Isaac's bubble. "*Stopped* him?"

"What?" Isaac's heart raced.

"Isaac, that's far beyond what we discussed. You can't…" the fingers holding the threading needle stiffened as she paused and took a deep breath. "We risk leaving a bigger trail for the police to find."

"It's helping people, though. I could help more."

"We need to *focus*." Kara jolted the last thread to suture Isaac's wound. The sting provoked Isaac to jump. "I care about you. I do. No matter how good, those actions have consequences.

Commander mentioned Isaac being on his radar after the attack on Clayton's dealer. Had it not occurred, tonight's mission would've gone smoother.

Kara continued, "Promise me this ends once we find the leader and end him."

"I…" Isaac stammered. "I don't know." His anger boiled, lashing out. "What if I want to continue? What would you do?"

"Don't put that on the table. Please don't. There are other ways to help."

The frustration became an unbearable implosion. He didn't want to scream at her. He didn't want to fight with the one person in this mission with him. Instead, he headed upstairs and laid in bed, staring at the ceiling. The line between now, this reality, and the ending he envisioned began to blur.

***

Isaac and Kara remained distant for the next few days. He tended to his normal schedule as the police aimed their sights on the vigilante. Study with Todd, exercise at Obadiah's gym and spend time with Rosemary.

Todd was nowhere to be found. Isaac texted him to check in and apologize for his disappearance. No response.

He followed with another text. Nothing. This wasn't like Todd.

At the cafe, Isaac watched Rosemary stir her strawberry lemonade. Isaac sipped on his chamomile tea. An attempt to ease his nerves. The acidity from the lemon made the drink more tolerable.

"How's your dad feeling?" Isaac asked.

"He's doing much better now. Thanks. Rosemary smiled.

"I'm really glad to hear that."

"You should meet him one day. I feel like you guys would get along. Do you know how to fish?"

"I can pretend I'm a pro who's having a bad day of fishing."

"How about tomorrow, then?"

"I…have another project to handle tomorrow," Isaac fibbed.

"Oh," Rosemary's pitch dropped. "I understand."

"I know, I know." Isaac bowed his head. "I'm sorry."

Rosemary fell silent. It was enough for Isaac to analyze his own words. He hoped Rosemary would understand his good intention.

Isaac's thoughts drifted to Todd's disappearance. "Hey, have you seen or heard from Todd lately?"

Rosemary squinted her eyes. "You seriously don't know?"

"What do you mean?"

"He was attacked."

Isaac's heart halted for several seconds. He stood up and exited the café to breathe. The air in his chest thinned, igniting a frightening sensation as panic rose.

# XXIII
## DIABLO

### November 5, 2022, 4:35 AM

Diablo had succeeded in his mission at Oswego. A crowd of dark navy rushed in; their guns raised at the drug lord cosplaying as the vigilante. The replica gear was easy to find online. He unleashed one of his largest infernos, obliterating the squad. Afterward, he tossed the gear into a fire.

Part of Gus's plan was lying low for a minimum of eighteen hours. No lodgings of any kind. Then, the best course would be to travel by foot and bus, landing in Syracuse to hide in the warehouse, blended in with the workers.

In the middle of the dusk, where dewy blades of shin-high grass were at their prime, a mile of Diablo's trek remained. His current clothing – a rare choice of tank top and sweatpants with the usual dress shoes – allowed more breathability despite clinging to his body from the humidity.

The phone rang, Gus's name displayed on the caller ID. Diablo presumed it was him checking to make sure his trek held no issues. He picked up the phone. "Almost there."

"Sirens heading to Syracuse," said Gus.

"What?"

"You need to get away from there."

Diablo checked his revolver and reloaded bullets into the missing chambers. *'The documents of the mutations,'* Diablo thought. Evidence that could incriminate him.

"I need to clean evidence," he told Gus.

"Are you burning down the location? There's no coming back to it."

"I'd rather conserve." The inferno Diablo launched had taken more stamina out of him than he expected. It was a first to feel this, in his essence, significantly shitty.

"You remember the bunker?"

"Barely…"

"By the corner of Henry's Sandwich shop, you'll come across a sewer grate. You jump down there and keep walking east. Find the loose stone, and inside the crevice will be a key. If you continue walking down, you'll find a pronounced slab of concrete. The keyhole will be somewhere there to open the pathway."

"Right, got it."

"I'll meet you there." Gus ended the call.

Diablo reached the peak of a small hilltop. In the short distance, past Lake Onondaga, was the warehouse surrounded by police cars. He approached with the plan to sneak around the back and climb through the window to grab the documents.

Officers marched in and out of the location, apprehending many of the workers, handcuffed in packs with many stationed on the front and left sides. Diablo had no time to ponder if they were worth saving. He circumvented around the perimeter, vaulted the fence and leaned around the corner with the rear window in his sights.

Looking through the window, police descended from the level above, carrying boxes of materials.

Diablo vaulted up to a nearby dumpster and hopped up to a small balcony leading to the window of his office.

A quiet approach was necessary. Diablo focused on the windowpane, forming a mental image of oozing lava. He hoped exerting this action wouldn't be as heavy as something explosive.

The window's surface turned viscous. It disassembled into a syrup, dissipating downward until the opening was fully created. The drug lord entered, careful to step over the extremely hot material.

Diablo managed to feel decent to continue as normal. His mind made wary, however, of excessive use. All guards remained stationed at the ground floor. He searched through the drawers. All empty. He lifted the bottom of each one, finding his documents.

———

*'Jackpot. I'll hide out in the bunker and wait for this to calm.'*

The ceiling creaked to the side, catching Diablo's attention. In the newly formed was a young man scowling down at the drug lord. His loose shirt hung from his back, leaving a wide opening to see his chest from the angle he was perched.

Diablo tilted his head with a single squint, catching sight of the shiv held in the young man's hand. The blade pointed at Diablo. The loose collar shifted more, revealing a portion of a tattoo to the office's light. Blue scales. The image of a blue koi fish with a dragon's head flashed in Diablo's mind.

The symbol of the Yakuza. Another mole was in Syracuse this whole time.

The young man leapt, slashing Diablo's chest as he sidestepped away.

The Youth slashed the air between him and Diablo, twisting and bumbling. Diablo unsheathed and hammered his revolver into the Youth's face, forcing him to collapse to the floor. The Youth let out a shrill scream for a second before Diablo covered his mouth to prevent an eruption. He continued hammering his forehead until the skull cracked and caved in. A rage channeled through a whisper, lower than the police chatter and crashing waves.

The traitor laid on the floor motionless, his face now an indecipherable blob. Diablo stood up, cleaned the blood off the revolver and his pants, and went back out the window and down with ease.

*"Don't. Move."*

His lips pressed flat with a sole squint at the sudden sight of a mob of armored officers, weapons aimed in an arc formation. They were cautious. Of course they were cautious after a batch of their comrades died a horrible death, whether brave or stupid.

One officer advanced, keeping a steady rifle aimed with one hand, the other hand holding a pair of handcuffs. "Raise your hands and face your back to us," the advancing officer said. The tainted eye still fogged with fatigue. But it didn't matter. He placed himself in this scenario. He'll get himself out.

An orange light engulfed the advancing officer in flames. The effort nearly nauseated Diablo, but he focused on the instinct of survival. He fired more consecutive bursts, two hitting the ground as it led to three bombs engulfing the mob.

Diablo circumvented away, using the walls as a crutch. Reaching the front, officers rushed to the source of the explosion before a couple spotted him, calling the other officers. The restrained workers clamored with victorious chatter within the vans, knowing the mark of their boss.

He used enough of his energy to vault over the fence and sprint for several minutes down to the corner of Henry's Sandwich Shop.

As Gus instructed, Diablo turned to the hollow alleyway and lifted the sole sewer plate.

No one in sight. Diablo paddled down the ladder, almost slipping from the oil-like muck glistening on the sewers' concrete. No surprise that it smelled like Satan's tainted asshole.

He fought against the sewage currents slapping his shins. With the comfort of the darkness, his pain in his vision lessened. Although, the ringing in his ears lingered.

*'I'll recover from this mess.'* A rare reflection while drops of blood fell from his face. *'And I'll make sure we're prepared next time.'* Soon, Syracuse would be back in shape. This couldn't be the end.

He dragged one hand on the wall until finding and gripping onto a loose chunk of stone.

Diablo ripped out the stone, emitting a glow into the crevice with his eye, revealing a tiny silver key through the cobwebs. He picked it up and shoved the brick back in its place.

The path spiraled deeper. Echoes amplified. Even his orange light didn't reach an end. Then, Diablo found the pronounced slab of concrete. He perched down to his elbows and knees, finding a tiny indentation.

Diablo twisted the key into the insert, clanking a vast mechanism that echoed beneath the surface, revealing a half-mile tunnel. It narrowed as Diablo continued, with one light flickering at the end.

He reached a white door at the end, an anchored lamp being the source of light. Inside, a small room–about fifty square feet–housed a chipped wooden table, steel cabinet, and a flat mattress stained with yellow blots.

Diablo opened the steel cabinet to find bags of snacks, a jug of water, one sedative, a plethora of cocaine and a spare, bone-white suit.

*'Convenient.'* Diablo changed out of his ragged clothes for the comforting suit. He left the suit jacket hanging.

He recalled keeping the one-of-a-kind sedative here for his discomfort over small spaces. His fatigue worsened the phobia.

The idea of cocaine numbing this rising panic excited him. Diablo ripped out the plastic bags and, one by one, laid his nostril against lines of white powder and inhaled in an instant.

First came the sting, followed by the euphoria.

Diablo's mind flew past the ceiling, into the clouds, grinning as every ounce of worry washed away from him like a high tide. He danced–jumping, screaming and smacking the walls until his hands welted from the roughness around the square room. Imagining victory in his grasp.

Then, a creak sounded from the door. The vision vanished. The grey surfaces and dull areas returned. Erratic fear burrowed into his skin like parasitic worms. He imagined the NMPD behind that door now, ready to kill him silently without remorse.

Diablo acknowledged the fear of being caught. The fear of losing everything. That euphoric sensation of victory remaining a dream.

No one would get in his way.

Without hesitation, he pulled his revolver and shot four times at the door.

A thud followed. Minutes passed, for what felt like hours. No one entered.

The lightheadedness from before finally overcame Diablo. He dropped his revolver to the floor and fell onto the mattress.

He awoke, drenched in cold sweat with the faint recollection of a dream. A vision of himself, older but with a beautiful young wife and their child, on a date in the park. The fragments felt more like the salvaged pieces of a burnt film. Wetness trailed along his fingers, forming a small river of blood to beyond the doorway.

He ambled over and opened the door, tracing the river to four bullet holes plastered on a lifeless Gus.

"Gus…"

Diablo crouched down for a closer look. Gus' skin lost all color. His pulse was thin and faint. He hacked up bare strips of air.

There was a want to feel some kind of remorse and shame.

"We need to go to a hospital." Diablo tried to express sympathy.

Gus nudged his head left and right. There was no need for words to understand why. The risk would be too high now.

Like droplets from an ajar faucet in the middle of the night, a sadness leaked through.

"I'm sorry," said Diablo.

He wanted Gus to say something. Keep talking. Say what would be recommended next or tell him to stop lying. But the light in his eyes faded. The fibers in his limbs had already lost tension.

Diablo absorbed this new silence for the next several minutes.

He needed to contact someone. Velcro would be the most viable option. Diablo shuffled through Gus's suit pockets, finding his wallet and phone, unscathed from the gunfire to Diablo's rare luck.

He rose to his feet and clutched the phone tightly before letting out a furious scream – an echo so violent it shook the door. Three stark realities slammed him at once. Gus, his one loyal colleague, was dead. Syracuse was gone. He was alone.

He dialed the phone. "Yes?" Mr. Velcro answered.

"It's me," Diablo bemoaned. "NMPD ambushed my H.Q."

"Yes, some of my subordinates made it out and relayed it to me."

"How nice."

"You're usually much more vocal. Are you that shaken?"

"Just help me. I need a base." It became likelier of why Velcro would even help Diablo. Why not just abandon for his losses? What would make him want Diablo on the board at this point? He sat through the long pause, waiting for the rejection.

"There's an underground warehouse in a sanctioned zone between Brooklyn and the main city," said Mr. Velcro. "I have men there that I will inform about your arrival, and they will follow your orders. Please refrain from killing them."

Diablo was stunned. Velcro said it as if he had it already prepared for him.

"Wha…really?  Syracuse is gone."

"And we will regard Syracuse as an experiment gone wrong. Now, memorize the following address."

As instructed, Diablo memorized the address, repeating the words mentally.

"Lie low for as long as you can. And then go there."

Velcro hung up the phone as soon as he finished. A metallic smell engulfed his scent and taste buds in the tight space.

***

The phone was able to last for some time, indicating three weeks had passed. Rations and grief made the living conditions unique.

Diablo found himself repeating the address and conversing with Gus' corpse. How many children he would like to have, where he would like to meet his wife. His ideal proposal being at the park. A dream home, made of bricks with enough greenery for the good air. An idea he got from the old homes in Charleston he once saw.

Then, the phone buzzed with its remaining charge.

"Who is it?" Diablo answered.

"Boss?"

*"Who. Is. It."*

The man stuttered. "We got the masked guy here like you said. It's a shitshow. Police are gonna come and ambush soon."

Diablo's eyes widened.  "When the hell was this planned?  Explain."

"Gus told us. Bonnie and Clyde got caught by him and told him about the warehouse in Massena. They told Gus, and Gus informed the police."

Diablo was delighted at the idea of having the vigilante and the NMPD both in one warehouse. An ingenious idea by Gus he couldn't let go to waste.

"Keep him occupied. I'm going there now."

"But…Boss, this guy's in a frenzy."

"Keep. Him. There. He better be there when I arrive."

Diablo tossed the phone to the floor. He grabbed the glimmering silver sedative out of the steel cabinet and stowed it into his sleeve and exited.

The devil's eye glowed orange, filling the inside of the room with flame. The heat bounced off his back as he gave Gus his final farewells.

# XXIV
## Isaac Sage

**November 26, 2022, 1:03 PM**

"Clearly, you have every right to be upset. I would be–"

"Of course, upset. I'm pissed!" Isaac fell back into the dark green velvet chair.

Dr. Bukowski kept his hands folded together, beaming at Isaac with a scolding look. The carpet's damage, as Isaac noticed while digesting Dr. Bukowski's silence, had been replaced with brightened stains. Most likely scarred from improper cleaning.

"Sorry," said Isaac. "You didn't deserve that."

Dr. Bukowski resumed. "I would be too, in your shoes. But who exactly is it you're mad at?"

Isaac recalled pounding on Todd's apartment door for minutes after learning that he left the hospital as soon as he woke up, against doctor's orders. The nurse had explained the event that transpired.

The inner rage amplified the more Isaac imagined the scene: his friend, beaten to near pulp by two people, no chance to fight back. No one brave enough to stop it.

After banging for several minutes, Todd opened the door, disgruntled. His body was covered in bandages over welts and bruises riddled on his body.

Todd shared what happened in a flat summary of few words. A stark contrast to the details the nurse shared.

When Isaac asked for clarity, Todd pointedly told Isaac to leave with harsh brevity, claiming he had work to catch up on.

"I'm mad at the ones who hurt Todd. I'm mad I wasn't there, said Isaac. "I want to find them and make sure they never do something like that ever again."

"And?" Dr. Bukowski asked. "What would that benefit, Isaac?"

"They've probably done the same to others. I'd break a cycle." Isaac tapped his foot, trying to convince himself of his own words.

"And if someone wished to pursue you?"

Instead of responding, Isaac festered in his thoughts. *'If I hadn't been so occupied with this agenda,'* Isaac thought, *'I would be at school. If I had been at school, I'd be more focused on the project and being alongside Todd. Then, maybe…'*

"You're doing it again, aren't you?" Dr. Bukowski stated.

"Doing what?"

"Clinging to past events. Thinking of what could've been when it's already set in stone."

Isaac exhaled his frustration. "What should I do instead?"

Dr. Bukowski leaned back. The silence gave Isaac a moment to analyze his own wild emotion.

"You've mentioned Todd's smart," said Dr. Bukowski. "I'm sure he processed it. He saved that man's life. He's a hero."

"No one who's left to die in an alleyway, or in the middle of their apartment, is remembered as a poor soul and nothing more." He paused, gathering his thoughts. "I'm tired of letting this happen in my life."

"Do you, the one who lost his family, still believe you can control this?"

Isaac caught his aggressive glare at the doctor, and instead calmed himself It allowed him to sift through his cluster of emotions. His anger toward his own self outweighed the other. "I…Todd hates me. I apologized. I should've been there. I need to be accountable." Going after the ones who went after Todd wouldn't change his feelings.

"Then I think time will be the best medicine."

"Other things have left my mind spinning, doctor."

Dr. Bukowski tilted his head. "Such as?"

"I know, we're on time, so I'll bring it up quick. I…had my first blackout recently."

Dr. Bukowski straightened his posture. "Don't worry about the time. How?"

Even if Isaac tried hard to meditate on it, no clear answer came to him.

"It just happened while exercising. Would the medicine have any effect? After prolonged use?" Isaac asked.

Dr. Bukowski took his glasses off, examining the rims. He pulled out a cloth and wiped each of the lenses.

"When I spoke with several medical experts and experienced therapists about the procedure…" Dr. Bukowski put his glasses back on. "We put a lot of care to ensure this method was both safe and effective. Your medicine's sole design was to resurface the memories linked to your trauma. It was reviewed by many groups of experts."

Isaac sighed. "There's no chance if there was a mistake in the compounding?"

"The odds are very slim. But you must be prepared for things out of your control."

"Honestly, my actions lately have made me feel more in control than ever. It's been a tug-of-war. But…has it seemed better from your end?"

"You talk less about that part of your past. And you share more recent stories even if you're not around as often. It must be working."

Isaac nodded. *'It has to.'*

"I would reduce intake of medication for now. To be safe. That way we know the issue."

The timer buzzed. Dr. Bukowski shut the timer. He continued. "And considering those actions…Every action stems from an origin. Every effect stems from a cause. So where does each action stem from? And how have those actions affected those surrounding you? Especially the ones you value most. Think about that."

What he found most valuable. He thought about his parents.

Kara. Todd. Rosemary.

His career.

Control over his life.

The mission.

Massena.

***

Isaac focused on his studies again as a distraction. And for falling so far behind.

At New-Gen Chemistry, the professor delved into the durability of M.A.D. A student asked the professor how a stable M.A.D. compound could be destroyed. "Is it by something acidic? A different bacterium?" asked the student.

"Fight fire with fire. You would have to create an identical compound to the T.Dohrnum," the professor replied. "Albeit flammable."

Isaac raised his hand. "How does that work?"

"Let's say, in theory, there is an unbreakable red worm. No matter what, you cannot cut it, nor pour acid on it, nor incinerate it. You *can* set it on fire, let me be clear on that. Flames will sprout from it. But it won't disappear, or even degrade.

"What you do is you create another red worm. Identical in properties, but flammable. A faux worm, if you will. Get them close, and the red worm will biologically assess it as its own. Even when you ignite it, the red worm will not assess the threat because of the properties."

Isaac wrote the notes down. "So, you trick the compound with a fake lookalike?"

"The fake needs to have most of its properties, but yes. Sometimes, you need to fight fire with fire, even if it means creating an inferno."

Isaac rapped his knuckles along his pen after jotting the notes, unable to shake off the innate adrenaline spurring within. A visit to Obadiah's Gym, to dissuade the adrenaline, was then in consideration.

***

Isaac and Obadiah geared up and took their positions in the center of the ring for mitt training.

———

Every hit, Isaac imagined the mitts as the back of his enemy's skull, impaling it with each hit. He continued, shouting with every punch, weaving past each hook, reaching a state of flow until Obadiah commanded Isaac to stop.

"Everything good?" Obadiah asked.

"Letting off steam, that's all," said Isaac.

"That's cool. There's bags for that. But you can't let your emotions get the best of you in the ring. Then you telegraph your hits. And then you look like an idiot when you get hit. Clear?"

"Clear." Isaac continued his training, holding back out of respect for Obadiah, his advice, and his facility.

Massena. Massena was where *he* should be. This could end tonight.

***

Isaac returned home later that day to the noise of the tree branches outside crackled from the breeze. Kara stood beneath the sturdy oak tree, observing the open patches of land next to the estate.

Maybe Kara was right. Maybe once this was over, his rage would vanish, and the vigilante life would no longer feel desirable. He could visit the nightlife, study in the day, travel outside the city to some country that didn't have a speck of concrete.

Isaac tried to sleep on these thoughts. Hours passed, with the idea to raid Massena and stop the boss tonight making him toss and turn.

He twisted out of the comforters, his surroundings blanketed by darkness with no light cast from the outside. He turned on the light and opened the map of New Manhattan, pinpointing Massena.

Isaac suited up, stowed his helmet into a backpack, and walked toward the main entrance, bag in hand. Kara passed by from around the corner of the stairway.

"Hey," said Isaac.

"Hey," Kara replied. "Listen, I'm sorry about what happened the other day. I do care a lot about you. That's all."

Isaac lowered his gaze, filled with shame over his headspace. "It's okay. I'll…be back later." He exited without looking back. "Be safe."

***

Isaac took a shuttle bus to the town of Massena due to its long distance. He slept on the seats, torn where the padding protruded out, for a brief hour until his heightened nerves made him awake for the remainder of the trip.

The small town lacked late-night activities, with most, if not all, of the residents asleep, leaving the town's streets in nothing but a blanket of white snow. It was easy for Isaac to imagine sitting by a cozy fireplace as the frigid winds forced his teeth to chatter.

Isaac checked his phone, finding a glitter of notifications. Missed calls and text messages from Rosemary, some unknown spam calls and one missed call from Kara.

*'Once this is all over. . .it'll be back to normal.'* Isaac assured himself. He found a narrow alleyway and took the helmet out of his bag. With the mask snapped on, he tossed the backpack underneath a nearby dumpster.

His helmet's interface scanned the surrounding area, interfacing it into his GPS. With the town housing three large buildings–a hotel, an automobile manufacturing site, and a three-story office–he first aimed for the automobile manufacturing site. Isaac could understand a small workshop for cars in a small town, but a large factory seemed out of place.

Isaac climbed to the factory's rooftop via an adjacent fire escape. He peeked through the landscape window panels. The vast teal layout of the building contained conveyor belts and automation, lit with artificial blue lights.

The workers sprayed a tiny plus sign on the cars laced with M.A.D. just after bounding the plastic packets between the car doors' interior shell with medical tape.

He thought about Todd, lying on a hospital bed. The leader still roaming the city. His focus dwindled and breathing turned thin with tightened fists ready to unleash colossal damage. A stagnant smell of sulfur filled his nostrils.

Suddenly, an orange flash overcame his vision, accompanied by a tremendous force that sent him tumbling across the ground.

He realized he was now on the factory's ground floor. *'Another blackout.'*

A silhouette stood in the orange glow, shimmering like a strobe light. To Isaac's left, a corpse lay on the ground. Its body charred black.

Canisters of smoke shot over the teal ceilings. From around the corner, two men dressed in SWAT gear blocked Isaac's path, rifles aimed at him.

Why were there NMPD officers in Massena? Was this a trap? His blood-drenched fists trembled. That terror of the unknown was apparent, albeit intensified more than ever.

Before the officers could fire, bullets pierced both of their heads.

Isaac sprinted away and maneuvered over the conveyor belts, taking cover behind a grand piece of machinery. The blood on his gloves disabled the electric currents.

A nearby light shattered. Followed by another, and then the next one, forming a pattern that led to the one, sole light above Isaac.

Someone as skilled as Gus and as strong as Commander, a leader of the cartel, should've been enough of a hint. Isaac was out of his league. It was time to take flight.

Isaac examined his surroundings, struggling to hold back his perspired body from overheating. The waxed reflection on the floor, refracted by the lone blue light, assisted Isaac's blind spot to find an exit straight down.

Nothing on his right, nor his left. Straight ahead was the exit.

He counted in his head for the right timing to make his escape. Leave too soon, and Isaac's haste could prove to be useless. Too late, and this could be his last thought.

One.

The footsteps increased their pacing.

Two.

The heat invoked a strange chill. Like the oncoming symptoms of a fever. The accumulated sweat on Isaac's face stung his eyes.

Three.

Immediately, a force gripped onto his left arm, pulling him back. His vision shifted to a bald man in a tattered, white suit.

He would've fought away from the man instantly. But the sight of his right eye had paralyzed Isaac. It was deteriorated. Near-rotting with a visible layer of flesh pulsating around his twitching, narrowed iris.

Isaac's head intensified with a burning sensation. A pain that was somehow nostalgic.

A sting against Isaac's arm followed, freeing him from the paralysis. He swung his free arm across the man's face. The devil-eyed man released his grip, and Isaac slipped to the ground, stumbling into a frantic sprint.

Flames erupted from the floor, dancing around Isaac to form a circle with a ferocious, discordant yell in the background. Wild embers clasped onto his clothes, with Isaac's H.U.D drowning in static. A proneness to overheating. Something Isaac didn't consider.

The flames from his past flashed in Isaac's mind. An inferno engulfing the escape stairwell and Gemma with it.

He hyperventilated. *'Not again...'* The memories flashed, his body feeling another re-immersion coming on. *'Not this!'*

The energy in his legs focused into a dramatic leap over the flames. His vision weakened. His feet landed just outside the last inch of flames, letting the desperation and fear inject him with one last, miraculous burst of energy, leading into a hurdle and dive out into the snow.

He rolled around until the frost extinguished every ounce of heat in seconds, and ran, hysteric. It may have been two miles, or more, until Isaac's mind sobered to find himself in the middle of a vast snowfield.

Endless sheets of blank whiteness, set beneath a dark blue sky, surrounded Isaac. Not even a tiny dot representing Massena or another town was in his sight. The nerves slowly woke, receiving the bitter cold of the frost.

Panic filled his voice. He called out to the abyss. "Is there anyone out there? Anyone! Hello?!"

No one. Aimless, and nowhere to go, the only option now was to walk forward with the hope that some sort of haven would be around soon to call for help and find warmth.

The orange flash remained embedded in Isaac's mind. All that came to him was a forgotten memory resurfaced from the day of the incident. As a young Isaac watched the spire fall, a blurred, white silhouette gazed in the distance.

# XXV
## John Saint

**November 20, 2022, 3:00 PM**

The soft surface beneath Saint eased an oncoming wave of soreness. It was a dull ache bringing instant certainty he was still alive and in the real world.

His blurred vision adjusted, separating the light from the dark and revealing silhouettes standing around him. The silhouettes defined themselves as Edoris, Billows and Briggs standing around him.

He curled his fingers and squinted his eyes. Any movement stung his entire body, as if his joints rusted in place.

Saint attempted to speak, managing to let out a strained gasp of air.

"Something's wrong," Edoris said to the others. She called to the nurse outside the hall. "Nurse, my husband, he's not breathing right."

The nurse entered and checked his vitals. The doctor entered minutes later. He instructed Saint to stare at the stick held in his hand. He moved the stick left, right, up, down. Saint traced his right eye to where the stick was positioned each time.

Then, a realization sank in. His left eye was dark. His fingertips felt the left side of his face.

"Mr. Saint, you are in the hospital," the doctor said. He moved Saint's hand away from his face. "Careful, that wound is still healing. Can you repeat to me where you are?"

His fingers glided along jagged ridges on the side of his head, leading to his eye, to which the doctor instructed to stop.

"Saint. Answer my question," the doctor commanded. "I know this is a lot. Focus."

As Saint tried to speak again, he was met with another strained gasp of air.

The nurse calmed Saint, reminding him not to force his breathing. The doctor turned to Edoris and Billows. "He will need some time to recover. There's a likelihood that he may have gotten cerebral hypoxia from the fall. We'll continue to examine him."

Saint adjusted his vision, noticing Briggs leaning against the wall opposite him with a lowered head. His eyes kept a steeled gaze on Saint, whose heart began racing.

His mind flashed back to the last frame of Carmichael. *'Is she…?'*

Briggs broke his silence through a low, gravely tone. "You're a goddamn mess…"

Billows turned his head away to the window, while Edoris' eyes flared, welling up the longer she looked at Saint. Wisps of shaky air spilled through her lips.

"What's done is done," Billows said to Briggs. "We can't turn it back."

Briggs scoffed at Billows. "Alright. Then tell our dear detective what happened, Jackson."

Billows looked inward. He took a deep, sharp inhale and turned to Saint.

"Look, John…" Billows began, "The raid on Oswego was a botch. Someone dressed in a grey hoodie and black mask sat there, waiting. He emitted some kind of explosion…not sure if that was Diablo, or some kind of person related to him. But eighteen out of twenty died. The other two on life support."

Saint's face paled. A lingering stab in his stomach intensified, twisting around, as Briggs beamed a furrowed glare. Regardless, Diablo and his cohorts proved smarter and more vicious. The underestimation was amplified by his impatience for greatness.

Briggs stomped toward him and snatched him by the collar. "You pale piece of shit!" Briggs shouted. "You knew it too…It's all over your goddamn face!"

"Easy, Chief," Billows said, "He didn't know–"

"Shut up and sit down!" Briggs commanded vehemently. "So many lives *gone* in one day. Fathers, mothers, some that were far too young."

Ashamed, Saint fixed his sight to the blanket draped over his legs.

"Look at me, John," Briggs' voice drew closer.

The nurses heard the commotion. One walked up to Briggs, warning him to leave the room.

Briggs continued, unfazed. "Their families aren't seeing them again. Now, all they get is a tombstone, a framed photo and baggage. I would much rather have had my life sacrificed instead of all of 'em.

"And Carmichael…" The sharp tone in his voice trembled. "She should've survived until retirement.  Because of *you*. A Saint of all people."

Saint lowered his head.  Briggs's words confirmed his last sight of Carmichael as true.  Even if the detective could speak, he was at a loss for words.

"Thank God your father's not around to see this," Briggs said before departing, making it in the clear in the stomping growing distant. He said to someone in the hall, "Don't worry, he won't see me again."

"He's processing a lot," Billows said. "Saint, you did what you had to do. I learned enough about you to know that."

They were hollow compliments trying to fill the bitter air like powdered cream for bitter coffee.

"It'll be alright," Billows continued. "Things will–"

"Leave…" Saint finally managed to speak through incredulous effort.  Another strained gasp followed. "Please…"

Billows' sympathetic expression turned somber. "Understood." He left without another word.

It was only he and Edoris now. She leaned in to embrace him. Though tender, it suffocated him due to his weak state.

"I was so worried you wouldn't wake," Edoris whispered into Saint's ear. "No more. No more of this."

His lone eye welled up, unable to see. Saint buried his face in Edoris' shoulder, wetting her blouse with tears from both eye sockets. Every twitch and fraction of movement unrelenting in searing agony.

She tightened her hold on him. After everything in the past months, Saint affirmed he didn't deserve Edoris.

An image of his father formed, looking down on him. "I'm…sorry…" Saint wept against Edoris, unable to finish his sentence. "I'm so sorry."

Edoris rubbed his brittle body amid his silent weeps. From the corner of his lone eye, the window looking out to the city was fogged with glittering dots of white.

***

Edoris brought Saint home after another three days of hospitalization since awakening from his coma. Saint received instructions from the doctor that although his recovery improved where he could walk again and be on his own, he would need to take caution in his nutrition and voice. Saint covered his missing eye with a black patch.

The doctor also wrote in his closing notes, "I've come across people who've experienced similar trauma. I highly recommend, for your sake and your wife's that you seek therapy."

For the next week, Edoris was more protective than ever. She checked in on Saint every other hour. Sometimes it would be direct by asking him. Other times she would simply look from afar, ensuring his wake state

By the end of the week, Saint had enough energy to walk in the park with Edoris. It brought a fresh, calm serenity to his routine after being cooped up in the house for so long.

Minutes into the walk, the calm then felt jarring. It twisted his nerves with restlessness through fidgeting or muttering silent gibberish. What was an enjoyable feeling, letting him breath with ease, became a frantic reminder. Something needed to be finished before he can enjoy the calm.

***

On the week prior to Christmas, the funeral service of those lost in the raids was broadcasted, including Catherine Carmichael. Briggs spoke at the eulogy in a black suit with several officers standing beside him, including Billows at the far end. Saint watched the broadcast in the living room, understanding of this imposed exile.

Briggs first went into detail about Carmichael's beginning as a cadet. She climbed through the ranks and succeeded in a lot of big-name cases. Her name was as prominent as Jacques Saint. Her fire inspired the mantra of the newer training programs, a little after Saint had graduated. *Live this life with full certainty.*

Carmichael's legacy would be lived on by her only daughter. Briggs then called the names of the other officers.

For the first time in a while, Saint dreamt about what it would be like to die. Not the act of it, but the feeling of what would happen after eyes, lungs, heart and brain ceased.

Did they wake up in a sandy plain faraway from cities, being filled with the thought of their last moments until a specter approached them? Did they end up in a white space where they met the Creator and recalled each of their past lives?

He reflected on Carmichael's words prior to the raid. "I like to have all the answers right before events like this."

Carmichael had been in this line of work longer than Saint by ten years to learn the maturity of accepting premature death. Because of that, she lived a full life as long as she had all the answers that satisfied her curiosity. He hoped so.

Did she follow a routine that left her satisfied? Like kissing her daughter good night, or sending her a message to let her know her true feelings every day?

There were then mental images, near indecipherable and lasting a nanosecond. His father's lips curling downward for a mere twitch. His body, standing in a dark hallway, where he bowed his head towards the shadows. Looking at the city's horizon with bitterness instead of awe. As if he too wondered if he could've done more. If he had done enough.

His subconscious, renewed with energy and feel to revise his wrongdoings, affixed onto the next thought, fueled further by the guilt of the fallen officers: *'I can go back out there.'*

Whether it was lounging on a chair, laughing with Edoris, paying attention to Smokey or resting in bed, the idea pervaded his mind for weeks like a fruit fly's ceaseless buzzing.

***

On Christmas Eve, Edoris gifted Saint a small, blue box bounded with a golden ribbon.

"Shit, I didn't buy you anything." Saint kissed Edoris on the forehead. "I'm so sorry, honey. Thank you."

Edoris smiled and reciprocated the kiss. "You can repay me later. Come on, open it! The tension is killing me."

"Alright." He chuckled. "Let me take a seat before I'm blown away." He sat down and placed the box back on the table with care. He readied his fingers on the folds of the ribbon.

It was the relaxation and peace of mind Edoris always brought to him. Calmness.  The same calmness that once again triggered that frantic reminder ever since he started those walks in the park. It recalled the one idea that clung to his head ever since being reminded of the fallen officers.

"Edoris…" He unfurled his fingers away from the gift. "I have something to say. I'm… going to finish the case."

Edoris' smile decayed. "What?"

The act of saying and hearing the reaction felt so quick.  He thought, for some reason, he'd have more time to convery his reason.

"I…" Saint tried to find the right words.  "I feel this. He's still a free man. I'm responsible for making it worse. I can't let him win."

Edoris exhaled. She batted her eyes away and paced to the living room. After a minute, she walked back to the kitchen, shaking her head.

"No," she said. "There are *plenty* of other people at the NMPD that can do this. You are *not* the man for the job, John."  The last sentence challenged Saint. Now he sat in the chair, simmering over his supposed inadequacy. It stockpiled atop the other days of being cooped up with his thoughts. "For the love of God, John–"

"I can't sit here!" Saint erupted.  "You want me to sit back and think they can catch this man?  They couldn't even get him–"

"Don't!" She yelled with clenched teeth.   She followed with a lowered tone of the same ferocity.  "*Don't* have the audacity to undermine the hard work they've done. To yell at *me* when I tried to understand you after all this time. Why…*Why*?"

"I may have messed up, but I do have it in me to finish the case I started." He pointed one hand to his eyepatch. "I won't let my mistake stop me."

Edoris' lower lip shook. "John…You've handled several cases over the years. Wanting to prove yourself. And I was by your side. You have done so much. Why can't you see that? I know the past couple of years cases had dwindled. You're getting to your fifties now. We're getting old. For God's sake, is it asking too much that I want to rest with you by my side."

"Edoris…"

"Right now, you're thinking insane. Truly. If you're talking like this, then you haven't imagined, *truly* imagined, the nights where I can't sleep because you're not there, or you're not waking up and I'm wondering when or *if* you'll wake up. The same nights I imagine something god-awful happened to you and a doctor will tell me that... Now you're doing it again." Edoris' eyes welled up. "Be honest. Jacques died young, right? He was a hero, but he was a stubborn hard-ass."

"He was a good man."

"Right. So why are you spiting him?" Saint raised his brows. "Don't act surprised," Edoris continued. "It's always been a goddamn race with him. Or is it that you're obsessed? You never say it, but it's there. Follow in your dad's footsteps, but better. And you think, to do that, you need to land that one case. One more big, fucking case."

Saint exhaled. He sobered from the initial eruption, replacing the rage with sorrow.

"I don't want to fight with you."

"Neither do I. I tried to be understanding for this past year. I don't need to remind you that. What's it gonna be, John?"

Saint fell silent. He bowed his head, locking onto the ornate gift. Even with the visceral truth, he imagined what his father would do. That he would be able to conquer this.

"I guess that's it," said Edoris. "Then you can't live here. Go." She walked toward the front door, her arms folded. Her gaze didn't meet with Saint's.

Saint clutched onto the gift and stood up. He collected his phone, wallet and coat before approaching the door.

"I'm sorry," Saint said.

"You're not."

The detective exited the house. His heart shattered with no initial plan of where to go.   Specks of white perched on Saint's shoulder.

***

Saint called Billows from a payphone a few blocks from his house.

"Saint?" Billows answered.

"Hey, Billows. Merry early Christmas."  Saint leaned against a nearby stop sign.  "Do you have a free spot I could stay at?"

"Yeah, what happened?"

Saint explained to Billows with full honesty. Billows fell silent. Saint was hoping to hear an enthusiastic reaction.

"Anyway…I want you with me on this case, Billows."

Static tapped the coin slot amidst the seconds of silence.

Billows finally replied. "Is there not enough oxygen going to your brain still?"

Saint sighed. "It's my decision. And it'd be best that we see this through to the end. We started this case together, and we finish it. We still have what it takes."

"Listen, I get your frustration of not finishing this, I do, but you're in imagination land right now, buddy. Go back to Edoris and apolo–"

"Look," Saint cut Billows off.  "We took an oath, Jackson. We learn from our mistakes. You know what happens with Briggs and his habit with stale cases."

"John…Sorry, but no. No one is above the law. And right now, I got a badge I earned to prove that."

Those words were a knife stabbing into Saint, followed by a slow twisting.

Billows continued. "I…I think you should go see someone. You're not in the best place mentally. You got a family…"

227

"I'm *not*…" Saint's pain reached a breaking point. "I'm the sane one, *alright*? When I had *my eye cleaved,* and fell from that building, spending the rest of the past days slowly giving up without even realizing it, *that* was when I was insane…I'm not doing it again!" His anger rattled his whole body, from his vocal cords to his limbs.

The unresponsive static angered Saint more, fogging his mind. He thought Billows would be one of the few to understand.

"Goodbye, friend," Billows said.

The call ended. When Saint re-dialed, it went straight to voicemail. He slammed the phone and tightened his coat as the winter breeze intensified.

***

Saint invested his remaining funds into a used laptop he purchased from a tech store and a room in Motel '76. Minutes away from Central Park, it was one of the rare motels that didn't overcharge tourists for profit.

A tiny yellow room, complete with a bed, TV and an 'out of order' coffee machine.

The limited budget could keep him here until April, at best, if he conserved on a meal per day.

Saint spent the entire Christmas Day researching on the laptop. He compiled all clues in his possession into sticky notes, anchored to the motel room's wall by colored thumbtacks, connecting each related clue with red strings of yarn.

*'Make sure the manager doesn't get pissed off by these tack holes,'* Saint thought.

His new web of clues canvassed one entire section of the wall, juxtaposed to the TV, circulating the entire M.A.D. trade case.

Late that night, Saint laid in bed. He stared at Edoris' unopened gift. Eventually, he unfolded the wrapping paper, layer by layer, until he reached the box.

Inside was a photo frame, facing down. He pulled the frame and turned it around to find the first photo Edoris and Saint ever took together as a couple, during their sorority dance in college. The youthful Edoris made Saint her plus-one after losing a bet. She held the same bright, radiant smile, sans wrinkles, while Saint was slimmer all-around with a sharper jawline.

When he turned the photo to a certain angle, the picture changed to a recent selfie. It revealed two elders, wrinkled but radiant as ever down to their smiles.

Edoris' handwriting was embedded behind the photo. It read, 'If God told me to restart from zero, I would never have it any other way. Even if you were somehow the worst option. I love you always.'

*'The worst option. Always.'* Those words meshed into his head as he reflected on the past. He clutched the frame to his chest and glanced at the web of clues. His gaze shifted to the one window in his room, the view covered in nothing but snow.

# XXVI
##  Isaac Sage

### November 27, 2022, 11:11 PM

The light snowfall intensified to a blizzard. The field of snow raised to just below Isaac's knees, requiring immense energy to trudge through the field. Hunger and thirst were on the back of his mind, with surviving the harsh cold at the forefront. Wrapping his arms around his torso was the most he could prosper. An instinct reminded him that stopping would only worsen the cold into frostbite, or worse.

For a moment, Isaac lamented on his critical mistakes. But the key was to persevere and adapt. He had assessed his greatest threat head-on. He can plan a counter. For now, he would maintain the resilient mindset that something would arrive soon.

Give or take, a full day had nearly passed. It was uncertain of whether the blackouts had taken place during this trek. He saw the layers of deceit casted by this blank field. Such as the delirious thought of being on a sandy beach in the day, more intense on the eyes as the light bounced off the white canvas. Instead of cold, he felt a firm warmth as if his bare feet walked along the wooden pier 35.

In the dark, the sounds of the wind were sometimes mistaken as some sort of unearthly tune, coming from a presumed predator.

Re-immersion therapy had at least made him attuned to deciphering these as hallucinations, such as noticing the subtle distortions or lack of logic in senses like smell, sight, or hearing.

Because of this, the small speck of light that appeared in the horizon amidst the dark brought him hope. The speck became larger as he continued moving toward it, running further, ignoring the weary mind and body.

Eventually, even the snow that was once engulfing a third of Isaac's body lowered to just his ankles, eventually thinning into a slippery driveway. The curving lane traced up to the site of the lit building.

It appeared to either be a warehouse or a motel.  For Isaac, it didn't matter. It was a sign of warmth.  And a sign to call for help.

Isaac walked along the driveway, careful of the icy surface, and entered the building, met by its low-lit lobby accompanied with furnishings and coffee table magazines.  With the low lighting and the vacant receptionist's desk, it appeared as though Isaac arrived during after-hours.

Behind the desk was a wired telephone with a lone light hovered just over it. *'I should make the call now before I rest,'* Isaac thought. He called out to see if anyone was around.  Then, he rung the bell on the desk.  The weariness in him made him impatient after seconds passed, choosing to walk around the desk and use the telephone.

He tried calling Kara first, met with an immediate dead tone.  Then, he tried Rosemary.  Another dead tone.  He couldn't afford to rely on Todd again.  Not that he would answer anyway.

Bukowski, the good doctor, came to mind.  Call him to send help.  He dialed the number and waited for the rings before static emerged from the other end.

"Isaac?"  Dr. Bukowski answered.

"Doctor, good evening," Isaac replied to his relief.  "I am so sorry to trouble you at this time but I need help. Please, I'm lost and–"

A timer had suddenly rang in the distance.

"Isaac," the doctor lowered his tone, "We've tried everything, haven't we?"

A sudden sharpness sunk into Isaac's gut.  All the stress, fatigue, hunger and thirst faded.  What did it matter about the methods the doctor tried?  What did he mean by trying everything?

"I…I need to go home," Isaac muttered.

A boom emerged from the other side of the entrance, constant in rhythm. Isaac hesitated for seconds, registering an eerie nostalgia from the sounds.  The tone on the other line turned dead.

The banging raised in tempo the longer Isaac waited, followed by an intense rattling against the door.

———

Someone could be freezing out there now, the doors having locked by accident after Isaac entered. He approached with caution and opened the door. Instead of the driveway with the dark, snowy fields in the background, he was met with vast blue skies, stricken with vines of charcoal smoke, instead of the familiar hallway. Below him were a ruined maze of grey cubicles.

And instead of the building he had assessed just minutes ago, he now stood on top of the Sage Foundation tower. It was the Hellfire Incident. The senses were all accurate. There were no distortions to dictate whether this was truth or fiction. Like clockwork, Isaac, reverted to a child and found his parents by his side shielding him from the destruction.

Samuel removed his coat and covered Isaac as an intense began to singe his skin. The Sages sprinted with a sea of workers to a nearby stairway. Some attempted to jump down stairwells or rappel out the window. The cacophony of screams wouldn't stop.

They descended further, step by step, until fire erupted from the adjacent wall. A blast of heat brazed against Isaac's body.

Isaac and Samuel turned to find Gemma engulfed by the flames. He couldn't hear her. Gemma's voice repeated in his mind, melodic in a strange distortion. "You'll…you'll be okay. You'll be okay, won't you? Are you sure? Are you certain?"

A chill trickled through Isaac's spine. This shouldn't be happening.

"Gemma!" Samuel screamed in anguish. Isaac's coughs intensified, but his expression remained frozen at the sight of the inferno. His eyes dried and lips chapped from the intense heat.

Samuel leapt past the flames, his arms clamped onto Isaac the whole time, racing and evading the debris plummeting from above.

The final hurdle led to the outside where firetrucks were already stationed firing beams of water to stop the expanding hellfire.

Samuel handed the young Isaac to a firefighter, exclaiming that he had to find his wife. Isaac screamed for his father, overwhelmed and terrified.

He looked around for answers. For something to say this wasn't real. For someone to wake him.

Far in the distance stood a man in a white suit standing amid the inferno and cacophonies of screams. His entire silhouette was nothing more than a smudge on a painting from how far he was.

An orange light engulfed the man's body, inciting an intense sensation of hot knives digging into Isaac's head.

Isaac cried out for his parents, turning a gargantuan plume of black smoke tainting the blue sky instead of the spire.

The debris' slow expansion accelerated, consuming Isaac. Nowhere to see, unable to move and the deafening screams still overpowered this horrific storm.

Voices, the same as the ones who continued screaming, suddenly whispered one phrase repeatedly. *"Do I trust her?"*

'*Her?*' A mental image of Kara manifested. She sat in the mansion, alone, phone in hand. The numbers 9-1-1 flashed on the screen.   He plunged deeper into the darkness, fixated on that mental image.

***

Isaac's eyes opened to white, padded walls. A black square, centered on the farthest wall, contrasted the full-white surrounding.

He found himself still wearing his suit, his body bounded by iron chains. Braces were clamped tight on his ankles and wrists.

The truth, upsetting enough, was a slow realization as Isaac's memories returned. Isaac never left the warehouse. He never stepped back on the bus.

A mistake could be mended. This was worse. Isaac had lost.

# XXVI
## ISAAC SAGE

~~December 9, 2022, 11:11 PM~~

## XXX, XXX, XX:XX

There wasn't time to mull over this devastation. No clock, nor a hint of daylight or dusk, could depict time.

Isaac scrunched up and used his core to try to catapult his body upward, but the chains binding him restrained his movement.

The more Isaac tried to fight the chain, the more it forced his spine to curl forward. Even then, the nightmare continued to repeat in his head, causing more struggle. Almost as if he was in limbo between reality and sleep paralysis.

He fell onto his elbows and knees, crawling towards the door. The metal of the restraints clanged with a booming echo with each motion.

A shadow appeared behind the window, bobbing up and down before stopping. Isaac froze.

His helmet was still on, easing the stealth of pretending to play dead.

The shadow twisted around, seemingly peering through the window. Then, it continued moving until it vanished out of sight.

This space could very well be in a different city or country. *'There has to be way out,'* Isaac fought his exasperation for air.

A hollow clank resounded from behind the door. It creaked open to reveal a man covered in SWAT armor. And behind him stood the man from Massena.

*'It...It has to be him,'* Isaac thought, struggling to steel his breathing. *'The boss.'*

They entered the room, grabbing Isaac by the shoulders of his cloth. Isaac tried to fight back, but his depleted energy made every action futile.

He was dragged back to the indentation he formerly sat on, forming a stricken trail of grime against the white padded flooring.

The man with the devil eye waved the other armored man off. His white suit blended with the rest of the room.

He paced around Isaac in a semi-circle. "I had no idea the sedative would work for that long."

"Se…dative?" It took extreme efforts to speak. Isaac's head sizzled like someone forced his head into an active oven.

"It's *super* powerful. Not even a lethal injection to the neck was necessary. I pricked your hand, and you went out about ten seconds later."

Isaac gritted his teeth, now recalling the prickly sensation. The moment Diablo grasped his hand. A checkmate Isaac didn't realize.

"You're…" Isaac gasped. "You're…the leader?"

"I am. Name's Diablo. AKA the man you keep trying to fuck over for some reason." His tone remained neutral yet bright and carefree. "Y'kno, they have a name for you, too." Diablo waved his hands through the air. "Asesino fantasma."

Diablo pulled out a revolver from his suit jacket. "But now you need to introduce yourself. I've been trying to pry off that mask, but I guess there's some stupid tech making my guys seem more retarded than usual. I could melt it off, but that could kill you. We don't want that yet." He aimed the revolver at Isaac's helmet. "But I will if you waste my time."

"The…chains," Isaac murmured.

"The what now? Speak up."

Isaac raised his voice. "The chains…I need my fingers."

"Alright." Diablo grabbed a key with his free hand and unlocked a portion of the shackles. The wrists and ankles were still detained, but now the chain allowed Isaac to stretch his back and extend his limbs.

Isaac paused, staring at the revolver aimed at his face. His hands trembled with rage. There was no chance to strike back. Isaac raised his fingers to his helmet, pressing the sides.

"Open," said Isaac. The helmet released its grip, falling to the floor.

Diablo's eyes widened as a huge grin filled his face. "Son of a bitch. No way. No fucking way." A breath of fresh, shameful air blasted over Isaac's exposed face. "The Sage kid! Wow." Diablo scoffed. "Mistakes happen, but damn. I thought you were in therapy? Isn't that supposed to work?"

The nightmares flashed again. The tall man standing in the distance, his silhouette blurred from smoke and debris. The blaring orange light from then to the orange light Diablo generated. Two parallel feelings.

"You were there…" Isaac panted. "It was you! You burned the Sage building."

Diablo's smile faded. "I did."

Isaac struggled to remain composed. "They're all dead because of you."

"Part of the job." Diablo stroked his chin.

"The…" Isaac exhaled through his nose. "The business cards?"

"Right, those. Y'kno, I kept their business cards as a trophy keepsake."

The adrenaline swelled up inside Isaac. His tense muscles contracted.

"There ended up being way too fucking many," Diablo continued. "Sometimes I lost track of where they got misplaced–"

Isaac propelled his head into Diablo's abdomen.

The rage exploded, re-fueling his body.

"Piece of shit!" Isaac shouted. He stumbled forward for another hit.

Diablo countered with a swift, simple telegraphed hook to Isaac's face. Every frame of the nightmare continued to pour into his mind.

Diablo tightened the chains once more.

Isaac rolled across the surface, mustering energy to scream. "You piece of shit, *coward*!" His voice turned hoarse, cracking into a whimpering cry. He found his parents' murderer, the very strength he honed and refined to deliver the final blow now restrained and helpless.

"I'll kill you!" Isaac snapped. "I'll kill you if it's the last thing I do!!"

Diablo gazed at Isaac on the floor. His smile was gone, as was the tempered scowl. He slammed the door shut. And, in an instant, Isaac's consciousness faded to black.

***

Isaac awoke, still restrained, finding Diablo crouched in front of him.

Diablo's forearms rested on his bent legs, balanced. Not a single wisp of breath from him. His deformed eye was calmer, the demonic iris focusing on Isaac.

"I've been through a lot of shit recently," Diablo said. "You should know that means something if I have to admit it. Especially since we've only just met."

Isaac pondered on what he could do to Diablo if he was freed of his shackles.

"And it has caused me to think—well, rethink a lot of things." Diablo looked inward. "What is fear?"

Isaac remained silent. *'What an odd, bullshit thing to ask,'* he thought.

"What an odd, bullshit philosophical thing, right? It doesn't feel like the right timing, but I need to vent. Do you fear me?"

Isaac's tone strained with contempt, inflicting pain onto his lungs. He hacked up some air in the process. "Fuck you."

"Good. Good, good." Diablo balanced on his toes. "I accidentally killed my friend. Well, I considered him a friend in retrospect, at least. He only shared a hint of fearing me once. Every other time, when others flinched or cowered as I exploded like an atomic bomb, he was unfazed."

Isaac rolled his eyes.

"He could've hid it, right? A lot of people hide what they feel, because, you know, professionalism." Diablo gazed around the room. "He could've left at any time, too. Not the most ethical job." Diablo let out a light chuckle. "So, you don't fear me. Do you respect me?"

Isaac locked eyes at him. "I would strangle you to death and pummel you over and *over* until your face turns to vapor. I'd stop to let the pain set in. And just when it turns dull, I'll start again. Does that answer your question?"

"To tell me that must be some kind of respect." Diablo sighed with a shrug. "I'd apologize, but then I'd be lying."

Isaac stared, so perplexed at Diablo's mannerism that it left his expression vacant. Sorrow, for a moment, filled his voice.

"Why kill them?" Isaac asked.

"I told you. Part of the job."

"Why?" Isaac repeated.

"I'm not repeating myself."

"Were they a stupid thing you got mad over? With your fucking child tantrum? So, you made it your job? Was that it?"

"They were extra pocket change, kid. That's it."

It was the worst day of Isaac's life. For Diablo, it was another Monday to freelance.

Isaac sank his head into his knees and let out a gut-wrenching shriek. Release all the pain bounded within. Instead, it returned tenfold. He screamed again, too weak to sob.

As the silence returned, Diablo resumed. "I think I learned the subordinates and partners that feared me, never respected me. But you do." He stood back up, towering over the hunchback Isaac. "You tried taking down my empire. You know the impact I bring. You knew what you were doing."

Diablo kicked Isaac's head. The momentum slammed the latter's body to the floor.

He continued, "I'll make sure every ounce of your body hurts. For every every dollar you made me lose, I will spend a day beating you to near death. Maybe I'll take a note from your approach to beating me to a pulp."

Every hit was harder than the last. From bruising to ruptures to bones turning brittle. Isaac caved, his mind only able to question when the pain would stop.

Eventually, the blows stopped. Half-dazed, Diablo, now a blurred blob, dissipated in the air. Once again, Isaac passed out.

***

Thinking about time in this room contributed to a growing insanity. The longer Isaac was awake, the more likely he had to not think about time. The nightmare returned in inconsistent beats.

Every passing minute, Isaac tried to focus on breaking the chains. He ignored the rings of blood forming on his wrists, the excess seeping downward. The more he yanked, he thought, the more they would wear down to the point of breaking.

He caught a reflection of his face on his helmet, frail in a sickening pale hue. Every torture corroded Isaac. Every meal was scheduled before Diablo's torture so Isaac could regurgitate it, leading to malnutrition.

Multiple punches across his face formed stacks of welts. The swelling made it difficult to breathe. Repetitive kicks against his core intensified this with nausea. Sometimes, Diablo pulled out brass knuckles that resulted in lacerations.

Near the end of every session, Diablo injected something into Isaac's neck. Whatever it was made Isaac restless, unable to discern reality from fiction.

"I never tested it before," said Diablo. "Shocking, I know. I'm told an animal takes over." He grinned. "I'd love to see the damage it'd do."

He was right. Something turned his mind into a nonstop frenzy. People popped in and out of his vision playing out full scenarios, affecting his cognition. All he could think about was every person that wronged him. Even the tiniest inconvenience filled him with an irrational rage. To be clear-headed was nigh and far more difficult than what he'd experienced so far.

Some thoughts managed to slip through before the primal discomfort, such as the oddity that they didn't take the helmet for research or safekeeping. Or where in the world is Kara? Is she okay?

In later sessions, Diablo instead spewed words of his own prides and passions. His brother, his production. How his father was a hypocrite for being disappointed in his line of work. Something called a unicorn. Diablo mentioned Sage Foundation once, though Isaac struggled to remember the full sentence. It was hard to keep track of things now in his state of mind.

On one session, Diablo arrived with a few photographs in hand. He tossed them on the floor.

"Take a look at what my guy shot," said Diablo.

———

Isaac's blurred sight examined a worn building, cracked and covered with vines, shot from different angles. Other photos showed a woman seen through the window of the vine-riddled building in one photo, and then walking around the city in a couple of others.

His eyes widened as his vision's clarity returned, connecting details to memory. The building was his mansion. And the woman was Kara.

"No…" Isaac muttered. He screamed again in denial.  He tried to struggle out of his restraints.

Diablo shoved his shoe into Isaac's mouth mid-scream. He flashed an intense grin.  "I wonder what we could make her do. Or how long before we get a picture of her corpse."

Diablo dislodged his shoe and walked out. Isaac screamed in denial.

After that, Diablo refused to bring up the photos again. Perhaps he was waiting for new photos. Or maybe he knew the thought of uncertainty alone would drive Isaac mad.

Kara. What would she do?  What could she do?  She could be forced to confess about Isaac's vendetta. Or she would be so terrified that she would reach out to the NMPD for help. This, and the accompanying nightmare left Isaac in his own terror.

*'Kara knows. She knows.'*

In the continuous, inescapable cycle of pain every notion of rationality was slipping.

***

More torture sessions continued. And soon, the gap of time stretched. Longer and longer, wrestling with his own thoughts in the white void.

A continuous, endless stretch with no one stopping by, not even in his hallucinations.

It was then Isaac realized through his frenzied mind: Diablo stopped showing up. The burning sensation hadn't occurred in his head either.

The gap of time stretched further. Enough of his consciousness returned to decide: Escape was now or never.

Isaac rolled around, moving his arms and legs into and away from his core, jittering the chain. His emaciated muscles tore with every pull, pushing Isaac to the verge of screaming.

The metal grinded for so long. The parts of his body embedded by the chains had turned so malleable that he feared the chains would saw through him, like a sharpened knife on the finest cut of meat.

But he paid no mind to the exhaustion, or the fear. The worst would be to stay here and do nothing.

As long as it took to break. It could've been minutes or hours. Screaming and tearing in this obnoxiously white bubble smeared by the numerous footsteps.

Then, a metal snap echoed through the entire room. His wrists, still shackled, moved toward his chin. His legs stretched out to alleviate the prolonged stress on his body. The chain broke.

It was the most utter disbelief Isaac had felt in ages. Was it a trap?

For now, Isaac yelled in his room for several minutes to catch someone's attention.

On the last note of his tired lungs, an armored guard slammed open the door.

Isaac kept his back turned on the guard. He hid the loosened restraints around his hands.

"Being so damn annoying, and now you're quiet," the guard spat. "You miss your torture, huh?"

The guard moved closer. A foot away, Isaac whipped out the chain, wrapping the guard's ankles. With one strong, swift pull, the guard fell.

Isaac wrapped the chain around the guard's neck, keeping his distance from the flailing hands.

As the stress amplified, the hallucinations returned. Isaac fought hard, focusing on his strength on the chains tightening around the guard's neck. There was no opportunity to lose again.

Tighter, using every fiber of every muscle in his body, the chain extending in each direction, until–

A harsh snap echoed through the room, leaving Isaac breathless. The man's hands fell limp.

This entire struggle spanned a few minutes. All it took for this man to die was a few minutes. Or was it hours?

He looked at the man three times, waiting for him to move.  But nothing. Not even the lungs expanded his body. A sudden, trembling remorse welled up throughout Isaac's body.

"I'm sorry," he muttered, before the frenzy blanketed him once more.

Isaac equipped his helmet, grabbed the guard's rifle and exited the white room into a narrow, musty-yellow corridor.   The wall's pores smelled of oil and gasoline. The curved path made it difficult to peer past any blind spots.

As others sets of footsteps were getting louder, Isaac sprinted around for the exit. The alarm began to blare through the facility, bathing the yellow halls in red.  The footsteps turned to stomping.

He turned every corner, passing by a map with a notable empty building marked 'Unicorn.' Diablo spoke about Unicorn.

As enemies appeared, Isaac wildly sprayed rifles, keeping his momentum until he stormed through a door, leading into darkness.  The darkness soon turned into a stony street beneath a navy sky, surrounded by neon lights.

He looked back while running.  An abandoned tunnel.  It was underground.

At the corner was rusted sign, labeled '127th St.' Across from there, a board-ed train station, labeled 'Queens – 127th St.'

No one was behind him after a few blocks.  He finally slowed down and cut right, knowing by impulse it would take him into the active part of Queens.

Dehydration and starvation took hold of his vision and muscles, blurring and cramping respectively.  Although he was conscious enough to direct his movement, and sense everything around him, his mind began to disconnect. He watched himself move in this out-of-body experience. Like controlling a char-acter in a video game.

*'Diablo knows,'* he thought, still fixated on the nightmare.  *'They know. Is Kara safe?  Kara knows. Is she okay?  She knows.'*

The rage once again fell in and out, uncomfortable as his bodies twitched and flexed out of his controls. His thoughts slipped between conscious and unconscious.

The streets soon cluttered with people. The neon multiplied in intensity. A television on a display window caught Isaac's eye. An active newsreel played over a car accident on the freeway. The report highlighted the date.

Isaac's dismay sobered his vision for a moment. The blurred numbers solidified into crisp digits.

It was March 3rd, 2023.

# XXVII
## Kara Culver

## December 25, 2022, 8:02 PM

Snowflakes stuck to the kitchen's windowpane, the lit Christmas tree caught in its subtle reflection. Kara swirled a glass of red wine in her hand. She set a plate of cookies to the side. A gift from a retirement home she volunteered to work overtime. Underneath a tree was one gift she wrapped for Isaac.

There was no answer or sign from him. Even Rosemary, who Kara met for the first time, stopped by to check on him. She lived in higher stages of fear and worry with each passing day. Every minute turned into an eternity of thinking about where Isaac was now.

Rosemary's kindness and company subdued those feelings for a while. On some days, they spent the day conversing on clothes, complimenting each other's beauty, music, movies and any other minor thing that came to mind.

The more Kara learned about Rosemary, the more she recognized the potential in a woman that was capable of conquering anything she set her mind to. When she realized it.

But with each passing day, Rosemary had continued to ask for Isaac. With each the day, the answers remained the same. That he was still on his trip, or he'll back eventually. The latter used to reassure both Rosemary and her.

Eventually, Rosemary no longer showed up at the mansion. It may have been the waning confidence in Kara's words that made Rosemary assume this was an indirect way of saying he wasn't interested.

If only, Kara felt, it was that much simpler. Of course, one could only spend so much time waiting for someone until it reached a breaking point.

***

January 25th, 2023. Noon. Kara took initiative to re-scout the warehouses Isaac explored. The Tipsy Tapp, Queens, the coastline, and many others. Isaac had mentioned finding the boss' location, but never shared the specifics.

The adrenaline booster she had kept for him was left at the mansion in his bedroom. If he had gone there, he was unprepared.

If he were alive, where was he? If captured, what could they be doing to him? If dead…Kara didn't want to continue that question.

In exchange for the subtraction of sleep, focus and calmness was her waking routine filled with multiplied panic and insomnia.

The searches ailed Kara with worse news rather than beneficial results. She needed to stop and wait. She needed to distract herself.

As always, Kara turned to gardening for therapy. The herbs were reaching their full bloom. Tree saplings Kara had planted earlier in the year were sprouting. The oak trees needed to be trimmed eventually.

Her fruit trees over the years had grown to be resilient to the cold weather. Even now, they bore fruit, with the leaves rich and vibrant.

A chirping whistled from her lemon tree. Kara examined deeper to find a trio of blue jays nested within the tree, huddled together against the chilled temperatures of the day. Kara smiled. The first sweet thing in a while. To create a safe environment for someone else. It was happy. It was simple.

From the corner of Kara's eye, something glimmered from afar in the dark green shade down the cobblestone road.

It was a black circular lens. Some kind of bush shifted behind the lens in an irregular pattern.

Kara entered the mansion and went to the kitchen sink. Perhaps her mind was playing tricks after sitting in the daylight for too long.

She peered through the window once again to find that black circular lens. Then the bush rose upward, revealing it to be a lanky person holding a camera. He stumbled away.

That photographer…it would be too much of a coincidence for him to be connected to Isaac's disappearance. Or could it?

She rushed out, trying to pursue the photographer. But by the time she ran a third of the way out into the road, the photographer had already disappeared into the green horizon.

***

There was no sign of the photographer since that day. But ever since then, Kara's caution and paranoia skyrocketed. Every hour or half-hour, she'd check her outer surroundings to see if anyone was watching her.

Any bizarre noise or visual prompted her to assess and identify the source before continuing her normal routine, even if it took several hours.

She balanced her routine schedule to focus on gardening in the mornings and continue forth with her day searching until the sun set. Now, in the night, she was compelled to sleep with the lights on.

The chirping became a comforting sound filling the morning's quiet. Kara tended to her lemon tree to find the blue jays growing their nest and family. They'd even fly together around the mansion's nature like a tiny murmuration.

On one morning, Kara's reprieve was cut short with the sight of a stranger dressed in a brown jacket and slacks.

He didn't hide like the photographer did and instead stood in the middle of the road with a casual smirk. The expression formed wrinkles on his forehead, pointing to his thin, black head of hair.

Kara stood up and walked to the mansion's back entrance. Her plan was the moment she'd enter, she'd lock the doors and wait. Isaac's promise rang in her head whenever she thought of even calling the police. She needed to have faith. Wait and hide.

As Kara reached the backdoor, the man ambled in from the other side of the rear door. She froze, her hand hovering over the scuffed handle.

The moment she touched the handle, the stranger yanked the door open and snatched her hand while maintaining that same, alarming smile.

Kara's eyes locked onto the gripped hand for several seconds. Her heart raced with uncertainty. Curious, she darted to the man's other hand, finding it armed with a black pistol equipped with a silencer.

Kara's lips shuddered. She controlled her hyperventilation as much as possible and conjured the confidence to speak.

"Please…"

The hitman exhaled through his nose. "People want you dead."

"I swear I won't bother anyone or anything…" Her breath shuddered. "*Please.*"

The hitman locked his squinted, blue eyes with Kara's. "How much?"

"How much?" She asked, stunned by the question.

"Boss isn't paying much. You got that Sage money, though. I want that." The hitman gestured the gun to handle. He entered the mansion and shut the rear door. "Go on then."

If this hitman was here for her, what did this mean for Isaac? This had to be the culmination of his actions. A misstep that Kara allowed.

Kara guided the hitman into the living area. He rubbed his chest, half-wincing with each circular motion.

"So, where's the safe?" He kept the gun aimed at her.

"I…" Kara needed to think fast. The money was an easy alternative, but there was a strong feeling that no matter what she did, it would all end with a bullet through her head or heart. "I have a trust account."

"Fair enough," the hitman nodded. "Set it up."

Kara grabbed her laptop and sat down at the kitchen table. The hitman stood behind her, rubbing his chest once again.

Discomfort in the chest. Could he be sick?

Kara revealed her bank info. $187,622. Residuals of money saved and funds Isaac sent her from his trust account.

The hitman peered over Kara's shoulder. "That can't be Sage money."

"Doesn't mean I have access to his money…"

The hitman pressed the gun against Kara's head. "I'll count to ten for you to come up with something. One… Two. Three. Four."

"We have a safe full of jewelry," Kara fibbed. "You can sell it."

"Why didn't you say that before?"

"It belongs to them…I don't like touching it."

The hitman shook his head. He yanked her up by the elbow. Kara jumped from his ice-cold touch.

""They're dead and you're letting good jewelry sit and collect dust. *Now* my patience is thinning. Get the fuck moving."

Kara led the hitman upstairs. His chest discomfort returned. And his ice-cold hand from before…low blood flow. It could be a heart condition.

Another clue for a weakness would be sufficient. Halfway, she turned to get another look at the hitman.

The hitman fired a shot into the stairway. "Who said you could look back?"

Kara stuttered. "I'm sorry. I'm so sorry."

Then it clicked. A weak heart couldn't handle too much stress. A heavy load of intense energy. A dose…

The adrenaline booster. It was in the bathroom.

"Tell me…" Kara asked with a concerned tone. "Does this have to do with Isaac?"

"That ain't my job to say."

"Is…" Her tone wavered. "Is he alive?"

"I'm not playing these games."

"If you could just let me know–"

"I'm not. Playing."

Kara turned to the hitman and launched one kick at his torso. The hitman fell down the stairs firing another shot through the air. Kara sprinted up to the bathroom and locked the door.

She snatched the EpiPen, startled by the instant rattling of the door. Her first instinct was to unlock the door, and retreat to the farthest side of the wall. Pretend to be hysterical. She withdrew into the bathtub, crouched and covered her head.

The hitman slammed open the door.

"I'm so sorry," she sobbed.

He reached for her neck and slapped her with the back of his hand.

She continued sobbing. "I don't know what to do…"

"You either pay or end up dead!" The hitman spat at Kara. He gritted his teeth, the grip loosening for a moment.

Kara jolted past the hitman's loosened grasp and stabbed the EpiPen into his neck.

The hitman grabbed her wrist with his free hand and re-aimed the gun at her torso, pinning her to the bathroom wall.

Kara reeled back and headbutted the hitman's nose dead-on. The hitman fired two shots, both grazing her abdomen.

The hitman's grip loosened again, letting the pen inject into his neck. His thin breath hastened in an off-beat rhythm.

Kara snatched the gun from him and pushed him off. He slouched down, hyperventilating with half-shut eyes, the pupils dilating in similar fashion.

She lined the gun with his head and pulled the trigger, brought back to the days of forced into hunting deer with her dad.

The hitman ducked past the shot with ease. The adrenaline had already set in, enhancing his reflexes to the maximum.

Kara fired again, one of the two shots grazing the side of his bald head as he pivoted his body. His hands contorted into claws, wrapping around her neck before flinging her straight out of the bathroom.

*'Turn and make a point-blank shot,'* Kara thought dazed yet recovering quickly. Before she could, the hitman pulled Kara toward him and slammed her against the nearby wall. He repeated the action with more power.

A wet trail began to drip down her face as the actions repeated. He turned her around to look her in the eyes as he began strangling her.

Kara clawed into the hitman's hand, shedding lines of blood as a last resort. Every reserve of air dwindled. The hitman didn't relent.

"You asked if Isaac is dead," the hitman yelled. "Yeah, I killed him. Just… like…this!"

Seconds later, her fingers fell limp. She waited for the world to turn dark. To see Gemma, Samuel and…Isaac.

A sudden flow of air returned. The hitman, in contrast, heaved and gasped. He squirmed on the floor panicking.

The gun lay by the bathroom's entrance. Kara dragged herself to the gun, suddenly being yanked back by the hitman.

She retaliated with punches and kicks in the tug-of-war struggle, the gun within arm's reach.

Within second's worth of sudden energy, she was thrown to the side and the gun ended up in the hitman's hands.

He aimed at her head. Not even enough time for life to flash before Kara's eyes, when in a sudden nanosecond–

*Click. Click, click.*

Out of ammo. Kara stood up as the hitman's attention redirected to himself. He clutched his chest before collapsing, his eyes rolling to the back of his head. The remaining air in his lungs hissed out of his agape mouth.

Kara grabbed her medical supplies. The blood around her head stemmed from a small gash on her forehead. She stitched her arm, bandaged it, and then applied two bandages to her head wound and the graze on her abdomen.

She dug a deep hole and buried the corpse outside the mansion afterwards. The hardest part was getting the body down the stairs. Step by step, with caution to her own injuries, the corpse's slow tumble reached the base of the stairway.

With the gun being a rare relic of self-defense, Kara kept it in case any other enemies tried to approach her as this hitman did. She reloaded it with the little ammunition she found in the hitman's clothes before burying him.

The weakness in her limbs returned. Kara laid on the couch, resting and reflecting on what transpired.

Then, she wept. There was no signal, no build-up, other than recanting the hitman's words.

*'I killed Isaac.'*

The fractured state of her mind intensified the delirious feeling of losing it all. A feeling of no return.

***

February 27th, 2023. She found herself, in a trance-like state, standing in front of the glass entryway into the NMPD. The outside cold stung her face while her palms slickened with sweat. She could peer into the building noticing the officers either bantering or working over their desks.

All she wanted was to do the right thing for her and Isaac. The last remaining spark of optimism lingered in her. It all funneled toward one thought. *'He can't be dead.'*

She placed her hand on the door handle, ready to come clean and seek help.

Several seconds passed and it didn't budge. Neither did Kara. Her mind bounced back to the promise she made to Isaac.

Then, a female officer opened the door. "Everything okay, miss?" she asked, concerned.

Kara continued to stare, frozen speechless, peering past the female officer's shoulder. She then realized one of the officers inside was Billows. His arms were folded, catching Kara's stare from afar.

"I'm sorry, there's this bakery, my favorite bakery," Kara said, "the one right around the corner, and I saw someone stealing goods and I felt awful about it. I wanted to inform you guys, but maybe the shoplifter was homeless and hungry, and I–"

"Say no more," the officer replied. "Stealing is no excuse for anyone. We'll take care of it. You get home and stay warm, miss."

"Thank you, officer."

Kara quickly departed for the mansion. After a block down, she fell to her knees in the middle of the concrete, uncaring of how shockingly cold it was to her body and broke into tears.

She couldn't stop them. For that final hopeful ember dissipated. It was coming to terms with her true reality: Isaac Sage was dead.

***

March 3rd, 2023. Kara strolled around the park as a murmuration of birds flew just above.

To her realization, she rarely traveled even though she had a mental bucket list. Like exploring the vastness of the Grand Canyon. Or the mystical nature of the Northern Lights. Perhaps she could get lost in Egypt or Hawaii.

One day.

Kara arrived home later in the evening. She made dinner, rested with some wine. A slow, regrettable return to normalcy.

Later that evening, Kara flipped through channels to find something interesting. Her eyes grew heavy with each passing click.

A sudden boom shook the mansion, startling her awake. It came from the front entrance.

The gun was in the bedroom upstairs. She jumped, sprinting straight toward the kitchen to grab the largest kitchen knife.

She crept to the entrance. The door was wide open with no one in sight.

Another sound emerged from her left. She gripped the knife tightly and shifted to the direction of the sound: a man of familiar build and clothing stood huddled over the stairway's railing.

He dropped his helmet onto the floor, revealing a tuft of messy yet familiar brown hair. Her eyes welled up.

"Isaac?" Kara ran toward him, examining his face. Worn, fatigue. Looking as if he was at death's door. It was him.

She guided him up the stairway. His entire body trembled with the effort to ascend.

She embraced him. From the bony shoulders to the paper-thin stature, he felt so fragile. It provoked a worry that he would break with even the most moderate pressure.

"Oh my god, Isaac…" Kara held back the tears in her eyes.

"Is…" Isaac said, "What day is it? Please…tell me it's only December."

His mannerisms appeared disconnected, focused on one thought or action. Rest and reprieve were important. She carried him over to his bedroom.

"It's March 3rd. 2023," she said.

Isaac banged his fist against the door frame, scaring her. "No!" he screamed. He sped over to the bathroom, turning on the faucet. "No, no, no, no, no."

Isaac slapped himself with water. The harshness turned his cheeks blistering red. "A dream…still a dream," he muttered.

"Isaac, what happened?"

"There was no…no time." He leaned against the sink, using it as a crutch. His state of mind made it difficult to communicate. The image intensified the horrors he endured.

This couldn't happen again.

"I'm sorry, Isaac, but this has gone too far," Kara relented. "This never would've happened if I stopped you in the beginning."

"What?"

"We were in over our heads. I was about to tell the police that you were missing. Or dead, or, fuck, I don't know. Had I done it sooner, you would've–"

"You…" Isaac once again mustered up the energy to regain his voice, "You were never supposed to be a part of this."

"But I was, Isaac. I suffered, and you suffered for it. We can't do this. We have to contact the police about this.

Isaac's face grimaced. His bottom lip trembled.

Kara continued, "They can handle it. I'll tell them everything. I can't see you–"

"Why would you say that…"

"What? Isaac, you know how much I care about you. You deserve to live. You deserve what's bes–"

Isaac roared from the top of his lungs. *"Why would you say that!!"*

Kara jumped back. He kept his still eyes locked at the sink, hunched over like a beast.

She'd never seen this side of him. It was a feral violence pooled in his eyes. A willingness to stop anyone in his way.

Anyone.

———

"I…I didn't mean that," Kara said. "I'm tired. And I know you must be tired too." She paused, trying to find the right words to bring Isaac back to normal. "I'm sorry. You should rest…We'll talk about it tomorrow."

She entered her bedroom, slipping underneath the comforters to slumber. Frightened, she convinced herself Isaac came from a good place. He needed to rest.

*'We'll rest,'* she thought, *'and then we can talk about what to do next.'*

She thought about the murmuration of the birds from earlier today. The one and only time she would see that soothing motion. There would be no turning back.

Nearly lulled to sleep, something suddenly pressed her down into the bed before every sense in her body became nothing. Still silence.

# XXVIII
## DIABLO

### February 9, 2023, 12:05 PM

When the first six days of Isaac's torture took place, an electric sensation of ecstasy surged through Diablo. The person that tampered with his plans was in his grasp. And now, he was an entitled brat. An entitled Sage brat whom stepped into the underground world dressed up for a revenge mission. It was comical.

Diablo bled that comedy into his torture methods. He found joy at the idea of making his life worse. Had he continued life in normalcy, the consequences would be granule like sugar ants.

The joyous feeling, however, came and vanished like the snap of a rubber band.

Grief overcame Diablo afterward. As if his torture was adding to his loss rather than a victory. He'd wash his bloodied knuckles off in the restroom, staring at the welts painting the rushing water to a red hue.

Mentally, Diablo decomposed into a frail shade of his former self. Physically, his body drenched in its own sweat, even in the coldest environments.

Then there were the spiking headaches, accompanied with fatigue and clusters of bright, snow-like white spots in his vision, like damage on a film reel. The cocaine stopped numbing his pain.

The intent to keep Isaac locked up and tortured diminished as his worsening health signified an ominous fate.

He thought the tortures would bring some clarity into seeing his own actions as something good. A step forward rather than backward.

But the warehouses were being raided. The income was falling. Diablo's men were scattered, with these random substitutes wandering this loaned facility.

Gus, an essential glue to the business, was gone. The vision of his empire, to be a staple part of Sage Foundation, was fading.

He decided to leave the facility for a scenic drive around the city after the 2 months of Isaac's torture.

He drove to areas he visited often as a kid. The old elementary school he attended. The pier his family relaxed at and had ice cream until his father forced them to scurry back home.

Even the obscure corners of some intersections brought Diablo back to when he counted skyscrapers with Carlos as they waited for the crosswalk signal.

Diablo refused to return to the warehouse until his health improved. Even after several days, the improvement never occurred.

On February 14th, Diablo thought of a benefactor to pass his legacy on to. Someone that had been established in the underground. Someone who held the right balance of power, passion and potential.

He called Mr. Velcro, inquiring if he knew where Commander was located. Mr. Velcro provided his last known whereabouts, while inquiring if Diablo was aiming to collaborate.

"Something like that," Diablo muttered before hanging up the phone. Commander stowed himself in a textile factory 30 miles out northeast.

When Diablo entered amid the loud machinery, Commander was standing on the upper railing with a Rubik's cube in hand. His unzipped high-collar jacket revealed a vibrant, cartoon shirt complementing his blonde braids.

He paused at the sight of Diablo. His calm face contorted into a scowl.

"The fuck do you want?!" Commander shouted. His workers turned to him.

Diablo raised his hands. "You're not gonna ask how I got here? We have no beef."

"You're in the black market, obviously you knew a guy that knew a guy. And bullshit. Don't think because you're head honcho that my guys won't fuck you up."

"They know not to."

Diablo examined the glaring eyes and the machinery before a current of air blasted just past his neck. The indirect force brought some pain to the affected area. He shifted back to Commander, whose metallic-laced arm aimed at Diablo.

Diablo emphasized his raised hands as a peaceful gesture.

"Stop playing," said Commander.

"Just wanna talk."

Commander sparked a wide grin. "You signing off your last will to me?"

Diablo lowered his brow, keeping his gaze on Commander. His lips impulsively frowned, out of his command.

Commander's grin faded. He assessed Diablo's expression for a minute. "Take the stairway up here."

Diablo followed Commander's direction. The stairs led straight to where he stood, looking out at all the kinetic movement in the factory.

At a closer glance, Commander's face showed discolored bruises. There were also patches of bandages around him, using the same skin color.

"You look like shit," said Diablo.

"Taking notes from you and that stupid eye."

"So you do admire me."

"I do admire the guy that looks like he wanted to be a man-cat, and backed out just at the eye."

"That…makes no sense."

Commander flattened his lips and leaned his upper torso over the railing. "Why're you here?"

"You want a piece of Sage Foundation? I could put in a good word for you."

"I freelance. And besides, I think I'm gonna take a sabbatical for a while. Maybe a year max."

"Must be nice. What about my warehouses? We've had a history where you tried to smuggle my stuff. It can be yours."

"Is your life on the end? Is this a set-up?"

"Neither," Diablo fibbed. It was his own volition to not place his death on a plate for everyone to salivate over. "Just putting perspective on careers."

"I don't need hand-me-downs."

"That so?"

"Besides, maybe you got a point for once. There's always shit going down in this market."

Diablo remained silent.  He digested Commander's refusal.  A bit of a surprise, really.

"We could always fight it out," Diablo finally spoke.

"There's that psycho talk."

Diablo sighed. "Who am I kidding? We'd end up blowing everything to kingdom come anyway.

"That's how our last scuffle went."

"Almost died."

"Yep."

"We're all gonna die.  Might as well die the way you want with everything you could do. My brother, uncle and cousins would've liked to die *years* later surrounded by family."

Diablo assessed Commander's last words. He wondered if he made the most out of his life more than his father.  His brother certainly did. He turned back to the stairway.

"Offer's yours if you come back and no one's usurped my throne," said Diablo.

Commander scoffed. "Aw, shut up." He kept his gaze in the same direction, but his tone began to tremble. "I'll keep that in mind."

***

February 15th. Diablo pulled up to Carlos' driveway. The sunlight beamed against his car's waxed surface.

'*Shit,*' Diablo thought as he glanced at his reflection in the side view mirror. He forgot to add makeup to his malformed eye. He covered his bad eye with one hand, walking to the front door.

The rhythms of Salsa clamored from within the house. It was no surprise for his brother to be playing music in the middle of the day.

Diablo tapped on the door. No answer. He stepped back onto the lawn, looking through the window from afar to find Carlos and Vanessa in the house.

In their arms, caressed between them as they danced, was a smiling newborn wrapped in a white cotton blanket. His soft, round black eyes were identical to Vanessa. His wide, goofy smile was a copy of Carlos.

Carlos offered his index finger to the newborn, who pulled it back and forth. His tiny hands wrapped around half of his index finger. The newborn broke out in giggles while both Vanessa and Carlos smiled at their child with this look of happiness. Gratitude. Peace.

An envious thorn prickled at Diablo's heart. He had no idea the baby was born. The baby was beautiful. They lived this free life to dance in the middle of the day.

It was…happy. The happiness was backed by a certainty that Carlos' life, moving forward, would continue to flourish.

Diablo imagined his own presence at the hospital the night Vanessa gave birth. He dropped the hand covering the scarred eye.

Diablo turned back to the car. With one hand clamped onto the handle, he waited for a minute with the naïve thought that some voice would call to him.

That, in gradual realization, was pointless. Diablo entered his car and drove out past the blessing his brother was able to manifest.

***

March 3rd. Going through the building protocol, and stepping into the dark office, Diablo found Mr. Velcro sitting at his desk basked in the purple light.

Velcro remained focused on writing in the same giant black book. His bodyguard Emin stood by the far corner.

"You ever move from that spot?" Diablo asked.

"There must be a perfect reason for you to show up unannounced." Mr. Velcro locked eyes with Diablo.

"Don't worry. I won't take long." Diablo bent his neck left, emitting a hollowed crack. "Sage Foundation isn't for me."

Mr. Velcro raised his brow. "What made you conclude this?"

"Business is dwindling. I know when to fold."

Mr. Velcro returned his attention to the book. "I won't try to convince you. But you understand you're calling it quits before the race is finished?"

"Like I said," Diablo tried to refrain from bringing up his health, "I know when to eject."

"Coward," Mr. Velcro spited. "You have my men and a base while you recover from the fallout. Yet you choose to grovel at your own failures and let that define you."

Diablo sighed. "I'm also 99% sure I'm dying."

Mr. Velcro stopped writing in his book.

"Glad to know that gets your attention," Diablo continued. "Every day it gets harder to wake up. My adrenaline is fading. I'm going blind."

"Even though I tried, a premature death still follows you."

"Sure."

"What do you plan to do?"

"I'm gonna wire my remaining money over to my family. As for everything else…beats me."

Velcro looked up at Diablo. "You had potential. You know that right?"

"Coming from you, that's something," Diablo said through a deflated tone. "I think past me would've tried to shoot you in the head for saying that." Diablo paused, processing the reality of his words. The flare of energy he had before was gone, even with adrenaline-inducing drugs. "And that saddens me."

Diablo observed with his lingering vision a slight frown painted on Mr. Velcro's face. He wandered back to his book.

"One of the most saddening things to see is the fire in someone's eyes dying out, when they're still breathing and standing."

"What are you trying to say?"

"Aren't your enemies still out there? The NMPD. The Yakuza. Your other nuisances."

Diablo leaned back in his chair. "What about them?"

———

"You should leave a permanent mark of your wrath. Even if you don't decide that, allow Emin to help you." Mr. Velcro motioned Emin over.

"Are you sure, sir?" asked Emin. His German accent was soft, set in a deep bass.

Mr. Velcro smiled. "I'll be fine, Emin. Go with him to the facility."

Emin nodded and met eyes with Diablo. "Whatever you need," Emin said. "Boss' orders."

Diablo nodded.

"How you conduct yourself in your last moments is how you will be remembered," said Mr. Velcro. "We might not have talked much, but it was fun watching your progress while it lasted, Mr. Diablo."

"Can I make a request?"

"Go on."

"The Unicorn is stowed away in a building. Use it. It's all I have left as a legacy."

Mr. Velcro paused, then nodded in agreement. "I'll honor it."

Diablo readied to leave when the information regarding Isaac Sage popped up in his mind. He leaned toward Mr. Velcro.

"One last thing."

***

Diablo returned to the warehouse on March 4th. He was resolved to tackle what he could do for the next few days.

Unfortunately, more misfortune followed. One of the main infantrymen approached Diablo, accompanied by his squad. They informed him of Isaac's escape from captivity the night before.

"He killed one of the guards. We are looking into the captive's whereabouts across the city."

Diablo had not told them about his true identity. But it wasn't their business to know anyway. It was, however, their business to make sure he didn't escape.

Diablo shot the vocal guard 5 times out of impulse. His body buckled to the floor, bleeding to death as the rest of the squadron looked on, standing frigid in their V-shaped formation.

Diablo pointed at the man in the middle of the row. "You're leader now. Clean this base out," he commanded. "I need all our supplies gone. Get whatever extra hands you need; I couldn't give a shit. Go!"

The men saluted in unison and branched out. Diablo cut past a corner of the hallway and entered a bunker room. The room was littered with junk and a few lockers.

If Diablo were Isaac, he would return to the facility to settle things. Isaac's vendetta was clear. The emotion behind it was true. War was approaching his doorstep.

While the men scurried back and forth across the hallways, dumping shipments and equipment tied to drug trading, Diablo paced with a surreal calmness in the bunker.

There was a new ending imagined: One imagined by Velcro's acknowledgement of his potential. The potential to bring a roaring inferno to his enemies.

Carlos' life molded to his desired dreams.

Commander's words to die in your way. A chance not bestowed onto many dying lives.

Diablo opened the middle locker, revealing multiple syringes of M.A.D, ranging a wide spectrum of colors. Some included prototypes of the Unicorn compound–a more lethal volatile version. Guaranteed adrenaline and much, much more.

The vials stared back at him, signaling a reminder of his beginnings. The start of his career, his rapid ascent and his mistakes. Every step that brought him here.

Alongside his planned finale, Unicorn would be part of the legacy he was proud to leave behind.

Footsteps echoed in the room, prompting Diablo to turn around. It was Emin, standing by the entryway.

"What do you want?" Diablo asked.

"Assuring you're safe."

"I'm fine." Diablo glided his hand along the vials. "Velcro's got a lot of trust in you, Emin."

"He does."

"I have a bad feeling we may be facing an army soon. Can I trust you to help without fail?" Diablo was certain Emin would fail with the rest of Velcro's troops. But he would be a useful pawn, nonetheless.

Emin scowled at Diablo. "I can handle it. Do you have a plan?"

"I wait and take the lead when the timing's right. I'll keep these generous donations at bay until I choke the necessary ones into a corner."

"When will the timing be right?"

"Don't worry about that."

Diablo grabbed a syringe and pulled liquid from one of the vials. He placed a cap on the syringe and tossed it to Emin.

Emin caught the vial.

"Use it as a last resort," said Diablo. "Give me some privacy."

Emin departed, examining the vial in his hand with skepticism.

Diablo injected his neck until the syringe was emptied. There was no change. No rise in power, no altered mutation. Diablo was certain he needed more.

He injected the second dose, gritting his teeth as the feeling of acid waste coursed through his blood. The skin around his eye burned as if it was planted onto a warming stove top rising in temperature. The crown of his head, however, cooled with an aloe vera-like sensation.

Diablo rolled up his sleeves, drowning in both heat and perspiration. Welts and red blotches formed where the sensation of burning occurred.

*'It's not enough,'* Diablo thought, questioning his current state of power. Diablo continued injecting, escalating his symptoms to experience direct fire on his teeth and tongue.

The final dose gradually amped his entire body to a boil. His arms and legs were now covered in milky welts and red blotches, scorching from the inside. Portions of his body revealed charred bone.

But Diablo felt no pain. His vision was sharpened tenfold, and the distorted sounds from prior solidified to crisp and clear notes.

In his reflection lay a far noticeable deterioration around his face. His right half was now grey, decaying at a rapid rate. Thin, corroded veins branched toward the other half.

The malformed eye transformed from bloodshot red to a neon blood-orange surrounding his cat-eye iris. A red glow emanated through the charred bone.

There would be no prisoners this time. The empire would be no more. But Diablo assured himself the hell he was bestowed with will leave no person the same as they were before.

# XXIX
## Isaac Sage

### March 4, 2023, 10:06 AM

Isaac awoke, dazed and curled with a blanket of shivers. His mind gradually cleared enough to register he was laying in the corner of his bedroom. The sun, at its morning peak, cracked light through the windows.

He retraced his memories to confirm which past events were a reality or nightmare. But it was all still a blur, including how he ended up here.

The lingering aches resonating across his torso connected to the starvation and pain at the white room cemented the capture was real. Parts of his limbs were also stiff after being restrained for so long.

Isaac rubbed the sides of his forehead. He shifted down to find dried blood on his hands, most likely belonging to a guard escaping the facility. The thought of having killed, even when blacked out, weighed Isaac's mind with a mourning.

*'It had to be done,'* he assured himself.

Isaac stumbled out of the bedroom. His eyes shifted back and forth, looking for Kara. Maybe she was asleep.

At the foot of Isaac's bedroom door, a streak of blood trailed across the hall, leading to Kara's room.

Isaac leaned onto a nearby column as his vision tilted and senses unfocused. He suddenly felt lightheaded with a heavy heart.

In that moment, a patch of a memory from last night re-surged.

"No, no, no, no," he muttered.

He remembered contemplating what to do now that she had lost his trust. His hand reached for the knife from the kitchen, an animalistic impulse to survive.

Until he found the gun on her nightstand. The rest of the timeline was blank.

---

He ran into her bedroom hoping to be wrong. That what he remembered was a nightmare.

Inside, Kara's head was covered by a pillow blotched with one bloodied hole.

The air in the room thinned. She was still. She was too still. She should be breathing.

Excess blood seeped into the bed.

He collapsed to his knees. There was no energy or will to stand. He meekly crawled to the edge of the bed, examining every inch of her body again and again.

*'Medicine. Home remedies. Hospital.'* Isaac continued listing things that could correct his grave assumption.

He reached for her arm. The flesh was stiff and frigid. He hastily shifted his palms, in sync with his sudden hyperventilation, looking for warmth or a pulse. The hands, neck, anywhere.

Then, his mind lit an idea: CPR. Enough resuscitations would do the trick. He knew the bare basics, repeating what he'd seen on movies and school safety videos as he got on top of Kara's body.

He placed both hands onto her chest and began the motion. Counting with each press, followed by waiting for any change. He repeated what may have been a dozen times, reaching a breaking point of frustration. The frustration only fueled him.

*'This was right.'*

He pressed three more times with stronger force, screaming in desperation.

*'This was the right thing to do. There's still a chance to bring her back, and then I can apologize to her directly.'*

Once again, he applied pressure through desperate roars until a cracked resonated from within. A dent formed in Kara's chest.

His face cracked into a horrendous weeping, out of the blue with no warning. Almost as if it was subconsciously pent up.

The weeping contorted into screaming, interlaced with apologies as he hugged Kara. He checked again for a pulse, as if it miraculously returned.

———

Nothing.

Isaac curled up by the foot of Kara's bed, with only enough will to weep and recant apologies through low whispers. Loud enough for Kara to hear.

The prior malformed thoughts of mistrust and betrayal now felt irrational. In pure conscious thought, Kara was the one person who did understand. Kara deserved better.

The shock of being trapped in that room for months had now been replaced with the shock of feeling trapped in this irreversible tragedy.

He lamented on every action that led to this. He thought about his parents. The friends and acquaintances he neglected to focus on satiating the desire for revenge. Closure.

Kara wanted that too. The mission, however, was now nothing but an indecipherable dead pixel. He remarked how young she was. Perhaps, at this point, close to the ages of when Samuel and Gemma passed away.

His tears began to irritate his skin. His eyes dried from the constant rubbing. His mind, blank, observed the floor stained with the dry trail of blood.

A knock against the window snapped him alert. The sun was going down. He rose back to his feet and turned to Kara once more. His first thought was to see if she had awaken. Or if at least some sliver of a breath fell from her lips.

It took another few hours for Isaac to return to some form of consciousness. He considered the least he could do, for now, was give her a proper burial.

He shook the idea. *'I can't bury her,'* he thought, feeling the tremble in his lips. *'I shouldn't. She can't wake up buried in dirt. She'd be terrified.'*

Once she woke up, he would say they won't have to do this anymore. That he'll study, go to school and focus on his career. They can be a family and live in the mansion together, where Kara could take care of his future family if she obliged.

All she had to do was wake. *'She's still in there. She can wake somehow.'* But then, he assessed the vacancy of expression as the little light pouring through the mansion's window dimmed to darkness.

The soul was long departed. This wasn't Kara anymore. He conversed with himself internally for another several hours with ne side refuting this thought, thinking of other ways to bring her back. But the other side was the one that had lingered with him for years. It had sedated him with the ultimate truth that time solidified as it did with his parents. The truth that overwrote those little white lies of them being trapped somewhere in the rubble or his parents were simply on a top-secret mission, implying some chance of return.

That sunken truth returned for Kara as morning cracked through the windows once more. She was gone. And there was no way of bringing her back.

Isaac ambled back to the room, staring at her–no, her body. Her corpse. She needed a proper burial. To remain with the house she had lived in and taken care of for so many years.

Isaac wrapped Kara's corpse in the same blood-drenched comforters and sheets, strapped a shovel to his back and carried her out into the vast acres of the mansion's backyard.

To his left were dense forests, the cityscape just on the other side. To his right, vast green landscapes stretching to the horizon. The emptiness and restricted boundaries left him certain he would be alone.

Kara's lemon tree stood like a monolith near the mansion. She always tended to the plants around the mansion, and thus deserved to rest in that natural setting.

Isaac trekked out, accumulating sweat after the first minute from the intense sun and unexpected heaviness.

By another mile and a half, he placed her on the grass, paying care to her head and began digging.

The hole reached four feet deep about an hour later. He climbed out of the hole, weary and tired but committed to finishing this now. He picked up Kara's body and then hopped back down into the excavated hole.

The landing was sound, but his body was weak. He tripped, dropping Kara onto the ground. He rushed down to make sure she was okay.

Her face was now visible. Cracked pieces of blood scattered around the skin. The bullet hole on her head glared back at him. The stillness of her calm expression welled his eyes. He recalled each memory, understanding, with intense sorrow, he would never expect to find her sleeping in front of the TV or waiting for him by the stairway. He would never find her tending to the trees, and asking how her day was just to hear the small details. She would no longer be by his side.

He climbed out and shoveled the dirt back into the hole until it leveled with the grassland's surface, Isaac folded his hands atop the shovel handle, then sat by the fresh grave.

Calling the police would be simple. They can arrive, and Isaac would turn himself in. Be done with everything. Let the news inform Todd and Rosemary of what happened to him if his disappearance didn't burn those bridges. This surely would.

Suicide still felt like the easy way out despite the amount of grief and guilt. And as he battled with other notions of what to do next, he watched the sky saturate before it dimmed and darkened. He didn't pay mind of bringing his own light.

His body was finally beginning to shut down from the lack of sleep. He stood, anchored the shovel into the ground and walked back to the faint outline of the mansion in the distance. A fifteen-minute trek with his senses and thoughts in darkness.

Half a block away, Isaac tripped over something. This wasn't the path he took before. He felt around the ground, feeling the raised, subtle mound that caused his fall. Isaac rushed into the mansion for a light and ran back out to investigate the mound. Only a careless walk would have caused anyone to discover this. It wasn't the typical size for plants trees or vegetation.

This investigation could've been an aching for curiosity or a yearning to distract himself. He dug up the mound to eventually reach a patch of color, different from the rest of the surrounding dirt. His heart stuttered yet continued removing the dirt.

It was a stranger. His bald skin revealed varicose veins around open red eyes. His mouth was agape and pooled with dirt.

The sight of the stranger at this mansion brought back the memory when Diablo revealed a photo of Kara taken by their hitman.

Kara must have fought back.  It must have been terrifying.  It must have been even more horrifying when he screamed at her with a blind, primal ferocity. He considered how long she waited for him.

He recalled not feeling that way until Diablo injected that drug several times during the drug.  Every action Isaac had conducted within this past year all rooted from a single action Diablo paid no second mind to.  Diablo's action, his influence, led Isaac to blindly killing Kara.

Rage returned to the surface as the name repeated over and over with an image of Diablo suffering by Isaac's hands.

Suddenly, every memory followed of where the facility was.  The location, and the inside, and the bunkers. The white room. The path he took from the facility to the mansion.  He remembered everything with such abnormal clarity.

More would come now that Diablo knew Isaac's identity.  Before Isaac decided his own ending, Isaac would ensure Diablo's ending would be met.

***

On the late night of March 6th, lingering questions still kept Isaac awake.

The first question was whether Diablo had any concrete, incriminating evidence. Maybe there were eyewitness accounts, but that wouldn't be enough in the court of law. The ideal scenario, additionally, wouldn't be jail. It'd be a personal execution.

The second question was what caused the blackouts? Dr. Bukowski made it clear it wasn't the prescribed M.A.D.  A question like this, to his admittance, should have been a priority matter as soon as it happened after that night with Commander.  Another poor mistake. He needed to make sure the blackout wouldn't happen again.

Finally, as much as Isaac didn't feel deserving of help, support was necessary to counter Diablo.  Who, or what, could he rely on?

All possibilities had to be explored and all questions needed to be answered for certain victory.

In his bedroom, Isaac re-analyzed the small leftover traces of the compound he retrieved from the warehouse in the Tipsy Tapp. Opening the drawer, the entire compartment reeked of rotten eggs and sulfur. Isaac covered his nose with one hand, picking up the plastic container with the other and placed it on the side with slow, steady caution.

Before he proceeded the analysis on the compound, he pressed a needle syringe into his shoulder, collecting a dot's worth of blood. He placed the blood onto the clean petri dish and rested the dish on the stand beneath the microscope.

The red cells had been tinted with tiny black dots, mirroring the pattern of a quail egg. Isaac further examined one of the black dots. The dots were composed of a molecular structure resonating a low, familiar vibration.

Isaac halted all motion. The memory of the compound's vial shattering on the floor after being caught off guard by Todd. Through sheer exposure to the air alone, the irritated compound X had taken root –perhaps, even fused– into Isaac's bloodstream. Infected for several months.

Extreme intensity may have triggered the vibrations, leading to the blackouts.

Hydrogen Sulfide, usually a gas, had a chance to cause headaches, nausea, and eye irritation. Using it as a base to mix with the compound of M.A.D. could lead to a variety of different effects that could either intensify, do the opposite, or something random.

It all depended on the scientist at the other end of it through all its creation. But without the scientist, it was all pure conjecture. This theory aligned with Compound X's unstable vulnerabilities to a natural, dangerous reaction with the right amount of agitation.

In his breaks, Isaac cleaned the blood-stained flooring and sheets. He created his own cleaning solution of bleach and vinegar to try to remove the stain. Instead, a brown-red blotch etched into the white sheets. A poor imitation.

*'Poor imitation…'* an idea lit in Isaac's head. He recalled catching a glance of the map. A nearby detached building was labeled with *'Unicorn.'*

The drug lord had also talked about his pride in Unicorn before. This compound in Isaac's possession must be it, if not an earlier prototype draft at the very least.

Isaac then pulled out his notebook, flipping to his most recent page of notes. 'Create a flammable duplicate of the compound to ensure full incineration.'

As a kid, Isaac was no stranger to making small, harmless explosives with Todd. The materials for an explosive were possible to acquire. Enough to destroy a building's worth of Diablo's prized business. Brass caps, steel pipes, electrical fuses, a trigger and a set of transmitters and receivers to work. And the final piece: a faux hydrogen sulfide compound.

The city would have the supplies he needed. Gathering them would need to be done in spontaneous batches as to not arouse suspicion. Research on where to acquire the proper molecules was necessary. The task felt grand.

*'It'll work,'* Isaac persuaded himself. *'It has to work.'*

***

March 8th. Given that Isaac's vigilante self was still a prime suspect, having the support of the NMPD seemed impossible.

He recalled, however, the news stories of John Saint subduing a sniper related to a cartel case. The same detective who questioned Isaac.

The case he was on…chances were high that it had to be related to Diablo. If that was true, he and Saint may share the same vendetta.

It was worth trying. He sent his email, through a private VPN, to the detective's found email address.

There was no time for rest. He returned to his room and began to repair his gear. The process was messy due to his naïve experience. Scrunched up parts of clothing forced Isaac to undo and re-sew his sweater and pants. He attached patches of fire-retardant fabric to his gear to better prepare his defenses.

He re-wired his gloves, followed by his battered helmet. The scuff marks and cracks on the surface remained etched in, albeit rarely visible.

His limbs eventually lost feeling, as his eyelids became too hellish to keep open. He threw himself into bed. A sudden shock of wake kept him tossing and turning, filling him with sorrow.

*'It's not my fault,'* Isaac repeated to himself. A poor attempt of a white lie to lull himself to sleep. *'I have to make this work.'*

Enough had been lost because of these actions.

———

# XXX

## John Saint

### March 9, 2023, 12:24 PM

Complimentary watered-down coffee and day-old bagels held a value to be treasured. The outdoor pool was an occasional second office. Martha and Brando, the two employees of Motel '76, were now pleasant people to hold a conversation instead of stoic staff to either pass by with a simple nod or stiffly ask for help. Even the incessant hum of the air conditioner in his room lulled him to sleep instead of keeping him awake.

It took four months, but Saint had finally acclimated to Motel '76 as his temporary home.

Despite taking advantage of all amenities, Saint paced around his suite in a bathrobe, draped over nothing but striped boxers, for most days. It was a positive compared to the sweat accumulating in the professional attire he wore at the NMPD for multiple hours. *'Being comfortable helps with the thinking.'*

But in exchange, a negative emerged. As an ex-detective, he needed to remain more covert than ever and avoid any overlap with officials. Saint had even learned about the DEA busting a surplus of warehouses across the states, followed by the country and then extending to neighboring territories like Canada and Mexico. The task of acquiring new evidence and getting ahead became increasingly difficult with each day.

Despite their efforts, no records of any critical arrests were made. There was no announcement of the prime suspect. Perhaps it was to ensure safekeeping of their progress to capture him.

An uneasy tension rattled him. Some inner voice affirming the stupidity and wrongness of his actions. But another voice, expressing necessity, said otherwise. His rationale agreed with both.

Clues were necessary. Saint scoured the internet for any breaking news in one window.

Another tab showed his savings plummeted to $8,528. In about a month, he wouldn't have anywhere to conduct his business. Saint shook his head.

"What the hell am I doing?" he said aloud. A way to vent the uneasy tension rattling him within, affirming the brash stupidity behind his decisions. Even Brando and Martha had their fair share to say whenever Saint vented with tired thoughts at 5 o'clock in the morning.

Martha's advice held some level of understanding. "Do what you gotta do. But make it quick. Everything has an expiration date."

Brando, however, bluntly responded once with a single line. "You know *you're* lucky to have her, right? Not the other way around?"

Saint urged himself to stop wasting time on self-reflection. Be done with this now. Explore the city, find new prospects and get closer to cornering Diablo.

He switched to his inbox for anything new, skimming through the promotional offers from retail stores, fast food joints, and 'sexy single women in his local area.'

In the dense spam, one email caught his attention. Saint's fingers floated over the keyboard. His heart began to ache from the sudden rising adrenaline. The message read:

*Subject: Diablo's the culprit*

*[DO NOT RESPOND]*

*I have the lead you need in your case. Everything needs stop by the end of this week. Please come to the abandoned rooftop of Mick's Toys, on March 9 at 11:59 PM sharp. There will be an unlocked door on the side to the stairway. I hope you take this into consideration. Every ounce of help is essential.*

If true, this would be the most substantial lead Saint had caught wind of in months. The odds of getting something like this were slim to none.

Saint deleted the e-mail and prepared himself for the night's meeting.

With his issued gun having been revoked, he invested in bronze bracers and a metal bat. Be prepared for the worst scenarios. Hopefully, they lacked firearms. Ambushes, traps and anything similar. He washed his clothes, hanging them atop the hotel door by a single hook.

In his preparation, while going over his clues, he wondered what Edoris was doing right now. Any time he thought about her, his current pursuit made him feel sick. He then wondered if his father was ever this nauseous.

Depending on what happened tonight, everything could change soon. The sooner, the better. He took some sleep medication to rest for the remainder of the day.

***

Saint departed the hotel at 11:00 PM sharp. He re-tightened the straps of his eye patch. The bracers were snug in his pocket and the bat strapped in-between his trench coat and shirt. He took the train routes to Brooklyn, where Mick's Toys was formerly located.

Closed two decades ago, the 5-story building remained standing after multiple attempts to invest and re-open. Unfortunately, it always ended up being a terrible investment due to its location in the blackout half of Brooklyn.

After a stop off the last train, Saint walked from the lit partition of the city to pitch-black roadways. He used a flashlight to guide past any debris or injury-prone potholes. The sidewalks were littered with trash and nests made of twigs and newspapers for rats and other homeless pets.

Saint reached Mick's Toys, indicated by its so-big-you-can't-miss-it sign. He circumvented around the building, finding the side door open as the e-mail specified.

The staircase inside spiraled around the walls, missing small chunks of its former architecture in-between. Some floors remained intact. Others, completely gone. Saint ascended each level, traversing the gaps with caution until he reached the rooftop. The dead zone shared the glittering night skies with ones only found in nature.

*'Edoris would like this,'* Saint thought. *'Maybe a blackout date could work...maybe not. Even if she would agree to be with me.'*

The rooftop door's loud creak broke Saint's focus. He readied his bracers.

A male silhouette, veiled by a black helmet, emerged from the doorway. His grey sweater, padded pants, and boots formed a bizarre large, yet slim stature.

*'Wait,'* Saint thought, connecting the dots on the man's appearance. Was this the masked man at the coastline? Did he kill all those officers?

But he was attacking that warehouse. Common, street-level thugs chased after him. Why would he guard a warehouse connected to the same one he was trying to attack?

Saint approached the man with caution. The masked man approached in a familiar mannerism.

"Are you the one that was attacking the warehouses?" Saint asked.

The vigilante nodded his head.

"It's vigilantism," Saint said. "Obstruction of justice even, given how much that interfered with my case."

"I was trying to help," the vigilante said with a distorted voice. "Sorry if that caused any trouble for you."

Saint let out an irritated sigh. "I have to be certain and ask this too before we continue…did you kill our team at Oswego?"

"Not at all," said the vigilante. "I'm not capable of what *he's* capable of."

"That's…"

"You know. The guy we're both after."

Saint paused. He was right. The fiery explosion. The two critically injured who confirmed the explosion came from a light. Diablo probably hoped his explosion had killed them all. Luck wasn't entirely on his side.

"I'm sure you have more questions," said the vigilante. "I'm all ears."

"What's your reason?" Saint asked.

"I have personal matters to settle. When he's done, I'm done. That's it."

"So, why come to me?"

"The news painted a bullseye on your face. I need help but since the NMPD has me as a prime suspect still…Maybe you could convince them otherwise."

"Well, I appreciate the thoughtfulness," said Saint. "But I can't bring the NMPD on board."

The vigilante was still and silent. It was hard to interpret his expression behind that black veil.

———

"Why's that?" The vigilante asked.

He pointed to his eye patch. "Call it creative differences."

The masked man's head tilted down at the floor. "I think we can still help each other out. I need back-up. In return, you get information on Diablo's whereabouts."

Saint still held his suspicions high. People with vendettas held ulterior motives.

"What happens to Diablo?"

"You arrest him. He's locked up for…well, I hope for the rest of his life. That's that."

"Your personal matters won't get in the way of that?"

The vigilante nodded.

Saint couldn't place a hint of deceit in his distorted tone. It was like talking to one of those bots on a toll-free call.

"You got a name I could call you by?" asked Saint.

He shrugged. "Your choice."

"Alright, Freddie Mercury, let me hear your information. I have some ideas, too, if it's legitimate."

Mercury, the vigilante, pulled out a sheet of folded parchment paper from his back pocket. Unfolding the paper revealed a map of New Manhattan. A blue circle was marked around a portion of Queens.

"I was holed up here for months. His underground haven, currently."

"You're sure that's his only hideout? He was rotating before."

"I doubt it. Maybe the police's operations pinned him into hiding. New Manhattan would have a lot of issues at this point if there were more of these underground havens too."

"Have you seen our sewage?" Saint remarked.

Mercury looked up with a blank expression.

"I'll take what I can get with these reactions," Saint continued.

"Sorry." Mercury pointed to the blue circle on the map. "This is the area I came out of. It's a closed tunnel dipping underground."

Saint scratched his ear, confused. "Your plan? Go back in there?"

"And gather evidence on Diablo's connection to the drug trade. Find him, arrest him, and lock him up using said evidence."

Saint gave Mercury credit for making the plan sound far easier than its actual execution.

"Was it heavily guarded?"

Mercury nodded. "High-grade weaponry, too."

"Jesus." Saint rubbed the center of his forehead. "We need back-up, then."

"You don't think we can handle this on our own?"

"You're kidding, right?"

Mercury shrugged.

"I think I know someone willing to help," Saint pulled out his phone, ready to call Billows. "But he'll need to meet us here to follow through. You alright with that?"

Mercury nodded in his statue-like stance. "Go ahead."

Saint dialed for Billows. The latter answered in a half-dazed tone.

"He…Hello?"

"Hey," said Saint, "Could you meet me at Mick's Toys?"

"What the hell? Saint? In Brooklyn?" Billow's groggy baritone revved to one of dismay. "What the hell are you doing in a dead zone? I swear to God, if you did some stupid shit again…"

"I'm fine, I'm fine," Saint replied. "I got a lead. It'll help all of us. Can you come?"

Billows let out a sharp, hiss-like exhale. "You've got some balls to be…"

Saint turned his back to Mercury and whispered. "I messed up. Is that what you wanna hear? I messed up, and I've been paying for it these past four months. But this'll be everyone's best shot in closing this case. For good."

A pause. It lingered for seconds.

———

"Billows…" Saint pleaded.

"Alright…Alright, I should be there in 20 minutes. Do I need to dress nice?"

Saint beamed at Mercury's unique outfit. "No."

***

While they waited, Saint asked more of Mercury's plan. "How will this evidence put Diablo behind bars?"

"My best-case scenario," Mercury replied, "is we need to have him occupied with his own drug resources. Hydrogen sulfide was something I caught traces of across the warehouses. This compound sparks with a purple flame, though more harshly and far more acidic than others if my research proves right. It's mixed with M.A.D."

"Of course, it is," said Saint. "A unique substance with sporadic properties…"

"We make sure he's pinned to it without any doubt," said Mercury. "Then…"

"I see your point, but that could surely go wrong," said Saint.

"I'm aware," Mercury's tone lowered. "In many ways."

"Man…Back in the day, it was cops and robbers for my dad. Maybe a few serial killers in the mix. But mutations. Vigilantes. This is something else."

"My mother told me to follow my dreams as long as you're stable and happy. I think she's turning in her grave."

"I imagine my father is scratching his head and asking for more whiskey while he watches this shit show unfold. Hope there's whiskey for him in heaven, at least. What a shame the Sage's invention turned into this."

"I…maybe if they were still around, they would've mitigated that," said Mercury.

Saint smirked over that hypothetical. "Big fan?"

"We need some optimism."

Minutes later, the door creaked ajar.

"Don't move," Billows' voice emerged from behind the door. His gun pointed at Mercury through the narrowing opening.

Mercury raised both his hands, an act of surrender.

"He's good, Billows," Saint said. "He's the lead I told you about."

Billows poked his head out from the side of the door. "So he didn't bomb the warehouse?  Are you sure?"

"I assessed it," said Saint. "It was Diablo pretending to be him.  To trick us into taking down another one of his enemies.  I'm sure of it."

Billows digested the information.  Slowly, he lowered his gun. Mercury lowered his hands.

"Alright, so what the fuck are you wearing?" Billows asked Mercury. He turned to Saint. "What is he wearing, Saint?"

"I need to keep my identity a secret," said Mercury.

Billows squinted his eyes. "What?"

"Billows, this is who I refer to as Freddie Mercury," said Saint. "I'm letting the whole mask thing slide since Mercury has information on Diablo and where he's hiding."

"Are you serious?" Billows directed his attention back to Mercury. "You realize you're holding back crucial information from the NMPD. I could arrest you right now."  He pointed between Saint and Mercury. "In fact, I could arrest *both* of you. What, are we blackmailing, bribing? What is this?"

"Be honest," said Saint.  "They haven't made progress, have they?"

"Who?" Billows asked.

"NMPD, DEA," said Saint.

"Fuck if I know," said Billows.

Saint raised a brow.  "We both know how Briggs gets when a case hasn't made progress."

Billows scoffed.  "He knocks. Or taps?"

"And he paces around while he does that," Saint continued.  "He's been doing that, hasn't he?"

Billows paused, then nodded.

Saint gestured to Mercury. "Mercury was captured by Diablo," he briefed Billows. "He escaped the facility a few days ago. He has the location, and he's also familiar with a specific compound Diablo's organization has been handling."

"A map?" asked Billows.

Saint shook his head. "This is as close of a clue as we'll get. You know this as well as I."

Billows rubbed the back of his head. His eyes closed tight before reopening. "Alright then. The plan?"

"We find the evidence first," said Saint. "Then find Diablo. Either capture him or wait for back-up to arrive."

"Since we'll get smoked," Billows contemplated. "The risk factor feels…I don't know."

"We may not have any more time to re-plan," said Mercury. "What's certain is that we can end this operation."

Billows turned to Mercury. "You're a bit shorter than I perceived."

"Fair," said Mercury.

"I don't even know what your motive is for this," said Billows. "What if you're a rival for another operation? *Who* are you?"

"You won't see me after this is done."

Billows peered closer, examining Mercury's helmet. "I'll do it if you show your face."

"I'll do it. After Diablo is apprehended," said Mercury.

Billows shook his head. "No, show it–"

Saint grabbed Billows into a huddle, their backs turned on Mercury.

"Take it easy," Saint whispered.

"Back off," Billows whispered back.

"Listen, arrest him after. I'll help. He won't escape." Saint knew this was the only way to seal the deal if it meant bringing in Billows, and as a result, the NMPD on this mission. "Mercury mentioned they have high-grade military weaponry."

The scowl in Billows transformed to one of confusion. "How?"

"No clue. But this *cannot* be deferred elsewhere. Who knows what they're gonna do next…a city war?  Worse?"

Billows broke away from the huddle, staring at Saint, then at Mercury. Another hiss-like exhale came from him.

"Fine. Let's get these fucks out of our city."

Billows reached his hand out to Mercury. "I'll hold you to your end of the deal, Mercury," said Billows.

Mercury reciprocated, shaking his hand. "Thank you.  Thank you both."

"I guess we got our impromptu black ops team now." Saint extended his hand to Mercury.  "You got more of those fancy helmets? Get a bit of a uniform going on."

"Uh…no," said Mercury. His stance stiffened to a pause for a moment before shaking Saint's extended hand firmly.

It felt like Saint was interacting with some socially awkward teenager.

"I propose we meet at the entrance of the tunnel in Queens," said Mercury. "As of now, being March 10th, we head there in two days. March 12th. 2:00 AM."

"I'll ready my side of things," said Billows.

"See you in two days," said Saint.

Mercury departed.

Billows turned back to Saint.  "You want a ride back?"

"No need. Thanks, though. You didn't have to pick up that call."

Billows pressed his lips.  "I know. See you in two days."

Saint took a seat on the roof's boundary as Billows departed.  This was it. The vast stars, and a conclusion for the case on the horizon, brought a sense of liberation.

# XXXI
## ROSEMARY DIER

### March 9, 2023, 3:48 PM

**B**right, navy-blue waves swayed the ferry in a subtle flow. Rosemary hadn't realized her susceptibility to motion sickness until now.

Mikey stood by her side, trying to control his baggy clothes from being blown by the breeze. He tapped Rosemary's shoulder and pointed at the Statue of Liberty, the size of her index finger.

"Focus on that, trust me," he said.

The perception of the back-and-forth motion slowed to a stop. The nausea settled. And with that, she simmered back in her reality.

Isaac stopped contacting her. Any message she sent was met with no response. No callbacks either. He was never present at the mansion, for all the days she spent with Kara.

From the way he spoke and spent time with her, it didn't make sense. Was it boredom, or something she said? The theories from her thoughts never gave her a satisfying answer.

M.A.D. relieved some of her stress. But the main reason for using it –her connection to Cher– was diminishing. Her angelic, detailed appearance blurred, and her sweet, consoling voice turned incoherent.

Even with an increased dose, it gradually faded.  Even as she brought her father back, she was losing her mother once again.

Rosemary never shared this with Mikey. But he carried an intuition for her mood. He planned today's surprise trip to cheer her up. Buying ferry tickets and enjoying some hot dogs while strolling through museums.

By the end of the ferry ride, Rosemary wanted to go home and let her body sink.

"I'm not feeling well," she said. "I'm sorry.  But can we please go back."

Without hesitating, Mikey obliged.

***

When they returned to Mikey's apartment at 7:50 PM, Mikey went straight to his nightstand drawer, where he kept his drugs and handgun.

"We'll light up a bit and order pizza," said Mikey.

"I'll take pineapple on my half," Rosemary replied.

"Pineapple? Seriously? I can see why Isaac ghosted you." Mikey let out a playful grin.

Rosemary scowled at Mikey.

Mikey flustered.  "Sorry. Too soon."

She smirked.  "I'm fucking with you."

They each grabbed a pipe and took a small round chunk of grassy sediment. Rosemary began to pray for her mother's return.

She added more M.A.D. to her pipe, fighting against her trembling grip.

With one light and puff, Rosemary and Mikey laid in silence. Bits of dis-embodied, incoherent voices visualized as enchanting wavelengths cutting and interlacing into each other, creating a DNA-like helix pattern in front of her eyes.

Her soothing thoughts rechanneled to her anger with Isaac. She imagined pushing him into traffic or humiliating him in public with a slap to the face.

"I fucking hate that guy," she said aloud.

"What?" Mikey muttered.

"Who the hell does he think he is?"  she shifted to a mocking tone, "'Oh, let me do whatever the fuck I want because I'm rich, and my parents are dead.' Piece of shit."

"Um…What kind of music are you in the mood for?"

Although Rosemary heard him, she focused on Mikey's couch. She rolled onto her stomach and screamed into the leather couch.

Her issue with Isaac was minor. Like a sprain, it'll heal. She affirmed all would be fine. Her dad was back, and she had Mikey around. That's what counted the most.

Mikey had always given her a place to stay too. He didn't spite her for taking, or linger over her head how she came and went. The more she assessed, the more she realized how rare of a kindness he held.

"Y'kno Rose," Mikey interjected as he paced around the living room in an unrhythmic, slurred dance, "You ever think of the career paths we could take?"

Rosemary shrugged. "I mean, we have another year or two in college. Why?"

"I don't know if I see myself doing this forever."

"The courier stuff?"

"Yeah. And what if I do, right?" Mikey perched up from the couch. "It pays good, but I always think about the side effects more."

Rosemary's body turned dull and irate. The effects should've hit by now.

"Is this the same stuff we've been smoking?" she asked.

"Yeah. You've been smoking this every day, Rose. You're desensitized.

"I guess you're right."

"You never worry you'll go through…the same issue as your dad?"

"No," she said within a snap. "I'm better than that."

"Right," Mikey's turned somber.

"Are you this kind to other people?"

"Wha?"

"Sorry," Rosemary softened her tone. "I started thinking a lot about it. This trip, me taking the gun, giving me a place to stay. It's so much. Why?"

"I…"

"Is it…do you like me?"

"I just get it. That's all."

"You get it?"

"I just get it. If it's okay, I don't wanna talk about that."

Rosemary sank into the couch, the material feeling grainy like sand. She embraced the feeling while swept by sorrow, imagining what transpired for Mikey. She had never thought of asking.

She replied, "Well if you ever need to–"

A sudden rampant knocking boomed against the door. *Stuck In The Middle With You* by Stealers Wheel played in the background.

"Is the pizza here already?" Mikey opened the front door to find a person in a suit, unnaturally bulky and rectangular. A bulbous, rooster helmet sat atop their head. The person towered so high that the upper half of their helmet was veiled by the door's top frame.

The expression on Mikey's face drained.

"Mikey," Rosemary said through her dullness, "Am I tripping out? Is that a rooster-man?"

The Rooster leaned down and glared its hyperbolized, oval blue eyes at Rosemary, stunning her silent.

"Money," the Rooster spoke to Mikey with a deep, bass-like tone, yet an ambiguous femineity interlaced underneath. "They've given you enough time for it."

"They said I had another month," said Mikey.

"Things change," said the Rooster. "And I'm in a bad mood."

Mikey lowered his voice. "You can let my friend leave, and you can...*we* can talk this out."

Rooster forced themself inside, brushing past Mikey.

Mikey continued, "Look, a couple more months, I'm–"

The Rooster interrupted Mikey with a harsh back-hand across the face. He stumbled backward before crashing into the nearby nightstand.

Rosemary sobered from her dull trance.

Rooster thrusted their leg into Mikey's torso repeatedly, offsetting the song's energetic tempo. He screamed with every harsh kick against his core.

"Mikey!" Rosemary jolted off the couch.

Rooster continued kicking and stomping. For a moment, Rosemary thought she heard a bone crack.

Her limbs froze halfway, like back in the cobblestone alleyway with her father and the dealer.

*'Not again.'*

She forced herself to charge forth, attempting to push Rooster off Mikey.

Unflinching, Rooster lifted Rosemary off the floor by her neck, and slammed her down. The blow blew the little air out of Rosemary. The M.A.D. intensified her stun as she gasped for air.

She tried to extend her hands, an attempt to claw off Rooster's mask. The static, cartoon face, swung another massive hook against her face.

The first hook hurt. Severely. Rosemary could feel her face swell from the blow, the skin distorting into a bruise.

The pain intensified with each hit. But she didn't relent. She had to save Mikey.

She forced herself out of Rooster's grasp, enough to crawl halfway to the nightstand where the gun was, only to be punched in the back of the head by Rooster.

"You! Fucking! Idiot!" Rooster shouted with each punch.

Rosemary loosened her leg enough to wind back and kick Rooster dead-center in the mask. Rooster's head reeled back with a resounding *thunk*, followed by the rest of their body falling back several inches.

It was luck. Pure luck. And now, she didn't know how to counter.

Rooster's breathing hastened to hostility as it broke into a bull-like charge, shaking the ground with each stomp.

A gunshot filled the room. The stomps slowed to a halt, frozen over Rosemary. *Lay Lady Lay* by The Byrds began to play.

Rosemary rolled to the side. The cartoon head shed a chunk of ceramic from its left eye, leaving an enlarged crack. Its body swayed side to side until gravity brought it down to the floor, shaking the apartment.

Rosemary turned to find Mikey holding the gun, trembling.

"Self-defense," he repeated to himself. "It was self-defense."

---

She ran to Mikey. "Mikey, are you okay? How bad are you hurt?"

He winced while trying to speak, pointing to the side of his abdomen. His breaths turned shallow.

She continued. "We need to go to the hospital." Sirens blared nearby. *'Already?'*

She could patch him up where they could then run away. Although she held little to no medic knowledge to patch broken bones. And if he were bleeding? A simple internet search might do the trick.

Then, Mikey touched Rosemary, catching her attention.

"You don't deserve this, Rose," Mikey murmured.

"Stop being nice! I was supposed to help *you*. For once." Recounting every moment made her spite her oblivious perspective evermore. "It's not fair."

The freckles on Mikey's face scrunched together from his smirk. The sirens were approaching closer with rising volume.

"You need to go," Mikey mumbled, dazed.

Her heart raced at both the sirens and Mikey's weak state, forcing her eyes to dart around with sporadic motion. She ran out of the apartment, promising herself she'll see Mikey again.

***

Rosemary slowed to a stroll underneath the dimming streetlights. Her chest caved with worry and shame amidst a swarm of shivers.

*'Why did I run,'* Rosemary spited herself. *'I should've stayed. I should've chosen to take the fall.'*

Rosemary arrived at her house to find her father's bedroom door wide open. He splayed across the bed, snoring a calm bubbling tempo. Drool spilled onto the mattress.

The bare movement of his torso reminded Rosemary of the Rooster's corpse. From the last frame of living and breathing to the first frame of being motionless.

She gasped, nearly forgetting to breathe. She walked over to her bedroom and plopped straight onto her bed, destitute. In need of rest.

Slowly, letting her misty, irritated eyes, close and ease into calm.

A stampede, muffled from the carpet flooring, echoed outside the room.

Rosemary's heart raced again. Police? No. The uneven stampeding was a specific kind of cadence she'd become accustomed to for survival's sake.

She exited her room and found her father, draped in a blanket, staring down into the sink.

"Dad…?" She muttered.

"Rosie," Clayton muttered like something was stuck in his throat. "That calendar is wrong, right? That date is wrong?"

Rosemary shook her head in denial of what was happening.

Clayton's face widened. He turned back to the calendar, his back facing Rosemary.

Rosemary snapped herself out of her denial. There was still time to stop this. *'I'm in control,'* she thought, *'I can make this better. I am better than this.'*

She tiptoed over to her dad. "Hey. Everything's okay. Let's take you over to your room. You should rest."

"*Don't.*" Clayton scowled. As if Rosemary were some robber invading his home. "Don't. Touch. Me. You're not my Rosie. Look at that shiner on you."

The bruise from Rooster. Rosemary forgot.

"My Rosie isn't…she's still a young princess, you fucking bitch."

The vile tone unsettled her to the point of tears. She found herself cowering, once again.

"Where's my wife? Did you kidnap her?" Clayton confronted her, maintaining the scowl. He grabbed her shoulders. "Did you kill her, huh? Out with it!"

Rosemary's lips quivered. "Dad…it's me." She motioned her hands to her racing heart. "We went fishing. You love orange blossom candles because of mom. An Old Fashioned is your favorite antidote. You let me be on top of your shoulders even when your back hurt. It's me."

Clayton grabbed Rosemary's hands and pulled her into him. "You…" He pushed her into the wall near her bedroom. Her body, injured from before, screamed in pain.

She couldn't stop his relapse. She couldn't reconnect with Isaac. She couldn't bring back her mother. She couldn't save Mikey.

The pattern was so incessant. Like a beep she could hear in the darkness, unable to switch it off. So tiresome. Irritating. A sudden emotional fire flowed through her shaky limbs.

Clayton roared like a bear. But it was a muffled echo as Rosemary, through tunnel vision, stood up and pushed Clayton down with her whole body's force.

She cursed down at him in pure anger, blaming him for all these years of giving up. Her rage went to chucking glass on the floor, denting the wall and ripping anything within her reach. Sheer, blind wrath.

"She's dead! She's never coming back!" Rosemary screamed. Words for him, and her.

Her feral gaze locked onto a shattered photo frame picture on the floor. It was her as a child, with Clayton and Cher smiling. In the background was a shimmering blue waterfall, veiled by a rainbow.

Clayton grabbed her by the shoulders, forcing her to look at his panicked gaze. She was ready to fight back.

"I saw him, Rosie," Clayton said.

Rosemary squinted her eyes, confused by what he meant. Was he back to his senses?

"Him?" she asked.

"Your boyfriend, I saw him in the rain. It's him. He's the masked man."

"What? What do you mean?"

"November. I needed it again that night. To calm down. He was after me before, and I think he won't stop."

The masked man at the alleyway…was Isaac? Rosemary struggled to process the new string of information.

"You tell me this now? Why now?"

"I thought you knew!"

Rosemary reacted with an aghast expression.

Clayton stammered, "I…I think we can move, start new, I can find a new guy for it."

"Do you even realize where you are?" She pointed at the surrounding mess with her eyes.

Clayton loosened his grip, looking around. His mouth lowered. "I was in the bedroom…" His eyes dilated. "Where's Cher?"

Rosemary yelled, throwing her father into the glass-covered floor. She picked the photo out of the broken glass and folded it into her pocket, leaving into the night.

***

It was 12:05 AM. March 10th. The one thing she learned about the desire to be in control was that it was futile. No matter what, there would always be something, whether it was her own instinct or another event, disrupting that yearning.

If she could at least confront one more thing, it'd be Isaac. Her ghost of a boyfriend and the supposed masked man.

It began adding up, from his disappearance to his concerns for her. Rosemary walked to a train station, departed the subway after a few stops and walked to his mansion.

Upon her arrival, the mansion felt grander with the moonlight cast over its dark architecture, void of light, creating a haunting yet imperfect silhouette.

Rosemary battered against the rough, thick door. "Open up!"

She rattled the doorknob, only to realize it was unlocked.

Rosemary explored the empty living room, kitchen, bedrooms and the bathrooms. She checked Isaac's bedroom. The comforters were tossed all over the mattress, but the floor of the room was spotless.

On his desk was a microscope with a sample reeking of a potent scent similar to…rotten eggs. When she examined the substance, its rigid shape and rough texture was identical to condensed M.A.D.

The scent relayed a memory. The night Mikey offered her M.A.D. after her father had his memory loss episode. Mikey had gotten this from a dealer.

And then the dots connected from past clues to this. Her father was right.

It all went back to M.A.D. A parasite that burrowed into her life and those around her, guiding to a chaotic ending with the same, familiar hallucination.

Her mind sobered up, clear from her rage, and disgusted over letting herself turn blind.

Rosemary walked to an adjacent bedroom, empty of sheets. She decided she would sleep here. Wait for Isaac in the morning. And make the decision for closure.  Her way.

# XXXII
## ISAAC SAGE

### March 10, 2023, 4:47 AM

Anxiety-stricken shocks forced Isaac awake in the middle of the night. The countdown neared closer to March 12th, 2:00 AM. Even after the mission, the reality of getting a full night's rest was a far yet hopeful dream.

Through extensive research and careful construction, he had successfully crafted a bomb capable of incinerating Diablo's compound. A trigger was also made for remote detonation.

Testing confirmed it would work. But what else could happen? Was there anything else to prepare for?

After tossing and turning restless, he passed out. His sluggish mind woke from adrenaline at 9:00 AM. It must have been roughly two hours of sleep.

His stomach fought with his urge to go back to sleep, eventually winning. Isaac ambled down the stairway to the kitchen. Eggs and coffee would be his remedy.

He grabbed two fresh eggs from the fridge, cracked them into a dark ceramic bowl, whisking the yolks together.

Any action he performed in the mansion resonated with remorse. He was ready for Kara to pop from around the corner, talk about their mission. Maybe something she saw on the TV the other day.

"Isaac," a familiar voice spoke.

Isaac jumped, dropping the ceramic bowl of scrambled yolk onto the counter. Bits of yellow egg jutted out.

He turned to find Rosemary standing across from him. Her frizzed locks tangled together. The morning light glowed against her skin, revealing a dark, matte bruise around her eye.

---

Isaac's heart floated at the split-second sight of her. A split-second later, it had sunk in, realizing how long it's been since they last spoke.

"Jesus Christ, I…" he managed to thread some words as the shock settled. "Rose. What happened to you? Are you hurt? When did you get into my house?"

She remained stoic. Her gaze was cold, hollow, unblinking.

Isaac continued. "I know, I have a lot to explain. I'm sorry. I was–"

"Front door was unlocked. Slept in the other room. Where's Kara?"

Isaac tilted his head. "How do you know Kara?"

"I met her while you were away. Visited here a few times." Rosemary's stare thickened the surrounding air with tension. "So?"

Isaac broke his stare away, looking at the spilled bits of yellow egg on the counter.

"She's on vacation."

"How long?"

"I don't know. All I know is she left for Denver."

Rosemary's tense expression fell blank. She crossed her arms together.

"I had all this…rage and sadness and concern before seeing you, and now… I'm disappointed."

"You wanna yell at me, hit me, do something to vent, I get it. I still like you, Rose."

"Then why didn't you talk to me again? Why the hell did I have to find you here? That's not liking someone. Give me a reason why."

"I…I was tired from my work. I can't really justify other than I didn't want to talk to anyone. At all."

"Even me?"

"I'm sorry."

She folded her arms, leaning against the wall of the kitchen closest to the front door.

"You're the masked guy. Right?"

Isaac locked eyes with her. An unprompted twitch triggered in his left eye. He forgot. All this time, he forgot that night when Clayton saw him.

He wanted to hear it from her to be sure. "Who said?"

"My dad told me. He relapsed."

Isaac lowered his head. He was frozen, unsure of what to do with his body or what words to emit.

"Mikey had M.A.D. like what was in your bedroom."

"The Mikey that goes to our college campus?"

Rosemary nodded.

*'I could've gotten the sample from Mikey,'* Isaac thought. *'For fuck's sake…'*

Isaac refocused. Was a bluff even effective at this point? He raised both his hands.

"Alright. What of it?"

"What's your whole deal suiting up? Wearing a mask and terrorizing warehouses?" Rosemary's tone sharpened. "Are you starting your own cartel? What the *fuck* is going on in your *head*?"

His lips trembled.

"I…" she continued, "I really liked you…"

Isaac's eyes glossed at her melancholic expression. "I did too."

He felt the need to at least defend his actions. Instead, Isaac shut his eyes and pinched the bridge of his nose. To rationalize felt menial compared to the plan occurring in two days.

"At least give some closure," said Rosemary.

He locked eyes back at Rosemary. "You wanna know why I've been doing this, Rose? Those warehouses are linked to the guy that killed my parents."

"They weren't killed."

"That's what I thought for all, *all* these years!" Isaac snapped. "It's as simple as that."

Isaac registered the changes in Rosemary's expression. Then, she erupted into a cackling laugh that lasted for seconds.

"Fuck you," she said through her giggling grin. Isaac remained stoic.

He presumed his expression was what finally sedated Rosemary's humor.

The corners of her grin contorted downward.

"*Fuck* you," she repeated, albeit with spite.

"Should I explain more?" Isaac asked.

"So, killing the NMPD is a part of this revenge?"

"I was *framed* for that. In a couple of nights, that'll change. I'm not someone wasting my life awa–"

She slapped his face, leaving an awful red sting. It reawakened the stinging nerves from his recent scars.

"Fuck you! You had your life set. Why would you…?"

Isaac rubbed the sting on his cheek. A pain so sharp he recalled on his recent shortcoming. The time wast– no, invested– in his vendetta, including his capture. Then, Kara's death. His worst downfall.

All those mistakes compounded into the need for a conclusion. "If there was a person that tore your family apart…he was alive, within reach. The police and the law kept him walking for all these years. Everyone that had the power failed to stop him. Wouldn't you take it upon your hands? So, if not me, then who?"

Rosemary stepped back.

"I know this. I stop now, I'll always be restless. I'll never live it down. So for some peace of mind, this is what I'll do. And then…well, that's it."

"Why even be with me if you were set on this?" Rosemary dragged one foot back, moving out of the sunlight and removing the glow off her. It appeared as if she had struggle sleeping.

A sudden melancholy washed over Isaac. "Bad timing. I was hopeful to reset when this was over. I did like you."

Rosemary kept her distance. She turned and spoke.

"Goodbye, Isaac," she said before departing.

Isaac felt compelled to say more. He thought of his words being amateurish and dull.

———

He washed his hands from the egg residue and rubbed it off the counter. Through the window, the oak tree's branches were almost touching the ground. No one was around to trim it.

*** 

As the countdown continued, Isaac shuffled through the amount of mail sent to him. One of the envelopes had Darwin's scrawled name and address. The contents of the letter invited Isaac to the grand opening of the new Sage Foundation next month.

He questioned himself standing at the grand opening, welcoming every face with a smile after everything that transpired. It felt jarring, like eating something that used a substitute ingredient.

*'What do I actually do next after all of this is over?'*

The idea of fitting into normalcy felt more like a faraway fantasy now. It would have to be re-assessed once the raid was over. Thus, the plan needed to be successful.

Isaac – disguised with a black nylon mask and hoodie – planted all the pipe bombs around the abandoned apartment complex near Diablo's hideout on the early morning of March 11th, before the sun had risen.

Peering through the gaps between the boarded windows confirmed no sight of any squatters nor the compound itself. The contents must have been hidden within the building, such as floorboards or walls.

With the final bomb placed, Isaac returned home as the sun cracked through the horizon.

*** 

Isaac laid his gear out on the side of the room, the day rolling into evening.

The helmet –now repaired and layered with a flame-resistant coating– combat boots, electro-gloves, padded hoodie, undershirt, pants, and finally, the trigger. All of it ready for the oncoming night.

He cooked a light meal, wary of avoiding the humiliation of collapsing due to a stomachache. After, he meditated. His wandered to the progress, once again, made. And the progress to come after.

Images of Kara's decomposed body, covered in dirt and maggots, filled his mind. The following screams of someone berating Isaac as a monster instantly startled him out of his trance.

Turning himself in wasn't something he considered. In fact, it was a bad future he wished to stay astray from. Tonight had to right his wrongdoings. It had to change everything.

Isaac took one last power nap, waking at 11 PM. He took a cold shower and then suited up, leaving the helmet, gloves and trigger for last.

It had been a while since he examined his reflection. The last time, to his recollection, was his first date with Rosemary. All the recent cuts and bruises had scarred into his skin as darkened slivers and crescents.

Isaac equipped his remaining gear. He stowed the trigger into his pocket and set the GPS for Diablo's hideout in his helmet. The trek would be illuminated by a crescent moon tonight. With few grey clouds floating underneath.

***

March 12th, 1:02 AM. Within half an hour, Isaac arrived at a rooftop near the tunnel entrance. A sedan was parked from across the entrance.

Isaac saw the familiar square head and sharp jaw belonging to Saint, sitting in the sedan. He was glad to see the detective's eagerness reflected through his early arrival. Though, it could've been anxiety. Or both.

1:55 AM. After recovering his stamina, Isaac scaled down to the front of the tunnel.

Saint exited the sedan shortly after, dressed in a mustard button-up and dark pants hoisted by black suspenders.

"So, in there," Saint said, gesturing at the tunnel's depths.

Isaac nodded.

"I'll be honest. Hard to believe I could rest once the case closed and this guy is locked up."

Isaac's goal to make Diablo die a harsh, painful death remained certain. But he needed every ounce of assistance.

"I'm happy to help arrest him," Isaac replied with a diplomatic lie. "When you think of it, he would still have to go to court and be on trial for his actions. Who knows how long that would take."

"Ah. You kidding me? He'll have enough evidence pinned on him with all the drug trades. I bet with all the stuff we'll find in there, too…That son of a bitch is gonna be enjoying a lifelong prison diet."

"I would like to see that." Another lie.

"Me too. More importantly, things will go back to normal after this. Maybe get back on duty."

"You'd still wanna work after this?"

Saint nodded with some hesitation. "I mean…for now, it's all I got."

"Come on," Isaac scoffed. It seemed doubtful that this was all a 40-something year old detective had.

"What? You got some wisdom, Mercury?"

"You seem like a nice guy. Why don't you just enjoy your life?"

"Coming from the guy fully dressed up from head to toe when it's not Halloween? I've got passions, kid. It's a matter of balance."

Isaac shrugged. Considering those thoughts, he compared Saint's willingness as a detective to his willingness to accomplishing his vendetta.

Saint changed the subject back to the plan. "Billows should have a spare gun for you. What are you good with?"

Isaac felt his face warm. "I…don't use guns."

Saint squinted his lone eye.

Isaac continued, "I have protective armor for gunfire."

"And?"

"And what? I do better with my body."

"Take a gun anyway."

"I'm good. What good would it do if I have shitty aim?"

Saint narrowed his squint. "Seriously?"

Isaac slowly nodded.  "Seriously. Not my style."

"You gotta be…Alright. We'll discuss formation when Billows gets here."

Billows arrived in a black sedan at 2:02 AM.

He stepped out of the car, dressed in a bullet proof SWAT vest worn over his dark blue button-up.  His hair was even more slicked back than it appeared the other night. The vest was equipped with a walkie-talkie, and additional ammunition was anchored to his belt. Pistols were holstered on both sides.

Billows approached Saint and Isaac.  "This is it?" he asked.

Both Saint and Isaac nodded.

"Alright…" Billows took a deep breath, "I let the NMPD and the DEA division know about the situation. Told them we found the kingpin, and back-up will be necessary. They'll be here in 5 to 10 minutes. Let's scout around and make sure there are no traps."

"Roger that," replied Saint.

Billows unsheathed a pistol and extended it to Isaac. "Standard issue."

"He's against guns," Saint jeered.

"I didn't say that!" said Mercury. "Guns are not my forte."

Billows paused with a shocked expression. He smacked the side of his shaking forehead.

"Christ almighty…" Billows muttered.  "Take the gun, Mercury. Please."

"It'll be in better hands," said Isaac. "Not my first rodeo."

"Yeah, they all say that until they see how fast a bullet hits them," said Billows.

Billows made a good point. Although Isaac had the helmet to predict future nerve patterns, it was ineffective on bullets, even if encountering a firearm was rare.

Regardless, Isaac reassured them.

"For formation, Mercury, you should take center," said Saint. "Billows, you take the front given your protection, and I'll cover the rear."

"You'll be good with one eye?" asked Billows.

"I've gotten used to it," said Saint.

"Let's begin," said Billows.

In a single-file formation, the trio entered the tunnel. The echoes of their footsteps reverberated as they continued through nearly full darkness.

Not a single guard in sight. Not a hint of a sound either other than the echoed footsteps.

"This place is fucking dead," whispered Billows. Saint's eye turned skeptical. "You didn't get confused with the route, Mercury?"

"Of course not," Isaac whispered, "You don't forget the place where you were locked up and tortured."

They reached the door to the hideout, filled with light from the other side. Isaac confirmed with a hand gesture this was it.

Billows opened the door, using it as a shield while his gun was readied by his chest.

He leaned his head in and examined the surroundings. The heavy forces could be waiting inside. Isaac clenched his fists. Saint readied his gun.

Billows signaled all-clear with his free hand.

Billows directed another sign to Saint and Isaac, in the form of an index finger pressed on his lips. No talking.

Isaac and Saint signaled back with a thumbs up.

The room's interior and the rest of the gritty yellow dome-like corridors were barren. Once again, no level of counter-measures. In fact, it was too vacant.

They continued marching, each step echoing faster with Isaac's rising panic. For a moment, he thought he heard another pair of footsteps intertwined with theirs.

No remnants of any M.A.D could be found. The previous crates and canisters had disappeared–Still not a single person in sight.

Then, a purple light glowed through the hallway from around the corner.

Unicorn? Hydrogen sulfide M.A.D? The source, as they continued, was through another door. The purple light shined through the center window.

Something was off.

Isaac checked his helmet's HUD to ensure it was detecting all movements accurately. Billows and Saint's wireframe movement were subtle. Aggressive actions would alert the helmet.

The formation walked to the door. Billows repeated the same procedure again, confirming another all-clear.

Isaac soured behind his helmet over the sudden pungent scent of rotten eggs. Saint covered his nose with his arm, while Billows pinched his nostrils.

In the room were two lockers and a few purple rocks, the origination of the glow.

"What the hell…" Billows murmured. "Mercury, where the hell is everything? Where are the guards you mentioned?"

"They…they were here." His heart palpitated from fear. "I swear it."

The alarm of the base began blaring throughout the facility.

A trap.

"Back-up should get here soon," said Billows.

"It's been more than 10 minutes," said Saint. The detectives readied their firearms.

Isaac reached in his pocket for the last resort: the trigger. At least if they didn't make it out alive, Diablo would suffer. He pressed the button and…

…No explosion. It wasn't far. If the noise was insulated, then the room still should've shaken from the power. *'The walls,'* Isaac realized. *'It must be laced with a lead or something interfering with the signal.'*

"We have to go outside." Isaac spoke over the alarm.

Saint screamed. "Hey, hey, freeze!"

A strong force broke against the side of Isaac's helmet. Isaac collapsed to the floor. Before he could hit the floor, his vision went black.

*'We have to go outside,'* Isaac thought. His blood boiled, struggling to force his body to move. *'I must find him. I need to find him.'*

Screaming clambered his eardrums. The unease continued with the thundering of several gunshots, followed by shattering sparks of electricity before he faded to unconsciousness.

303

# XXXIII
## John Saint

### March 12, 2023, 2:23 AM

A silhouette, snug in the shadowy corner of the room, struck a harsh familiarity in its outline. The patches of light shined around a decayed portion of a face, revealing a mix of raw flesh and blackened bone.

But the most noteworthy and unforgettable element was that eye. It pulsated an orange light as if it crawled out of the lavas of hell. Saint could recognize the eye that stared down on him during his time being tortured.

Before Saint could warn the others, Diablo had already extended his gun at Mercury.

He grabbed Diablo's arm, swinging the revolver upward as the shot fired, grazing Mercury's helmeted face.

Saint grabbed his pistol with his free hand and fired from the hip at Diablo's torso.

Diablo wrapped his palm around the barrel of Saint's gun and forced it out of line.

The bullet pierced through the adjacent locker as Diablo rocketed his knee into Saint's gut. The visceral force pushed the energy out of Saint's body, forcing him to wheeze for air and loosen his grip around Diablo. A strange warmth radiated around the point of contact.

The orange light intensified, and rising heat encroached the room. Diablo was going to set this place to flames.

In a split-second, Billows finally lined his aim and fired at Diablo's face. The bullet shot through Diablo's mouth, leaving a hole in his cheek.

Billows continued firing.  Diablo sidestepped the other shots before he shot the hanging lamp.

The purple glow of the sediments fizzled out amid the conflagration of more gunshots, each accompanied with a split-second flash.

Diablo flung the door open, his silhouette sprinting out into the yellow luminescence.

"We got two men down, repeat, two men down," Billows yelled into his walkie-talkie. He followed Diablo into the yellow halls.

"Billows!" Saint screamed. The pain and uncomfortable heat from the blow lingered across his torso and lungs. He used the wall as a crutch to stand back up.

The injuries restrained his movement, but this wasn't a stopping point. Mercury, he hoped, wasn't fatally wounded.

Sweat dripped from the brim of his scowling forehead. Of course, it was an ambush. Mercury departed, leaving Diablo to prepare. And based on the vigilante's vendetta, Diablo prepared a defensive strategy.

A shriek from down the hall froze Saint. Perhaps it was Diablo. Or Billows…

Saint pushed past the blunt stings, running with as much strength as possible.

'Fight the pain, you gotta fight the pain,' he encouraged himself. The shrieks lingered and the heat climbed.

Then, the shrieking stopped after multiple, distant gunshots. Saint was getting warmer.

In fact, the hallways were getting hotter.

The curving hallway broke into a three-way intersection. Forward, left, and right.

Though not as harsh as before, a grating scream echoed again, closer to the right.

Saint turned right, sprinting to a body slouched against the wall in the distance. From the dark color of his clothes to the hair, it was, to Saint's horror, Billows. His unconscious head was sunken into his chest.

Saint rushed to Billows. "Hey, are you alright? Did he shoot you anywhere fatal?"

Billows raised his face, showing the right half brimming red with threads of smoke. The upper-right portion of his vest was incinerated into charcoal.

His eyes were aimless, the nerves having accepted defeat. The pain coursing through him must have unimaginable. Every twitch provoked grit teeth and stifled screams.

"Jesus…" Saint's sweat grew more irritating. His friend needed assistance now. "We need to– Wait."

A swirl of air whistled through the hallway. Saint turned to the source of the sound to find Diablo at the far end of the intersection. Upright, blood dripped down his calm limbs to his fingertips. The winds whistled louder, thundering through the halls.

An orange light crackled out from Diablo's eye, followed by yellow and red. The whistles heightened into an eruption of booms. It thundered through the halls with the heat intensifying tenfold.

Saint's lips dried, his lungs struggling for air. His clothes felt heavier.

Sparks of orange, yellow and red conglomerated into a sea of infernos surrounding Diablo before it funneled through the hallway toward Saint and Billows.

Saint heaved Billows over his shoulders.

"Move, move, move!" Saint shouted to himself, running through what felt like a 500-degree oven.

Orange embers caught on to the tail end of Saint's pants, inches away from the intersection. The flames crept closer. He was more concerned about the flames reaching his weakened partner.

He cut right, bracing he and Billows as the inferno crashed past the two. Saint verified both to be safe as he laid Billows down.

The sea of fire continued through the hall for another minute until it left nothing but charred floors, scarred walls, hot steam and thick smoke.

Saint fought through his coughs. Billows, wheezing threads of exhales.

"Why the hell didn't you just…" Saint shut his eyes, re-assessing the major flaw of this operation. The dangers he underestimated. Two people already out of commission. "It was my fault."

Billows paused before taking a deep breath and moving to detach his vest and belt.  He winced in pain, implying the burns were more than just the face.

"Ammo," he strained to say.  "Finish…it…"

Saint grabbed two smoke grenades and one flashbang, stowing it into onto his belt. He spoke into the walkie-talkie informing the NMPD of Billows' condition.

Saint crouched down to his friend. "You took a sniper bullet. This is nothing, yeah? I'll see you at the end of all this."

Billows reacted with a quick smirk before returning to focus on his wound.

Saint turned into the charred hall and made his way to where Diablo formerly stood.  A trail of blood was evident.

He followed the path through this maze, eventually reaching a grand circular room. The room branched out into ten different pathways, and a ladderway at the center.

This underground warehouse was overwhelmingly grand. Did it actually belong to Diablo?

The blood trail led to the ladder steps. As Saint approached the ladder steps, a burly man in a tank top interrupted his path. He fashioned fingerless gloves and loose-fitting pants. His short brown hair, swept back to the side, fitted around his narrow jawline. He wielded a tonfa bat in each hand.

Saint pulled his gun out. "Hands up–"

The man, with no hesitation, uppercut Saint's elbow and followed with a hook to Saint's left rib, ending with a slamming roundhouse into the detective's blind spot, propelling him across the floor and far from his gun.

"Son of a bitch…" Saint sighed. "I tried, I tried."

Saint got back up, forming a boxer's stance. Elbows and chin tucked in, his right hand snug close to his cheek with the left raised higher, shielding the blind spot. He inched closer as the Burly Man protected most of his body with his tonfas.

"I figured Diablo's other guy would be here," said Saint.

"Emin." The man said with a German accent.  "What's your name?"

A pause. Saint had never heard of an Emin being with Diablo. And he wasn't here for introductions. He equipped his knuckle bracers.

"I like to put a name to my victims," Emin continued. "What's your name?"

Saint lunged at Emin with a one-two-three combo. Hit with the left jab, then the right straight punch, followed by a solid left hook. Emin deflected most of the damage with his tonfas despite stumbling a little.

"Just nobody," said Saint.

Observing the counter allowed the detective to assess several disadvantages, in favor of the German youth. He was handicapped with one eye. The previous efforts of running taxed a portion of his energy. And he could feel the rust, already relying on mere thin strips of air after only three hits.

Emin appeared to have no gun. In the underground world, few hitmen relied on their unique weaponry out of pride. But for Saint, a firearm was his key to ending this early in his favor.

Saint leapt for his gun. His motion was quickly halted by a leaping ax kick. Saint rolled out of the kick's path by a hair, the dirt on the floor bouncing upward.

In another setting, or a moment in the past, Saint would've been on equal footing. But Emin's breathing maintained a calm tempo, controlled and silent. His strikes were instantaneous, cutting through the air.

Saint couldn't quite put a label on his fighting style. An onslaught of attacks, with a brief pause for defense and counters.

Emin rushed in and followed with five successful body shots against Saint. He stumbled a few steps back, held up by some reserve of adrenaline. Emin soon followed with lateral hops. Almost playful as he mixed between feints and actual lunges.

Saint mimicked the feints in frustration, offering his own furrowed scowl. He spaced himself from Emin's reach by jabbing in the air with his left hand to measure the distance.

*'A little closer,'* he thought, readying his next jabs as direct hits.

Emin maneuvered a step ahead, locking in another two hooks against Saint's left ribs. Pride seemed to be less of a thing as Saint noticed Emin aiming for Saint's blind half.

Although, it was never meant to be a clean fight. Instead of wincing, Saint flashed a variant of Emin's crooked smile. He latched onto one of the tonfas and pulled Emin toward him. Emin countered with a relentless offense.

Saint took hold of the near-crippling blows, with one blow bashing his sole eye to temporarily blind him. Alas, his hand grasped onto the flashbang on his belt. He released the trigger and let it fire close range.

There was no time to let his blurry vision sharpen. Saint leaned his upper torso back and lunged forward. He landed a direct headbutt on something, inflicting him with more damage.

As he recovered, Emin was on his knees, mumbling and shuffling his hands around the floor for his tonfas. The blow landed. And it may had been concussive.

"Don't." Saint pulled out handcuffs and rubbed the center of his head.

The German fighter scowled. He yanked a syringe from his pocket and plunged it into his right upper thigh.

He screamed in German. "Zukommen! Zukommen!"

Saint restrained Emin by force, frustrated over the time wasted. "Enough!"

Suddenly, a blunt force slammed into his right jaw, sending him onto the dirt floor.

Half-dazed, Saint gazed around for the new enemy. No one in sight.

He adjusted his eyes. Emin's body stood next to a silhouette covered in fragmented glass. The interior lights bounced off it, creating a bizarre glimmer.

Emin began yelling in German, beating the floor in the process with his right hand. The crystal body swung its right arm up and down.

Emin switched his spite to Saint. This crystal body also approached him with an extended hand.

The body was sharp and rigid like crystals. One direct hit and Saint would be bleeding out from the inside.

If he wanted to see Edoris again, he needed to survive and face this. Running wasn't an option.

Saint re-focused with a right hook aimed at the crystal's face. In that moment, Emin sprinted from behind, countering Saint's blow with his tonfa.

Emin and the crystal threw hooks from both sides, careening toward Saint. The energy in Saint's legs was diminished. He was unable to evade the shots. There wasn't enough time to absorb the blow.

Rapid footsteps approached.

The source of the rampant steps, in the form of a dark blur, launched a hook into crystal body. The momentum of the hit threw the crystallized silhouette into Emin.

The blurred silhouette solidified to reveal Mercury. The vigilante positioned himself beside Saint with raised fists.

He turned to Saint and handed an epipen to him. "Adrenaline shot."

The detective, although hesitant, he'd be dead weight without it. He pressed the epipen into his neck. The sudden burst of energy prompted him to rise to his feet in shock.

Mercury proceeded to attack Emin and his crystalized component. The synchronized duo recovered back to their feet and readied their stances. Both sides exchanged strikes, with Mercury able to counter and avoid several of the hits for a minute straight.

Saint was perplexed at what appeared to be a choreographed sequence. But it became apparent Emin was still adapting to this–*phenomenon*. Saint couldn't formulate the thought to describe this other than a *crystal duplicate*.

The crystal waited for its turn, about a second of delay, positioning itself away from Emin. By the third minute, the crystal mirrored Emin's attacks simultaneously from its new position as a pincer maneuver.

In short order, the simultaneous attacks connected repeatedly, leading to an overwhelming pummeling from the duo against Mercury. His pace had somewhat adhered to the new flow but still struggled.

Saint forced himself to stand up and run to the conflict to help his ally. He grabbed his gun from the floor, clutching the barrel as a melee weapon.

He ran, swinging at the crystal body in his boxing stance, now blending his punches and elbow strikes with gun shots. Every successful shot chipped away some of the crystal in the form of shattered dents.

Saint shot a hook, only to be intercepted by Mercury, and then smacked with a direct blow from the crystal.

*'What?'*

Unknowingly, their fighting circles had overlapped.

Mercury didn't respond. He continued attacking Emin followed by the crystal.

Whatever Mercury was using to counter, it was detecting *all* movements. And it was a huge reliable asset in his toolkit.

In that moment, Saint caught a smirk from Emin. The detective launched more jabs, his motion suddenly cut short by Mercury's interference again.

Saint shoved Mercury. "Watch it!" he shouted. The distraction led him to take another clean hit on the cheek by Emin's tonfa.

Emin was an all-around tactician. He analyzed the behaviors of both fighters and utilized those weak points to the fullest.

There was a reason why *he* was blocking that ladderway and no one else and it showed in this adaptability. This wasn't a last-minute adjustment.

Mercury pushed Saint aside and swung wide, wild attacks.

"I can handle this!" Mercury yelled.

If Saint had to deduce, having fought alone…Mercury had no experience recognizing allies mid-conflict.

He couldn't pull Mercury to the side and have a nice one-on-one chat. Any time Saint tried to move away, one of the two opponents would command the ring to bring him back in Mercury's vicinity.

Soon, Mercury seemed to be holding back because of the confusing stimuli. Emin lunged a direct strike at Saint's eye.

His breathing stuttered to the point of not returning to optimal health. It was slow damage building up. Saint, blindly, made for a leap of faith, wrapping around Emin. He forced his injured eye open by a sliver, catching the blur of the German mercenary in his grasp.

Emin struggled, unable to release himself from Saint's grip. The crystal launched a straight punch at Saint. However, a direct spark-fueled power punch from Mercury proved to be faster. He impaled the crystal's head, the strike at Saint falling limp before making contact.

The remainder of its body combusted into a pool of glass.

———

"Now!" Saint shouted.

His grip loosened, giving Emin the window to release himself. Mercury, mid-range, threw two electricity-surged hooks against Emin's stomach.

The first made contact, while the second was interrupted by Emin breaking free and launching both feet into the air, striking Mercury in the direct center of his core. It prompted a forced, thin gasp of air out of the vigilante.

This was Saint's chance. A half-pivot, moving to Emin's side. The latter was semi-conscious due to the continuous electric shock.

From the corner of Saint's eye, the crystal reconstructed, beginning its movement to flank.

No time to think.

Saint hit Emin with an uppercut. The crystal connected a straight punch against Saint's battered face as he landed the hook. Its jagged edges sank into Saint's cheek, stacking the bruises.

Saint pushed on for the final hit. He reeled back, carrying all his momentum from his legs and back into this punch.

The crystal tried to step into its path to intervene. But a second shock of adrenaline, most delayed from the EpiPen, allowed Saint the senses to careen his past the crystal and into Emin's face.

Emin flew across the floor, ceasing all movement. The crystal by Saint combusted into microscopic shards, the detective standing injured yet tall.

Now, the path ahead was clear.

# XXXIV
## 
### Isaac Sage

## March 12, 2023, 2:45 AM

Isaac rose to his feet and met with Saint, letting the adrenaline-fueled instinct settle.

"You alright?" Isaac asked, panting.

Saint nodded. "Would've lost a lot more time without your help. Thanks for the adrenaline shot, too."

"I'm processing it now. We fought a literal, walking crystal."

Saint reloaded his gun and placed it back into his holster. "When you meet an invisible guy and a guy spewing lava from his mouth, your expectations are open to anything."

Isaac took their opponent's tonfas to use as his own.

"Excuse me?" Isaac asked.

"A story for another time." Saint approached the ladder. "Let's be cautious. This guy didn't pop up out of the blue."

A planned trap. Diablo expected Isaac would initiate this plan. But how could he have anticipated it as now of all days? A hidden camera or sensor Isaac hadn't considered?

The vast surroundings felt barren compared to everything else. Isaac turned back to the ladder. The steps, upon closer examination were laced with infrared lines. Saint extended his hand to the closest step.

"Saint, wait!" Isaac shouted.

As his hand touched the step, an alarm blared. Clamors of noise approached from where Isaac entered, and two of the other ten pathways, the noise climbing rapidly as it approached. Mobs of gangsters and guards clad in dark purple armor flooded out of the paths, forming a circle around Isaac and Saint as they ran for cover behind a nearby pillar, cut off from the ladder.

Saint fired his gun to keep them at bay. "See why you need a damn gun! How many can you take?" He asked.

"As many as it takes to get to that ladder," said Isaac.

Saint's pistol clicked.  He chucked a grenade from his belt into the crowd. "Wish I had your optimism."

More noise followed from two different pathways. The enemies would be flooding the entire center area at this rate.

Instead, the ring broke. Enemies turned their attention around, pulling their weapons and attacking, firing their guns. Few attacked Isaac and Saint, all dismantled in quick succession.

Dark blue bled into the ring of dirty shirts and dark purple gear. Glances of golden badges popped out as they clashed in wild motions. 'NMPD.'

Billows's back-up had arrived. The crowd closed around Isaac and Saint, suffocating their movement. And then, emerging from the dense crowd in a controlled, wrecking motion was Chief Briggs, laced in his own SWAT armor.

Saint called out to him. Briggs turned back with a look of shock. He looked at the ladder, then back to Saint.

"Can you make the headstart?" Briggs asked.

Saint nodded.

"Then we'll join you once we handle these guys."

"Yes, sir." Saint turned to Isaac, confirming their march for the ladder. Briggs assisted Isaac in making a path by bashing back as much of the swarm with his baton and physical mass on one side, while Isaac enacted the same goal on the other side with electric force.

He joined Saint at the base of the ladder and commenced their ascent. Briggs, joined by three other officers, blocked off the path to the ladder, keeping the ouroboros of conflict on the ground level.

The ascent emphasized the weariness on Isaac's limbs already. As much as he wanted to deny it, the effects of the torture still kept his body weaker than it had initially reached. He could only imagine what Saint may have been feeling. But he didn't show it. Instead he continued ascending without stopping.

For that reason alone, Isaac commanded his body to keep pushing. After a few minutes, they reached the balcony at the peak. The flimsy narrow path, clamoring with each step, led to a large steel door.

Saint gestured at Isaac to remain silent and pointed at his ear and then to the door. Isaac leaned closer. Behind the door was a subtle murmur of foley. Isaac assessed it as a metallic object tapping against something. Few wisps of air being inhaled and exhaled. Straps being re-adjusted.

Before Isaac could reach for the door's handle, Saint plucked a smoke grenade off his belt, cracked open the door, and tossed the live grenade down the hall. About eight people were seen through the sliver, equipped with weapons and armor more advanced than what he had encountered at the warehouses.

The hissing smoke filled the room with a foggy haze. Isaac charged in, followed by Saint. Both hugged against the walls while a conflagration of gunfire rained out of the smoke against the steel door.

The vigilante marched farther before he jumped into the smoke, pinpointing his enemies at close range. He battered two enemies with electrified fists, and dove while twisting his body away from the new line of fire directed at him.

Four of the remaining five charged at once against Isaac. He unsheathed his tonfas and fended off the simultaneous assault. The four stood in unison, their wireframes remaining still on the HUD. Isaac clanged his tonfas together.

The wireframes signaled all four proceeding with another simultaneous charge.

'*Space them out,*' Isaac strategized. He focused on harsh, crippling blows to launch two away. He tripped the third, and paralyzed the fourth, with two smacks against his neck, making him wheeze for air.

Isaac was suddenly forced against the wall with a barrage of strikes against the face, abdomen and crotch. The frantic speed and bursts of static filling his HUD made it as though it could have been anyone. The third guard possibly recovering from his fall or a new unknown enemy.

Isaac reeled back with little space and launched a headbutt, followed by two jolted fists slammed against the third's ears. His eyes rolled into white.

Static lingered. At this point, the muscle prediction system was damaged. He switched off the system, seeing the clarity of his surroundings when another guard rushed to Isaac, a jagged shiv equipped in his hand.

Then, a gunshot left the guard stumbling to a near-frozen state. The energy drained in his face. Then, his aggressive stance loosened before he collapsed.

# XXXV
## John Saint

## March 12, 2023, 3:02 AM

Smoke exhaled from the muzzle of Saint's gun. The remaining cartridge had been unloaded onto the guard pressuring Mercury. The remaining two Mercury had initially incapacitated were restrained by the detective's feet.

Mercury's helmet was further scuffed from the fight, the cracks becoming enlarged. He picked up the tonfas and sheathed them into a belt socket behind him. His hyperventilation arrhythmic and sparse. Seemingly exhausted.

Saint didn't mind the lack of politeness. What he did mind the lack of teamwork.

"What's with you charging ahead like that?" Saint asked.

"Habit," Mercury said. "It's not like we had time to plan."

"We did. Diablo's gonna kill us out there if we don't fight with some kind of plan. He's already chipping away at our stamina." Saint gestured to the gun. "You still think you don't need this?"

Mercury shook his head. "Would you handicap yourself with something you're not skilled with? I'll adapt with what I do best."

"There won't be *time* to adapt. You've been almost gunned down twice."

Mercury's visor fixated on Saint, motionless for a few seconds. Then, he started a robotic-like pace toward the end of the hall, as if not affording to waste energy on this conversation.

Saint examined a reckless vigilante, bent on reaching his desired goal no matter what. He saw this silhouette marching down the stained hall as someone who was self-driven enough to cause more harm than benefit for others. A person who felt, subconsciously, he was better off to handle this work seldom.

---

For a moment, it was his own reflection walking down the path, just as alone and isolated.

Had he allowed the events around him to go differently, Diablo could be arrested by now. Or it could at least be the DEA's issue. Saint could be relaxing at home with Edoris, debating on whether to watch a romcom or documentary special. He could be sharing a drink with Billows instead of being riddled with anxiety over whether his partner would survive those injuries.

It was strange, Saint thought, that now was when his true moment of clarity swept him off his feet.

They lumbered to the end, reaching another ladderway. At the end was a hatch with a rusted gold-green rotary handle. Mercury gripped the smooth parts of the handle and swung his arm, letting the handle spin.

The spin halted after several rotations. Mercury pushed the door upward, climbing to an outside platform beneath an open black sky. Orange infernos inflicted a large, vivid contrast in the dark canvas, as if miniature suns combusted one by one.

The danger made him think of Edoris one last time before he stepped into the warzone. Steps away from one final test.

# XXXVI
## ISAAC SAGE

## March 12, 2023, 3:28 AM

Every explosion boomed like a delay after the eruption of a firework, unrelenting in its rapid, nonstop pace. Without a doubt, it was Diablo's work. They descended the platform's adjacent fire escape to the lower main atrium consisting of ten small, pyramid skylights.

Isaac's entire body twitched with goosebumps. It was excitement for seeing this finished. Anxiety from worrying over that one small misstep. And undeniably, fear of a painful demise.

There was the brash passing thought of what he exactly he would do to the man that murdered his family, tortured him, and scarred his mind to the point of destroying the last sentient remnant of his past.

He had thought about it several times before. But nothing quite amounted to something that satisfied this vengeful craving. Another moment to reflect inward was, however, impossible.

His entire energy focused on approaching Diablo. Even the detective seemed to have his mind homed in on the threat ahead.

They maneuvered around the pyramid skylights toward Diablo, who visibly stood tall by the corner edge of the roof. Blackened, decayed cracks of dry blood, bone and veins stretched across his skin, like damaged concrete. Blotches of dirt stained his suit.

Each orange flash created multiple narrow concave shadows around his deteriorated skin and narrow-slit iris, taking on the appearance of a zombified creature of the night. A trail of old blood stemmed from an apparent wound. His cheeks appear to have been cauterized, making them appear taut.

Diablo gazed down at the sea of fire. The screams, sirens and blind gunfire below reached the top of the building.

Isaac pondered how much M.A.D, or what sort of experiment, provoked such a sickening transformation in this short span of time. The back of Isaac's head itched with a burning ache.

"They don't know a damn thing…" Diablo said, his gaze affixed to the sea of fire.

His breaths wheezed as if he struggled to reach for the air around him, letting off tremendous sweat.

"I'll give you guys ten seconds to either fall off the building or go back down that hatch," Diablo turned to Isaac and Saint. "My only kind warning."

Saint raised his gun and fired three shots. Diablo flashed his trademark orange light. The light faded, revealing the bullets vanished.

"Come in easily. Get some medical attention. Stop being a *damn* coward and do something right for once."

Three new pools of silver liquid pooled on the floor of the rooftop.

Diablo smiled. "I'm gonna enjoy killing all of you."

This heat had become so intense and visceral they melted the bullets. Diablo manifested another orange glow, directed at the stunned detective.

"Saint, move!" Isaac screamed.

He grabbed Saint and leapt past the sudden eruption of flames. They ran to the farthest skylight to use as cover.

"Or kill some essence of you all, at least. Your friend was able to walk away with a scar!" Diablo chortled. "If he didn't bleed to death, anyway."

"We need time to think of a counter…" Saint said to Isaac.

Another flame-spewing geyser shot against their cover, shattering the glass of the skylight. Unlike Massena, Diablo was far more chaotic. The fires still spurred a panic within Isaac.

No time to think. This needed to be done quick, with no time to brainstorm counters. If anything had to be brainstormed, it should've been done earlier.

"I'll get his attention and make call-outs," said Isaac. He sprinted to the next skylight and then the next, hearing Saint's shout of frustration. He was prepared to be met with an eruption of flames with every dash.

Even if the embers struck, the flame-retardant gear would provide defense for some time.

Isaac froze on his way to the third skylight, standing in open, vulnerable air. Paralyzed by a sudden shock of intense, fever-like boiling in his head.

Diablo crept closer. The glow of his eye intensified. Fire was the presumed sole power of Diablo. Now, Isaac struggled to measure his true limits.

Two shots fired from Saint's direction, enough to distract Diablo where Isaac broke free of his paralysis to head to the next skylight.

The heat around Diablo's vicinity amplified. His gaze focused on Saint, the latter froze in place with grit teeth.

Isaac leapt atop the skylight's peak and launched one tonfa at Diablo as he zoned toward him in a spiral-like movement.

The tonfa, inches away, froze mid-air before turning to hot, plastic ooze just as Isaac reached the busy demon at the back of his head and smacked the other tonfa.

Instant contact turned the tonfa so hot, the upper half melted. A prominent scent of burnt plastic mixed in the air with the charcoal.

Diablo snapped his focus to Isaac. Close-range. He covered his arms, pushed back by scalding gusts of wind. Isaac crashed against one of the sky-lights. Shards of brick and glass embedded into his back and shoulders. Most of his gear, gloves included, were charred black.

*'I should be dead,'* Isaac thought. A new bullet hole was visible on Diablo's shoulder for a second before instant cauterization closed the wound. Another stray bullet from Saint must have stopped Diablo's full power.

The last shots Saint fired managed to either hit or graze Diablo. *'The heat shield could only manifest in one or two directions,'* Isaac deduced as a blind spot. A burning sensation built on his forearms.

"Gotcha!" Diablo's roar caught Isaac's attention. First came the split-second of warmth, followed by intensified heat amplifying into flames combusting across Isaac's body.

He rolled around the rooftop's rough floor in the hope he could dampen the flames. Yet, the flames wouldn't diminish. The flame-retardant layer was reaching its final thread.

A grenade landed at Diablo's feet. Saint fired a bullet at the grenade, prematurely combusting it into smoke.

Diablo discharged another blast just as the smoke released. The combination resulted in a tower of flames imploding within Diablo's vicinity for eight seconds. Enough time for Isaac to roll out the flames covering him.

For a moment, a chilly gust of wind had flown through the sky, overtaking the intense heat. Isaac's teeth chattered amongst his searing skin. Parts of clothing on his limbs were vaporized. The gloves were discolored, but miraculously worked.

He tried to focus less on the pain.

Diablo, hyperventilating, clutched onto his body. He had the powers of something unearthed from Hell, but he was still only a human with limits.

Isaac's limbs twitched as he gathered energy to rise from the floor. Fatigue from the previous fights was taking hold. Diablo unsheathed his revolver and swung the gun around, looking for Saint.

Saint flanked Diablo's blind spot. Close-range bullets to ensure the shots made complete damage? Isaac wished he could read Saint's mind.

Diablo pivoted around simultaneously, flashing that same, annoying orange strobe light from his eye at Saint. Building up for another fatal attack.

*'I need to help,'* Isaac managed to raise his pained body to one knee.

Saint aimed his glock underneath Diablo's tainted eye and pulled the trigger.

Immediately, Diablo's expression turned aghast, the bullet maimed his eye with a deep gash. The orange light burnt out. The key to his power, extinguished with a single bullet.

Diablo dropped his revolver and screamed, panting from exhaustion.

Saint whipped out a set of handcuffs and clamped them around Diablo's wrists. "You're under arrest. Anything you say can and will be used against you in a court of law."

The detective grabbed Diablo by underneath his left armpit. "You have the right to an attorney. If you cannot afford an attor–" Saint suddenly screamed, releasing his grip.

A thin haze rose from his palm. A smoky aura exuded off Diablo's body. The handcuffs had melted into a pool of silver.

"You should know better than anyone…" Diablo flashed that wide hyena grin. The lingering orange from his tainted eye faded around the bloodied gash. Then, orange bled through his uninjured eye before the pupil narrowed into an iris, emitting an eerie auburn glow. "You gotta use *both* eyes."

Isaac sprinted to Saint. The vigilante admitted his own self-sabotage. He should have remained working together with Saint from the beginning.

Isaac approached within reach of the standoff. The orange light blinded his vision while he reached for Saint.

An instantaneous massive force sent Isaac and Saint flying across the atrium, skidding across the floor until it hit the base of an intact skylight.

Isaac found the back of Saint's head covered in blood as the light faded. A large portion of his right shoulder and arm was also burnt, revealing mostly bare flesh.

The vigilante smacked the side of his head once. Then, another two times in pure anger. "Fuck. *Fuck!*"

Gunfire rained down from Isaac's blind spot. An unknown voice called out confirming a man down. Diablo spouted a blood-curdling roar as more eruptions followed.

Isaac rushed Saint over to a nearby stairwell entrance, far and out of Diablo's sight. He propped Saint against the wall and and placed two fingers on his neck. A faint pulse reverberated through his fingertips.

Isaac tore off a few pieces of fabric and padded the wound on Saint's head. Had it not been for Saint, Isaac would've died far sooner in this fight. He couldn't die. He couldn't.

He rushed out, in another hurrying sprint, and found Diablo occupied with two officers – one of which being the Chief that helped them earlier, wielding a shotgun. Five other officers laid dead, covered in flames.

Diablo incinerated the adjacent officer with another beaming glance. The Chief lunged in and fired his shotgun. Diablo countered with one swipe up the air, enveloping the Chief's left arm in flames. Isaac closed in and wound back to launch an electrified left hook, surprising Diablo with an agape mouth.

Chief used his flame-lit hand to grab a flashbang off his belt and shoved the flashbang into Diablo's mouth.  Isaac veiled his eyes from the explosive light, as did the Chief.

Another grave injury couldn't be afforded. And, he couldn't leave Saint to bleed out and die. Isaac took the Chief and brought him to the same stairwell.

Just as they reached the stairwell, the Chief pushed Isaac off.  He winced over his scorched arm.

"I don't know what the hell your problem is, but I have a job to finish!" The anger in his voice faded as he noticed Saint.  "No…no it can't…John?"

"He has a pulse," said Isaac.  "Please take him to the medic.  Get yourselves treated."

Chief shook his head.  "He killed my men.  All of them. They were my responsibility.  I need to see to it that he pays the price."

A line of thought abruptly came to his mind without conscious reason other than the sight of the fire. "You have a family, don't you?  Does he have a family?"

The Chief nodded.

"Be mindful of them. Your men are already gone.  Saint has a chance. At least save one.  This one."

Diablo roared off the sides.

"You'll stay behind?" The Chief asked.

"Yes."

"My one and only request, after all this shit that's happened…I don't care who you are.  Make him pay." The Chief picked Saint up with his right arm, the latter gritting his teeth, and made his way for the stairwell.

Isaac turned away and approached Diablo. The drug lord struggled for air, yet it seemed as though his power would return soon.

The HUD was still broken. One electro-glove was working at half-capacity.

Diablo's focus set onto Isaac.  The passion in his bloody grin made it clear he still had energy to muster.

He fired a shot, grazing Isaac's shoulder with a streak of flames.  The drug lord's stance nearly crumbled.  He was a glass cannon.

Alas, Isaac had nothing to steer Diablo's focus away.  At this distance, Diablo maintained the advantage to survive and win.

Suddenly, Obadiah's lesson re-emerged.  Controlling emotion.  Emotion turned a man into a predictable algorithm.

The pipe bombs Isaac had planted were intended for this.  He lamented over the trigger when his eyes widened.

He was outside, with nothing to restrict the signal.

Isaac approached Diablo and pulled the trigger out of his pocket.  Miraculously intact.  Hopefully functional.

"I'm getting real tired of seeing you," Diablo seethed.  "Do they even know who you are?"

Isaac remained silent. Diablo most likely referred to Saint.

"Answer!" Diablo shouted.

Isaac remained silent.

"You're lucky I didn't kill you sooner," continued Diablo.

"Me?" Isaac questioned.  "I've been unlucky. For 16 years. You've been breathing for 16 years too long."

"Poetic."

"Say their names."

Isaac pressed the trigger. Diablo stared, bewildered at the action.

Three sets of detonations exploded from afar, one following the other. An explosion of purple flames erupted within sight from the rooftop.

Diablo turned to the sight. "That's…" He said, "those purple flames…that smell…the Unicorn."

His breath shuddered.  He flailed his arms, with trails of flames sprouting across the rooftops in congruence with every swing of his arm. "No, no, no! No!"

Diablo snapped back to Isaac with the flames rising around him, "You… you ruined everything!  That was all—"

Isaac rushed in and landed a headbutt square on Diablo's forehead. His decayed body stumbled a few steps back.

Diablo immediately retaliated with a straight right punch. Stiff, easily tele-graphed.

Isaac continued with each passing hit, landing a string of combos. Diablo's counters interlaced in-between the hits failed. He turned predictable. His eye turned to a fog. Could it be this was the sign he could no longer focus his power? That this was strictly a hand-to-hand fight.

Isaac's own body was then wrung back by fatigue. The command to push through couldn't reach to any part of his body.

Diablo landed two clean hits against Isaac's face, lighting the vigilante awake. He launched at Diablo. His stance sloppy and animalistic. Their colli-sion a string of back-and-forth beastly hits.

The murderer wasn't fazed. "Come on!" Diablo shouted with hoarse breath. "Again! Again!"

Isaac fired back harder. A shout interlaced with every punch. Every punch echoing a flashing, vivid memory of what happened so many years ago.

"Again!"

His parents, the burning building, the dense crowds surrounding a lone Isaac. The sight of him enveloped in an orange glow. The punches began to dull the shine behind Diablo's aura. His limbs became less responsive, the eyes turn-ing heavier and the blood shooting across the floor with every hit.

Then, Diablo shined that bloodied grin once more. A flash of life returning to his face. A reminder of Ibrahim's liberating, bloodied grin.

Isaac smirked behind the mask for a split-second before furrowing his ex-pression and channeling the fury across his body. He swept Diablo off one foot, forcing him to his knees. Isaac instantly followed with a barrage of continuous, rage-fueled hooks. One normal. The other electrified. All backed by the mo-mentum of his body carrying into a power that either shed blood, welted flesh, or cracked bones.

Within a split-second, the fog in Diablo's eye disappeared. A patch of fire erupted off Isaac's left shoulder, the embers shorting out his glove.

Isaac fell backward, coughing for air. Diablo pinned him down with one foot, preventing the flow of breathing.

"That's enough!" Diablo roared. The orange glow blinded Isaac. The high-pitched whining of the emitting light grew louder. And so did Diablo's hyper-ventilation.

Isaac's limbs were concrete. The familiar regret returned. He apologized to his parents, Kara, and to everyone else he had failed.

"I'm…I'm tired." Diablo panted. "I'm so tired of this."

The glow snapped. A pressure of air erupting with flames, banging against Isaac's eardrums. Yet, no new pain emerged other than the throbbing burns.

There, Diablo stood. Motionless. His silhouette engulfed in a pyre of flames.

Diablo stumbled back. Isaac looked on with a stupefied expression, unsure if the man he sought his revenge after was still alive or already gone. Scraps of his clothing dissipated to ashes. The flames ate away his skin to reveal the rest of his decayed flesh and charred bones.

Isaac expected a vivid, painful expression from Diablo, complete with him shrieking in misery over what had come to him. To lament over his own demise. But the visible portions of his face were void of any kind of pain or emotion.

Diablo, in his meandering stumble, reached the rooftop's edge. His torso leaned back farther and farther past the boundary.

The kind of execution akin to a premature flatline or climax. The kind Isaac didn't envision nor desire.

Isaac ran to the edge and reached for the collar of Diablo's flame-lit body, now suspended in mid-air.

"No!" Isaac screamed.

The reach was so far, his shoulder almost popped out of its joint. But Diablo's body plummeted off the edge and vanished into the inferno.

Isaac screamed in anguish. It should've been days of agonizing pain and not the near-peaceful expression that was on his face.

Diablo was gone. In exchange was a wish for a far more nightmarish demise instead of the void expression left on his face.

There was no group to return to. And there was no kind of group to meditate over what had occurred. Instead, Isaac sullenly walked back to the entry stairwell and descended to the ground level. He nearly tripped over some of the steps.

He paid no mind to his surroundings as he departed into the night, heading for the mansion, shifting to his memories. Memories of what were, and, more vividly, memories of what could have been.

***

Isaac arrived at the front doorstep. He brainstormed what else he could have done differently. And what caused the spontaneous self-combustion to occur. Diablo would no longer be around to disrupt the city. The lives of many would be safe now. That was the mission. There should've been happiness to Diablo's demise, Isaac admitted.

He ambled up the stairway. Inch by inch, the high-stakes energy that moved him before faded. He tossed each article of clothing to the side, landing either on the steps or over the railing. He cursed at even the slightest thread rubbing over his bruises, cuts, and burns. Especially the burns.

Isaac removed his helmet, holding it as he fell onto the bed, his perspective peering out to the darkness.

His burn-ridden body cocooned to a fetal position. The injuries, despite the severity, could be tended to in the morning.

He raised the helmet to his eye level one more time to assess the damage. His glossy reflection was warped amid the scratches and split in two by one vertical crack.

Then, the sudden correlation clicked. The mystery of Diablo's demise.

"I'm tired," Diablo's last coherent words echoed. At the brink of exhaustion, his own reflection laid before him as he conjured that final blast.

A spark of contentment from this realization, however brief, allowed Isaac to fall asleep for the first time in a long while.

# XXXVII
## John Saint

## March 14, 2023, 7:31 AM

Saint awoke in a bed draped with thin white sheets wrapped over him. That mixed with the white, fluorescent lights and sterilized scents all felt like a sickening déjà vu.

To his right, a 'Get Well Soon' balloon tied around a bouquet of white orchids were set atop the nightstand. NMPD officers patrolled the halls from the corner of Saint's eye through the window.

And in the center stood Chief Briggs, speaking with one of the officers.

Briggs turned, shining a bright smile through his wrinkled face. His left arm was fully covered in bandages. He walked into the room and approached Saint.

"Look who's up," said Briggs. "What timing."

"Good…evening Chief," replied Saint.

"You might wanna check again," Briggs pointed to the curtains, brimming with pockets of sunshine.

"How long has it been?"

"You've been out for two days."

"I see…" Saint suddenly gasped. "Billows! Did he make it out? What happened to Diablo?  What about the vigilante?"

"Billows is also recovering. You two can't get enough of this hospital. The vigilante, we haven't seen.  No sign of his corpse was found.  So, here's thinking he's alive."

A relief filled Saint's chest. The aching re-settled.

"We're lucky to be here. You haven't mentioned Diablo…" He lowered his tone, accompanied by his dropped head, expecting the worst.

---

"You two did…tremendous." Briggs grabbed a nearby chair and sat down, heeding caution to his bandaged arm. "Diablo was pronounced dead. His special production of M.A.D. was destroyed. All of it. No one will be using that sick shit. Majority of his men were arrested, too. We even found a mole in our ranks prior to heading out. Some random dumbass. I should've seen it coming."

Saint grimaced. "Casualties on our end?"

Briggs lowered his head. "We were prepared to the bone, John. And he still had a lot more crank in him than what we anticipated."

Saint lowered his head, ashamed. Not only was Diablo dead, but the death toll should've been only at least one or two. "I'm sorry."

"They were my responsibility, John. Not yours. They knew what they had signed up for, too. The ones that survived…we all got scars for it." Briggs waved his bandaged arm. Saint assessed the bandage care around his right shoulder and bicep. "And it'll stay to remind us of what we had to sacrifice to take this guy down."

Knowing that Billows was okay, all Saint's mind attracted to was one person.

"But, no melancholy," Briggs said. "We should be celebrating. Their deaths weren't in vain."

"Right." Saint clutched the thin white sheets. Sitting on the couch with Edoris, or strolling with her through Central Park, was all he wanted.

"Any visitors?" Saint asked.

"Sorry?"

"Did anyone else stop by to visit? If you know."

Briggs shook his head. "No, none that I know of."

Saint lowered his head and laid back in bed. "Then, I should get back to rest, Chief."

Briggs rose from his seat and patted Saint's chest. "You deserve it." Briggs walked to the door, then paused. "I'm sorry for my behavior the last time we interacted in a hospital room. Just…"

"No, I deserved *that*. Carmichael…"

---

"No, you didn't. Carmichael, look–she and I were close. That's why I said what I said. But she knew what she signed up for. We've been in this about 20 years longer than you, Saint."

Saint exhaled through his nose. Briggs' expression turned melancholic. Perhaps he had finally acknowledged the reality that the old era was fading.

"I should rest more," said Saint.

Briggs flashed a smirk. "Be seeing you, buddy."

Soon after, every life that died because of Saint's actions suddenly collided with him, forcing his gut down. He grabbed a nearby bin and vomited from the overwhelming feeling of the emotion.

He remained in bed for hours, silent. Instead of rest, Saint learned where Billows was staying from a nurse. He entered the room where Billows laid in bed with half his face and both eyes covered in bandages, staring at the sun-lit window.

"Man," Billows groaned. "We end up in this hospital way too fucking much."

"You can see me?"

"I can *smell* you."

Saint and Billows laughed.

"Well? How do you feel?" Billows asked.

Saint smirked. "We did good." He assessed Billows's injuries. "I'm sorry for what happened."

"Ah, don't apologize like you planned this to happen. Know that you didn't force me."

"Right."

"I mean it. It was better this way. I told you before."

"About the raid?"

Billows nodded. "There's a lot of burials on the way. But at least I can know I did my best. Doing my best save a couple lives more from being lost. I guess." He shifted back to the window. Patches of light cracked through grey skies. "What's next?"

Saint sighed. "No more hospitals."

***

It took a week for Saint to return to full physical shape. Billows remained in the hospital for another month. While Saint and Briggs managed to recover with less invasive procedures, Billows would be prepped for a skin grafting procedure, as informed by the doctors.

Saint returned to the NMPD HQ, where Briggs walked with him around the building and informed him of all the updates regarding the case's resolution.

A plethora of silver hearts were rewarded to the 42 officers that perished during the 3/10 Raid. And although a different division, the firefighters were given courageous merits for their efforts to clean out all the fires, including the mass of purple flames caused by the Unicorn explosion.

News media also reported Diablo's havoc, the alibi being that the explosion by the buildings was a sort of distraction to escape and to send a message of anarchy. It was labeled to the whole world as "A True Act of Terrorism."

Then, Briggs informed of one final, critical piece as they made a full lap in the building and reached the middle of the cubicles. Despite Diablo's death, there had been inside sources confirming his warehouses still existed, hidden. His reign of terror could soon expand through the city's underground once again.

Saint's heart dropped.

"What do you think?" Briggs asked. "A lot of sleuthing work for a good detective like yourself?"

"I...I did what I could do. Right?" Saint responded. "It meant something, right?"

"What do you mean?"

"That what we did at least had some kind of impact, right?"

"Oh, absolutely. It disrupted the balance. But we have to make sure that disruption doesn't reset." Briggs raised one hand and backtracked. "Sit on that thought, I got something."

***

Briggs returned, handing Saint a silver box. The officers and detectives in the building all gathered to the middle, circling Saint. His heart dropped.

"What's this?" Saint asked.

"Open it and find out yourself," said Briggs.

Inside the box was a silver medal in the shape of a heart, personally adorned with his name.

Briggs continued. "Call it the purest symbol of your all-defining justice. You deserve this, John. Billows will be getting one as soon as he returns, and every officer that laid their hearts on the line. You worked hard even when you were pushed so far back to the wall that you fell through."

Briggs began applauding, followed by the rest of the officers. He continued, in a lower, more personal tone. "You know Jacques would be proud."

"What are we doing after this, Saint?" One officer spoke aloud. "Celebrating?"

There was something inspiring in the tiny details of the box's craftsmanship. The fine grooves of the heart maintained a sleek shine. It was beautiful. The grooves formed a harmonious cycle.

More work needed to be done. But for Saint, that one person remained in the back of his mind.

Saint smiled. This was no longer his battle. "I'm retiring."

The crowd responded with bellows of laughter. "That's what I'm talking about! A vacation to Florida, eh?"

Saint kept his smile, silent.

Briggs' joyful expression faded, gaining an understanding in that frigid silence. The crowd looked perplexed.

Briggs commanded the crowd to disperse. He approached Saint.

"This is what you wanted John. You were supposed to be in my shoes come five years from now."

"Times…have changed. My life's focus is on different things."

Briggs joyous smile returned, expressing a feeling of understanding. "Live well with her, John."

———

Saint turned to the door. "You can clear whatever's on my desk. Thank you all for everything."

It was the first case in the detective's ages, revealing the messier flaws that lingered with him. At least, now, Diablo's death provided some closure for the fallen comrades of the NMPD and DEA.

Later that day, he stowed every trace and detail of the case in his motel room and stuffed it all into tiny trash bags the hotel provided. The minute this case reached its closing statement, everything would be out of his sight, either in the trash or with the NMPD. It didn't matter. There was a sense of relief in feeling that it didn't matter.

His next spot was where that lone spark was calling to him. Hopefully, it wasn't too late to fix it.

***

Saint reached the doorstep of his former home and pressed the doorbell.

Edoris opened the door after he waited a few seconds.

Saint cracked a tiny, awkward smile.

Edoris slammed the door shut, stunning Saint.

A few seconds passed. Edoris opened the door once more. She commanded, "Get. Inside."

Saint complied, with haste.

Edoris shut the door. "Are you here to argue how you have to deliver your justice?"

Saint shook his head. "I was wrong."

"Tell me what you were wrong about."

"Well, first, I don't think I was wrong to deliver justice."

"I don't think that either."

"We're on the same page, then."

"For the most part."

Saint sighed. The light strained his lone eye. "It wasn't the deliverance but the matter of the pursuit. I was left asking a lot about myself. The way I behaved, the things I did. Why couldn't I trust others to handle this case? I'm a veteran, for God's sake. Why couldn't I let go of what my dad represented to this line of work? Why couldn't the other cases I did have satisfied me? They helped people. And I couldn't figure out why it kept gnawing. But what kept coming back stronger was I wanted most in this life…"

Edoris stared at Saint, looking as if she was trying to subdue the urge to claw him to death. She gazed into his eyes, trying to read into his true frame of mind. If what was said was the truth.

The subtle rage faded. "You look tired."

"I am." Saint lowered his head. "Would it be alright if I had a cup? If you decide what I say isn't enough…I'll be gone."

Edoris sighed. She shifted to the coffee pot, preparing the grinded coffee beans and the clear tank of water to brew. The aroma sifted into the air while the machine bubbled for minutes until it reached completion.

She handed Saint a hot cup. They sat down at the tiny roundtable, where Smokey stealthily rubbed her body against Saint's leg.

"The cat missed you," said Edoris.

Saint scratched behind Smokey's ear. "Me too."

Edoris looked out at the window, her ear turned towards Saint. "Go on then."

"The case is moving to eliminate the remnants of Diablo's operation," said Saint. "They say it's hidden somewhere. But I'm retiring."

Edoris' eyes widened. "Really?"

"It's over."

"What made you decide that?"

"I guess one way to put it is I added more fuel to the fire rather than extinguishing it."

"Okay."

"I'm sure you're able to describe many other ways I messed up."

"What's more idiotic is that you're smart. So, for you to do things this stupid…it's like going to your favorite bakery, where they nail it perfectly every time. And then one day everything tastes like shit." Edoris exhaled her frustrations. "I admit, I was naïve. You did fuck up, John."

"Those are mistakes I'll live with. To be honest, it doesn't matter if the world is going to combust in flames. There'll be others to put it out."

Edoris kept her eyes fixed to the window.

"The truth is," Saint continued, "the one mistake I'd struggle to live with, whether I'm watching the world burning or another sunset, is not living the rest of my life with you. As a simple life." He looked down to his cup of coffee. "We can focus on building that family. Maybe adoption. All I know is that I…" Saint inhaled.

Part of him felt Edoris was ready to say no, no matter what Saint would say next. He poured all his heart into these words, reciting his wedding vow from years ago.

"I want us to fall asleep side by side. I want to hear about your dreams. To stay up late, doing whatever the hell we want. I want us to get healthy together, then get sucked into all the junk food and relish in that. I want to see the wrinkles form on your face and still see the youth that made me love you the first day I met you."

Saint could remember their wedding day. It made him ramble more and more, until that spark of a hand touched his scuffed hand. There, he could see it, caught up in his own regrets until now. The wedding ring was still there.

He looked up to find Edoris' eyes glistened with tiny teardrops. One drop fell onto her wedding ring, refracting light to create the bright shimmer before Saint's eyes.

"For fuck's sake…" Edoris rubbed her tears with her free hand.

Their fingers intertwined together, folding into a firm, comforting lock. Saint kept his thumb loose, massaging one part of Edoris' hand.

"I'll have more time to water the plants," Saint smirked.

"You're actually retiring." Edoris turned to him. Her lips were still pressed together, but now forming a big smile. "You also know you're cooking for the next year, right?"

"You're gonna put up with *my* cooking for a year?" Saint chuckled while Edoris covered her mouth as she laughed.

*'I missed this,'* Saint thought.

"Maybe we broaden our horizons and travel again," said Edoris.

"Next month, Canada?"

"Call me cliché, but maybe Paris?"

"We got a bucket list to go through now."

Saint leaned towards Edoris, embracing her. For the first time in a long time, his past concerns were dissolved with not a shred of doubt.

"Attagirl," he whispered.

"Attaboy," she whispered back.

***

Briggs and Saint agreed to appoint Billows as the leading lieutenant for pursuing the Diablo operations. He deserved it for his sheer ethic alone.

For the rest of the month leading to his retirement, Saint added closing details to the case's aftermath. Briggs wanted information on the backstory of Diablo from other sources. It could also help the continuing case of finding the remaining operations.

Since his body disintegrated from the fire, no DNA tests could be performed. But security traffic footage from all around the city's local stores managed to map out one house Diablo would visit.

Saint visited the house to not interrogate nor intimidate, but to receive an honest perspective on Diablo.

He met Carlos Gonzalez, alongside his wife and their newborn son. Carlos was welcoming, from his open-armed body language to his energetic tone. He maintained a polite professionalism, allowing Saint to speak with him in his living room, while Vanessa tended to the baby upstairs.

Their house was modern, renovated with vibrant palettes that felt like a home.

"So, you heard about the news then, by now?" Saint asked Carlos.

Carlos nodded.

"All the reports?" he continued.

"Yeah. It was shocking for us," Carlos' somber tone contrasted with his initial bright aura. "He had erratic tendencies in the past. But never anything as far or extreme. And Diablo? Jeez, that name? No. He was David to us. Not this monster terrorist the news says."

"Well, it's what he called himself. Although I want to be unbiased. Maybe you didn't know his monstrous side."

"I stand by what I side so I can answer other questions. If that's alright."

"We'll move on then." Saint continued with a series of questions, learning about Diablo's childhood, and some of his early adult life. Most of which involved an abusive yet loving father. A mother that even Carlos was left uncertain of what happened to her. A spiraling rollercoaster of a life for what Diablo and he endured.

The more Saint talked to Carlos, the more he was surprised by the contrast between his life and Diablo's, even in the younger years.

"He told us about a different job," said Carlos.

"And what about the eye?"

"No kind of tainted eye from what they described. He looked fine."

"So… To you, he was good."

"Sir, I mean no disrespect. But I know for certain that I could bet my son's life on it, that…David only wanted a simple life."

Carlos caught his breath. "I guess I have been fibbing a bit," he continued. "The last time I saw David was out on the front lawn. He was heading back into his car. I had no idea how long he was there. By the time I opened the door, he already drove off. Now I wonder what could've been. If I said the right thing, or went out and talked to him directly, would he still be…" Carlos's eyes welled up. "You know? I don't know if I'll ever sleep not thinking that."

After a silence that lingered for too long, Saint concluded the interview. He thanked Carlos for his time and left with confusion over a sinking sorrow, pooling together a grey empathy for Diablo's fate.

# XXXVIII
## TODD HYME

### March 31, 2023, 2:05 PM

Flowers were scattered around the doorway of the unit two doors down from Todd. Rows of tiny plastic candles emitted an artificial warm, golden flow along the apartment's lot. The bulbs all surrounded a framed photo of Todd's neighbor.

As Todd would learn, his name was Oscar Paz. A line underneath the frame read, 'A kind son, brother, human. One of the brightest architects.'

For several months, he focused on his key concept after receiving approval from Professor Beige: the nanobots. Blueprints were in place, and trial and error had been the key focus. The memorial acted as an additional light through the window.

The strive to catch up on lost time had turned into something therapeutic. Todd picked out kinks, developed and tested the app numerous times. He connected each loose wire to its respective frame, slowly building the bot to fruition.

He fought with insomnia, hysteric voices from the lack of sleep, and errors.

Errors were abundant. Misconnected wires, app errors and concepts not thought through fully. This was the therapeutic realization, however. Every problem, Todd found, had a solution. Errors were not a setback, but a lesson learned. And these lessons were the actions within his control.

He was incapable to save that man in the alleyway or stop the attackers. And he was more incapable to save Oscar. He committed to living with this reality for as long as possible, or until there was a chance he would forget through natural time. For there was a lesson to remind him of his purpose.

One night Todd surfed between channels during his self-imposed break. He switched between a report on a major incident involving a drug lord, Sentai shows and half-baked yet entertaining reality TV.

Then, a feature interview on Rudy Vel Gallagher, the mind behind the revival of Sage Foundation, appeared. Gallagher was a frail elderly fellow dressed in a dark purple and black suit. His eyes, however, evoked the radical opposite of fragility compared to his slightly withered skin and thin grey hairs.

The interviewer, Marley Darwin, and Gallagher divulged on his beginnings with Velcron and the new endeavor to continue with Sage Foundation.

"So, Rudy," said Darwin, "a lot of what's on other people's minds…why bring back the name, the brand? You're not a Sage."

"An astute observation," Gallagher smiled. "I'm not. But I understood, and so did the board, that we are bringing back a revolutionary product to the public market. People would know right away of its symbol in that spire and the meaning behind it. Instead of trying to compete with the name, we'd rather inherit and honor it. Simple."

"Some have commented on how the tower feels like a ghost watching over them. Nearly 1-for-1."

"I can understand that. It was felt, and agreed, that the tower shouldn't be new. It should remain what it once was. And, with that, a more vivid reminders of the tragedies that came." Gallagher then adjusted in his seat, dart his eyes to the corner before looking back at Darwin. "We have to remember it wasn't just the Sages we lost, but many good, innocent people."

"See, that feels more like the real answer."

"I didn't want to lead with too much sadness."

Gallagher and Darwin chuckled.

He continued, "It's a good moment, right? That's what I hope we're all able to embrace from this."

"I agree. Now, the next question is, how was this even possible? What trademarks did you have to handle?"

"Many overlook that I was a 5% owner of the former company. The name was just as much mine. I worked with Samuel and Gemma." Gallagher looked at the gold rings on his index and ring finger. "They were wonderful."

"It's been your calling since then?"

"Oh absolutely. Every time I create, it's from the soul."

"And what you're creating is really going to inspire others."

———

"Well, I don't mean to be prude, Marley, but I can't say I care much about inspiring others."

"I commend your honesty," Marley said through her off-pearl smile.

"Sorry, it's not at the forefront or why I do this, to inspire, no. It's what lights me up. Creating something *essential*."

"Has that ever been interrupted? Or has there ever been a period where you didn't create?"

"When I was discovering myself, I thought more. Thinking, well…Frankly, I thought too much."

"You thought too much?"

"I froze myself. I thought I needed to do things the right way, or go about something a specific way, and I was too scared to tackle the different avenues and realize everyone has their own way. Do you know what else resides with the soul?"

"A lot of things, but I assume you have an answer."

"Overthinking. And that's why it's so dangerous. It resides with so many other realms, including creation. Overthinking leads to the death of creation essentially. So, I found a frame of mind to avoid overthinking."

"Which is?"

"I become a servant of the creation. The creation will serve others, but I will be indebted. Willing to bend with the flow instead of asking why or how else things should be. Such is the sporadic nature of the soul, the calling of an inventor."

"The younger generation would do wonders if they had you as a teacher."

"If I had the attention span," Gallagher chuckled. "There are others far more capable than I. Again, I'm just a servant."

Darwin concluded the interview and reminded all the viewers that the Sage Foundation would be commencing its public grand opening on April 10th. Gallagher's words reminded Todd that choosing between logic and passion wasn't the issue. It was the act of not creating a new avenue, and thus avoiding the trap of being in frozen thought. Anything else, or choosing one over the other, was detrimental. Finding this new avenue was Todd's role as a creator and an inventor to the world.

The same philosophy applied to Isaac. It wasn't of Todd's volition to force Isaac into a box. Isaac held a conviction confident enough to take matters into his own hands. A confidence to make others' lives better among his own. He wondered if Isaac was alright now.

Todd switched back to the news. A new report had surfaced of a man found dead. The cause of death correlated to overdosing on a black-market variant of M.A.D. Out of what was found in the house was a ceramic, cartoon pig head. Reports further confirmed this head was evidence as one of the two assailants that burned down Isaac Sage's house back in June 2022.

His mind flashed to the alleyway. The man in the pig head. Then, Isaac's missing finger and his story about the fire.

Although he tried to show some respect for a lost life, Todd couldn't help but smile. He tended back to the finishing touches on his five prototype nano-bots. They resembled silver flies, each equipped with ocular lenses. The lenses shined with a sapphire hue atop the tiny metal structures. Their limbs, thinner than a needle, allowed them to land onto surfaces without being detected. A bare-bones app was also created to command the nanobots.

The restless nights could pause. The voices and hot flashes from the lack of sleep could stop. It was time to move forward.

***

The following day, Todd received a text from Isaac. A request to meet him on campus grounds. Todd was willing to hear his friend out. On April 2nd, he arrived on campus and waited at a bench shaded by a few oak trees, waiting per their proposed time.

Isaac arrived shortly after. On time, shockingly. Although most of his body was veiled by baggy, long-sleeve clothing, his skin was several shades paler, and appeared dehydrated, as if his body was made of sandpaper. Parts were either yellowed with faded bruises or discolored as if healing from burns. The latter was much less noticeable. His friend had seen better days.

Isaac waved at Todd and took a seat beside him.

"Long time, huh?" Todd asked.

Isaac flashed a smile before a sadness overtook his expression. "I'll get this out the way now. I was out of line. And I know I'm kicked out of the project; I spoke with Beige a little while ago. There's no issue with that. I wanted to \

[ay sorry. I was, and still am, a piece of shit."

T;odd looked at Isaac with a vacant expression, registering his words. The shade helped him focus with full clarity.

The thoughts he formed were right.  And from the injuries, they leaned toward one truth:  Isaac's convictions were a part of him.

"It's okay," said Todd. "We're both accountable. I should've confronted the whole situation. And I think I get where you were coming from before. I should've been more understanding."

"I mean…"

"Don't get me wrong, you're *definitely* more at fault here. Big piece of shit vibes."

Isaac's face flustered.

Todd chuckled. "We're good, man."

"I'll make it up one day."

"Dude, like I said, we're good. No need to say that like I'm your lover, God forbid. Life happens."

Isaac turned to the floor with a look of defeat.  "Well, I think I failed that class. Hard."

Todd patted Isaac's back.  "You can retake that class a hundred times with your money."

"A habit I wouldn't prefer."

"What we could do is hit the arcades tonight. Grab a slice of pizza, take a stroll through the streets."

"Are you asking me out on a date?"

"You're too ugly for my standards."

"It's enough of a compliment for me."

———

Todd shifted to a serious tone. "I gotta ask one thing, man. I think I connected the dots, but…I'd rather hear it from you. Why the sudden 180 this past year?"

Isaac remained silent. He was sweating underneath the heavy clothes.

"One day," said Isaac. "I just need time. Please."

Todd nodded in respect. "I'll wait for that."

***

The late nights, to Todd's dismay, were still filled with restlessness. And, worse, the voices were still prevalent.

Todd tried to not acknowledge in his mind the details of the voices. But often, they played the tones and phrasing of his family and friends originally, or memory reels as Todd would frame it.

But eventually, the voices framed as their own unique tone and frequency. They spoke fits of curiosity, pride and anger. Especially anger to the point of frightening Todd.

Tossing and turning, Todd soon jolted up to the recanting of one phrase, whispered next to his ear:

*I choose not to sleep. I choose to change the world. To change, I choose to create.*

Todd examined his surroundings. He walked over to his nanobots, polishing the mechanics.

# XXXIX
## ISAAC SAGE

### April 3, 2023, 2:31 PM

In healing, there was time to meditate on the near future. The March Inferno Raid, as the news media called it, did not detail any appearance of 'Mercury.'

The waves of ache, stinging and discomfort through Isaac's body reminded him of the reality of that night.

Now, he waited for the day of feeling renewed, expecting this to arrive once he completed his mission. He would notice the skies move with a heightened vibrancy. The city would be livened with smiles and laughter, and his mind would focus on strengthening his career and restoring his bonds.

Instead, there was a void. From fog in his mind to the stone in his movement and a dullness lingering in the air around him.

His thoughts leaned to his parents and Kara. He hoped, and prayed, they would be proud of his actions and forgive him for the mistakes he made. For now, he would continue through life, hoping this renewal would come.

***

On April 3rd, Isaac received a C- after presenting his fake neuro-helmet. Better than expected, but the grade combined with the missing assignments led to Isaac officially failing the class with an F. Todd received an A+ along with a 'well-expected recommendation.' As for his other classes, Isaac failed Business Administration with a D and passed New-Gen Chemistry with a B.

Todd told Isaac at the café he planned to start looking for companies to pitch his inventions to. A way to network and expand his portfolio.

As they spoke, Rosemary made a passing appearance from afar. Isaac's heart shot with contrition. It was, of course, a not-so-subtle reaction, as Todd began to share words from around the grapevine.

She apparently left her father's home and moved into a boarding house. Before Todd could share more, Isaac changed the subject. All he could think about was his last confrontation with her, and the future he once believed he could have with her.

Like a drawing in the sand erased by high tide, that possibility was gone. And, once again, the question branched to, "what now?"

Isaac returned home that evening. He scanned his inbox to find another invite from Darwin about the Grand Opening of Sage Foundation, scheduled for April 10th. She expressed her desire for him to speak for the grand inauguration, or, at the very least, make an appearance.

He had denied ever being involved in the past. But, a thought compelled him to reconsider. That perhaps this was the push he needed to feel that sense of renewal. Perhaps he, a Sage, can ensure his parents' legacy was handled right.

***

The anxiety, paranoia and guilt mixed into something tar-like. The restless nights impacted Isaac's breathing now to the point of waking from suffocation and then staying up for hours from a rushing beat in his chest before he could let his tired eyes fall asleep.

He called Dr. Bukowski on the late night of April 7th and requested a last-minute appointment for the following day. The doctor, to his surprise, answered and obliged with the same kindness as before. He was able to provide Isaac a 15-minute slot.

Isaac arrived early the next day with a clean appearance. A contrast to his disheveled mind. Dr. Bukowski met with Isaac as if nothing had changed. He complimented Isaac's appearance and was eager to sit down and talk with him.

Isaac used every ounce of his focus to breathe. He didn't bother to feel the grooves of his chair, or to appreciate the orange-red hexagon pattern of the carpet.

Dr. Bukowski locked onto Isaac's face with a kind and welcoming aura.

"So, how are you doing, Isaac?"

"I'm okay. Yourself?"

"Good. You never call that late. You even sounded worn out."

"We can dive into it, if that's okay."

"It's what I'm here for." The doctor smiled with an aura of comfort.

"I…I've been grieving. Horribly. I feel like it's relapsing again. I need only advice, not the immersion stuff. Please." Isaac wished with everything in his power to avoid the painful cycle of the re-immersion once more. He knew his words were rushed and unorganized. But he had hoped the kind doctor would understand his urgency. "I'm so sorry again if I screwed your schedule up, but I'm at a loss."

Dr. Bukowski's gaze stiffened. His lips pressed flat. An apparent dislike for Isaac's choice of words. He leaned forward and clasped his hands together.

"I know you've doubted the process of these sessions, and I can't help but somewhat understand," said Dr. Bukowski. "I promised at one point it would be quick. I failed on that, and I'm sorry. I think you need to reflect on those pains-taking memories haunting you, Isaac. Remind yourself you're still alive. For that, you need to heal and be alive for them. And to do that…"

Dr. Bukowski raised his eyes to the ceiling. As if thinking what different thing he could say now that hadn't been repeated the past several years. The smile, along with the comforting aura, faded the longer he waited.

The doctor continued. "We've asked before where can Isaac Sage fit into life now to accomplish that? You need to accept that future. And accept that past. Then, the present in healing comes."

*'Accept?'* Isaac's heart rate increased as his nails dug into the chair's grooves. None of that quelled his mind. He tried to remain composed. The timer buzzed.

"That's all?" Isaac asked.

"That's all you can do now, and all I have to offer. Goodbye, Isaac."

***

———

The morning of April 10th. A limousine picked up Isaac, dressed in a fitted black suit.  The vehicle cruised out of the roundabout, down the pebble road, easing into the city roads cramped with traffic.

Two days ago, Isaac obliged to present an inaugural speech on behalf of the Sage legacy. He muttered his memorized rehearsal, backtracking whenever he froze or forgot a word. He had nailed most of it.

The main reason for freezing in thought now came with the same idea: What next?  And, more importantly, would this next event ease him of this feeling gnawing at his appetite and his yearning for sleep.  He hoped he at least didn't look too dead from the insomnia.

The limousine reached the sidewalk adjacent to the stairway of the new building. The obelisk tower gleamed with that same green, oasis-like tint.

Isaac exited the vehicle where Darwin, fitted in a sage green dress revealing the freckles on her shoulders, approached him.

"You made it," she said with a soft embrace.  "Thank you, Isaac."

"I should thank you for letting me be a part of this, still," said Isaac. "After everything."

"Where's Kara?"

The doctor's words had recanted in his mind.  *'Accept the past.'*

 "Vacation. Denver," said Isaac.  Recanting the alibi was corrosion at this point.

Darwin shook her head. "She's missing out on this."

"I know." He kept it brief, wishing to let the subject change on its own. They ascended the stairway.  Production crews readied the podium, audio and cameras.  They tidied the sage green ribbon to be cut at the end of the ceremony. People began to form and fill the vast front entrance.  What first felt intimate had now been overfilled with an overwhelming sensation.

Darwin guided Isaac to a stylist tweaking details on an elder's purple suit. He flashed a smile, saying something with a charmed tone that made the stylist flush red.

"Isaac, this is Rudy Vel Gallagher, the man behind this resurrection." Darwin stood in the middle between the two while the stylist focused on her work. "Rudy, this is Isaac Sage."

"Mr. Sage," Mr. Gallagher replied with a confident tone. "I'm a bit of a statue, but it's for the best as I've already made Katie mess up…what is it, six?"

"Might be seven," said the stylist.

"Lucky me, seven times." Mr. Gallagher extended his arm halfway out with a smile. "It's a pleasure to finally meet you and have your grace for this company."

Rudy Vel Gallagher had some relation to Velcron Empire. That was the most Isaac knew due to a lack of interest to research further.

"Thank you for having me, Mr. Gallagher," replied Isaac. He struggled to reciprocate the same energy Mr. Gallagher did.

"I should be thanking you. I've been meaning to meet with you personally so you could hear it from me, especially since, well, you don't know me."

The stylist flashed a thumbs up as she stepped away.

"Thank you, ma'am," Mr. Gallagher continued at Isaac. "We respect what your parents brought forth and desire to continue their vision. I worked closely with Gemma and Samuel. Fantastic people."

"They were," said Isaac. "Thank–"

Mr. Gallagher checked the time on his watch before Isaac could finish. "I must get going now if you don't mind, but we should continue this another time. Good luck with your speech!" He scurried back to the other side of the building.

By 10:00 AM, a sea of people accumulated at the base level of Sage Foundation. News cameras stationed at the far back. Everyone clamored to see a dead remnant of the city's past being revived.

Isaac rehearsed his lines one last time before striding to the podium at 10:30 AM. In front of him, some of the faces in the manmade sea looked on with eager attentiveness. Others were bothered by the heat. Many held their cameras and phones high.

Isaac tested the microphone with two taps. Then, he spoke, the first words met with a whining screech:

"When the board of directors approached me to write a speech, I decided to, of course, consider how my parents would write this speech. My mother would most likely record her lines in a messy web of different talking points that would sound like…"

Then, an unsteady pause. Painful memories surged through his mind.

The silence filled with a low ring. Isaac's brain processed every eye locked at him—dilated and microscopic pupils, eyes colored like honeycomb, indigo, green and brown. He felt as though they could see every facet of him. From what he showed on the surface, to what was beneath him. The insecurities, the trauma, the rage. The guilt he tried to hide. The guilt that held his truth.

All eyes on Isaac Sage.

He pushed on. "The most awfully edited movie plot, but still somehow making sense."

The crowd chuckled, relaxing Isaac.

"And my father, Samuel, would organize lists filled with different pros and cons. How many ways the speech can be structured, arising venue-related factors and anything else that compelled him to pull his hair out.

"I loved them with all my heart, and…and I miss them dearly. I am a Sage. But I can affirm I'm not my parents, and I will never be like them. It is with that in mind that I provide my perspective as their son in their honor."

A brief exhale.

"I'm…nervous. I'm concerned about the future of the new Sage Foundation. My family's legacy, represented by this name, this business. The mission of that legacy was to cure the world so humanity can evolve to be better."

His heart increased in pace. Near the end with no destination in sight. No, he wasn't his parents. They held a great responsibility in bringing a wonder into the world. They sacrificed so much.

"But fear can hold many back," he continued, "We, including myself, must give this group a chance. So, to Mr. Gallagher and the rest of the board…"

The question recanted. *'What next?'*

*'To be better,'* Isaac thought. The kind doctor's words once again followed. It continued uprooting a subconscious conflict. *'Accept the past.'*

Not just the loss of his parents. Kara flashed in his mind. First, her youthful self. And then, her bounded body buried in the dirt.

Then, a light bulb in the form of an idea of where he wanted to head, the path he should take to be better. This would be his price to pay for forgiveness.

"Congratulations. I look forward to the new innovations and success of this company…" Before the applause could erupt, Isaac spoke over the claps. "—as a shadow to the board of Sage Foundation." The crowd applauded in a roaring fashion. Isaac waved to every person. "Thank you."

Darwin, standing to the side of the entrance, mouthed the words "Oh my gosh," while applauding.

As Isaac departed the stage with beautiful, thunderous applause, Mr. Gallagher took over with an exaggerated grin plastered on his face.

***

Once the ribbon was cut, Mr. Gallagher guided Isaac to the inside of the building. It was an eerily similar palette pulled from the past with some modern alterations.

They entered the elevator. Mr. Gallagher pressed '42' from the array of buttons.

"That was quite ballsy of you to do that," Mr. Gallagher said.

The elevator commenced its ascent. "I apologize if I stepped on any toes," said Isaac. "It felt right, to do what my parents left behind. If you'll allow me."

Mr. Gallagher turned to Isaac. "I haven't seen anyone do that to me in the years I've worked. The people like it. They're already making headlines. The kind of spotlight we need." Mr. Gallagher extended his hand. "Welcome aboard."

Isaac blinked, registering this gesture. He shook his hand.

"Thank you, Mr. Gallagher!  Really, I…wow. Wow, I'm shaking." He laughed.

The elevator arrived at the 42nd floor. "Let me take you to your desk. I had my assistant prepare it last-minute."

On the way, Mr. Gallagher introduced Isaac to all the scientists and specialists occupying the floor. "They're working extra hard to ensure production is smooth. Over time, you'll have the pleasure to meet everyone in the building."

He led Isaac to his office, approximately 100 or so square feet, fit with a stained walnut desk and a computer. His view, behind his desk, held an awe-inspiring cityscape of towers stretching to the grand horizon.

"What is it they say? The daylight helps with your circadian rhythms?" said Mr. Gallagher.

Isaac, almost lost from the pleasant vista, suddenly felt his soul crumble. Like the floors once again quaking, turning his legs into jelly. His lungs turned tight with the vision of sleeping and eating well dissipating.

He turned back to Mr. Gallagher. "What's next?" Isaac asked.

"Well, if you want to climb in the ranks, you must learn the trade around here. You'll learn how we manufacture the pharmaceuticals, how we market and communicate with our visual advertising." Mr. Gallagher leaned against the desk, folding one leg over the other. "I must ask, though. Why? Because what's next for you after this?"

"Well, because…"

Isaac searched. He searched in the several seconds that dragged like one of the most excruciating hours.

The grandness of this win, instead, inflated the sense of regret tenfold. A regret over Diablo's outcome. How he wished to scream in his dying face that he beat him. What bloomed higher, taking form of thorns pinning into his soul, was immense regret for Kara.

The subconscious had become fully conscious. He wanted to smack his head beyond the point of his hands blistering, until the brain became torn asunder from excessively bashing the skull.

Mr. Gallagher stared with a raised brow. "I don't have all day."

Isaac felt a sense of mourning when he spoke. *'They would've wanted this,'* Isaac thought. *'Wouldn't they?'*

*'Accept the past,'* the thought returned as its answer.

"I…I don't deserve this," said Isaac.

Mr. Gallagher squinted his eyes, souring his expression with disdain. "What the hell do you mean?"

No ambience filled the office as silence dragged for several seconds.

The slow trembling in Isaac's hands flowed to his heart, then to his lips. "It was…" he fought back from weeping as he conjured his memories of Kara once more. "It was all stupid. I thought *this* would make every stupid thing I did the past year better."

"I said, I don't have all day," Mr. Gallagher's tone sharpened. "Speak properly."

"I found him…I found the one who blew up this building…who killed my family. And he's dead now. He's dead because I used people to get to him. He's dead because I tore through so many to be stronger! And now…now, she's dead."

"*She?* You said it was a man."

Isaac continued, near-delirious from the clogged trauma pouring out. "I could blame it on so many things. So many factors. But she's gone. I took that away from her. Because I killed her…" Isaac hyperventilated, feeling a sudden liberation of saying this. "I should go to jail. I should look at nothing but concrete walls and just die slowly. I'm not a good person. I'm *not* a good person. This isn't where I should–"

Mr. Gallagher slammed onto the desk's surface, forcing Isaac's train of words into a crashing halt. Isaac expected this man who was nothing more than an acquaintance, or a mere stranger, to hound a look a disgust. To brand him a monster by calling him such directly or calling the police.

He looked up to find a soft smile painted on Mr. Gallagher's face instead.

"I feel your remorse," he said with a similarly soft empathy. "But what good would that do?"

"Would…what?" Isaac asked.

Mr. Gallagher maintained his tone. "You go to jail, or you die. You get your just punishment. Suddenly, the weight is lifted, isn't it? Even the thought of being in jail or dying feels nicer than having you sitting comfortably on the 42$^{nd}$ floor or resting in that mansion."

Isaac nodded.

"And it must've been nice to speak of this. I'm the first, aren't I?"

Isaac nodded, quicker.

"And it's safe with me.  Because neither of those are the right punishment. The act of withholding and keeping it silent, continuing through life while this weight is pressed on you–like Sisyphus rolling the boulder or Prometheus being eternally devoured–*that* is the rightful act."

Another pause of silence lingered.  Isaac was uncertain of how to react to it.  There was the shock of Mr. Gallagher uttering those words in such a kind tone.  There was also the sudden epiphany of how right it was.  That the sleepless nights would continue.  The food and movies he enjoyed before would be dull. The choice to surround himself with people would never outweigh the decision to remain in isolation.

The bloodied, crescent smile of Ibrahim, the sign of liberation, was out of reach. The answer to what was next had finally cemented.

Mr. Gallagher patted Isaac's back with a bright smile.

"Look ahead, Isaac. Get used to your new future." He gestured Isaac to the desk. "Your first day will be tomorrow. Good meeting you."

He departed, leaving Isaac in this grand new place to explore. Isaac sat at his desk and let Mr. Gallagher's revelation sit with him.

Autonomously, he sifted through the drawers. Pens, staplers and the other typical office goodies. He opened the third drawer, locking onto a parchment neatly rolled up.

Curious, Isaac grabbed the parchment and unrolled it across the desk. The first sight was a title written, 'As of 03-13-2023' set atop an abundant array of lines, overwhelming Isaac.

He analyzed every line and symbol, conscious thought overriding autonomy. A sense of calm before a heightened ramp in alarm. The lines arranged a wireframe map of New Manhattan. A few were crossed with black X's, multiple marked with crimson O's.

His heart dragged downward the longer he looked at the map, realizing he'd seen most of these locations before. They were warehouses ran by Diablo.

A legend on the upper right corner denoted the ones marked with X's were defunct warehouses. Courtesy of Isaac and the police. The O's marked warehouses that either continued or restarted their operations.

Isaac's hands shook, uncontrolled and visceral enough to tear the paper by accident. His back arched upright against the chair. His dull olive eyes darted between every blood-tinted circle, unresting.

A high-pitched noise buzzed through Isaac's eardrums. Diablo's legacy continued. A madness compelled him to pursue.

Unresting was the madness, like an inferno fueled from the eternal flames. A storm so indistinguishable from the pyre that forever changed his life.

# THE STORY CONTINUES

---

## STORIES WITHIN THE MAD UNIVERSE #1

If you want a full dive into the MAD Universe, then these
supplementary novellas are for you!

## MAD VIGILANCE

*The path to a life reset with prosperity is long and treacherous. But will it cleanse the blood on your hands?*

**On Sale at Amazon and other participating sites in Digital and Paperback**

**OR Sign up for Victor Vahl's Newsletter to receive the novella for free!**
**(Scan the QR Code to be taken to the page!)**

For the past six months since the events of *Mad City*, Isaac Sage has been waging a personal, covert war to eradicate Diablo's legacy in the shadows, all while leading a solitary, routine life by day.

When his longtime friend Todd returns, a new enemy emerges—an inhuman force led by a father determined to claim Diablo's throne and eliminate anyone in his way.

Faced with this life-threatening adversary, Isaac grapples with a harrowing, heavy decision choice: to end a young boy's life or find a way to save him. Is it his responsibility to be the judge, jury and executioner? Is it his burden to live this part of his life alone?

**In Victor Vahl's action-packed, gritty novella, Mad Vigilance bridges the gap between *Mad City* and *Mad Virus*. Order your copy today to continue your journey into the MAD Universe!**

# BOOK 2 OF THE SAGE'S LEGACY IS COMING...

## MAD VIRUS

*An infected vigilante.  A superpowered terrorist.  A virus doomed to devastate the entire world.  One chance to do things right.*

### OUT WINTER 2025!

Two years have passed since the events of *Mad City*. Isaac Sage, now a hardened vigilante, has dedicated to erasing the remnants of Diablo's legacy. Though he walks this path with acceptance, he is constantly haunted by his sins. Even with his position in Sage Foundations, he struggles to envision a future different from this one.

His path takes a sudden turn, however, when a mysterious terrorist known as Rickard announces that the M.A.D. compound has been tainted with a deadly virus, set to infect anyone in New Manhattan who has ever ingested it within hours. In seven days, the infection will spread worldwide, bringing certain death in the process—including Isaac.

As chaos erupts, the NMPD and military scramble to contain the outbreak. Todd Hyme learns his mother is among the infected, pulling both he and Isaac deeper into the epicenter of the crisis.

It's no longer a choice. Isaac, fighting past self-doubt, pursues to stop the virus and save Todd's mother alongside every other infected in the process.  Or die trying.

New allies and enemies emerge.  Familiar faces return. Each with their own mission in this high-stakes race with the countdown ticking away.

Will a hero rise to save the world? Or will a large chunk of humanity take its last breath, leaving a permanent mark of horror ingrained into history?

# ACKNOWLEDGEMENTS

## - 2024 -


I had to learn a lot of appreciation for the small steps in making this novel into the version I had desired it to be in the beginning.  The first time ever publishing was finding my way on the playground and chucking sand around with some form and finish.

This time, it was taking steps back, spending most of my time behind the scenes in isolation. A lot of mistakes, overthinking, and imposter syndrome taking form.  I won't get into the nitty-gritty as there's a good message at the end of this all. Re-analyzing, recrafting, admitting what sucked and what was okay.  Rinse and repeat, over and over. And now we're here.

It really came down to this.

**Thank you to all the supporters** that stuck through to see an old book shed its skin to form something new.  I truly hope you enjoyed it enough to see the characters within this world continue their journey.  I will truly do my best, with everything in my power, to make that come to fruition.

**To my friends and family:** It means the world to me when I see you share your support vocally, and even personally share with me milestones that humbles my journey as a writer.  And to those silent supporters, you know who you are.  You are just as much appreciated.

**To Gabriela Guzman:** She was the designer responsible for the design on the front cover of *Mad City* , which was inspired by the painting series "World Trade Center As A Cloud" by Christopher Saucedo.  Gaby is a fantastic artist, and I'm so thankful for the work she put into this cover.

**To BF, my editor:** Thank you for diving into this story.  Your feedback helped me finally find the footing to push my creativity across the hurdles we came across thanks to your feedback.

**To all the beta readers. Especially Angie, Anja, CJ, Mark and the many other patrons that engage with my newsletter:** All of you had a unique perspective to this book. And, once again, helped me realize the vision I wanted to achieve this book and its future sequels. You invested time into this and, from the bottom of my heart, I am forever grateful in helping me sharpen this book.

As this very special person was mentioned previously, last but not least...

**To my wife, Daniela:** You often tell me that you're the luckier one in our marriage. While I believe that's not true, I also struggle to find the right words that better convince you otherwise.

Should I convey that the current version of myself would have taken decades to become without your presence? Should I explain how your love has nearly cured my imposter syndrome, which has followed me since childhood? Should I explain that you've stabilized parts of me that I believed were designed to be permanently broken?

The stakes are higher, but I feel grounded. The responsibilities are heavier, but I feel lighter. The obstacles we face now can be harsher at times, but my future feels safer. I can feel all of this because you are by my side.

There are two things I've learned since we've been together: love means finding satisfaction and forgiveness for who I am, and it also means considering you in nearly every thought I make more instant than twitching the lightest nerve.

Now, learning to be a better writer and crafting every book with the right care isn't just for me. Building a safe, peaceful home, maintaining our health, and providing isn't just about me. Every action and thought is for you as well. Undoubtedly.

Love means following through on these actions without regret or annoyance. My love for you is about cherishing our memories and the feelings that began long before you invested in my passion. Thus, these memories and feelings will last longer than the ink on this page.

# THERE'S MORE? YEP, THERE'S MORE

Sometimes, it's tedious to find more works written by the same author, after laying one's eyes on their first work. (and, well, enjoying it!)

If you are someone who enjoyed this book, you can find all my other currently published works on my website, linked below.

There is also a newsletter you can sign up for on the website, where you can stay connected with me and check out special promotions, exclusive benefits, behind-the-scenes content, and any other content I find fun to share.

## WWW.VICTORVAHL.COM

# ABOUT THE AUTHOR

You would expect awards here, or credibility, or some kind of background like any other writer (as Vahl himself has done in the past). But, pushing past the courses centered around creative writing in Florida State University, some skills in graphic design, copywriting, video editing, and being a self-proclaimed cookie connoisseur, no. You won't find that here.

Vahl is simply a guy that loves stories. From the craft and execution to enjoying and being inspired. Vahl's true paradise is either getting lost in his daydreams, brainstorming new ideas, reading books, petting his dog and cat simultaneously, cooking, or watching movies with Mrs. Vahl.

You can stay connected with Victor Vahl here:

facebook.com/thevictorvahl

twitter.com/thevictorvahl

instagram.com/thevictorvahl

goodreads.com/victorvahl

bookbub.com/profile/victor-vahl